MONKEY IN THE MIDDLE

MONKEY IN THE MIDDLE

JOSH PRYOR

CARROLL & GRAF PUBLISHERS
NEW YORK

MONKEY IN THE MIDDLE

Carroll & Graf Publishers
An Imprint of Avalon Publishing Group Inc.
161 William St., 16th Floor
New York, NY 10038

First Carroll & Graf edition 2003

All of the characters in this book are fictitious, and any resemblance to actual persons, living or dead, is purely coincidental.

Library of Congress Cataloging-in-Publication Data is available.

ISBN: 0-7867-1173-6

Designed by Paul Paddock

Printed in the United States of America
Distributed by Publishers Group West

For Grandma Betty, Grandpa Gene, and of course Jocko
who taught us the larger meaning of family.

What song the Sirens sang, or what name Achilles assumed when he hid himself among women, although puzzling questions, are not beyond all conjecture.

—Sir Thomas Browne

MONKEY HOUSE

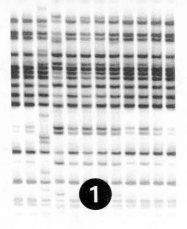

1

FROM OUR CONVERSATION ON THE PHONE that morning, I had expected Dr. Janus, cofounder and CEO pro tempore of Acteon Corporation, to be a little test-tube happy, but in an eccentric-genius sort of way, not a total freaking nut job lurking in the steamy twilight of a man-made grotto. Here I was in the middle of downtown Los Angeles, and you would've thought I'd stumbled ass-backwards through a hole in the asphalt into a land forgotten by time. Outside, it was all sunshine and car exhaust, freeway killers and fitness clubs. But inside . . . This was like one of those life-size dioramas in the central exhibit hall at the Museum of Natural History, a dark depository of forms and flora held over from an epoch remembered only to the slouching beast pacing in the shadow of civilized man. The walls, a sweating aggregate of jagged black lava rock bristling with anemone ferns and spidery bromeliads, gave the impression that I was standing at the base of a slumbering volcano—20,000 years of geologic hibernation giving way to a precarious ecosystem poised on the brink of flash extinction. Everything but a thick-browed basher-in of skulls robed in animal skins, and his slack-jawed sister-wife with a feral infant gnashing at her droopy tit. This was the beginning. Ground zero. And yours truly, Captain Dutch Harlowe Flowers (U.S. Army Ret.), standing two-thirds upright in that low-ceilinged microcosm of genetic drift, head carouseling with questions and an instinctive distrust of offers that sound too good to be true.

Janus's office was not exactly what one expects of a *Fortune* 500 top executive. If you ask me, it was all a bit over the top—the epitome of L.A. chic—which is pretty much par for the course in the land of aerospace and make-believe. Imagine me trying to get my bearings in this dubious paradise while Janus, a corporate heavy-hitter I didn't know from Adam, was trying to sell me on the idea that one of his pedigree lab chimps was a budding Charles Manson. Although the good doctor was clearly in need of a little psychiatric calibration, what with the diastolic sound loop of the jungle canopy cricketing overhead and his apparent aversion to electric light, I had to consider the possibility that he was actually serious. I've seen enough in my thirty-six years on this planet that nothing surprises me anymore. The crackpot's Bigfoot is the cryptozoologist's missing link. Besides, money is money. The presidents don't get any deader because of the company they keep. Ask Mr. Wonderful, the evil son of a bitch with a contract on my head. As long as I deliver his monthly installment on time, my balls don't get nailed to the bedposts.

"So let me get this straight," I asked Janus, running the numbers as I spoke. "You're offering me fifty thousand dollars—*in cash, tax-free*—to tell you whether or not one of your monkeys is a murderer."

Janus spoke, cool and fugue-like, his words trickling like water over wet stone. "Chimpanzees, Mr. Flowers," he affirmed resolutely. "Anthropopithecus. Mankind's *closest* living relative. *Cousin*, if you will."

A humanoid silhouette padded toward me through the artificial dusk, the shaggy ground cover crackling lightly with each step. I tried to make out the features of the man who had yet to divulge exactly how he had tracked me down, but he broke off his approach and resumed the conversation from the waxy blind of a banana plant. His voice was strangely soothing, almost hypnotic. There was a modulated newness to it, a precise coupling of syllables and ideas you might expect of a visitor from a far away place not entirely fluent with his borrowed tongue.

"I'm sorry if I seem a tad bit skeptical, Doctor, but this isn't exactly the sort of thing that blows up my shorts every day. I'm a private detective, not a pet psychologist."

"Don't take my word for it," Janus pressed forward with a note of chagrin. "I am offering you a unique opportunity to observe for yourself. Remember, Mr. Flowers, this is a place of science. Faith, as I imagine it to be in your line of work, is of little use to us here. Doubt is the scientist's greatest tool. In the laboratory, the heretics are those who suspend their disbelief."

"Say I accept. What's the catch?"

"You are a suspicious bunch, Mr. Flowers. Once you have determined who the murderer is your work here will be complete. We will take over from there. Then, and only then, will you receive your money."

"Why not go to the police?"

"Involving the police would be like amputating an arm to cure a hangnail. The costs would far outweigh the benefits."

"Why come to me? I'm not exactly up to my ass in laurels these days. There must be a dozen other guys in the area who could handle a case like this."

"Secrecy, Mr. Flowers. What we are doing here is very cutting edge. State-of-the-art. If the media caught wind of our experiment, the negative publicity would set us back decades. The truth is, we looked at several candidates; however, you seemed to be the perfect fit. No offense, but even if you were to go public with the details of our work, chances are no one would listen."

"You don't pull any punches, do you, Doc?"

"Not when it may affect the outcome of our mission."

"Tell me, what exactly is it that you do here?" I asked, trying to make sense of my untamed surroundings like a hopelessly lost expeditionary.

"Quality of life, Mr. Flowers. We seek to improve it. Myself and a handful of others at Acteon are not convinced that natural selection has had the best interest of our species in mind. We simply wish to speed along the inevitable."

"Tell me this isn't about finding a cure for baldness."

"Ah, vanity," Janus mused coolly. "Although Acteon's research is dedicated to the field of applied genetics, the hairless need not apply. Here, our concerns run much deeper than the follicularly impaired."

"Say I take the case and there's no murderer to be found. Then what?"

"The road from the eye to the intellect should not pass through the heart, Mr. Flowers. As I stated earlier, I am offering you a chance to see for yourself. If your suspicions are confirmed and, indeed, there is no murderer, then I fail to see how you could be any worse off than before."

Smart money said that Janus had a file on me a gigabyte long. Every word I had ever muttered in my sleep, every election ballot I had ever punched, every twist and turn in my lower intestine had no doubt been mapped out for him courtesy of the information-superhighway data mongers. Those too-good-to-be-true ads you see offering five compact discs for a dollar . . . Book-of-the-Month Club . . . Carpet shampooing absolutely free of charge. . . . Come-ons devised by information gatherers that make the boys in the federal crime lab look like weekend hobbyists. Janus knew damn well that I was in no position to haggle. He knew that I knew. Since the *Times* had run a serialized exposé on my tribulations in the Persian Gulf, I couldn't get a sniff from anyone other than the vultures recruiting for the talk-show circuit, a short-lived tour of infamy whose limited revenue earning potential had been quickly exhausted by Mr. Wonderful's ever-increasing fiscal demands.

"Give me twenty-four hours to think it over," I said, knowing damn well I'd strip for Turkish sailors if that's what it took to keep my would-be assassin off my back.

The deepening twilight had given way to total darkness. The door through which I had entered the grotto was no longer visible, nor was the ground underfoot the same consistency as in the reception area just a few strides away. It was soft and spongy like the infield at Dodger Stadium after a hard rain. My feet made sucking noises as I rocked nervously from side to side. The unwholesome air smelled of mulching vegetation and standing water, pestilence and decay. An ironwork cresset illuminated vague outlines on the vine-clad walls: stick-figure hunters hurling spears at herds of grazing herbivores. Imaginary rain crackled on the impenetrable canopy overhead. A bird ruffled its feathers. I could hear Janus's breathing, his deep nasal intake and slow curling release.

"Anyway," I continued, my voice a pitiful echo of the virile mating calls of impossibly distant tree-dwellers, "what makes you so sure it's one of the chimps? Maybe you have a disgruntled worker on your hands."

"Impossible. No one enters or leaves without my direct authorization."

"You run a tight ship, Warden."

"Six months ago, one of our staff accidentally left his cellular phone in one of the habitation modules. By the time we retrieved it, the chimps had received several calls from outside the enclosure. It seems the strange voices beamed into their midst awakened them to a previously unimagined consciousness. They have not been the same since."

"You're not suggesting? . . ."

"The concept of God is no less arbitrary than the position of hands on a clock. Things are not always what they seem to be; nor are they otherwise."

"I'll make sure to hang on to my car keys."

"Be that as it may, you will be conducting your investigation from a vantage outside the enclosure."

"Things would go a lot more smoothly if I was allowed access to the crime scene—get a feel for who I'm dealing with."

"Correct me if I am wrong, Mr. Flowers, but astronomers can tell us the composition of distant worlds without actually setting foot on them, can they not?"

"Of course, but—"

"See Mr. Shackleman on the way out. He will provide you with biographical information on the control group donors. I imagine this will be your starting point."

"Sure. Great."

By now the darkness had acquired texture. It was thick and velvety and as pure as the space between galaxies. What little I could make out in the grotto was eerily incongruous with the well-lighted world of concrete and steel and glass to which I was accustomed. Dangling creepers bobbed like snakes in the orange black nimbus of a single guttering flame. Although half-blind, I was instinctively aware of Janus's presence very near to me. The quickened beat of my pulse was interrupted when something soft and gooey struck me in the side of the head. I bent over to see what it was. A partially eaten banana lay sluglike in the muck at my feet. A strange half-human keening boiled out of the darkness like deranged laughter. Born and raised in the city, I was highly susceptible to the enervating properties of chlorophyll. It awakened something inside of me, a carrier gene, primal stirrings, a core connection to a long-dead band of hunter-gatherers who had foraged on the savannas wearing animal skins, and who had wrested lice from one another in the smoky firelight of a communal cave. As much as I wanted to disavow my ancestral leanings, I was possessed of an ancient déjà vu.

The rain let up and the still was shattered by the crypt-like grating of stone against stone. White light knifed through the rear of the grotto, silencing the *bwoop-bwoop* of lovesick tree frogs and the sonic curlicues of bloodthirsty mosquitoes dive-bombing my exposed flesh. As I moved toward the exit, Janus called out to me, his voice grave and direct.

"A word of caution, Mr. Flowers. Think what you will of the rest, but do not underestimate your killer. Evil is an intelligence unto itself."

Given what I had seen, or rather not seen, I had not dismissed the possibility that this was all part of an elaborate, smoke-filled dream, the sensory flotsam of my shipwrecked nervous system.

"For fifty thousand dollars, I'll take my chances," I replied, edging toward the reassuring light of the reception area.

"Ah, yes," Janus drawled wearily. "Greed, the mark of humanity."

Shackleman, a bespectacled apostrophe of a man with bad posture and flat lusterless eyes, was flitting nervously about the reception area when I emerged from the grotto. He had the gaunt misplaced look of a forced laborer. His graying hair had been cropped back to the scalp as if to prevent the spread of parasites. His ears, small cartilaginous twists scarcely capable of supporting his eyeglasses, had apparently offered little resistance exiting the birth canal. I placed him somewhere between forty and sixty years of age, but to narrow it down any further I would have had to cut off one of his legs and count the rings.

"Dr. Janus didn't say anything about giving blood," I remarked offhandedly, scratching the bug bites pimpling my forearms.

"So that's what he's calling himself now," Shackleman hissed, the slack muscles of his neck tightening. *Doctor!* That's a laugh. He can't even tie his own shoes."

No sooner had the words crossed Shackleman's thin pink lips than his gaze snapped upward where it settled on the Damoclean eye of a surveillance camera peering downward from the ceiling.

"You'll have to forgive me," he grumbled, turning away from the camera and fixing me with a troubled smile. "I quit smoking last week and I'm not myself. But no excuses. When we cease to be civilized, we're no better than they."

Shackleman must have realized that I had no idea to whom he was referring because he offered me an explanation totally out of context with his office's vinyl-veneer assemble-yourself Scandinavian appointments. "The animals," he reflected sourly. "Our civility is what separates us from them."

"According to my wife, it's bubble baths and bikini waxing."

Shackleman frowned and pulled up his shirtsleeve. His arm was festooned with adhesive nicotine patches.

"These things," he informed me scornfully, "are supposed to dull the cravings. They don't work. I'd kill for a cigarette."

"Don't quit," I suggested. "I've never understood why anyone would want to live past sixty anyway."

I'm the first to admit that the years, particularly the last few, have knocked some of the shine off me. Every now and then I'll catch a glimpse of myself in a storefront window, and it will take me a second or two to realize that it's me standing there dumbfounded, eerily transparent and older than I could have ever possibly imagined. It's not the slashes of gray streaking my hair or the creases at the corners of my eyes. There's an aura of fatigue about me, the ashen pall of a terminal illness or, as fate would have it, the brow-beaten patina of a marked man.

"Company policy," Shackleman explained. "The *doctor* thinks a smoke-free workplace is good for morale. He says that humans are the only species on the planet to knowingly indulge in self-destructive behavior."

"Show me an ape that doesn't believe it's going to live forever and I'll show you a drunk in the making."

Shackleman fixed his gaze on one of those uplifting motivational prints corporations hang in the break room to brainwash their employees into believing that they are serving a higher purpose. It was centered on the wall opposite his desk next to a framed *Time* magazine cover picturing Ham, the first chimpanzee to be launched into space. Beneath a photograph of a wall-eyed lungfish wriggling across a soupy mudflat, perhaps the lowest order of vertebrate to make its home on land, was the caption ADAPTABILITY IS NEXT TO GODLINESS.

"If you'll excuse me a moment," Shackleman explained with a strained look, "I need to use the restroom."

He was out the door before I could respond.

I felt sorry for Shackleman—his ugly little apostrophe body, calcium-poor bones and nasty overbite. However, not sorry enough to waylay my deepening concerns about my own problems. Thirteen days until the last Sunday of the month, and Mr. Wonderful would be looking to collect his blood money.

Shackleman returned from the restroom a few minutes later. His face was damp and his color was off, the unwholesome yellow of chicken fat. He breezed past me and retrieved a crisp sheaf of papers from his desk drawer.

"Sign where highlighted and initial at the X's," he said.

I didn't see the point in taking the time to read the fine print. You don't talk knots when your neck's in a noose. What, I reasoned, could Acteon possibly have up its sleeves that wasn't surpassed tenfold by Mr. Wonderful's bone-numbing "pay up or elses"? For now, I had to put common sense on hold and go through the motions of a murder investigation as contrived and pointless as interpretive dance.

As I applied my John Holmes to page after page of rhetorical mumbo-jumbo, Shackleman hovered over me like an ailing billionaire waiting to take possession of my vital organs. He stunk. Badly. Worse, I imagined than the filthy chimps to whom the fruits of his labor were offered up in bitter supplication. It was brash and musky. Hormonal. While he checked to see that I had crossed the Ts and put little happy faces on the Is, I perused the titles in the bookcase beneath the lungfish print: *The Naked Ape*; *In the Shadow of Man*; Darwin's *Origin of Species*; *Quiet Massacre, Animal Testing in the Military and Beyond*; *Descent of Man*; *King Kong*. For the most part, the collection was ape-oriented, which didn't strike me as particularly odd given the identity of my employer's research subjects. Upon closer inspection, I discovered that most of the titles had apparently never been read. Their spines, conspicuously unbroken, crackled with newness when I turned back the covers to glance at the pages within. I was thumbing through a saddle-stitched doctoral dissertation entitled *The Thirteenth Apostle*, when I realized that Shackleman was again breathing down my neck.

"See any you like?" he asked, his query barbed with playful contempt. "Janus picked them out himself. He regards this one as something of a bible."

Shackleman handed me a book with a photograph of an immaculately groomed ape gracing the cover. The dapper beast had the deep-seeing eyes of one who has dedicated his life to philosophical inquiry. I had no doubt that the startling image was an illusion perpetrated by a clever photographer, but even so I could not help feeling as though it would have taken countless volumes of abstract discourse to capture the essence of the look in those omniscient, dead-ahead eyes branding my soul with uncertainty.

"Take it," Shackleman offered forcefully. "I want you to have it."

"I couldn't," I protested feebly.

"It's a gift." Shackleman fixed me with a savage grin and thrust the book into my hands. "I insist."

The fact is, that although I skimmed through it with an air of indifference, I wanted to hurl the book across the room and storm out of Shackleman's office. It was the kind of thing displayed for a buck a pop at carnival peep shows. Who could say what brand of dementia the book's fingerworn pages espoused, what lunatic theories abounded in the copiously annotated text? Unlike the others, its binding was badly worn as if it had been read and reread a thousand times by a thousand seekers of some unidentifiable truth. *Bobo, An Autobiography.* Even by talk-show standards, it was a low blow.

Virtually every man, woman and child with access to a television had seen in some way, shape or dissemination, my interview on the *Spalding Penzler Show.* In addition to myself and comedian Robin Williams, Bobo and Bobo's handler/ linguistics coach had been among the show's guests that afternoon. With the help of host Spalding Penzler, an erudite homosexual who had been incensed by my line-item rejection of his jaunty backstage advances, the zoologic duo had been bent on stealing the spotlight while making a monkey out of yours truly. In a few short minutes, any pretense of journalistic integrity had fallen victim, and me with it, to a savage three-way roast with Bobo at the helm. Scarcely had Bobo's chaperone dubbed my ordeal, by way of Penzler's pointed prologue, into sign language for his simian charge when the smart-ass mountain gorilla began cracking jokes about my mishaps in the Gulf. The studio audience roared with laughter as Bobo's translator voice-overed the ape's flamboyantly communicative gesticulations for the good people in TV Land. Whether Bobo had orchestrated the cutting burlesque himself, or if he was merely an innocent pawn of an elaborate bit devised by Robin Williams (in no way himself an innocent bystander), did not matter to me. I hated Bobo. I still hate Bobo. I will always hate Bobo for having the common sense and wherewithal to disassociate himself from me.

"So this is what it's all about," I fired bitterly, slamming the book on Shackleman's desk. "Let me guess—you're filming some kind of follow-up special. Janus is Spalding Penzler, right?

That's why he wouldn't let me see him. I thought I recognized the voice."

"I have no idea what you're talking about, Mr. Flowers."

"I'll spell it out for you. The contract, the money, the absurdity of the so-called investigation. . . . The bullshit in this place is so thick I can smell it." I spoke into the camera. "This is quite a spectacle you've devised here, *Doctor* Penzler, a real top-notch mindfuck." I was rolling, gathering momentum. "But don't think I won't go along with it. Give the people what they want, right? Why don't I just slit my wrists right here, right now, and get it over with? That's what it's all about, isn't it? None of you will be happy until I'm rotting in the ground!"

"Please, Mr. Flowers," Shackleman pleaded. "You have to stop this. The offer's legitimate. The case is real."

"Take your best shot!" I challenged, thumping my chest for the camera like the imaginary chimps I had been duped into investigating. "Make a monkey out of me! I submit. But don't think you're any better than I am. You're the monsters! You're the ones who should be ashamed. They'll turn their backs on you too, Bobo. Don't think for one second that they won't. They'll find a dog who surfs or a skydiving horse, and they'll stick you in a filthy cage somewhere with an old truck tire and a bunch of rotten bananas. You'll see. I was a hero once. Now look at me!"

"I'm begging you!" Shackleman pleaded. "Get hold of yourself. He might be watching. I know all of this sounds impossible, but you have to believe me when I tell you that what's going on here is terribly real!"

As much as I wanted to call Shackleman a liar and storm out of the office, I was anchored there by the sheer desperation in his eyes. He was no actor; he was afraid. I knew that look better than anyone. I saw it in the mirror each morning when I shaved staring back at me through the mentholated fog. Okay, maybe I was being paranoid. After all, the walls and the ceiling hadn't opened up to reveal a studio audience sniggering at me behind an inch-thick pane of soundproof glass. But don't tell me you wouldn't have reacted the same way if you'd been through what I had.

"Please, just take a look at it," Shackleman implored, forcing the accursed autobiography into my hands. "I've circled a few pages you really ought to see."

"Fine, but you're going to have to do something for me."

"Anything, if you'll just lower your voice."

"This stuff with the monkeys—it's on the up-and-up? It isn't some kind of twisted joke?"

"I swear," said Shackleman, knuckling his fists against the crush of pressures then unknown to myself.

"Then I want to know everything. From the beginning."

"Are you a religious man, Mr. Flowers?"

I thought about it a moment, unable to remember the last time I had set foot in a church. "I *can* be if the situation demands it."

"Forget what they taught you in Sunday school," Shackleman cautioned. "The rules have changed."

"What exactly do you mean?"

"We'll talk after your physical."

"No one said anything about a physical."

Shackleman reached for the contract where it lay on his desk, a little less innocuous-seeming than before.

"Fine," I conceded. "But I'm not taking off my clothes."

Dr. Dolmen was an imposing slab of a man—Czech maybe, or Ukrainian—as unadorned and impervious to natural forces as Stonehenge. He moved with the lumbering gravity of an Arctic herbivore, looming over me with the irrepressible contempt fostered in anyone who has spent his life staring into the many faces of disease. His hands were badly scarred and callused and profoundly cold. Crescents of grime underscored his fingernails. He did not wear gloves. When he examined my testicles for cancerous lumps, the sorrowful pouch withdrew like a hamster in the company of snakes. How grossly incapable and utterly pointless he must have thought my frost-bitten genitalia in contrast with the slack behemoths knocking around between his shot-putter's thighs like a couple of Idaho russets. Short-fused, with deep, aseptic eyes, he was not the type of man who readily entertains the word no. Not since the army doctors had sampled every fluid and tissue in my body had I been party to such a demoralizing battery of tests and analyses. Given Dolmen's menacing aspect and imposing physical stature, you can see why I was not more demonstrative with my unwillingness to produce a sperm sample when he handed me a specimen cup and pointed the way to the restroom.

"Great," I said, snatching the receptacle from his oversized mitt and starting for the door, "I'll drop it off with the nurse in the next day or two."

"Now," Dolmen rumbled, freezing me in my tracks. "You leave when finished."

"I'm a bit short on funds," I tried. "You know how it is—wild night with the missus. I'm all tapped out. Zero balance. You wouldn't want me to write a check I couldn't cash."

I scribbled in the air with an imaginary pen to make my point.

The man who had just swabbed my urethra for traces of venereal disease studied my chart blankly, the coarse handwritten characters writhing angrily on the sheet in front of him like the poison-pen legalese of a death sentence. He scratched something down and studied me with brutish indifference.

"Please tell me there's a stack of dirty magazines in there— *something*. Back in the old days, all it took was for the wind to change direction. Nowadays, I need a little persuasion."

Dolmen glared at me with his gray, glutinous eyes.

Again, I started for the door, this time less anxiously. "I really don't see the point—"

"Are you doctor?" he bellowed, his frustration boiling over in great baritone waves. "No, I am doctor! Go now!"

Although I was certain a high-res video of my autoerotic exploits would weave its way into the seamy fabric of the World Wide Web, joining the formidable canon of "celebrity exposed" Web sites on which I was already an unwilling pawn, I reminded myself that $50,000 was at stake, and with it my life. It wasn't so much performing the physical act that bothered me; it was knowing what the lab technicians would find when they examined my genetic code-carrying medium under the microscope.

Although normal-seeming to the unaided eye, magnification would reveal that the cup's sedentary contents stood about as much chance of impregnating a woman as a side of tartar sauce.

To my further embarrassment, the secretary, a woman built like an ax handle with a Quaker widow's sullen face, accepted the moribund specimen with a look of grave apprehension. Whether by coincidence or the notorious intuition of her gender, it was as if she knew without a shadow of uncertainty that the fire of my loins smoldered with all the intensity of a pile of wet leaves. She looked down her nose at the pearlescent sludge languishing in the bottom of the specimen cup—a veritable Little Big Horn of defunct cavalry—and dismissed me with a savage smile.

When I returned from Dolmen's office, Shackleman embarked on what felt like a guided audio tour of the facility and its unclear scientific objectives. With uninspired precision, he rattled off a bevy of anecdotal information and meaningless facts, from the "genetic miscue" blamed for the slayings to a sinister little fairy tale about needle-happy junkie chimps shooting heroin like seasoned pros. Truth told, it felt like window dressing for a much more beguiling product line.

"I'm not sure I get the point," I said, as uncertain of the experiment's purpose as I had been moments earlier.

"The point?" Shackleman echoed, fixing me with an ironic smirk. "I've been here from the beginning, and even I can't remember the point. Because we could, I guess."

"Because you could?"

"That's like asking why the universe, why all of this?" Shackleman made a sweeping gesture with his hands. "Maybe there never was a point. Maybe all of it was an accident. Maybe the point is that there is no point. Does it really matter?"

"I'd like to think that it does," I said. "Otherwise, it's all just masturbation."

The thought that all I had been through was random and without purpose was a hard pill to swallow. It meant that I was just as likely to die miserable and unredeemed as contented and vindicated.

"Ours is not to reason why," Shackleman recited blandly. "If there ever was a point, we lost it along the way. Now all we can do is put one foot in front of the other and see where it leads."

"Children," I said, grasping. "We pass our knowledge and experience down to our children so that they can succeed where we have failed."

"You mean so they can use it against us!" Shackleman charged bitterly. "I had a son once. He took what I gave him and used it to destroy me."

"What's with Janus's office?" I asked, changing the subject. "It's like Haiti in there."

"Janus believes that man lost his way when he left the jungle. If you really want to know the point of all this, he's the one you should ask."

So it wasn't exactly your typical case of murder and intrigue. Still, I have to admit the idea of a short-circuited lab chimp going postal on his fellow experimentees was not without a certain animal-cracker charm. One day I might even be able to write a book about it: *Monkeyshines—A Dutch Flowers Mystery Novel*. Parlay my experience into a runaway best-seller. For now, there was the issue of the bounty on my head. No matter how you sliced it, fifty grand would buy me time to figure out a way to keep Mr. Wonderful off my back for good. Already the pages were falling into place. Chapter One: "The Offer I Couldn't Refuse."

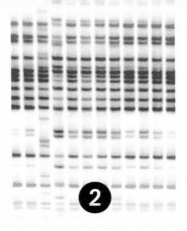

2

THE SAPIENS TRIALS FACILITY, or STF as it's known among the lab-coated technicians who monitor the chimps from concealed passageways, is a sort of hybridized ecosystem—*Brave New World* meets the Biosphere. It is the stuff of science-fiction novels, and as close to realizing his unrequited dream of colonizing the surface of Mars as some aging astrophysicist will ever get. The state-of-the-art genetics facility is located in the belly of the defunct Los Angeles Coliseum some fifty million miles from the inhospitable promised land of the red planet. There it resides in the heart of downtown, the ugly twin of its Roman sister, a concrete-and-steel homage to a civilization in the flower of ruin. Purchased in the late '80s from the city for a fraction of what it would have cost to tear the place down, Acteon slapped on a lightweight, nearly indestructible dome (the offspring of a fledgling alchemy that recycles nonbiodegradable disposable diapers—nearly 2 million pounds per day globally—into high-impact structural plastics and superefficient fiber-based insulates) and began experimenting with the building blocks of life. Now, more than a decade since hosting the 1984 Summer Olympic Games, the retrofitted megastructure showcases a different breed of contestant.

An eighth or so of the piecemeal enclosure is devoted to housing and feeding its esteemed subjects. The cleverly disguised network of false panels, camouflaged entryways, and sophisticated data-retrieval gadgetry is nicknamed the Haunted

Mansion. The remainder of the STF has been left to the whim of the exotic flora introduced by Acteon Corporation, a hothouse jungle known as the Enchanted Forest. Together, the Haunted Mansion and its roiling counterpart compose a working laboratory in the most ambitious sense. With a few notable exceptions, nearly every square foot of the STF, from ground level to the narrow catwalk encircling the convex firmament, is equipped for scientific observation and analysis. The place has got more one-way glass than an FBI interrogation center, a clandestine arrangement that lends a Darwinian wrinkle to the expression *Big Brother is watching*.

Those who spend their days analyzing and cataloging chimp behavior call themselves ghosts and seem entirely too comfortable with their supernatural status. They prowl the STF's sound-proofed corridors and observation conduits with an otherworldly inclination for stealth and secrecy. If you ask me, they're a bunch of peeping Jane Goodalls. Although the ghosts believe that the chimps are oblivious of their watchers, I am convinced that the accomplished performers of this preternatural theater-in-the-round are instinctively more cognizant of their audience than anyone cares to admit. No matter how you look at it, the place is fucking voodoo—Weirdsville—the chimps going about their daily activities while a bunch of undersexed microscope jockeys spy on them from the shadows.

Okay, maybe I couldn't explain some of the things I was about to see. It was going to take a hell of a lot more than a bunch of Ivy League knuckle-draggers and their gushing foster parents to convince me that I was witness to anything other than an over-budgeted zoo exhibit. From the way the ghosts were selling it, you would've thought I'd been given a front-row seat at the dawn of creation.

The first forty-eight hours on the job were pretty out there, but for the most part without incident. When I wasn't reviewing video of the so-called crime scenes, some pretty bloody footage to be sure, I spent hour upon hour observing the hairy prodigies via the camouflaged surveillance apparatus wired throughout the

STF: periscopic daffodils, bugged pussy willow, encoded tracking collars. State of the art intelligence gathering. And for what? Cut out the eyes on a second-rate portrait of some long-dead aristocrat, press your face to the back of the canvas, and you could have accomplished the same thing for a fraction of the cost. Remember, these are monkeys we're talking about, not KGB.

When a lion kills a gazelle, does that make the lion a murderer? Aside from the gazelle's widow, you'd be hard-pressed to find anyone who would respond in the affirmative. Although we share opposable thumbs with our loutish cousins, the propensity to kill for pleasure or to kill simply for the sake of killing struck me as a singularly human trait. Even if one of the chimps was responsible for the deaths of his fellow guinea pigs, did it make sense to call him a murderer? You don't throw the lion in jail for obeying his instincts. I was certain there was more to all of this than Janus was letting on. Either the murder instinct went farther back than I, in my cozy little world of useless facts and preconceived notions, had ever considered, or players yet unrevealed to me had their hands somewhere in the mix. If you can teach a monkey to ride a tricycle, how much more difficult could it be to teach one to swing an ax, handle an ice pick, discharge a firearm? From what I'd seen of the killings so far, the one common denominator shared by all was a distinctly human touch. Whoever it was seemed to derive satisfaction from his work.

Factoring into the equation that what I had observed of the STF's captive guests in my brief acquaintance was nothing short of miraculous—hell, they made Bobo look like Alfred E. Neuman—I was fairly certain that money of the Wall Street variety was somehow influencing the untimely slayings. Big business seemed a hell of a lot more likely than a homicidal chimp feeling his oats. Add that to the fact that I was not allowed any physical contact whatsoever with the chimps, and it didn't take a three-digit IQ to see that the procedural noose looped around my neck was custom tailored to protect anyone who might be working on the inside.

Only about a half-dozen of the fifty or so eggheads staffing the STF had access to the enclosure, an abbreviated list of suspects I abandoned quickly enough, having ruled out any possible involvement on the basis of a preliminary interview with each. And then, of course, there was Infusion Therapy, or IT as was its identity-less moniker at Acteon, the science of trickle-down genetics and reason for—or should I say cause of?—all of this.

To get a better feel for the killer's MO, I caught up with Shackleman in the lunchroom and picked his brain for information on the subject of IT. To catch a murderer, it is essential to know what makes him tick. I always say you can't spell pathology without path. I needed somewhere to start, a behavioral trailhead, what criminal profilers refer to as a *locus operandi*. Shackleman was sitting alone, devouring an open-faced turkey sandwich topped with ice-cream scoops of whipped potato starch and congealing flows of muddy brown gravy.

"Each strand of human DNA more or less consists of 128,000 haploid sets of chromosomes known as genomes," Shackleman panted between mouthfuls, attacking the food in front of him with a gusto fueled by his craving for nicotine.

"Could you dumb it down a bit?" I asked. "I haven't had any coffee today."

"If you promise to lower your voice," Shackleman growled, baring his teeth genially at the security guard standing next to the soda machine across the room. "I could get into real trouble for telling you this."

"You talk, I'll listen."

"Fine, but first I need to use the restroom."

Shackleman returned from the restroom much as he had during our previous meeting outside of Janus's office. He looked as if he had been carved from a bar of soap and left to dissolve in a bucket of water. Sweat glistened on his brow. His lips were thin and drawn. He produced an unmarked bottle of pills from his pocket, popped two into his mouth and washed them down with a swig of milk. "Now where were we?" he asked.

"DNA for Dummies."

"That's right. Genomes decide who we are, what we look like, what we're good at. The physicist who can draw a correlation between the energy signatures of subatomic particles in the emptiness of deep space and the expansion of the universe has the ability to do so because of the information encoded in his genomes. There are even those of us who believe that a man has as little to say about the leanings of his nature as the color of his eyes. There are those of us who believe that even the human soul is expressed in this manner—that the most elusive and prized of all human attributes is nothing more than a routine chemical process."

"Adolf Hitler was born bad," I suggested.

"Or . . . Liberace was born a homosexual," Shackleman confirmed. "If you subscribe to this school of belief—yes."

"So what's the point?" I wanted to know. "How do Acteon's shareholders get rich?"

"This isn't about money, Mr. Flowers. Acteon has spent the last two decades pioneering techniques for mapping and isolating behavior-specific genomes. Combining what we know with xenogenaltransmutation, a process also pioneered here at Acteon, we have succeeded in genetically engineering chimps who have a specified predisposition to any number of human psychological disorders and/or manias."

"Xeno . . . -*what?*"

"Xeno-genal-trans-mutation," Shackleman repeated. "We introduce human DNA into single-cell chimp embryos to create a sort of quasi-human lab animal."

"How do you decide which embryo gets what?" I asked, my mind spooling through a multitude of possibilities, each more fiendish than the one before. "Do you just point a finger at a test tube and say, 'Little Mookie here gets obsessive-compulsive disorder with psychotic elements'?"

"I wish it was that simple. Just because a predisposition exists does not necessarily mean that such a disorder will surface. More often than not, the manifestation of this type of condition requires some friendly persuasion. . . . The ghosts call it 'dooming and glooming.' "

"Catchy."

"Anyway, the more maladjusted a chimp is, the easier it is to evaluate the efficacy of a particular drug regimen. As you can see, we're trying to eliminate as much of the guesswork as possible."

"And I gave up duck hunting because I thought it was cruel."

"Don't be so quick to judge," said Shackleman, again lowering his voice. "For decades, your standard lab monkey was all that was needed to advance the science of pharmaceuticals. Prized for their physiological similarities to humans, researchers and scientists relied on our hairy friends to forecast the potential benefits and hazards of experimental treatments before they reached Phase III."

"Phase III is what, exactly?"

"Testing on human beings," Shackleman clarified. "If you could get monkeys through Phase II relatively unscathed, gaining FDA approval for Phase III testing was usually just a matter of filling out the forms and greasing the right palms."

I don't know if I was more horrified by hearing Shackleman go on about what I had known all along, or the simple fact that I *had* known all along. Animal testing was nothing new to me. It was one of those largely untalked-about blemishes on the underbelly of human society that we subordinate to our own selfish needs. Chemotherapy. Anti-wrinkle lotion. Non-dairy cheese products that don't require refrigeration.

"However," Shackleman went on, "with the sudden influx of space-age mood-altering drugs, the FDA really started cracking down. When you're talking about pumping chemical cocktails that are not entirely understood into the behavior centers of the human brain, the powers that be understandably get a little antsy."

"God bless American bureaucracy."

"*Anyway*, the FDA no longer regards your basic tree-climber as the tell-all barometer it once did. Nowadays, the required duration of Phase II testing is such that it becomes prohibitively expensive to test all but the most lucrative of potential drug therapies. Who can say how many revolutionary new drugs have been shelved while still in development because of cost overrun?"

"What you're telling me is that these are high-priced guinea pigs you're raising here."

"I know what you're thinking," Shackleman admitted. "But it's not like that anymore—at least, not for some of us. Originally, Acteon came up with the idea of genetically engineering chimps to meet the growing demand for nonhuman research subjects. Somewhere between the boardroom and the chimps becoming self-aware, the lines got blurred."

"It sounds to me as if you got more than you bargained for."

"I'm not sure whether it's good or bad, but this thing with the murders has left us at an impasse. We've leapfrogged a hundred million years of evolution in the blink of an eye, only to become divided as how best to exercise our newfound omnipotence."

"I'm not sure I follow you."

"This isn't Halloween candy we're talking about. These creatures are being handed souls. Imagine the unfulfilled longing they must feel, the lack of direction. They need spiritual guidance, Mr. Flowers. They need someone to show them the way."

"I suppose you have someone particular in mind?"

Shackleman shook his head sullenly. "Janus would never allow it. He calls them the last of the innocents. He's like an overprotective father."

"He mentioned something about a cell phone."

Shackleman brightened. "That's precisely my point—they know that something else is out there. Keeping it from them is a crime. It's immoral."

"How many of these superchimps have you created since the beginning of all this?"

"Eight hundred sixty-three."

"How many of those actually lived to see puberty?" I asked. "The mortality rate must have been through the roof while you worked out the bugs."

"Eight hundred sixty-three is the actual number of subjects raised to physical maturity since the project's inception."

The next question was obvious. "Where'd they all go?"

"Some were donated to universities," he informed me, somehow managing to slip the partially masticated vowels and consonants past the potato sludge in his mouth. "The rest were sold to private enterprise. Who, exactly, is writing the checks is kept strictly confidential. Only Janus and a few others have access to that information."

"What you're telling me is that there are nearly nine hundred chimps running around right now who might also be capable of murder?"

"That's not what I said!" Shackleman snapped. "Acteon is not the only genetics lab doing this sort of work. Ours is simply a variation on a theme. Other labs have been running similar programs for years. For all anyone knows, there may be thousands of genetically enhanced chimps out there. It's all very hush-hush. The STF is a prep school, Mr. Flowers. We program our subjects with the desired qualities and send them on their way. What happens to them after that is anyone's guess."

"It sounds awful," I said. "Aren't you the least bit curious?"

"If it will put your mind at ease there has been a recent shift in demand—what's hot and what's not, so to speak. It seems that our buyers are more interested in chimps whose, shall we say, genetic education is of a more classical nature. Don't ask me why, but it seems that they are more interested purchasing subjects programmed to excel in the arts and sciences than manic depression and Drug Dependency 101. Not that it matters. . . . Lately, Janus has been reluctant to let any of the subjects go no matter what the price tag."

The lunchroom was suddenly quiet. The men and women grouped around the gray Formica tables pushed their food around as if merely for show, slicing and seasoning and mumbling under their breath like convicts planning a prison break. The security guard watched over them, as totemic and foreboding as an Easter Island sentinel. His granite expression foretold an ageless wrath to any who dared defy his mute vigil. Shackleman looked around and fished a nicotine patch from his shirt pocket, removed the backing from the adhesive strip and applied it directly to his jugular.

"I've already told you . . ." he continued nervously, his voice sopranoing into a simian yelp before he could complete the sentence. His eyes bulged in their sockets and he brought both hands down on the edge of his plate, catapulting an arc of brown potato lumps past my head.

I realized quickly enough that someone had sent a bowl of scalding soup cascading down Shackleman's back. The security guard's swift intervention was all the proof I needed that the mishap was no accident. Scarcely had Shackleman's anguished cry dissipated than he was being whisked away into Dr. Dolmen's sadistic hands. Somebody didn't like what he was telling me.

As much as I wanted to feel for Shackleman—the swath of angry red blisters percolating along his spine and battery of Old World remedies he would be forced to endure as punishment for his garrulousness—I was more interested in whether or not one of Acteon's chimps may have been used to test-pilot pseuprezdid, the drug whose use the army doctors had insisted upon to better enable me to carry out Operation Slay Dracula. If this was the case, it meant that somewhere out there someone more or less like myself was every bit the unfeeling zombie I was. There was the remote possibility that I was not alone. More importantly, there was a chance that pseuprezdid's effect was reversible, or that its half-life, as intimated by my prescribers, was significantly less than the life span of the average man. There was an outside chance that one day I would be able to encounter a homeless person in the street and not think to myself, *Get a job, you filthy bum*. That one day I would hear mention of an Amtrak derailment on the six o'clock news complete with multiple fatalities and weeping eyewitnesses, and not find myself dreaming about the soothing *clakata-clak* of train travel and the green-gold panoramas of the American Midwest. The doctors were calling it compassion fatigue, an untreatable dysfunction flitting mothlike along the unresolved periphery of my soul.

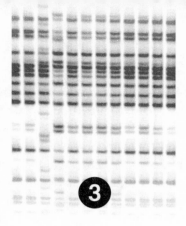

3

ANY IDIOT COULD SEE that what Acteon had achieved with the chimps was a bona fide simian renaissance. However, I could not overlook the fact that these were still only libido-driven higher-order mammals for whom a good roll in the hay and a postcoital banana was as close to experiencing God as any of them would ever get. The idea that one might actually be a calculating, cold-blooded murderer just didn't ring true. The chimps seemed to be capable of so much more than the senseless acts of violence Janus had attributed to one of their number. Although guarded with my admiration of their wondrous endeavors, I could not help but feel that they were better than this, eager young heliotropes with their gnomish faces turned toward the dawn of enlightenment. Murder was beneath them—uninspired, infinitely mortal, a human thing.

Of course I had been wrong before. A damnable industry of pulp peddlers and character bashers had arisen from the ashes of my debacle in the Gulf. Like a celestial body sharing the same cosmic neighborhood with a black hole, I was never truly free of their influence. It had taken neither my awareness of this fact nor Mr. Wonderful's looming presence to remind me that I was paddling my way through the heart of iceberg country in a paper cup. I knew with a certainty born of many such voyages that a dark catalyst lurked in the shadows of the STF, someone or some*thing* to whom neither jungle law nor the refined schemings of civilized man could be applied. On the surface, every subject within the STF was a contrast of extremes. As for what lay beneath, I've said all along that if I had been able to make sense of the chimps just a little sooner, things might have worked out differently. Lives might have been saved.

Take, for example, Leonardo 28, the elder statesman of the control group, who in spite of his exquisite work with the mechanics of flight and anatomically correct sketches of the simian form, was unable to rid himself of the parasites that regularly caused him to redirect his efforts with protractor and paintbrush toward the more urgent necessity of thinning the herds of body lice that rumbled over his hide like miniature blood-sucking bison. His genius, though formidable indeed, was ultimately subordinate to his primitive urges. Nonetheless, I could not picture the noble maestro applying the finishing touches to an inspired self-portrait and then taking batting practice on some poor slob's head with a tree branch. If I had not been blinded by the bright light shining at the top of the evolutionary ladder, I may have seen Leonardo's tortured duality for what it was. By receiving our DNA, the chimps had become every bit as confused as the fabulously wealthy tax attorney who commits suicide at thirty-five because he is so terribly afraid of dying. The chimps were beginning to understand what it meant to be human, and that rational thought as a viable route in determining one's purpose in life had been more or less a dead end since the discovery of fire.

There was Galileo 362, who with dates harvested from the tarantulean canopy of a medjool palm, had accurately charted the constellations projected onto the convex lid of the STF each simulated night, but was clearly dejected by their categorical exclusion of an invitation to be with them in the heavens. And let's not forget Marx 443 and Antoinette 68 who, though forever at odds over the distribution of resources within the enclosure, shared a mutual admiration for the work of Wright 351; a model city located at the foot of the habitation modules whose ever-evolving matrix of geodesic domes, tubular passageways, helical spires, and honeycomb ramparts evoked the futuristic structures science-fiction writers expect us to believe will one day house colonists on the inhospitable surfaces of the outer planets. 443 and 68 frequently set aside their differences long enough to reflect on 351's creation. It was as if they were envisioning a time in the not-too-distant future when they would leave behind the world of STF forever in favor of the utopian promised land dreamed by one of their own. Starry-eyed idealists, maybe. But murderers—I simply couldn't see it.

It was the behavior of Helena 12 that first opened my eyes to the possibility that these furry little men-in-the-making were every bit as capable of treachery as their human counterparts. Each morning the gregarious female would drink herself estrous on the fermented breadfruit sludge that collected in the rotted-out trunk of its parent tree. She would then throw herself at any male with enough blood in his body to get an erection. Call me sentimental, but 12 reminded me enough of my philandering wife, Janie, to consider early on that even when shopping for apples in paradise, it's not realistic to think that you won't find an occasional worm in the bunch. You have to remember these were the pet projects, the miracle births, shining prodigies who far exceeded Acteon's most ambitious expectations. These were not the carefully cultivated alcoholics, manic-depressives, and schizophrenics slated for potentially hazardous experimentation and clinical trials. Acteon had broken more than its share of eggs in putting together one hell of an omelet.

IT worked. So there was more to the chimps than met the eye. So they were artists and architects and scientists and philosophers. What about the nuances of human behavior? The little things? Acteon could pump all the smarts in the world into those wrinkled heads of theirs, but do you think for one instant that they could actually teach the chimps not to slurp their soup at the dinner table or how to spot the salad fork when appearances mattered most? What about posture and elocution? Sportsmanship? Honor among thieves? Was the veneer of civilization secondary to the thrill of uncultivatable genius?

Where were we going? Where had we been?

By day three, I was ready to pack it in. Yeah, I needed the money, but baby-sitting a group of chimpanzees who could paint the ears off Van Gogh, solve quadratic equations in a fraction of the time it took me to calculate the tip on a ten-dollar bar tab, and were getting laid more than me was not exactly good for my self-esteem. Believe me, if you'd had the kind of year I'd had, you would have felt the same way. Due in no small part to the fact that my doctor had diagnosed me as suffering from a rare and incurable form of sterility, my marriage to Janie was falling apart. Although I couldn't prove it, I was fairly certain the woman I had pledged my life to had been knocking pelvises with another man while the medical establishment made an emasculating case study out of me. Hell, I'd been bent over and rubber-gloved so many times that I had started to feel like an overgrown hand puppet. Naïvely, I had assumed that things couldn't get any worse.

X-Ray squad had been off active duty less than a year when the reports started coming in. Hell, we'd barely had time to shake the desert sand out of our boots when the shit hit the seven iron. First, Chopstix and Goof. Then, Bascombe, Chavez, and Neuhoff. After that, I lost track. Not a month went by that Saddam's assassins hadn't come calling on at least one of us. Of course we'd been aware of the risks when we had volunteered to take part in Operation Slay Dracula, but I don't think any of us expected the killing to follow us home. Of the thirteen Special Forces operatives the army had banked and bedrolled, only I was still paying taxes. The hunter had become the hunted. Ten to one, my face papered the walls of every post office in the Muslim world. I was a toe tag looking for a home.

The last thing I needed was to be upstaged by a bunch of monkeys whose future was a hell of a lot rosier than my own. I could see it already: me punching the time clock for some tin cup–carrying sidekick of an organ grinder who went home to a snifter of Napoleon brandy and his aerobics-instructor wife each night. The beautiful ivory-skinned Jane soloing on Cheetah's meat whistle while the recumbent beast laughed it up at my expense, the lowly blue-collar underling whose place on the evolutionary ladder had been leapfrogged while he scrambled to buy back his life in monthly installments from the transvestite son of an oil sultan. Don't think for one second that you wouldn't have been next in line. The writing was on the wall. Our species was up against a fate more sinister than extinction. Like the duck-billed platypus and cable TV, we were looking down the barrel of obsolescence. The fat lady may not have sung, but you can be damn sure that she was warming up her pipes.

Would man be the guinea pig of the future?

You can understand why I felt a glimmer of satisfaction on the morning of the fourth day when Kafka 99 turned up dead, hands pressed stiffly over his eyes as if death had found him in the midst of a game of peekaboo, an idiot's refuge from the violent end that had befallen him. An iridescent halo of flies, a portentous contradiction of the STF's alleged inviolability, gorged themselves on 99's pulverized remains. He had been discovered heaped in the shadow of a mulberry tree on the edge of the Enchanted Forest. A hands-on examination would reveal that 99's eyes were missing altogether, gouged from his skull and removed from the crime scene in a symbolic act of vengeance, no doubt. Although all of the chimps wore tracking collars that should have made establishing their whereabouts a simple matter of reviewing the surveillance files, there were apparent glitches in the program. According to surveillance, 99 had kept to himself the majority of the day in which he had been murdered. True, at one point the alphanumeric signatures broadcast by him and Helena 12 had occupied the same cyberspace grid, their overlapping pixels virtually indistinguishable from one another. Ultimately, however, the two had gone their separate ways: Helena 12 back to the Haunted Mansion; Kafka 99 off into the knotted bowels of the Enchanted Forest, where he would meet his death. For the time being, though, exactly how the perpetrator had managed to elude detection was of secondary importance to me. Something about the killing felt right. Deserved. In keeping with the cosmic order. Not murder, but necessary. It was as if natural selection had cast its vote in favor of the status quo, had upheld the verdict that man alone sit atop the food chain. It was when I saw the effect 99's death was having on the other members of the control group that something inside of me clicked. The parallel between the atmosphere of the Haunted Mansion and my own plight with Mr. Wonderful was inescapable. It was not so much fear in their expressions as it was a reflection of utter hopelessness. Their world, like my own, was nowhere near big enough in which to hide. I doubt they would have felt any differently had they realized the microcosm in which they had been raised from birth was only a tick nourished by the blood of a much bigger monster. The reality would have simply been that much more daunting, that much scarier, that much less manageable within the limited scope of their experience. The killer was as much a part of their destiny as Operation Slay Dracula and Saddam Hussein's many faces were of my own.

Nearly every homicide can be broken down into five integral elements: when, where, why, how and by whom? The goal is to determine as many of the five as possible and plug them into an equation. Basic algebra. Crunch the constants to nail down the variables. Usually, *where* is the most obvious. People tend not to get around as much when they're dead. Death is retirement in the strictest sense of the word. It's like Florida without the orange juice and hurricanes. So much for the law of averages. Surveillance had captured nothing out of the ordinary the night 99 was murdered. One sweep of the camera, and the STF was as calm and uneventful as a swan-boat ride; the next, it looked as if LAPD had revisited upon 99 a more savage version of the beating that had made a rich man out of Rodney King. Because of the location of the corpse, smart money placed the scene of the crime somewhere within the wooded enclave, but in no way was logistical probability a lock. I needed proof. Was it Albert Einstein who said that hypotheses make interesting dinner conversation, but it's hard data that pays the bills?

Equally discouraging was the condition of the body. The degree of mutilation opened the door for any number of answers to the *how* question. In many of the case studies I had read, the perpetrator of similar acts of violence had expressed a desire to kill that which could not be physically destroyed: race, culture, ideology. In these instances, physical murder was merely an outlet for the expression of a much deeper, more personal hatred. Kill the body and the spirit will die seemed to be the driving force behind such acts of wanton brutality. Of course, all the literature was derived from human subjects and could in no way be applied with certainty to Acteon's chimpanzees. So far, I was batting zero.

In spite of some persuasive wrangling, the ghosts were reluctant to get behind my suggestion that I be allowed to poke around inside the enclosure. The idea that a machete-happy trailblazer could accomplish anything a man with a discerning eye could not was absurd to them and moreover, I suspected, a not-so subtle jab at my investigative prowess. As far as Janus was concerned, the trail of blood began and ended in precisely the spot where the body of Kafka 99 had been discovered. He had dismissed my request for admittance to the STF with Dalai Lama–like airs.

"Without raising a foot, you are there already," he informed me breezily.

As for the *by whom*, I used what little footage there was to hammer out a list of suspects based on the process of elimination. When applicable, a good criminal profiler will reduce the field of suspects by doing some preliminary detective work. With Shackleman still recovering from his soup burns, a nasty second-degree job Dolmen was probably treating with a poultice of deadly nightshade, Janus assigned me a nerdy young research assistant named Lepke. Together, Lepke and I managed to establish the whereabouts of thirty-five chimps during the time period in which 99's murder had taken place. Although all of the chimps looked basically the same to me, Lepke was able to tell them apart with an ease and familiarity that left me feeling, for lack of a better word, bigoted.

After several hours in the surveillance booth, I had eleven suspects to go on, none of whom I could pick out of a police lineup should the need have ever arisen. Only later would I learn that Lepke had identified the rogue chimpanzees by the alphanumeric signatures broadcast via their ID collars. Throughout the day in question, each, including the now-dearly-departed Kafka 99, had randomly disappeared into the untamed nether regions of the Enchanted Forest. All but for the one glaring exception had yet to return.

"We've seen this sort of behavior before," Lepke explained, picking out encoded blips on a computer monitor with the tip of a mechanical pencil. "I guess it started around the time they found the cell phone. I'm sure Janus told you about it. Anyway, sometimes they'll be in there for days at a time doing God only knows what."

Lepke's skin emitted a sickly low-voltage light, the dull sunless tint of a ballooning cyberculture whose lives are spent surfing the Internet for free porno in the high end of the ultraviolet spectrum. His voice was unnaturally shrill for a man on the lee side of twenty-five, possessing neither the testoseronated rough-ness of post-pubescence nor the bass octaves triggered by the descent of the testes.

"Why not go in with a couple of chainsaws and cut the whole godforsaken mess down?" I asked. "It'll make your job a hell of a lot easier. Just don't let the tree-huggers hear about it."

"Nature versus nurture," Lepke replied. "Doctor Janus is a firm believer in the clinical benefits of an organic setting."

Although Lepke's explanation was too neat, too patently simple, I had my list of suspects. Totaling eleven, each could be circumstantially linked to 99's death. It could have been any of them. It could have been all of them. What if the chimps had simply stood by and watched, participated even, as one of their own was bludgeoned to death? After all were these bony-browed little men-in-the-making not that much less removed from the dark dawn of creation than ourselves and therefore more greatly inclined toward acts of the basest animal aggression? I'm no behaviorist, but it makes sense. So maybe I wasn't ready to tes-tify before a federally appointed Senate committee. As theories go, it made me feel a hell of a lot better than simply admitting that man has sole proprietorship over crimes of unspeakable savagery. I was drawn to the possibility that all I had been through since mortgaging my soul for a phony ideal was part of a much older and more deeply ingrained mechanism than I had ever imagined. There may have been no discernible purpose to the madness, but at least I had come by it honestly.

As for the *why* of 99's death—that was for God to sort out. I had enough on my plate already without having to unravel the mysteries of the simian psyche. Even with humans the answers are never as simple as you hope. Traumatic childhood, umbilical cord looped around the neck at birth, heavy-metal music—did it really matter why? The search for an answer presupposes that a reason is available. No answer is also an answer. No reason is also a reason.

Evidence gathering had not exactly been my strong suit of late. I suspected everyone and could finger no one. Take Janie's affair with Sasquatch. I was adequately certain that she had been running her fingers through the luxuriant thickets of hair on another man's back, yet I couldn't prove a thing. I had been stalking my own wife on and off for nearly a month and had not been able to place her in the same zip code with anyone suspicious enough to consider a suspect.

Half-hoping to confirm my fears, I had borrowed a friend's car and followed Janie to work one day. As much as I dreaded what I might discover, I was desperate. The thought that I was, as Janie would later charge, a paranoid nut, was in its own way more sobering than the possibility that my one-and-only was an adulteress.

I waited in the parking lot outside the law offices where she earned a good living as a paralegal. By the time she emerged for lunch, I had read the sports page twice and had called in to several talk-radio shows, anonymously voicing my opinions on everything from deadbeat dads to the woeful Cincinnati Bengals. Janie climbed into her car, checked her makeup in the rearview mirror, and drove off alone. So much for my theory that she was diddling one of the attorneys, a wild workplace affair consummated between legal briefs on overstuffed cordovan armchairs and in utility closets among the mop buckets and disinfecting urinal cakes. I tailed her anyway, hanging back several car lengths on the off chance that she was en route to some prearranged rendezvous. A few blocks later, my grim hopes were rejuvenated when she ducked into a corner liquor store and reappeared with a bottle of champagne dangling at her side.

The next leg of her journey carried her across town to the Nite Lite Motel, a miserable ghetto-adjacent dive advertising "sAniT!z d ooms aND hoUrLY rAt s" on its ailing marquee. I don't know what bothered me more, the idea that my wife was screwing someone else or that she was so goddamn cavalier about it. I was devastated at how premeditated all of this was for her: the long lunch, the bubbly, the seedy room at Chez Caligula with the condom dispenser on the bathroom wall and swaybacked vibrating bed. Add this to the fact that I couldn't remember the last time we'd made love and you can see why I was fraught with indecision and self-pity. Should I count my losses and write Janie off with the others, consider her MIA and etch her name among the many in the Wailing Wall of my heart? Or should I wait until her secret lover showed up? Kick open the door and catch them in the act, their heaving bodies torturing the bedsprings?

I decided that confronting one cornered animal was risky enough. To take on two was inviting trouble. After all, I only wanted my wife back. The less drama there was, the easier it would be to pick up the pieces and move on with our lives. The last thing I needed was some guy with a cock to his knees mediating our dispute.

I took a deep breath, prepared myself for the litany of accusations and counteraccusations I knew was coming and knocked.

"It's unlocked," Janie breathed expectantly.

I knew I'd been ambushed the moment I stepped into the room. The lights were on, the bed was made—the pop of the champagne cork, a fatal sniper shot. Janie did not look directly at me, but appraised my reflection in the bathroom mirror opposite where I stood reeling in the doorway as if mortally wounded. She stood at the sink, stripping the sanitized wrap from a plastic cup.

"A fake beard, Dutch," she remarked disappointedly, her expression summarizing our mutual shame. "How stupid do you think I am?"

For the first time since I had set out earlier that morning, I noticed the woolly prosthesis clinging to my face like an under-sexed raccoon.

"You look ridiculous," she continued calmly, filling one of the cups with champagne and holding it out for me.

"I thought I looked pretty convincing."

"If your intent was to look like a nut. You're going to scare people running around like that. I thought about calling the police when you were parked out in front of my work all morning."

Janie was right. I looked like someone out of a Russian fairy tale, a wild-eyed Cossack moonshiner who operates a vodka still in the hoary heart of a Siberian woods. Nonetheless, I left the beard on. The magician doesn't abandon the illusion because some loudmouth in the audience blabs the secret. It's all about showmanship, particularly when up against a hostile crowd. I accepted the champagne, smoothed the beard away from my mouth, and tilted back the stinging bubbles.

"At least now I know why I couldn't find my styling mousse this morning," Janie went on, her eyes resolutely fixed on my reflection in the mirror. "And I thought *I* was losing my mind. You must have gone through the entire can getting your hair to stand up like that."

"I guess we should talk."

"I don't like being followed," Janie replied flatly. "I'm not a case, Dutch. I'm your wife. Either trust me or leave me, but don't treat me like one of your low-life clients."

She studied me in the mirror and sipped her champagne.

We talked like that for fifteen minutes maybe, never looking directly at one another. No layers, no subtexts, no angles. Every-thing laid out flat. In the end we agreed that I wouldn't follow her anymore and that she would forget it had ever happened. She claimed the coarse black hairs and musky animal scent entrenched in much of her wardrobe came compliments of an overly friendly lab that belonged to one of her girlfriends at work. It was an honest mistake, she admitted sympathetically, baggage I had brought home with me from the Gulf.

Despite my shame at having been exposed, I was not able to shake the image of my cream-complected bride entwined in the embrace of a hirsute Adonis. That I hadn't actually witnessed her in the vicinity of the alleged canine she lovingly referred to as Poochie only meant that I was no closer to uncovering the truth. Either my beloved Janie was capable of greater deception than I had ever realized, or I was a lousy detective. If she was telling the truth then my investigative instincts weren't worth their weight in horsemeat on the Parisian black market. Although I'd have to go about it with greater stealth than I had previously imagined, I was more determined than ever to prove that the woman I loved was the adulterous fraud I knew her to be.

There were times when I wondered if Janie was right, that my suspicions were an ugly manifestation of the terminal uncertainty I had contracted while driving X-Ray squad through the heart of Old Testament country in search of a ghost. We had prowled our way among date plantations studded with antipersonnel mines supplied by our own government, through silver and green oases awash in toxic residue from the chemicals used to process the thick-as-tar crude into reformulated unleaded for the discriminating motorist. We shook our booties in nightclubs and in spots frequented by disco-dancing government bigshots and civic-minded dignitaries. We sipped hand-pressed apricot nectar and broke bread in the boulevard cafés of boomtown oil cities where the economy was good as long as Saddam Hussein said so, and where the bad guys shot it out with the Republican Guard in front of the auxiliary federal building and no one seemed to have any idea who was who. Thinning Hussein's stable of trained look-alikes, an operation plagued by indecision and second-guessing, had not exactly worked wonders on my ability to distinguish between fantasy and reality. Knowing this, it was still easier for me to blame Janie than to consider that my sanity was short-circuiting one synapse at a time.

● ● ●

On the morning of the third day, while the chimps clustered around the pulverized remains of Kafka 99, swaying and sizing up one another like happy-hour drunks staking their claim at the buffet table, I was in Janus's grotto debriefing the eccentric recluse on my findings and impressions of the first seventy-two hours inside the STF. His voice rose out of the darkness like jungle drums, its ominous intonation as mysterious and fore-boding as a declaration of tribal warfare. I couldn't get past the feeling that encoded within the halting aria of breathy vowels and rugged phonemes lay some cryptic agenda, a colossal scheme in which I had become hopelessly enmeshed.

"What you are telling me, Mr. Flowers," Janus clarified as if for my benefit as well as his own, "is that you have nothing."

"What I have, Doctor, is a corpse that looks like it's been kicked around the track at Santa Anita. With all due respect, sir, this isn't astronomy we're talking about. Distant planets don't bash each other's brains in. Murder is an up-close-and-personal business. Contrary to what you might think, criminal investiga-tion isn't an armchair science. I need to get inside, poke around, get my hands dirty."

In the blunted light I could make out the contours of a brooding monolith overgrown with shaggy vegetation. It was distinctly humanoid—an enormous skull or the bust of some long-vanquished pagan deity. As a kid growing up I had watched made-for-TV movies about islands inhabited by lost tribes who worshiped the airplanes that soared across the heavens like giant silver birds. Standing there in that dark and wild place filling my lungs with the moldering fug of rotting organics and the excre-mental rainfall of shiny-eyed tree dwellers, it was as if I had wan-dered onto the set of *Cannibal Island,* an accidental tourist in the lost and perilous world of my youth.

"Two hours," I continued, toe-testing the ground beneath me for a spot that wouldn't slurp and bubble each time I shifted my weight. "That's all I'm asking."

"Impossible," Janus replied flatly.

"It's not much, but I can get by with half that if I absolutely have to."

"I'm sorry, Mr. Flowers. You knew the rules when you signed on. The planets do not simply stop spinning because one man is unable to establish a foothold."

"You hired me to catch a murderer. So far, all I've done is spy on a bunch of horny, overachieving monkeys. I feel like one of those guys who plunks quarters into a booth so he can watch some cornfed Iowa runaway fondle herself behind an inch-thick pane of greasy Plexiglas."

I stood there for several moments awaiting Janus's response, sinking ever deeper into the marshy substrate that had already ruined one pair of shoes and was well on its way to making a mess of another.

"There is a Zen proverb, Mr. Flowers, that says, 'When you boil rice, know that the water is your own life.' If the water is not to your liking, then might I suggest you find a different pot in which to boil it."

"Fifteen minutes," I urged. "Not a second more. In and out."

"I will cooperate with you to the extent that it will not jeopardize the clinical integrity of the project, but no more. If I were to let you inside the enclosure, your presence would invalidate everything we have achieved so far. In case you haven't noticed, Mr. Flowers, you are witnessing the dawn of self-awareness, the coming of age of a species more closely related to your own than you might think. Every subject within the enclosure has been raised independently of direct human contact. Think of yourself as a contagion. The smallest degree of exposure could trigger an epidemic."

"So dope them up with vitamin C. They're chimpanzees, for God's sake!"

"No, Mr. Flowers," Janus corrected, "they are tomorrow's doctors and teachers and heads of state."

"You left out supermodels and commercial airline pilots."

"I can see, Mr. Flowers, that like most men you are only half awake."

I was tempted to hang it up, to simply walk away from the STF and never look back. However, the fact remained that I was still a few zeros shy of Mr. Wonderful's monthly installment.

Whether or not I gave a damn about the chimps was immaterial. The fact that I could not summon a nanoliter of pity from the stingy depths of my soul did not preclude me from valuing my own hide. The bitch meant business. Five of my closest friends—men who had watched my back and risked their lives for me—had failed to ante up and had paid with their lives. In a way, I envied the poor bastards—Chopstix, Goof, Bascombe—the hunt being over and all. No more checking under the bed at night, no more wetting my pants when the phone rang, no more hiding in the chimney every time a Girl Scout came a-knockin' with Pecan Sandies for sale. I tried not to think of my arrangement with Wonderboy as extortion, but simply as another cost of living, which isn't as far from the truth as it might seem taking into account the fact that without it I was fertilizer.

You're probably wondering why Mean Green wasn't watching my back considering my history of dedicated military service. Seven years in Special Forces and hung out to dry. The answer is simple: categorical disavowal. The "official" mission parameter of X-Ray's presence in the Gulf was simply to function in an advisory role, a benign shepherd in the interminable war against escalating gas prices and, of course, the tyrannical reign of the Middle East's most reviled supervillain since Ali Baba. No covert ops—just friendly good old U.S. know-how for our comrades in Kuwait. This was to be a war of principle and democratic ideals, a gallant stab at the heart of oppression. If the American public ever found out that murder, cold and calculated, was Slay Dracula's primary means of knocking ten cents off the price at the pump, the unequivocal hypocrisy of it all would no doubt resurrect the nagging ghosts of incursions past: Grenada, Panama, Vietnam. The bungled bid for the life of the dictator the American motorist loved to hate would make the fall of Saigon look like the wrap party for a B-movie.

Hours after Kafka 99 turned up dead, a six-man insertion team was sent in to clean up the mess. Outfitted in canary-colored biohazard suits and equipped with a suspect array of medical apparatus, the rubberized specters moved among the anesthetized subjects like CDC agents responding to an outbreak of the Ebola virus. While four of the six busied themselves with snow shovels and a body bag, the two others stood guard, tasers clutched at the ready. I could practically feel the nervous sweat runneling over their sealed-in flesh only to accumulate in the airtight booties guarding their penny loafers.

"From the way they're hanging onto those things," I said, nudging Lepke in the ribs, "you'd think they expected King Kong to come crashing out of the woods wearing a bib and waving a salt shaker."

Lepke winced.

"These *are* wild animals we're dealing with, Mr. Flowers," he reminded me. "The fact that their level of intelligence far exceeds that of any creature in the natural world only makes them that much more dangerous."

While Lepke and I steamed up the observation port with our noses pressed to the glass, 99's pallbearers worked quickly and efficiently, checking over their shoulders every now and then to see that their comrades-at-arms had not gone AWOL. By that time, I had reached a level of anticipation in which anything less than a 20,000-volt showdown between man and charging knuckle-dragger would have been anticlimactic. For the next several minutes, I looked on with a morbid sense of urgency like a ringside spectator at a heavyweight bout awaiting the clang of the bell, my hopes of witnessing a caste war between adjacent lines of hominids diminishing with each passing moment. Ultimately, it was my embarrassment at what I was about to witness that dropped anchor on my depraved little fantasy.

"Watch this," Lepke trilled hoarsely, his nerdy decorum surrendering to the forbidden rite enacted on the other side of the proverbial keyhole.

One after another the insertion team converged on preselected females to harvest viable ova—"Gen Twos" as they were called—and to abort any embryos conceived outside the careful supervision of the Acteon xenogenaltransmutation specialists. Armed with specula and a handheld vacuum, the ghosts went about their business with a mechanical lack of tenderness and compassion that would have left the pro-lifers foaming at the mouth.

I won't shame you with all the details of the undignified procedure. Suffice it to say that I was panged with guilt for having put Janie through a similar hell each time we paid a visit to the invitroist. Their work with the females completed, the ghosts moved on to the males, drawing blood and tissue samples and siphoning off sperm by way of electrostimulation—a quick zap to the testes with a cattle prod, and voilà! a half-dozen or so twist-tied condoms brimming with potential progeny. I cringed at the thought of Dr. Dolmen employing a similar tactic should I have been less cooperative with his forceful request.

Lepke assured me that the macabre ritual was absolutely necessary for the continued success of the IT project. However, it was plain to me that his interest in the proceedings was of a more perverse and personal nature. If you think for one second that he wasn't totally enthralled with the harvest's kinkier aspects, it is only because you weren't there to see the erection stirring lazily beneath the fabric of his trouser front like a newborn invertebrate yearning for admittance to the world.

After each procedure, the patient was dusted with insecticide to inhibit the proliferation of parasites and to keep a stranglehold on the spread of infectious disease within the STF.

"But it's a closed system," I pressed naïvely. "How the hell is anyone going to get sick in there?"

"Fleas and ticks, the foot soldiers of pestilence," Lepke explained with puritan zeal. "As you can probably imagine several of the technicians are dog and cat owners—soup kitchens for bloodsuckers if you ask me."

"The pets or their owners?"

"*Any-way.* . . ." Lepke continued. "Occasionally one of the little devils jumps ship, hops a ride and half the subjects come down with hepatitis. Fleas are like bloodhounds. If there's a warm body in the vicinity, they'll find it. Originally, we thought if we shaved the chimps bald—destroyed the fleas' habitat so to speak—we could better manage the problem. Fortunately, we realized our mistake before it got out of hand."

"Don't tell me, you had to knit Kojak a sweater so he wouldn't catch a cold?"

"Prejudice," said Lepke. "The other chimps nearly killed the shaved subject. Clearly, they no longer regarded him as one of the group. He was seen as an outsider, and therefore a threat."

"They probably mistook him for a human."

"Impossible. The chimps are as unaware of us as are we of the bacteria living in our digestive tract."

When you consider the surreal methodology of the specimen-gathering expeditions—the dozens of burgled ovaries and wicked-looking spinal taps—the harvests were suspiciously evocative of the alien-abduction scenarios recalled under hypnosis by undersexed housewives in the pages of supermarket tabloids. Lepke confessed that it was not entirely unheard-of for one of the chimps to regain consciousness during the procedure due to the imprecise manner by which the knockout gas was administered.

"It's really something to see—all that screaming and carrying on when they come to," Lepke intimated, his lilting voice acquiring a sadistic edge. "Imagine what's going on inside their heads—the suits alone, for fuck's sake." He shivered for effect. "*Brrrrr!* Just thinking about it makes me want to sleep with the lights on."

Here they were, a happy-seeming civilization of fifty-two minus the half-dozen now dead, snug in their own cozy little world, equally naïve in their understanding of the forces that lay beyond the periphery of everyday experience as we humans are of the indecipherable phenomena that constitute our most primitive fears. Imagine awakening half-drugged to find yourself hopelessly paralyzed and subjected to the whim of a team of rubberized entities armed with an array of sinister instruments and unfathomable intent. The chimps were ordinary individuals like you and me, forced to endure unspeakable humilities at the hands of a malevolently superior intelligence. I'd seen enough. Isn't it always the way? You find your conscience where you least expect it, and from that point on nothing's ever the same. Don't get me wrong. I didn't actually feel sorry for them. I couldn't have if I had wanted to. Pity simply wasn't in me, a character defect for which I have the army and pseuprezdid to thank. Nonetheless, I knew that I was supposed to feel sorry for the chimps and this alone was enough to get me thinking.

By acknowledging the fact that I was sick, wasn't I taking a step toward wellness? Does not the alcoholic have to admit his dependence before the healing process can begin? Deep down, I believed that if I could save the chimps from the twofold menace of the STF that I would be that much closer to exorcising my own demons. No creature, neither man nor animal, should be prisoner to the gross indignities they were forced to endure. Janus may have been right after all. Maybe the chimps and I were closer than I had previously dared to consider.

As the anesthetic wore off, the chimps awoke to a world that was much as they had left it: a botanical utopia minus the snow-shoveled remains of Kafka 99 that now awaited my inspection in an enormous Tupperware casserole like so much marinara. Although it was clear that the chimps were unable to pinpoint the precise nature of their artificially induced slumber, I got the feeling that they knew all was not as they had left it. Instinctively, they realized that they were not the same beings who seemingly only moments earlier had been huddled over their slain comrade now mysteriously absent from their number—victims of the phenomenon ufologists refer to as "missing time."

Of course there was the physical evidence, the corporeal residue of the wholesale violations committed against them while suffering the blank oblivion of the knockout gas. Nearly an hour after he had been revived, Edison 215 was still massaging the base of his skull where a large-bore hypodermic had been inserted to extract fluid from his brain stem. Curie 421, brow deeply furrowed and rubbing her abdomen, reclined against the trunk of the magnolia beneath which she had been impregnated by Mao 146 two months earlier. Sartre 376 and Frost 112 had awakened to resume their grooming of one another, only to find that not a single living parasite remained on either of them, apparent casualties of the bitter-tasting snow-fall of Diazinon powder now dusting their hides. Slapping their heads and tugging lamentably at their lips, they mourned the unspeakable loss, a tragedy that made the fate of the Donner Party look like a snowball fight run amok.

Then there were the more subtle signs: the heightened awareness of their surroundings, the uncertain footsteps and tentative caresses with which they seemed to test the solidity of their little world inside the enclosure upon first awakening from the dark, dreamless sleep. They knew. They had to know. How else would you explain the bowlegged exodus to the stream where one after another they crouched on its grassy banks, shrieking and splashing themselves with water as if to wash away the instinctive knowledge of the violations locked deep within their collective subconscious? If you had seen them carrying on like that, you, too, would have realized these were not the same happy-go-lucky primates who, a short while earlier, had been fornicating like there was no tomorrow and unlocking the mysteries of the not-so-natural world. They were not alone and they knew it. One moment they were grappling with the concept of God, the next, they were reevaluating everything they thought they knew about the universe and their place in it. Evil had wandered into the garden while their backs were turned and had upset the applecart for the second time in as many visits.

Eventually things inside the STF returned to normal, but as much as the chimps were not the same beings I had naïvely perceived them to be, I was not the same man who had been hired to identify the killer in their midst. I resumed my vigil with a greater sense of purpose than getting my hands on Mr. Wonderful's blood money alone could have inspired. I didn't have any children of my own thanks to what the medical establishment has cruelly designated "indolent" sperm, but as a former Special Forces CO, I had an acute familiarity with what it means to have others depend on you to keep them alive.

For some time I had been resigned to the fact that sooner or later the cost of living would overtake my earning potential, and that no matter how many convenience stores I robbed to keep Mr. Wonderful off my back, I was only delaying the inevitable. My father, rest his soul, once told me that every man must take at least one stand in his life to be counted among the righteous.

Considering that my lease on life was about to be canceled and that my opportunities at stand making were in perilously short supply, I figured it was now or never. I may not have been able to save Chopstix and the others from a lunch date with the Reaper, but I was determined to keep my defenseless charges out of harm's way no matter what it took.

So much for noble intentions. The next morning, in 100,000 watts of metal-halide daylight, Helena 12 was cut cleanly in two as she attempted—disoriented and bleeding profusely—to crawl into her habitation module. The motion-sensitive double doors had snapped closed prematurely, dividing her into roughly equal halves. It was no accident. The ID collars worn by the chimps were equipped with remote fail-safes that negated the possibility of such a malfunction. Sometime during the previous night, 12 had been badly beaten and both her ears torn from her head. Apparently this was done to facilitate the removal of the ID collar, the whereabouts of which was never determined. Transformed into a walking booby trap, she never knew what hit her. The postmortem also revealed contusions and tissue damage to the genitalia consistent with those found in cases of sexual assault. However, because of 12's checkered reputation, further inquiry was—particularly in light of the fact that she was already dead—deemed redundant and a waste of time. The ghosts were quick to remind me that she was no Ethel Kennedy.

Surveillance footage showed a collared 12 entering the Enchanted Forest at approximately 4:32 P.M., accompanied by three of her contemporaries. Seven hours later, she was picked up on night vision—sans collar—a wounded chimp staggering across the aqueous green landscape in the direction of the Haunted Mansion and the makeshift guillotine that would spell her death. As for the three who had accompanied her earlier that morning, they had been located via radio transponder, slow-moving blips scattered throughout the uncharted interior of the Enchanted Forest like survivors of a shipwreck swept apart by the ocean currents.

Everywhere I looked lives full of promise and possibility were being cut short. The STF's best and brightest had circumvented natural selection only to fall victim to a far less finicky predator. It had been slow going picking over the personal data files Acteon had provided me to help expose the killer. Replete with information on both the physiological and psychological makeup of those humans whose DNA had been integrated with that of the chimps, the files had proven too copiously comprehensive for snap analysis. At times fascinating, at others just plain tedious, the long-winded dossiers read like those epic biographies that are all the rage in the academic community, however are ill-suited to the fly-on-the-wall attention spans of the pulp gobblers responsible for the *New York Times* best-seller list.

The night of 12's death I was haunted by the paradoxical stares with which the chimp passersby regarded her booby-trapped torso lying on the ground some twenty feet below the antiseptic box she had called home. If these had been humans we were talking about, I would have sworn it was envy, brash and unrepentant, glinting in those unfathomable black eyes of theirs. Something was terribly wrong in the sunless depths of the Enchanted Forest. I could feel it in my BVDs. Like the canals of Venice, one had only to look beneath the surface to glimpse the malignant undercurrents gondoliers kept at bay with deliberate pole-thrusts. In less time than it had taken 12's thinking half to realize that she was dead, I had decided that I was going in.

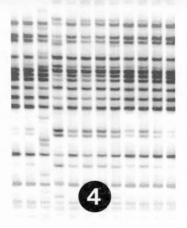

4

SATISFIED THAT SHACKLEMAN WAS ON THE ROAD to a speedy recovery from his soup burns, Dr. Dolmen had prescribed a yellow foul-smelling unguent and had ordered the miserable creature back to work. When I caught up with him in his office late that afternoon, he was sitting alone at his desk staring despondently into space. There was no doubt in my mind that he wanted to get rid of me ASAP and return to whatever rituals of internment he practiced as Janus's beleaguered chargé d'affaires.

"No," said Shackleman, burying his face in a stack of paperwork, a greasy rectangle of gauze covering the back of his neck. "Absolutely not."

"Anything I needed," I reminded him gently. "Those were your exact words."

"Yes, Mr. Flowers, I know what I said. But I'm afraid—"

"Of what?" I pressed. "That you'll get fired? If you ask me, it'd be the best thing that ever happened to you. For starters, you could stop wearing those ridiculous nicotine patches and start living your life again."

Shackleman lifted his head and cornered me with a debilitated smile. His eyes were bloodshot and watery.

"Have you been crying?" I asked.

"That's none of your business," he informed me abruptly. "Have you looked at the book?"

"Have I looked at it?" I echoed incredulously. "I can't put it down."

"What about the pages I circled?"

"To be honest I'm the sort of guy who prefers a good old-fashioned shoot-'em-up western. Cattle rustlin', hookers with wooden legs who carry derringers in their garters. I appreciate the gesture and all, but autobiographies really aren't my thing."

It was as if Shackleman had wandered into the focused beam of a death ray.

"You haven't read the book," he groaned weakly, his collar stained pus yellow from the topical analgesic dressing his wound.

"A woman died in there today!" I proclaimed forcefully, expressing a heroic conviction in no way influenced by my brain's comatose compassion center.

"12 was a whore!" Shackleman blurted, catching me by surprise.

"Why don't you tell me how you really feel?"

"I'm sorry," he continued, aligning himself along a different tack. "It's just that I'm in a lot of pain. 12's one of the lucky ones. Being human is not all it's cracked up to be. So many questions. And who are you supposed to turn to for answers? Philosophers? Your horoscope? Holy men? The pope is nothing more than a fortune cookie with a pretty hat."

"Then help me. Let me do something noble."

Shackleman glanced at the surveillance camera glaring downward from the ceiling like a high-tech gargoyle.

"I offered you my help and you ignored it."

"Give me another chance," I begged. "I'll do whatever you say. I'll read Bobo's book from cover to cover, if that's what you want."

"It's too late. There's nothing I can do for you that I haven't done already."

On my way out of Shackleman's office, I passed a guy in the hallway whom I had never seen before. Had it not been for the graphite swarf of hair hedged neatly above his collar, it would have been nearly impossible to guess his age, a figure I estimated to be in the vicinity of fifty. Other than the color of his skin, which was the dull pinkish-brown hue of a Band-Aid, he was tall and straight and fit-looking. Equal parts arrogance and leisure, his was the sort of face that pops up on brochures advertising luxury golf-course estates to wealthy retirees. It didn't take a hell of a lot of imagination to envision him zipping around between club tennis tournaments and martini luncheons in a convertible Porsche with a wife half his age in the passenger seat checking her face. He narrowed his eyes and fixed me with a cold smile as if I had just informed him that the timeshare in Aruba had already been booked over Christmas. Something told me that I hadn't seen the last of him.

I had been brainstorming various schemes to get my hands on the STF's access code for close to an hour when my eyes settled on the book Shackleman had given me. According to the banner printed across the top of the dust jacket in exclamatory red bold-face, the ape with the all-seeing eyes was a best-selling author. As much as I hated the thought of subjecting myself to such unabashed lunacy, I was short on leads. I began with the fore-word, as perplexing and mysterious an *éclaircissement* as has been penned since the Dead Sea Scrolls. No sooner had I gotten a feel for Bobo's eloquent prose than I remembered what Shackleman had said about marking the pages he thought I would find par-ticularly interesting. Skimming through the text, I came across four pages whose numbers had been circled in the same nonde-script blue ink favored by whoever was responsible for the baf-fling annotations crowding the margins.

   6, 43, 59, 82

To the layman's eye the numeric markers would have no doubt been dismissed as nonsense, their unfettered simple-mindedness deferring to the reasonable supposition that the hand guiding the pen was slave to an insane master.

   6, 43, 59, 82

As far as I could tell, the selections were consistently unnote-worthy. In fact, page 59 marked the end of a chapter, an expanse of paper virtually blank but for an enigmatic sentence fragment declaring ". . . lest we allow them to forget that one of ours was at the helm of the first *manned* space flight."

6, 43, 59, 82

Rather than boring you with an immodest catalog of the faster-than-light computations schussing from neuron to neuron within my brain, suffice it say that this was Shackleman's way of slipping me the access code. I had to hand it to the guy. 6435982. The idea was brilliant in its simplicity. Peanut butter and jelly. All I needed now was a diversion, something that would empty the building long enough for me to get inside the enclosure and have a look around.

I considered all the usual tricks: smoke canisters in the air ducts, anthrax scare, LSD in the water cooler. I weighed my options and decided to play it conservatively. Using my cell phone, I would call in a bomb threat from a stall in the men's room—throw in a few verses of the Koran to get their blood pumping. First things first. I needed to narrow down the field of suspects. If the Gulf had taught me anything, it was to know your target before going in, guns blazing.

The three chimps who had accompanied 12 into the Enchanted Forest on the eve of her death were also among the eleven I had circumstantially linked to the murder of Kafka 99. No matter how good you think you are, no matter how sharply honed your profiling skills may happen to be, you need to have a starting point. You just don't go for a walk around the block one day and find yourself standing in the middle of Eldorado, the buildings and streets dripping with gold.

Seventy-two hours would elapse between 12's death and the moment I would breach the pressurized threshold sealing off the enclosure from the outside world. Three days. Not a lot of time considering that I had nearly a dozen suspects to check out. Earlier in the week, I had called around to the universities to which Acteon had donated chimps. Fortunately, the corporate bookkeepers kept meticulous records of such charitable contributions for tax purposes. Apparently, this was a paper trail no one had thought to conceal from me; a simple oversight. I had hoped the lucky recipients of Acteon's dubious generosity could provide me with information about the nature of my quarry that my employers had failed to disclose. The phone calls were a bust. Of the seven department heads with whom I spoke, all seven confirmed that they no longer had Acteon's chimps in their possession. They were similarly baffled as to the whereabouts of the missing animals, all of whom had mysteriously vanished in the past year from the laboratories where they were being kept. The police still had no clues or leads as to who might be responsible for the disappearance of the chimps. Animal-rights activists seemed to be the most popular bet among a short list of possible suspects. Numerous requests from the universities had failed to procure a single additional specimen from Acteon, despite the fact that some pretty serious change had been offered up in return.

So much for jump-starting the investigation. I began the tedious process of elimination: reviewing surveillance footage, establishing timetables, eliminating the lesser of two probabilities, so to speak. The immutable laws of time and space had exonerated three of the eleven faster than you can say alibi— accomplices maybe, but certainly not the perp. For all their extraordinary talents, the chimps, to the best of my knowledge, were incapable of being in two places at once. Thus I began the arduous task of profiling each of the remaining eight suspects. I spent hours going over old medical records, news clippings, legal documents—basically, anything related to the individual whose DNA might expose the murderer survived in a chimp.

The first few were a snap. Tien Tzu 95's human benefactor had spent his entire life—one hundred twenty-one years, if the legends were to be believed—spreading the word of the Buddha in the oxygen-starved elevations of the Himalayas. Although you can't click on the six-o'clock news without hearing something about a neighborhood priest accused of fondling the altar boys, I wasn't ready to make the leap from seeker of wholeness and divine enlightenment to plunderer of eyes and ears without more to go on than the holy man's blind devotion to a grinning, potbellied deity.

Moving down the list, I learned that Rossini 232's human antecedent had been born with a degenerative spinal condition and had spent his entire life facedown in a hammock composing his celebrated fifteen-volume magnum opus, *Doctrines and Digressions in the Cosmic Parade* on the terra-cotta floor of his mother's Tuscan villa. It was conceivable that his simian reincarnate was acting out what Rossini, the man, had only been able to fantasize. However, this did not seem likely given the late Italian philosopher's famed respect for all living things. Regarded by many as the first practicing ecologist, Rossini had reportedly refused to bathe, citing that such a willful deluge would spell genocide at the microbial level for those organisms who depended on the harvest slough of dead skin cells for their survival.

There was Wilcox 156, who had washed out of the Oxford School of Medicine because he could not stomach the sight of blood, and Goebbels 311, the great instigator, neither of whom fit the hands-on profile of a serial killer. At first glance, Sing 49 appeared a strong candidate. 49's human forefather, the notorious Chinese outlaw, Han Wu Sing, had reportedly murdered a westward-bound family of six during a routine holdup. As I dug more deeply, though, I came across a xeroxed clipping from the old *Deadwood Herald* published nearly two years after Sing's death at the end of the hangman's noose. According to one P. Albert Merriwether, columnist-at-large, the "slope-eyed prospector turned bandit had run afoul of Lady Luck's ornery side that balmy afternoon in late July of eighteen-hundred and seventy-eight." The details were sketchy, but it turns out that the warning shots Sing had fired as he attempted to waylay the rickety Conestoga had spooked the horses and sent the entire rig plunging over the edge of a thousand-foot ravine in the Black Hills of South Dakota, killing everyone onboard.

So far none of the candidates possessed the calculating cold-bloodedness and hair-trigger disposition I was looking for. I'm talking about exposing a predilection for evil so deeply ingrained that not only had it managed to survive independently of the physical body for hundreds of years in some cases, but was now enjoying a sinister rebirth via the fledgling science of "trickle-down genetics," or IT as was its nondescript moniker at Acteon.

I had returned home that night hoping to spend a little

quality time with Janie, only to find the house conspicuously empty. There was a note on the refrigerator explaining that she was visiting her sister in San Diego and that it would be point-less calling her because she did not plan on spending any time near the telephone. She went on to explain that this was my fault because apparently I didn't know how to use a phone anyway— an allegation I interpreted as a metaphorical umbrella for my recent unwillingness to talk things out, more so than a jab at any demonstrated inability to grasp the push-button mechanics of telecommunication. Our relationship, as you might imagine, had not exactly been rich in productive dialogue of late. Although I have been told that I am easy to talk to, I am not exactly conversant in the language of togetherness. I have the uniquely human tendency of thinking with my head and speaking with my heart, a habit anyone suffering from acute paranoia will tell you is not an easy thing to overcome. For starters, it makes it nearly impossible for one to ingratiate one-self with loved ones. Because of this, I was left alone with my rampant suspicions and the brutal black hairs of my wife's lover, those inflexible shafts that surfaced, among other places, in our bedsheets every now and then like snippets of baling wire.

By midnight I had distilled the field of suspects to three. There was Tamara 324, Arbegast 131, and K'noon 538. Although it was true that 324's progenitor had lured many unwary travelers to their deaths, she had not exactly been proactive in her death dealings. A pretty song, a batting of eyelashes, an effortless shove out the window onto the jagged rocks far below. Calculating and cold-blooded, yes, but hardly the type to go looking for trouble. If you ask me, she was your basic spoiled rich girl, a trust-fund siren relying on the candy-coated artifice instinctive to her gender and that blissfully deepest of diversions between her legs. Besides, despite all their flaws, women just aren't serial killers. It's one of the few categories of meanness not indigenous to their nature.

A quick look at a police report filed in Point Barrow, Alaska in November 1981 was all it took to convince me that K'noon 538 was my man. Whatever. He had a rap sheet longer than the Book of Job: poaching, numerous violations of the Endangered Species Act, assault with a deadly weapon and, last but certainly not least, nine counts of first-degree murder. Although no one cared to speculate whether it was the relentless ultraviolet bombardment of the midnight sun, or the whale-blubber rotgut brewed in rusty Quonsets that had fried his brain, one thing was certain: the guy had antifreeze in his veins.

To make ends meet, the native-born Inuit had operated a small, modestly successful wildlife guide service leading weekly expeditions above the Arctic Circle where animal enthusiasts could ogle polar bears, walruses, and other subzero exotics in their natural habitat. When one such group went missing, the authorities concluded the whole kit and caboodle—tundra buggy, K'noon the great toothsome Eskimo guide and all nine paying customers—had fallen through the fragile spring ice and sunk to the bottom of the Arctic Ocean. In all likelihood, the story would have ended here, had K'noon not turned himself in nearly two months after he had been officially declared dead.

Following what was no doubt a rather rigorous interrogation by Point Barrow police, K'noon confessed to the murders of all nine members of his tour group, adamant that they had gotten what they deserved. As his health had diminished awaiting execution, so, too, had his resolve never to divulge just what had set him off on that brisk morning buggying over the frozen sea with nine red-cheeked rubberneckers in tow. Bit by bit, he painted a picture of the cultural malaise that had been gradually destroying his people and their frigid homeland. According to the man in the death-row cell adjacent to his, K'noon was like a scratched record, his mind skipping back to that fateful day again and again. Angrily, K'noon recalled how members of the group had complained about the absence of wildlife, an absence for which they and their kind were largely to blame. When he could no longer stomach their ignorance, he had shot all nine where they sat pressing their faces to the windows, and had sent the tundra buggy plunging into the glacial waters of the Arctic.

Like I said, at first glance all the pieces seemed to fit. On the surface he appeared to be the perfect suspect: patently unstable, violent in the extreme, seemingly remorseless. But something about K'noon bothered me. No two ways about it, what he had done was wrong. However there was a distinctly noble bent to his actions, an Arthurian sensibility that transcended the fiscal reality of oil pipelines and habitat-be-damned enterprise. The fact that within his community K'noon had been regarded as something of a martyr and a savior cooled me to the possibility that encoded within his DNA was an irrational and insatiable need to kill.

This left me with Arbegast 131, a special entry in the IT project I would learn soon enough was an eccentric billionaire's dubious attempt to procure an heir and bearer of the family name. Sparing no expense, Duncan Arbegast, II, CEO and controlling stockholder in Arbegast Pharmaceuticals, had sponsored an exhaustive search for his only child, Duncan Arbegast, III, who had vanished without a trace in the remote cloud forests of Papua, New Guinea. According to an exhaustive article published in *Newsweek*, the thirty-three-year-old college dropout was, among other less wholesome personas, a clinically diagnosed technophobe. The misdirected genius who had ritually mutilated neighborhood pets as a child would wet his pants at the mere sight of a computer. His pilgrimage to the mist-marbled highlands of the world's most primitive wilderness area was considered by those who knew him best—an eclectic smattering of heteroclites and antiestablishment extremists—as an escape from what he referred to as "the universal menace of technology" and a history of failed romances, whose lurid details routinely surfaced in the tabloids or legal depositions.

Although Arbegast II was intent on leaving "Dunkie" the entire family fortune, his son was not of similarly sound mind. In fact, Arbegast Jr. had told *Newsweek* that if he were to inherit his father's wealth, he would use every last penny to finance a "technocalypse," an all-out war against technology and its brainwashed disciples.

Although the disturbed young Arbegast had taken great pains to ensure that his itinerary could not be traced, a detailed how-to manual he had accidentally left behind provided several clues to his whereabouts. The unusual travel aid read like a CIA survival guide. The manual covered everything a man who planned on going native could ever need, including twenty-six ways to prepare tapioca root and an illustrated guide demonstrating the proper trajectory one's penile gourd should take when meeting with the chief of a rival clan. Too droopy and the chief might regard the gesture as an insult. Too erect and he might perceive it as a come-on. Dunkie's probable location, as it turns out, was extrapolated from a handwritten pronunciation guide for an all but defunct dialect spoken by no more than three Papuan tribes. According to the *Newsweek* article, the nuances of the language were such that a single mispronounced phoneme could be tantamount to a declaration of war. It was a dicey business living with the savages, but apparently Dunkie was willing to give up a life of privilege and wanton excess for a slope-breasted tribeswoman who would chip away the dried mud caked between his toes and lovingly tend to his jungle rot.

Although speculation of Dunkie's fate abounded in the international media, it was not until a year after his disappearance that conclusive evidence of his presence in New Guinea actually surfaced. While scouring the jungle highlands for rare and unusual specimens, an Australian kangaroo rancher turned zoo acquisitionist had stumbled into the midst of a bloody tribal war between opposing clans of headhunters. Kilter Cloud, a Botany Bay hand-me-down, had spent nearly a week as a captive guest of one of the clans. During this time he had observed the comings and goings of an exceedingly dirty Caucasian—" . . . mangy and wild-eyed as a Tasmanian devil"—who was actively participating in the nightly raids. Cloud recognized Dunkie from the pictures he had seen on the "telly." Nonetheless, it was difficult for him to accept that the "plucky school lad" and the "*feelthy* nose-boned sarvage" he had witnessed kicking around a rival clansman's head "like itwarra bloody coconut" were one and the same.

Cloud admitted that he had never actually spoken with Dunkie, though he was convinced that he would not have survived the ordeal had it not been for the intervention of young

Arbegast. That he was benefiting from the protective custody of a guardian angel would soon become eminently clear to him. During the night of Cloud's fourth day in captivity, Dunkie was kidnapped from his hut, his wife and balloon-bellied infant son murdered in their sleep. The following night, Dunkie's headless corpse was returned to the village. His mutilated body had been stripped of its ritual ornamentation and smeared with human excrement. Perhaps owing to the fact that Cloud and Dunkie were of the same skin color, the tribesmen to whom the eccentric runaway had pledged his loyalty presented Cloud with the corpse. It was as if he alone could oversee his kinsman's safe passage into the afterlife. Weak with hunger, Cloud scarcely managed to chew off a single genetic code–carrying pinkie finger from Dunkie's right hand and escape with it into the jungle. With a case of athlete's foot extending to his knees, a bellyful of intestinal parasites, and Dunkie's gnawed-on digit tucked safely away in the pocket of his trousers, Cloud crashed through the razor-sharp undergrowth for the better part of two days until he happened upon a band of loggers who delivered him to a tiny airstrip where he hopped a cargo plane back to Sydney.

Although Dunkie's pinkie finger was badly decomposed, the putrefying stub provided the Acteon geneticists with more than enough intact DNA to infuse an army of chimp Arbegast III's. Cloud, having squandered the million-dollar reward paid him by Arbegast Sr., had co-authored a best-seller inspired by his adventure in New Guinea and was currently in the midst of a twenty-two-city book-signing tour. Soon he would appear at the L.A. Book Expo, signing hardcovers for his adoring fans. I was anxious to question Cloud about anything strange he might have witnessed in Dunkie's behavior other than his apparently seamless reversion to savagery. It was essential that I cover all the bases.

It didn't take Charlie Chan to see that the connection to Arbegast 131 was a natural, unlucky thirteen coming and going. I had only to compare their file photographs to draw a similar and equally damning conclusion. On the one hand, you had Dunkie, a fluoridation conspiracy theorist *à la* Dr. Strangelove—a poorly proportioned little man with scarecrow limbs and a gargoylish face resembling that of a chimp. Then there was Arbegast—a wickedly handsome hominid who, but for the twisted scar haloing his left eye like a knothole, was physically nearer the stately form of Homo erectus. So what's in a picture, you might ask? You do the math. Over here you had Dunkie, the dark and cunningly adaptive but discernibly fragile Yin essence. Then take Arbegast: intense, ruthlessly direct, a real ass-kicker—the unbreakable Yang. You would have thought that in the close-to-perfect world of the STF, the two would have combined to form a precisely balanced entity, a harmonious union of disparate selves wedded under the watchful eye of Infusion Therapy. However, it was clear to me that something had gone terribly wrong with the equation. Either the guys in the lab had not followed the recipe correctly, or someone had spiked the punch. The end result was a dissonant chorus of blurred voices: calculating, antagonistic, totally evil. It was like mixing Kool-Aid with 190-proof Everclear. If you weren't careful you could wind up dead before your taste buds knew what hit them.

My suspicions did not end here. I was firmly convinced that the murders were the work of an insider—that the perp was operating from the sunless interior of the Enchanted Forest. This untamed wilderness was as far removed from the technological veneer of the Haunted Mansion as was possible in the abruptly finite world of the STF. It made sense that chimp Arbegast was simply picking up where Dunkie had left off insofar as his violent and reclusive nature was concerned. Anyone with the ability to read and an ounce of common sense could have fingered the perp for a fraction of what Acteon was paying me. Maybe it wasn't a fluke that one of Acteon's resident supergeniuses hadn't made the correlation between Dunkie's penchant for cutting up small fuzzy things and the murderous inclination that hung over Arbegast like an evil exponent. Wasn't it enough that I was going to collect $50,000? I could make the whole thing out to seem as suspicious as I wanted, but isn't suspicious just a gentler way of saying "paranoid"?

I had decided to take a hot bath before returning to the STF—a decision that would come back to haunt me on two counts—

when I had the idea that if I were to drown myself, just lie back and surrender to the soothing amniotic undercurrents, that Janie, the migraines and paranoia, my blood pact with Mr. Wonderful and general feelings of hopelessness, would be washed away. Don't think of it as suicide; think of it as self-actuated euthanasia. The impulse to check out was not as impulsive as it might seem. Since returning home from the Gulf, not a day had gone by that I hadn't sparred with the idea. I was sick of all the death, sick of living with my tail between my legs, sick of the man I had become. There would be no tear-streaked farewell note, no blameful declaration of fault, no plea for forgiveness. Here was an opportunity to achieve in death a measure of respect I had been unable to attain in life. I wanted to be remembered with dignity. In spite of my bitter disillusionment, I would honor the deal I had made with Acteon. Before I committed myself to the tepid medium of my intended grave, I sealed the information I had gathered regarding Arbegast in a manila envelope marked ATTENTION: DR. JANUS—DIRECTOR, IT PROJECT. I wasn't exactly saving the world, but as far as the chimps were concerned, I may as well have been.

I was buoyed with a sense of hope I had not felt since I had stood before the altar with my betrothed more than a decade ago. I retrieved the heavy bronze Janie had given me on our tenth wedding anniversary from the corner of my desk and relocated it to the bathroom, where I intended to apply a memorable coda to the furiously brief score of my existence. The bronze was of a rather astute-looking chimpanzee perched atop a stack of scholarly tomes contemplating the skull of Charles Darwin. I may have been suicidal, but this did not mean that I had lost my sense of irony. Clutching the learned primate to my bosom, a poor substitute for the child my dissipated semen had been unable to provide Janie (the fertility doctors had told me that nothing short of an outboard motor affixed to the back of each indolent sperm would propel my seed to the uterine headwaters), I slipped quietly beneath the surface and exhaled a long and deeply needed sigh of relief.

When I came to, choking and spitting up mouthfuls of

lukewarm bathwater, not only was I confronted with the over-whelming sense of failure that comes with a botched suicide, there was my sworn enemy, Mr. Wonderful, to consider. I found myself stretched out on the fringe of a porcelain and tile mirage, a genie-faced sun hovering impossibly far overhead speaking to me in tongues that only a madman could hope to fathom. The lifesaving assassin would later explain that he had been reciting the verses of a Muslim prayer, but at the time I was certain he was damning my soul to hell in preparation for a far more sinister end than the one I had envisioned for myself.

If Mr. Wonderful was to be believed, he had rescued me from the liquid shroud and resuscitated me with standard CPR. Although he denied it vehemently, I vaguely recalled there being an inordinate preponderance of tongue in the mouth-to-mouth with which he had breathed life back into my naked body. In fact, upon regaining consciousness, I could taste the cinnamony mélange of pigeon pie and mint couscous favored by the gourmet transvestite. I did not dare consider what other liberties he had taken with me as I lay unconscious on the pink tile floor of the bathroom Janie herself had remodeled in anticipation of my safe return from the Muslim holy land, a happy home-coming that now seemed like eons ago.

"You!" I croaked, coughing up sticky blood-laced water.

"Shhh, don't talk," Mr. Wonderful admonished me gently. "You almost drowned."

As I fought to catch my breath, I realized that Mr. Wonderful was astride the center of my chest, his shiny bronze kneecaps on roughly the same plane as his shoulders. The disconcerting bulge between his legs was aligned with my saliva-smeared chin in such a way that it implied an awful union. He was dressed like a cabana boy out of the slick pages of a Versace swimwear catalog, a fashionably loud ambassador from the land of bad taste: orange sherbet low-rise men's bikini briefs accessorized with a white patent-leather belt and a tight-fitting spandex top dappled with magenta narcissus. I couldn't help wondering what Janie would think if she happened upon the two of us on the bathroom floor like that: Mr. Wonderful's freshly Nair-ed buttocks wedded to my hairy chest—shivering, wet, and utterly naked.

"Why didn't you let me die?"

"Because I love you, baby," Mr. Wonderful assured me softly, his voice slipping along the periphery of my blunted senses like an oily tributary of a lake inhabited by monsters. It was raw and breathy, an incestuous pairing of the man he was and the woman he would soon be.

He was beautiful in a deadly sort of way, like a Portuguese man-o'war or a coral snake, at once inviting and lethal. He moved with the sinuous sway and hypnotic grace of a harem dancer. In his gold-flecked eyes swirled the might and mystery of the Middle East's turbulent history, its desert kingdoms and jeweled navels, a kindred reprise of Persian emperors and veiled princesses intact but for the lambent patina imparted by century upon century of cross-cultural osmosis. As much as Mr. Wonderful wanted to think of himself as purebred, he was as much a product of upheaval as his Byzantine cousins. His dyed-blond hair was black at the roots and flowed down the center of his back like honey alchemized from crude oil. Both his eyes and mouth were slightly too large, the evolutionary signposts of a creature adapted for the kill. Although self-consciously slender, he was rangy and well-toned, every bit the true predator as a jaguar or an anaconda. He wore too much eye shadow for my taste and his lipstick could have been a shade or two less intense, but women envied his skill with cosmetics. He could go the whole nine yards and somehow manage to avoid looking cheap.

"I was doing you a favor," I groaned into the caramel-colored delta of his bikini-waxed inner thighs. "Now get off of me."

"First," with a concerned look, "you have to promise me that you won't try this again. With you dead, how would I afford my surgery? I will be stuck in this horrible body forever with this awful *thing* between my legs!"

"I've got a pair of scissors in the kitchen," I grunted, struggling vainly to dislodge him from his perch atop my chest. "Let me up and I'll get rid of it for you. It's not doing *me* any good."

Mr. Wonderful's eyes filled with tears and he began to cry.

"Why must you talk to me in this way? I try to be nice and yet you insist on treating me like a common whore. Maybe I should have let you die," he crooned, lifting the monkey bronze from the edge of the bathtub and clutching it over my head.

It's uncanny how quickly the will to live reasserts itself even in the wake of a failed suicide. Minutes earlier, I had been lying on the bottom of the bathtub wondering what would become of Arbegast and the chimps, Janie and her hairy Don Juan. Now all I could think of was the phrase "blunt-force trauma"—the semantic light-years separating its clinically precise language and messy reality. There I cowered, instinctively shielding myself from his pouty wrath.

"Say you're sorry," warned Mr. Wonderful, the arch of his exquisitely manicured eyebrows foreshadowing the roundabout trajectory of the monkey bronze as he used it to crush my skull.

"I'm sorry, *Bunny*," I replied hollowly.

Choosing a new name and going by it, Mr. Wonderful had explained, was one of the hardest things he'd had to do after deciding to go through with a sex change. Kassem Al-Jelaluddin, one of the most ruthless killers to ever come out of Hussein's stable of assassins, had become Bunny Valentine. Mr. Wonderful was the nickname his comrades had given him shortly after he had announced his decision to become a woman. Bunny's assignment abroad was more or less a form of exile, though he refused to admit it. He was too good an assassin to waste, but required too much explaining to keep around. As long as I was still alive, he had a reason not to return to Iraq. His happy little world of denial would remain intact.

"There," said Mr. Wonderful, sniffling and wiping the tears from his eyes, "that wasn't so difficult, now was it?"

He got up off my chest and ran his index finger along the elastic seat of his orange sherbet banana hammock, liberating it from the crack of his ass.

"I've got eleven more days," I reminded him, my lungs inflating with a convulsive gasp. "Shouldn't you be somewhere coming up with new ways to spend my money?"

Mr. Wonderful stood at the medicine cabinet preening himself like a debutante. He raked back his hair with a fluid sweep of both hands and blotted runny mascara from his cheeks with a Kleenex.

"It's these fucking drugs," he cursed shrilly, tossing me a towel, which I draped over my lap. "They make me so damn emotional."

"Welcome to womanhood."

"Your wife seems to enjoy it," he remarked with a sniffle, repairing his makeup.

"What is that supposed to mean?"

"You're not going to like this," he trilled, his voice swelling with the thin portentous edge of a war cry.

"Tell me."

Mr. Wonderful paused, allowing my imagination to steep in the silence like a tea brewed from squashed hopes and black suspicion.

"Your wife brays like a camel," he said decisively, cruelly. "She and that creature of hers are at it all day when you're not here. *Haww-haww-haww!* I'm surprised the neighbors haven't called the police."

It was as if someone had blown the hatch on an interstellar flight—a violent *whoosh*, then the perfect vacuum of deep space closing in around me. It was suffocating. Cold. An airless tomb. My heart froze, a tortured howl crescendoing in its bloodless chambers like the call of a lovelorn coyote.

"You've seen them together?" I asked numbly.

"Oh, yes, many times," Mr. Wonderful confirmed moistly. "Many, many times."

"Who is he?" I demanded weakly, the feral sounds of their lovemaking turning over in my mind: wet, unabashed, animal.

I suddenly realized why I had never been able to catch them in the act. While I had been staking out places like the Nite Lite Motel, Janie and her illicit beau had been getting it on under my own roof. As much as it hurt, I had to appreciate the irony. Janie had done her best to get me to spend more time at home. In a way, I guess I deserved this, although it didn't mean I had to like it.

"Who? Is this really so important—to know who?"

With an explosive burst that surprised us both, I sprang to my feet, spun Mr. Wonderful away from the mirror, and was clutching him by the elastic lapels of the couture shuffleboard blouse I had paid for.

"Stop fucking with me, you bitch!"

"Careful," he cautioned wryly, "you're going to pop my buttons."

Even up close the assassin's skin was perfect, childlike, as supple and smooth as Demerara rum.

"Look, you son of a bitch," I snarled, oblivious of the pink anodized .22 automatic pressed under my chin. "Start talking or I snap your neck."

Mr. Wonderful appraised me woefully.

"Don't do this to yourself, Dutch. She's not worth it. Now let go of me before I paint a rose garden on the ceiling with your brains."

He cocked the hammer and backed me away from him. I was as loose-jointed and easily manipulated as a marionette. I collapsed on the hard, wet edge of the bathtub next to the monkey bronze. Cold, defeated, impotent. A portrait of humility. Mr. Wonderful disengaged the hammer and returned the custom double-deuce to its white patent-leather holster aligned just above the cleft of his ass beneath the spandex blind of magenta narcissus.

"Cover yourself," he ordered disgustedly.

When I reached for the towel, I first noticed the black radio transmitter affixed to my left ankle like a space-age parasite.

"What the hell is this?" I demanded.

"A solution to both our problems," he explained, returning to the medicine cabinet. "You no longer need to run. I no longer need to chase you."

He opened the mirrored door and searched the shelves, removing Janie's mascara and studying the label.

"That's very Christian of you, Bunny. But you're totally fucking insane if you think you can collar me like some sort of endangered species." I tore at the carbon-fiber manacle uselessly, my face going red with effort and shame. "Now, get this fucking thing off me before I strangle you with it. I'm a human being, you sick bastard—a man!"

"Relax, Dutch, it's for the best. I'm having surgery this week. I'm going to be laid up for a while, and I need to be certain that you won't try anything."

I pulled and twisted until my knuckles were white and my fingertips raw, but it was no use. A hacksaw, that's what I needed. Maybe in the garage buried amidst all the junk Janie and I had collected over the years: tennis rackets, books, collapsible beach chairs, Christmas decorations, the crib we'd bought one hopeful month when Janie was late and the home pregnancy test had come up a false positive, and all manner of things we had no use for but refused to give up on. Racked with grief, I plunged my head into the standing bathwater, determined to succeed where I had failed so recently, only to have Mr. Wonderful open the drain and thwart my efforts for the second time in as many attempts.

"Please," I choked, half delirious, catching sight of myself in the mirror: wild-eyed and feverish. "I have to know the truth, Bunny. Who is he?"

"Sometimes it is better not to know," Mr. Wonderful assured me grimly, uncapping the mascara and brushing one of his eyelashes. "Look at you now. You would rather die than face the unknown. Imagine what the truth will do to you."

"She's all I have," I said, sinking to my knees.

"I can't use this," he stated disgustedly, dropping the silver mascara capsule in the sink. "It clumps."

Mr. Wonderful regarded me with a sympathetic smile and strode from the bathroom, the rhythmic flip-flopping of his orange rubber-soled sandals merging with the ambient whisper-roar of rush hour.

"Come back here, you bastard!" I shouted after him. "Don't leave me like this."

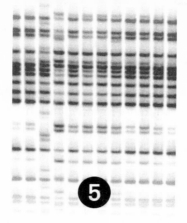

5

WHEN I RETURNED TO THE STF the following afternoon, the place was a fucking madhouse. The ghosts scampering around the observation tunnels looked as if they had spent the last twenty-four hours white-knuckling their way through the initial stages of crack withdrawal. My arrival was greeted with a mixture of heated rancor and unspoken gratitude. Apparently, there had been some sort of shakeup in my absence, and Janus had been on the warpath ever since.

Let's be honest. Their concern regarding my whereabouts was not entirely unwarranted. I am—or should I say was?—not an easy man to track down. For reasons of self-preservation, I make it a point to never stay in the same place for very long. Special Forces teaches you that there are two basic categories of target: moving and dead. In the last year, I have spent more nights in my car camped out in the basement of some abandoned parking garage than sharing a bed with the woman I love. Even when I am at home, it's just about the last place anyone would think to find me. My life exists in a perpetual state of upheaval. I never know what to expect from one moment to the next. Had you suggested twenty-four hours ago that Mr. Wonderful would one day rescue me from myself, I would've told you to get your head examined. So much for my grip on the random ebb and flow of earthly events.

Considering that I had given Shackleman a bogus phone number and a false home address, you can't blame the ghosts for being a few clicks left of center. I was their safety net and had gone AWOL as they walked a tightrope high above in the rarefied no-man's-land of genetic experimentation gone wrong. In a disturbing sort of way, the radio transmitter around my ankle was almost a relief. Ironically, it allowed me a degree of freedom I had not enjoyed for longer than I care to consider. All the running and hiding was suddenly pointless. Like the Arabian oryx or the California condor, I was now watched over by a round-the-clock baby-sitter. But don't think I didn't try like hell to get the goddamn thing off: black, inscrutable, vigilant. Captivity is not a natural state of being. In fact, I nicked my ankle with a butcher knife trying to force the issue. Nothing serious inasmuch as the severity of the wound was concerned; however, the deep crimson trickle of blood was enough to compel me to reconsider the urgency of my desire to be free of the passive restraint. As for Janus, he was downright spooky, his voice rising out of the grotto's darkness like an eerie echo of the half-formed creatures who stalked the earth before men were men.

"Where have you been?" he inquired coldly. "We have been trying to contact you. The address you gave Mr. Shackleman belonged to a diaper service."

The quicker I explained myself, the quicker I was out of there. I was being mobbed by swarms of stinging insects, their relentless assault on my exposed flesh ringing in my ears like the suicide whine of diving kamikazes.

"About that . . ."

"I'm sorry, Mr. Flowers, if I seem a bit put off by your obvious lack of concern for the project, but this type of behavior is inexcusable. Typical of your kind, but inexcusable nonetheless."

"*My kind?*"

I had a pretty good idea of where he was going with the callous indictment: deadbeat, flake, loser—labels applied and perpetuated by the international news media. Just because I'd heard them all before didn't mean I liked it.

"Understand my position, Mr. Flowers. Billions of dollars are at stake. More importantly," Janus continued gravely, "innocent chimpanzees are dying."

"I know who the killer is," I declared semi-triumphantly.

"Please, Mr. Flowers, I am not in the mood for guessing games."

"131 . . . Arbegast. He was arrested for performing surgical amputations on cats and dogs when he was eleven. At twenty-two he was charged with sexual assault, but the charges were dropped after a large cash settlement was agreed upon between the victim and Arbegast's old man. Classic signs, really. If I had a dime for every animal vivisectionist turned serial killer, I'd be sipping mai-tais on the beach in Tahiti with Brando."

Janus's voice flatlined. "Subject one-three-one is dead, Mr. Flowers. He was murdered while you were off doing whatever it is you were doing."

I was stunned. Worse than stunned. Cracked open, laid bare and quivering like an oyster awaiting a garlic-butter bath and the interminable slide down the esophagus. What little certainty I had managed to dredge up in the way of establishing whereabouts and predisposition imploded like a soda can bound for the floor of the deep ocean.

"*Dead?*" I echoed feebly.

"Yes, and I hold you partly to blame. If you had been doing your job, perhaps one-three-one would still be alive. I shudder to think what his father will say when he learns what happened here today."

"Who's father?"

"Have you not listened to a word I have said?" Janus snarled, his admonition precluded by an unusual high-pitched hooting that seemed to originate from a pantheon of nonverbal expression only distantly related to human discourse. "One-three-one's father, Duncan Arbegast Senior."

"Calling him the monkey's father is a bit of a reach, don't you think? We're talking apples and oranges here."

Considering the perverse nature of the IT Project, I would not have put such a union past Acteon's research department, no less invited confirmation of said practice had I not been absolutely secure in the inveteracy of certain standards of human conduct and decency. I was having enough difficulty accepting my diminished standing in the food chain without having to face the possibility that some of society's most respected citizens were getting it on with monkeys.

"It's not as if the old guy was doing the horizontal tango with a horny baboon."

Apparently Janus didn't see the humor in my whimsical little jab. For the second time in as many visits to the grotto I was bombarded with half-eaten fruit, a short-lived fusillade of gooey bananas and overripe figs.

"Do you have children of your own, Mr. Flowers?" asked Janus as I took cover beneath the lacy parasol of a towering tree fern. Although calm and controlled, his voice betrayed an edge of irritation not readily concealed.

"No," I said rigidly. "I don't."

"Are you familiar with the procedure known as artificial insemination?"

"I've heard of it," I replied distantly.

The truth is, Janie and I had taken part in variations on the procedure on three separate occasions and had failed to produce a single zygote. To make matters worse, each successive failure had initiated a revised opinion as to the degree of my sperm's so-called indolence. One of the doctors even had the audacity to refer us to a fertility specialist in Beijing—a veterinarian, as it turned out—citing his enormous success with a captive-breeding program whose goal was the reintroduction of the giant panda to the Chinese highlands. To be grouped with a species whose notorious aloofness was surpassed only by its lack of reproductive adroitness was a devastating blow to our marriage, not to mention my beleaguered self-esteem.

Janus went on: "Then certainly you must agree that the mode of transfer of genetic material precludes, and is therefore primary to, the act of coitus."

"If what you're saying is that it doesn't matter how the cake batter gets into the oven as long as it comes out done—then, yes, I agree," I replied sullenly.

"Mr. Arbegast's *cake batter* as you put it, albeit by way of Dunkie's rescued digit, was alive and well in the genetic blueprint

of subject one-three-one. Therefore, you see I am correct in referring to the deceased as the *son* of Mr. Arbegast. Based on current
standards of DNA analysis, I strongly doubt that you could find
a court of law in North America who would rule differently—say,
for instance, in a paternity suit." Janus paused, allowing me to
assimilate the data like a dutiful father explaining the perti-
nence of the infield-fly rule to his son. "Given the facts, it strikes
me that you are obligated to treat our benefactor's loss with the
accord and compassion due a grieving parent—*whether or not*
your range of personal experience has imbued you with this most
fundamental aspect of *human* decency. Frankly, Mr. Flowers, anything less is unacceptable."

Janus had me on a technicality and knew it. Arguing with him
would only lengthen the duration of my visit, something I
wanted to avoid at all costs. "Yes, of course, you're right," I said,
emerging from the cover of the tree fern. "What about leads?
Did anyone see anything suspicious? What time did the killing
take place?"

"I believe, Mr. Flowers, that these are questions we are paying
you to answer."

By the time I slogged my way out of the grotto, the insertion
team was busy tidying up inside the STF. The drugged chimps lay
where they had fallen, a chilling tableau of everyday life which
reminded me of the aftermath of the mass suicide at Jonestown.
Operating within the indefinite time constraints of the anesthetic, the ghosts worked quickly to extract 131's corpse without
compromising their own safety. One thing, however, was certain:
131 was a fraction of his former self, his wounds numerous and
mortal. Foremost was the fact that his head had been removed
by brute force—apparently twisted off—the soft tissue of his
neck bearing a pattern of helical striations consistent with the
suspected mode of death. Mysteriously, his trunk had been thor-
oughly eviscerated, the headless torso scooped clean like a
dugout canoe and set adrift on the sourceless waterway that
snaked its way through the STF like a lost tributary of the
Amazon. Sometime during the night 131's body had been

regurgitated from the mouth of the Enchanted Forest and become entangled in the roots of a mangrove approximately thirty yards upstream from where the denizens of the Haunted Mansion were breakfasting on one another's parasites. There, 131's body had remained until the insertion team had rescued it from the mangrove's clutches like baby Moses from the papyrus shoals of the Nile.

Once again nothing had been caught on tape. Lepke, the research assistant, proposed with a novice's flair for the obvious that 131 had met his maker in the black-bearded groves of the Enchanted Forest.

"Rivers only flow one way," he concluded smugly. "Therefore it's logical to assume that the crime was committed somewhere within the Enchanted Forest and that the body was dumped in the river."

"Good show, Mr. Spock! That's just fucking brilliant. You people are unreal. What good is any of this if all of your subjects are dead? I'm tempted to contact the police and let them know what's going on here. If they won't listen to me, I'll pay a visit to Animal Rights. And you can bet your ass *they* don't fuck around. If the SPCA catches wind of your little experiment here, there'll be so many protesters standing out front you'll need an armed escort to get inside the building. You think I'm playing? I've seen it before at the abortion clinics—secretaries carrying Glocks in their lunch bags just to keep the Jesus freaks from chewing off their faces."

Lepke's eyes jumped nervously from me to the surveillance camera monitoring the passageway in which we had watched while the insertion team tagged and bagged what remained of 131. Apparently some of what I'd said had struck a chord with the young neophyte, his voice skipping octaves with the unrestrained fluster of an imperiled songbird.

"I'm sure, Mr. Flowers," he warbled, "that if we work together we can get a handle on the situation without involving the SPCA. *Please*, keep things in perspective. We're doing the best we can."

"You want perspective? Fine, I'll let you in on a little secret. At this rate, you'll be working with poodles because there won't be enough goddamn monkeys left in all the world for you guys to poke and prod."

"Chimps," Lepke chirped meekly. "It's in your own best interest. . . . "

I was hot enough to boil lead.

"My best interest. . . . Do you have any idea who I am? No one's given a shit about *my best interest* since my mother let the family dog breast-feed me! You ought to start thinking about the *best interest* of your subjects. Without them you don't have a fucking experiment."

At this point, it was academic. I could carry on and shake my fists at the heavens all I wanted and it wouldn't change a damn thing. Someone was listening to what I had to say; they just didn't give a flying fuck. The violation of trust and subsequent legal penalties Janus had spoken of no longer constituted the moral dilemma it may at one time have presented me with. Take it from a man who's gone through a divorce. Trust is a two-way street, a covenant between individuals. If one crosses over the double yellow line, it is inevitable that both suffer the consequences. As far as I was concerned, Acteon had been lying to me from day one, either directly or by way of omission. I had given them my trust and they, like Janie, had repaid me with deceit. One way or another, the killing had to stop.

Shortly after midnight I dialed the STF's main switchboard and warned the operator of a vengeance that would make the bombing of Baghdad look like a glass of Alka-Seltzer. It worked like a charm. Surprised? Don't be. Nowadays people want to believe that they're bomb-worthy. It's a sign of the times. In a world where the global population is fast approaching double digits in the billions and anonymity is the next great epidemic, just getting noticed is tantamount to walking on water. The average citizen is little more than livestock branded with bar codes and PIN numbers while those unearthed from the rubble of federal buildings and foreign embassies enjoy an immortality and global renown unprecedented in the uneventful lives of

John and Jane Doe. We see the faces of the bombed on the six-o'clock news garlanded with broken concrete and twisted rebar, noble in their meaningful repose. We bow our heads at monuments commemorating their passive acts of heroism, the fallen infantry behind which others take cover from ideologies as random and disparate as the madmen who preach them. We know the names of the bombed, if only for a moment, better it seems than we know our own. Like the nickname of a high-school sweetheart, they are on the tip of our tongues, waiting to be recalled with a pang of nostalgia. We celebrate the dead and ignore the living. To be bombed is to stand for something. Their sacrifice is our shame. Their fame, our loneliness.

Within minutes, the entire facility was completely evacuated, the lab-coated researchers and their supporting cast of maintenance workers, technicians, and custodial staff scampering for the exits like frightened villagers sighting a Bengal tiger strutting into town. The place was so quiet I could practically hear my toenails growing. Shortly after 1:00 A.M., while the ghosts awaited the bomb squad's arrival, I donned one of the rubberized biohazard suits, keyed in the access code Shackleman had slipped me, and kissed good-bye to any possibility of collecting my fifty grand.

Locked and loaded, I committed myself to a world no less outlandish than that to which Charlton Heston had been exiled in *Planet of the Apes,* a cult standard that had experienced a mini-revival of sorts at the Beaux Arts Theater not five blocks from my unhappy home. With only the vaguest notion of a plan, I had wandered into a reality diametrically opposed to the one I had known only moments earlier. Unable to distinguish a single observation window in the star-spangled firmament above, I lost all sense of what lay beyond the vast enclosure. I doubt I would have been able to find my way out at all had I not left the door slightly ajar to avert any possibility of being locked in. I stood with my back against the unfiltered white light of the passageway beyond, my shadow stretched and disfigured like an interdimensional marauder spit from a tear in the fabric of space.

Moving through the untamed gardens—heavily perfumed thickets of primrose and thornless blackberry—I was staggered by the STF's sheer immensity, its labyrinthine geography and seeming infiniteness. With a few strides, I had put enough distance between myself and the entry port that I could no longer discern its luminous outline, the glittering trail of photons I had hoped would guide me back, gobbled up like so many bread crumbs by the vacuous maw of night. The bird's-eye view that I had enjoyed moments earlier was lost to me now, a figment of the godlike vantage I had forfeited upon pledging myself to the mortal world of the chimps. I stood on the fringe of a bonsaied forest every bit as dense and foreboding as its old-growth twin, the moon-illumined silhouettes of dwarf baobab, moss-bearded oak, twisted banyan, and shaggy fir looming before me like the grim specters of a fairy tale.

Guided solely by dumb luck, I stumbled upon one of the forest paths frequented by the chimps during their mysterious comings and goings. At first I was able to stoop my way along, ducking under low-hanging branches and sidestepping potential snags. Soon, however, the path narrowed considerably and I was forced to proceed on my hands and knees. I was stalked by the ghostly rhythms of my own breathing, raw and hollow-sounding, the rubberized crinkle of the suit's inflexible fabric striking an odd counterpoint to the snapping of twigs and fallen leaves beneath me. It was slow going along the girdling passage. Slashes of artificial moonlight knifed through the roiling wormhole of vegetation and illuminated the condensation droplets that traversed the interior of my face shield like silvery invertebrates. At times it got so dark that I couldn't see my gloved hands in front of my face, the mean glint of my .45 all but invisible to me. A flashlight was out of the question. It didn't take seven years of Special Forces training and countless insertions behind enemy lines to know that I was ripe for an ambush.

Images of the slain chimps danced at the periphery of my senses, their disembodied spirits whispering at my folly, awakening me to the untold perils lurking in the darkness. Gradually, the path opened on a small clearing and I was able to stand.

Ethereal blue green light illuminated the wooded rotunda, its inexplicable source I would later discover was derived from a bioluminescent mold that thrived in the Enchanted Forest's subtropical climate. Layer upon layer of the slimy illuminant had been smeared over the irregular colonnade of tree trunks, the telltale handprints as impossible seeming as those chronicling the lives of Ice Age hunters on the walls of Pleistocene caves. This was where the chimps had been congregating, crossing over into the realm of animal savagery that is so intrinsically human, narrowing the distance between them and us in eon-gobbling bounds. The hackles on the back of my neck prickled. I was not welcome in this place of primeval horrors. How long, I wondered, would it take Acteon to rescue me from what I was about to discover? Would they even know where to look? What would they tell Janie? Would they need snow shovels to collect my remains?

As my eyes adjusted to the creepy light, I began to see the clearing for what it was. I stood before an altar the likes of which had not been seen on earth since primitive man had abandoned anthropomancy in favor of divining rods and crystal balls. Skewered on the leafless branches of a jacaranda were the missing components of 131's dug-out corpse—heart, lungs, liver, kidneys, spleen—the ornamental viscera of a pagan Christmas. Looped over another branch on the same tree were several of the bar-coded ID collars used by the ghosts to identify the chimps. Calypso 87, Fossey 517, Pourdanesh 43, Dupin 88. It suddenly dawned on me that the headless corpse recovered from the marshy banks of the Rio Guachada had been identified as Arbegast 131 despite his ID collar's conspicuous absence.

The more I thought about it, the more I didn't like the way it was beginning to look. Having encountered a substantial number of bomb-blast victims while on active duty, I was aware of the difficulty facing those assigned the painstaking task of tagging the remains. Imagine trying to confirm the identity of a strange chimpanzee without a face to use for reference. I'd been hit with the news of 131's purported demise so abruptly that I had accepted it without a second thought. It now occurred to me that this selfless act of heroism into which I had entered so blindly was beginning to look more and more like a setup. Think about it. What better way for Acteon to sidestep legal liability than to get me inside under my own volition? So what if something terrible happened to me? When it came out that international scapegoat extraordinaire, Dutch Flowers, was involved, no jury in the world would hold Acteon responsible. I had taken the bait. Everything from the fine-print contracts I had signed to how easily I had gotten hold of the access code had been custom-tailored to suck me in. Either I could stick around and see if Acteon's fears were justified, or get the hell out of there and let them clean up their own mess. No dollar figure in the world was worth walking that line again. I could worry about getting Mr. Wonderful his money later.

I had turned to retrace my steps when something terribly familiar rolled out of the darkness and came to rest at my feet. My astonishment and horror could have been no greater than if I had just witnessed the reinvention of the wheel for the sole purpose of conveying the dead. There, like a lopsided and deflated football that had been kicked around a muddy field, lay the head of a chimpanzee. It was looking directly at me. Its eyes, although at half-mast, lacked the identifying stigma I had hoped to find. The mouth was loosely ajar, a ragged stump all that remained of the tongue. No secrets here. As I confronted the worst of my suspicions, a dozen shaggy silhouettes swaggered out of the blue green shadows and hemmed me in. Arbegast was the last to take his place among them, the crimped twist of scar tissue wreathing his left eye holding me fast with the inexorable pull of a black hole.

Sheer brutishness compensated for what the accursed brotherhood lacked in height. Standing just under five feet tall and gilded with 180 pounds of rock-ribbed muscle, they boasted the chiseled physiques of professional bodybuilders. These were not the same cuddly career-minded primates I had watched groom one another in the Haunted Mansion. These were sinister reflections of men reinvented in the image of their savage forebears, black-eyed and heartless emissaries from the glaciated valleys and peat-bogged lowlands of the Upper Cretaceous. Naturally, they saw me as a threat to their continued existence, a rival species vying for supremacy atop the food chain. Janus's earlier request that I see myself as a contagion suddenly acquired an urgent relevance.

As the circle closed around me and I made the fateful discovery that my .45's trigger guard would not admit my gloved forefinger, I was paralyzed by a sobering epiphany. I thought of the monkey bronze Janie had given me on our tenth wedding anniversary: Darwin's disembodied skull—the very seat of his consciousness—manipulated in the hands of his drag-knuckle shadow. In that instant, as the hopelessness of my situation became mortally apparent, I was able to slip outside my own body and see the future as envisioned by Acteon's genetics heavy hitters. I had been born into a world in which I did not belong. As though abandoned by my spirit in hasty departure, my head remained bound by the gravity of the earth below, an intoxicating curiosity pawed at and clamored over like a jug of moonshine in the hands of idiots. Hanging there, I stared destiny in the eye: a round table of retarded Adams grabbing for the dire fruit skewered on the jacaranda's organ-laden boughs beneath which the yammering fools danced.

ECCE HOMO

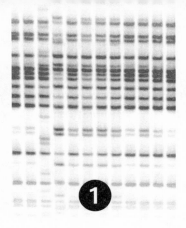

IF YOU'VE EVER WATCHED AN OLD BELA LUGOSI MOVIE, or for that matter most any flick boasting a befanged member of the undead, you are no doubt aware of the mandate that holds that if you drive a wooden stake into the heart of the master vampire, the souls of those fallen under his spell will be released to their rightful owners, the natural order restored. It was this bit of anecdotal wisdom—a time-tested favorite borrowed from as many vampire movies as covert military ops—that had served as the inspiration behind Operation Slay Dracula. The idea was to knock off Saddam Hussein and watch the Iraqi political infrastructure crumble like the walls of Jericho. How difficult could it be? Hussein was one man pitted against the awesome resources of the United States government. It was a noble idea, though hardly grounded in the reality of rogue-nation protocol. We may as well have been patching bullet wounds with Band-Aids.

Although Hussein was most certainly the catalyst behind his nation's bid for acknowledgment as a global power, he was simply one of dozens of Muslim visionaries with aspirations of erecting a holy counter-empire on the inveterate bedrock of Western sloth and excess. His would-be replacements were as preened and plentiful as French emperors; there had been, was, and always would be another "Louis" waiting to enumerate himself among the auspices of tyrants past. Assassinating Hussein would be like exterminating a single termite in a house held together by the onionskin layers of paint holding fast its brittle underpinnings. The real culprit was the American public—the hundreds of thousands of RV owners, weekend yachtsmen, motorheads and anti-carpoolists—who constituted the latter portion of the supply-and-demand equation for light-sweet crude. The proposed liberation of Kuwait was no more than a pretext to establish a fixed price at the pump, an agreeable dollar figure that existed within the universal standards of Anglo entitlement and human decency. Why risk thousands of lives and dump billions of dollars into an all-out war when the death of one mustachioed fanatic would give the freeway flyers back their wings? Do it like surgery—an incision here, a stitch or two there. . . . By the time anyone realized what had happened, the oil-hoarding cancer in the heart of the American motorist would be in full remission, Kuwait liberated and ready to crank up production.

Aside from the fact that Iraq was home to some 250,000 deeply loyal Republican Guardsmen clamoring to die for their beloved commander in chief, there was the irrevocable oversight that Hussein had gone to paranoid extremes to ensure that any attempt on his life be thwarted through as formidable an array of trained look-alikes as had been seen on earth since rumors had surfaced that Ronald McDonald, mascot and clown prince of fast-food's most celebrated dynasty, was a homosexual.

Acting on CIA intelligence, X-Ray squad was deployed in the fall of 1989. Knowing that the Republican Guard had a pretty good handle on ground operations and that the Iraqi navy was more flotsam than fleet, it was decided that we make our debut at the 30th parallel along the Shatt-al-Arab seaboard. It was in these waters, our mission scarcely begun, that the trail of tragedies leading up to my exile from society would realize its genesis. Even then I should have known that the mission had been albatrossed from the very beginning. Our fates were pointed down a path of no return like the web-footed vertebrates who had drag-bellied their way out of the evolutionary starting gate long before there were species capable of killing for ideological contempt.

With our dubious humanity in tow, the nuclear reconnaissance submarine *Beagle* ferried X-Ray into the Persian Gulf, flanked the eastern shore of Bubiyan Island, and slipped undetected into the placid waters off the ancient seaport at Umm Qaar. Once in position we were deployed via the *Beagle*'s torpedo tubes in one-man remote landing crafts, experimental technology, we would learn only after it was too late, that had never been tested beyond the binary aquascape of the army's foolproof computer model. Conceptually, the Submersible Ultrasonic Deployment System (SUDS) was fundamentally sound. However, confronted with real-world variables and plain old bad luck, its shortcomings were made tragically manifest to us all.

Of the thirteen handpicked specialists in X-Ray squad, only twelve of us made it ashore alive. SUDS 3, manned by gunnery sergeant Lance Schulters, an ace sniper and devoted family man who could shoot the testicles off a carpet mite at half a click, was accidentally fired into the rusted-out belly of the Iraqi fishing trawler, *Samarra*. The *Samarra* had lain motionless approximately two hundred yards off the *Beagle*'s starboard bow, her crew of eight lulled into a rockabye slumber by the gentle offshore rollers. Sonar had failed to identify the danger until it was too late. One second Schulters was whizzing along just beneath the oil-black surface, the next he was being hauled all but dead from his wrecked SUDS by the *Samarra*'s wild-eyed first mate, a deeply spiritual man for whom the freakish event had the unmistakable hallmark of the apocalypse. In the ensuing pandemonium, Schulters was dragged to the deck of the sinking boat, his broken body prodded at and puzzled over like a strange and horrifying sea creature regurgitated from the deep. The force of the impact and rapid depressurization of the SUDS capsule had caused Schulters's eyes to bulge from their sockets with an amphibian prominence. Alive against all probability and burbling in tongues, Schulters, the kamikaze frogman, had confirmed for the *Samarra*'s superstitious crew that diabolical forces were oiling the jaws of Armageddon.

At daybreak, when every muezzin for a thousand miles called

the righteous to prayer, an unearthly refrain filled the air with an impending sense of doom, the likes of which had not fallen on human ears since it was believed that a total eclipse of the sun foretold the end of the world.

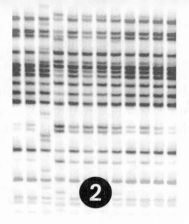

2

WHEN I FIRST REGAINED CONSCIOUSNESS, it was as if I had been set to rewind. The tangled conduit through which I had accessed the forbidden clearing raced by overhead. Through the fractured face shield of the biohazard suit, I could make out the hunchbacked silhouettes of my chimp captors dragging me by the ankles along the roughshod trail. Our destination was as unfathomable to me as it was a matter of terrifying concern. Pagan altars, human sacrifice, fiendish blood rituals. I lapsed in and out of consciousness, each time awakening to the sustained thwacking of the whiplike foliage tanning my rubberized hide. I could do little more than flail my arms against the savage momentum. I grabbed at exposed roots and stripped the leaves from hanging branches, clutching desperately for the handhold that would bring an end to my horizontal freefall and maybe—just maybe—give me a chance to escape.

After being nearly bushwhacked to death and having failed to decipher the bestial nonsyllables of my whooping escorts, I was dumped and left for dead at the fringe of the Enchanted Forest. I must have passed out again because the next thing I knew I was encircled by four stoop-shouldered ghouls attired identically to myself. They were as familiar and yet alien as the face of the man who had gone to the Gulf full of idealistic fervor and had returned an embittered middle-aged martyr who had lost everything: his career, his self-respect, and the woman he loved.

• • •

Within the hour, I was back inside Janus's office, the dank fungoid air and marshy landscape suspiciously reminiscent of the mold-illumined clearing where I had looked death in the eye a short time earlier.

"You lied to me!" I shouted into the darkness, the sudden swell of my voice unsettling an invisible flock of birds in the canopy overhead. "Arbegast isn't dead. The evil son of a bitch tried to kill me."

There was no reply, only the earnest mating call of a solitary tree frog.

"Janus, I know you can hear me! I want you to tell me what's going on here. I have a right to know. I almost lost my life in there. I'm sure the press would be interested in hearing about your little experiment. If you ask me, it's one hell of a human-interest story."

"And what about you, Mr. Flowers?" came Janus's godlike reproach. "What shall we tell them of your invaluable contribution to our *mission* gone wrong? I believe a precedent has already been established—wouldn't you agree?"

"You back-stabbing bastard! I'm here to help you. This is *your* fuckup, not mine!"

"*Help?*" Janus sneered. "By violating the conditions of our agreement, you may have forfeited everything. Two decades of research and development potentially lost."

A light rain began to fall. The tree frog's mating call acquired a new urgency. *Bwoop! . . . Bwoop! . . . Bwoop! . . .*

"If you'll just let me explain," I pleaded into the darkness. "I saw things in there—things I think you should know about."

"I am afraid, Mr. Flowers, that we have exceeded the usefulness of explanations. You have given me no other choice than to terminate your employment here."

"You've got to listen to me. Something incredibly fucked up is going on in there. What I saw . . . It's not natural. They're *organized.*"

Janus paused, exhaling slowly, the deliberate release of his breath unfurling in the darkness like an anaconda preparing to lasso an unwary passerby.

"Bravo, Mr. Flowers, it seems your investigative skills are not entirely without merit. I only hope that no one will be hurt—*or worse*—as a result of your transgression."

"I was only doing my job," I growled. But, oh, how terribly familiar the words sounded—the irreverent equivocation and unmistakable refrain of dismissals past. All that was missing was a stone-faced military tribunal and the taste of humility still fresh in my mouth.

"*Job*," Janus echoed contemptuously, momentarily drowning out the crackling rain-patter on the leafy umbrella overhead. "Your *job* was to catch a murderer, not turn one loose on the world."

"Let's not get carried away."

"When, Mr. Flowers, was the last time you saw your gun?"

"*Gun?*" I countered innocently.

"Please, do not insult my intelligence."

"You didn't expect me to go in unarmed knowing that a killer was on the loose?"

Although I had not seen my .45 since the renegade chimps had pummeled me to within an inch of my life, I had naïvely assumed that it was buried somewhere in the slurping muck of the clearing, an artifact-to-be of a civilization on the brink of extinction.

"In fact, Mr. Flowers," Janus clarified, "I expected you not to *go in* at all."

"I still don't see what my gun—"

"We have reason to believe that one of the control-group subjects escaped. Apparently, with your weapon."

"You don't expect me to believe? . . ."

"Given your pattern of behavior, I do not expect anything of you, Mr. Flowers. Because of your gross ineptitude, there is a murderer on the loose. We had hoped that you would be able to salvage some small bit of rectitude from the larger waste that is your life. However, it appears that history is simply repeating itself, as is so often the case with your kind."

The fallout of Janus's scathing observation blanketed me with shame. As impossible as it seemed, the swampy refuge became even darker. As I slunk-slurped my way out of the gloom, I was pursued into the antiseptic light of the reception area by the restless ghosts of X-Ray squad, their tortured faces forever frozen in the neural ice fields of memory and regret. But Janus was only half right. The history to which he had anchored me, a saga of mistaken identity and death, was simply extending itself by way of an alternate route. But there was still time and opportunity to realign myself with a more favorable legacy.

For now, though, I was left with a deeper issue to consider. Why had the chimps spared my life? What was it that had compelled them to grant me, a rival species so clearly bent on treachery and ill will, leniency? That it may have been an act of compassion, something of which I, Homo erectus, the purported apotheosis of "do-unto-otherism," was desperately incapable, only augmented my sense of self-loathing and doubt.

The surveillance video seemed to substantiate Janus's claim. With an easy loping gait, a single, rather large and princely chimp stole out of the darkness and padded quietly across the floor of the Haunted Mansion. This was not the awkward semibrachiation of a knuckle walker, but rather the stalwart perambulation of a creature hand picked by evolution to stand head and shoulders above the rest: proud, indomitable, arrogant. Mid-frame, the chimp paused, turned deliberately, and stared directly into the camera, as if intuitively aware of the omniscient eye spying on him from the twinkling firmament overhead: God, the devil, heavy-breathers in crinkly rubber suits. It made no difference. They were one in the same. Takers. False prophets. Strangers bearing tainted fruit. A fleeting glance was more than enough to confirm what I already knew from my brush with death in the Enchanted Forest. Arbegast! The leprous whorl of scar tissue encircling his left eye like a budding tornado was enough to send me hightailing it for the storm cellar.

"Handsome devil," Lepke remarked reverently, pausing the tape to admire Acteon's misguided handiwork. "Don't you think?"

"A real lady-killer," I agreed.

I couldn't help feeling that Arbegast was taunting me with those disingenuous black, retina-less eyes, that godless loose-lipped smirk. Despite my obvious embarrassment at having facilitated his escape, I was, at first, relieved. My .45 was nowhere in sight.

"Here's where it gets good," Lepke quipped heartlessly and restarted the tape.

I was slammed by a sickening wave of nausea. Something or someone off-screen must have caught Arbegast's attention because the aristocratic chimp suddenly ambled back the way he had come and ducked into a stand of brooding black oak. A moment later he reappeared carrying something in his right hand. Given the poor quality of the light, I could neither confirm nor refute Janus's claim. If it was my .45 wedded to the ape's trigger finger, I was in a world of shit. Not since the little Dutch boy had rescued the hash bars and storefront madams of Amsterdam from the wrath of a leaky dike had a solitary digit exercised such terrifying omnipotence. Horrified, I watched as Arbegast slipped out the door I had foolishly left ajar.

"You're going to have to do better than that," I said. "It's too dark. He could be holding a banana for all we know."

"Bananas don't put people in intensive care," Lepke countered. "While making his escape, 131 shot a police officer in the head."

"What are you talking about?"

"Look on the bright side. The man you tried to kill is in a coma. The doctors say he may never regain consciousness."

"You said yourself that Arbegast shot him."

"We know that, but the police don't. You can imagine trying to convince them that a monkey was responsible for the bomb threat. Naturally, they believe the one who made the call and the shooter are the same person. *Person* being the operative word here."

"You can all go to hell."

"Anyway," Lepke continued smugly, "there's no point getting all worked up over this now. Officer Blanks could remain in a vegetative state for the rest of his life. And if he's not dead, they can't try you for murder."

Although Arbegast was still at large and my .45 had not been recovered by the police, you can be damn sure that Acteon would roll over on me in a heartbeat if things got any stickier. Who do you think was going to take the fall should Janus develop an inclination to bring the case to a tidy close? Either Acteon could admit to fathering a race of evil superchimps that made Nazi Germany's experiments with selective breeding look like a kindergarten-class science project. Or they could go public with the gentler story of the fallen soldier whose life they had hoped to resurrect from the ashes by offering him a respectable position at their firm—a charitable undertaking, they would sadly confirm, which had ended in tragedy for everyone involved. The slug ballistics retrieved from the cop's brain was all any D.A. worth his weight in antacid would need to send me to the electric chair. . . . If, of course, Blanks cashed out. This was just the sort of sensationalism the press craves. I could see the headlines already:

A ROSE BY ANY OTHER NAME: CAPTAIN DUTCH FLOWERS—THE ASSASSIN OF ABU DHABI—SOUGHT IN LOCAL LAW-ENFORCEMENT SLAYING

Vegetative state. This was supposed to make me feel better. Christ almighty! I may not have been able to grieve for the poor bastard, but that didn't prevent me from realizing that some kid's daddy was strained peas and IV tubes, the cardiac bleep of life-support transmitting a futile SOS from the speechless realm of oblivion. I would have rather pulled the plug on him myself than watch as all that was once vital about him abandoned his wasted body like rats fleeing a sinking ship, the missus and Blanks Jr. crying their eyes out and leaking snot all over the hospital linens.

Who was going to believe me? Since my court-martial hearing had been aired on *Court TV*, a groundbreaking television event for which I had been financially well-compensated, I had about as much credibility as a Protestant whore turning tricks in the Vatican. There was only one way I could think of to keep the situation from snowballing out of control and landing me in the center of another scandal. I had to track down Arbegast and bring him back alive, expose the truth. If I could show the world what was going on at Acteon—the peril facing our species and subsequent tampering with the very essence of life—there was an outside chance that I could revive my public image and bring an end to the suffering I had endured as the poster boy for good intentions gone bad. With a little luck, I might even be able to parlay the story of my comeback into a lucrative book deal—a riches-to-rags-to-riches sort of thing. And this time, when I took a turn around the talk-show circuit, it would be under the banner of a victory lap, a triumphant reversal of the tragic misfortune that had landed me in the inauspicious company of such reviled public personas as Benito Mussolini and Shemp, the sniveling second-rate knucklehead who joined the cast of *The Three Stooges* in the wake of Curly Howard's passing in 1952.

Fortunately, a 180-pound male chimpanzee did not exactly fit the visual profile of one who could easily lose himself in L.A.'s vast and heroically depraved underground. Even the sex junkies and meth-heads were not so far gone that they would overlook five feet of prime circus attraction breaking bread in their midst. Had Arbegast still been wearing his collar, tracking him down would have presented me with nowhere near the logistical nightmare it did. Ironically, it was I who was electronically tethered to an inescapable watcher. One way or another, the key was expedience. The sooner I pinched Arbegast and recovered my .45, the sooner I could begin rebuilding my life. On the off chance that Arbegast killed anyone else (I had mistakenly concluded that Blanks's shooting had been a freak occurrence), my chance at redemption would all but disintegrate.

I returned home, down but not defeated, to the scene of my botched suicide and the resounding echoes of my estranged wife, Janie. It was heartbreaking: the wedding photographs, her hand-washed brassieres and silken finery hung out to dry like tobacco leaves over the shower rod in the guest bathroom, the sweet fabric-softener smell of her lingering like a memory of springtime in the bedsheets and bath linens. She was everywhere and yet she was nowhere, a ghost of good times past and aching reminder of the bubble of aloneness growing around me like an atmosphere unto itself. I thought about calling her at my sister-in-law's, but decided to wait until I'd had a chance to decompress. I had learned the hard way that it is better to hesitate on behalf of prudence than to err in haste.

I kicked off my shoes, retired to the kitchen table, and mixed myself an iced drink of Coke and the banana liqueur Janie had procured as the essential ingredient in a wonderful-smelling, low-cholesterol soufflé she had baked a few months back. Although I had been denied the pleasure of sampling the ambrosial confection gleaned from the pages of *Cooking Light*, she had assured me that it had elicited more than its fair share of oohs and aahs at an intimate dinner gathering I had missed on account of my fugitive status. For weeks, the sweet scent of bananas and caramelized unrefined sugar had lingered throughout the house like the candy-coated breath of a white-shuttered plantation home.

To track Arbegast, I needed to get inside his head, locate him via the poisoned neural pathways mapping his brain like the effluvial klongs of Bangkok. I needed to think like a chimp who thought like a man—keeping in mind that the DNA fueling his flight was patently unstable and therefore inclined toward random divergences from any one true course. I knew from the outset that it would be like tracking a whirling dervish through a crowded medina, a kaleidoscopic journey into the heart of chaos.

After racking my brain for nearly an hour and having laid to rest all that was left of the banana liqueur, I was fairly satisfied that I had developed a reasonable plan of attack. Certain basic needs, shared by men and chimps alike, are indelibly subordinate to sentient machinations. Food and rest, to name a couple. By now hunger and fatigue would have set in, and Arbegast would be looking to satisfy these animal necessities. Because Arbegast was not human, I believed that his ability to look past these primal urges was not as highly evolved as, say, a Special Forces combat vet trained to ignore the grumblings of his belly and function for days at a time without so much as a catnap. Multiplying approximate foot speed over unfamiliar terrain by the amount of time elapsed since his escape, I arrived at a radius of five miles, give or take, in which to focus my search. It may not have been much to go on, but it was enough to get me out of the starting gate and point me down the long road toward redemption.

Although it's not something I particularly enjoy, I have more than my fair share of experience when it comes to tracking fugitives. Artie Shank, a bail bondsman I know from all the way back in basic, gives me work whenever I need it. For the most part, it's pretty straightforward stuff. Contrary to what you see in the movies, your average bounty hunter spends more time checking phone records, bank transactions, and credit-card statements than in high-speed chases, strip-club brawls, and back-alley shoot-outs. Occasionally, I have to pack it up and move the whole shebang across state lines, but usually a few well-placed phone calls and a routine course of stakeouts are all that's needed to get my man. Although the experience hasn't exactly taken me to the ends of the earth, it has shown me one thing: People are not as unpredictable as you might think. No matter who the perpetrator, regardless of their criminal background, it all boils down to knowing their comfort zones.

I microwaved a couple of tofu hot dogs for dinner, spread out a map of greater L.A. on the kitchen table, and charted the evening's itinerary with a pink highlighter. Given the overriding sense of strangeness Arbegast must have felt when confronted with his new surroundings, it stood to reason that he would make a beeline for the place most closely resembling home. It had only taken Tarzan a single glance at the bustling streets and storefronts of Ye Olde London Towne to conclude that he was better suited for life in the jungle. I couldn't imagine that Arbegast had felt any differently upon first escaping from the STF into the palpitating heart of downtown La-La Land. I would start with what few parks there were, and if necessary broaden the search to include anything vaguely resembling a wooded area.

I had seen enough documentaries on chimp behavior that I was confident in my ability to track Arbegast by the telltale signs of his habitation. It is a well-known fact among primatologists that chimpanzees nest and that rarely do they bed down in the same location on consecutive nights, a prudent contradiction of our own blunted survival instincts. Who would have guessed that living on the run would have brought out the monkey in me? According to the research, I was looking for an area of matted vegetation ringed by discarded fruit rinds.

The last of the half-dozen or so parks I checked that night was essentially the same as those that had preceded it: an open-air halfway house for cracked-out junkies and drunken Dumpster-divers. The place reeked of stale beer and fermenting urine, an ammoniated draft that permeated the air and scuttled slept-on newspapers like the yellowing leaves of a hopeless autumn. These were not the pine-perfumed refuges of my youth—the smell of freshly cut grass and Sunday cookouts as sweet to me then as the seedy inner-city mélange was repulsive to me now. The sprawling ameba-shaped lawn that in happier times had been host to goo-goo-eyed picnickers and company sack races was balding in some places and overgrown with spiky patches of crabgrass in others. Scraggly palms hula-skirted from top to bottom with layer upon layer of dead growth towered over the forgotten happy place like Polynesian colossi. As I made my way across the sickly pasture toward the newswrapped bodies stretched out in the windbreak of a defunct handball court, I breathed as shallowly as possible, fearing that some airborne pathogen exhaled by the park's degenerate fauna would penetrate the ragtag defenses of my decimated immune system.

One by one I peeled open the makeshift cocoons, exposing the transient larvae within, most of them too far gone to notice me crouching over them with a penlight clenched in my teeth. Those less blottoed regarded me with the stricken look of bomb-blast survivors, the slow-blinking victims of a catastrophe beyond their immediate comprehension. I was about to throw in the towel for the night (I was still wrestling with the idea of calling Janie at her sister's in spite of her request that I do no such thing) when a strange noise caught my attention. A deep and sustained breathing emanated from the barrel of an enormous concrete sewer pipe next to which I had paused to check the time on my watch. Its methodical cadence rose and fell with the self-possessed air of a psychopath. Lurking just beyond the range of my penlight's impotent beam, I could discern the silhouette of something vaguely humanoid hunched in the darkness. Scattered about the mouth of the pipe were empty schnapps bottles: peach, blackberry, watermelon, passion fruit. Though these were not exactly what I had expected, they were, in a sense, latter-day analogues to the discarded fruit rinds for which I was searching.

"We can do this one of two ways," I called into the mouth of the sewer pipe, my voice flat and unconvincing in the dead still of night. "Come out peacefully and I take you back to the STF, no questions asked. Otherwise, it's going to get ugly."

My ultimatum hanging limply in the air, it occurred to me that I was negotiating with a chimp. I could see Arbegast's Quasimodoesque silhouette shifting nervously about, rocking from side to side like a sumo wrestler readying himself for battle.

"I'm only going to ask you once," I announced, still cowed from the earlier beating I had suffered at the hands of my taciturn quarry and his ecclesia of chimp thugs.

My nerves prickled with static electricity, the transmitter manacled about my ankle broadcasting my whereabouts via the ultrasonic frequencies that drive canines mad. Should anything happen, recovering my body would be a matter of simple triangulation. I transferred the penlight to my mouth so that I would have both hands free and entered the pipe. The limp beam scarcely illuminated the path ahead of me. The massive artery was ankle-deep with garbage, its walls inscribed with the graffiti of past tenants, the savage stench of excrement and urine I had encountered in the clearing concentrated in the filthy tract. It had to be Arbegast, didn't it? The odor was unmistakably animal in origin, a byproduct of living habits totally ignorant of the practice of personal hygiene and sanitation.

As I inched my way forward, it occurred to me that I may as well have been walking down the barrel of my own gun so high was the probability that one of the knuckle-sized .45 slugs would find me in the concrete cylinder. I paused to galvanize my nerves against the torrent of fear pumping through my veins. I could hear the agitated breath-grunts of the murderous beast hunkered in the shadows, his oxygen intake doubling in response to my approach. As I eclipsed the black hole of an opening, whoever or *whatever* it was hiding in the darkness at the opposite end of the pipe rushed me like a Moroccan carpet vendor. Before I could turn tail, he hit me with the full force of his momentum, knocking me backward from the pipe with a bone-rattling blow to the sternum. As the air was forced from my lungs I spit up the penlight clenched in my teeth and swallowed the four-tooth bridge of upper incisors loosely affixed to my gums. Choking down the costly hors d'oeuvre, I realized that it was not Arbegast clubbing me with his balled-up fists about the head and face. Although unshaven and caked with filth, the snarling creature going at me like a wolverine was clearly human. Not only was this not the gun-toting chimp I had expected, but there was something unsettlingly familiar about the man with whom I was grappling.

"Ehrlich, it's me," I cried out, covering up against the rain of blows. "Stand down, soldier!"

Immediately, my attacker's arms went slack, the fury of a moment earlier abandoning his body as if I had incanted the words necessary to exorcise the demons that had fueled his rage.

"Sir?" he responded, his voice stretched with uncertainty.

"You don't have to call me 'sir.' The war's over."

For a moment, the two of us just stood there, knowing in our hearts that the truth was much more difficult to swallow. The war, in spite of what it said in the newspapers, was not over. Not for X-Ray squad. It lived in our dreams and nightmares, in the places where we had once felt safe. It lived in our blood and in our bones.

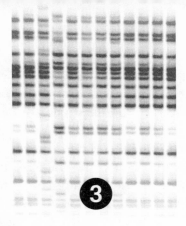

3

EHRLICH WAS A DEMOLITIONS EXPERT. The best. He could blow the door off an oven without knocking the wind out of the soufflé within. At the time of his disappearance, X-Ray had been in-country for three days, our mission overshadowed by a series of mishaps and mistaken identities that had pursued us across the forbidding desert landscape like the ghosts of camel caravans past.

Travel was not as difficult as you might think for an armed contingent of trained assassins sojourning in a hostile land. Our cover, as inspired a subterfuge as was ever devised, all but guaranteed our anonymity. We assumed the identity of a seldom-seen and little-understood order of Muslim holy men who emerged from a hidden desert temple but twice each century to inventory the sinful for Satan. Timing, as they say, is everything. Nineteen thirty-eight was the last anyone had seen of our mysterious alter egos, a band of robed disciples trekking along the outskirts of Ar Rutbah, a city of hookah-puffing arms dealers approximately one hundred clicks southeast of the Syrian border. You gotta hand it to the twisted fucks in Psy Ops: everywhere we went, men and women were dropping to their knees and kissing the earth in anticipation of the apocalypse the mysterious hooded figures in Reaper black were believed to portend.

Once every couple of weeks, Saddam celebrated his power by throwing an intimate gang bang for his closest advisors and top generals. Girls were flown into Baghdad from all over the world and shuttled via presidential limousine to a different venue each time. Early the following morning, the girls were paid handsomely, sworn to secrecy under penalty of death and shuttled back to the airport. The entire operation was very hush-hush, as much a matter of national security as the secret locations of the SCUD missile sites with which the Iraqis would one day soon rain death from above on the Allied forces. Islam did not exactly condone wholesale fornication among its followers. The Middle East was a veritable who's-who of civilizations toppled from their foundations of wickedness by the vengeful hand of God. If word got out that the country's leaders were laying the pipe to a bunch of Western she-devils, Iraq's fearful citizenry would most certainly trample each other fleeing her iniquitous cities lest they be turned into pillars of salt. To reduce the likelihood of security leaks the escort was kept to a minimum. Our plan was to hijack the convoy on the road outside of Hadithah and Trojan Horse it all they way into Saddam's love nest at Al Qa'im.

Rather than risk a conspicuous barricade, we used fear and superstition to bring the convoy to a halt. When the driver of the lead vehicle rounded the bend and saw us standing in the middle of the road shrouded in our voluminous black burnooses like sons of the occult, he nearly put his braking foot through the floorboard laying down a trail of sizzling rubber twenty yards long. Before the smoke cleared, the six members of the armed escort were on all fours French-kissing the sandswept asphalt like there was no tomorrow. Curious about the delay, the girls periscoped from open moon-roofs like the buxom honorees of a ticker-tape parade celebrating the wonders of silicone.

Although we could have simply climbed into the limos and driven off without firing a single shot, our orders were clear. All those with whom we came into contact were to be terminated, if for no other reason than to protect our cover. Ordinarily, the idea of a deeply revered group of holy men executing its devotees gangland style while they knelt in worship wouldn't have agreed with me. However, a rigorous course of pseuprezdid had instilled in me an alarming sense of clinical detachment. Uncle Sam had wired me to feel nothing. It was as if an internal switch had been flicked to deactivate the compassion receptors in my brain. Problem was, there were bugs in the program, synaptic short-circuits that, every now and then, allowed what little humanity I had left to rear its sympathetic head.

Things got a little crazy when we started popping off silenced 9mm rounds. Although none of my men seemed to particularly enjoy the heartless task at hand, there was an impersonal efficiency in the way they carried out the executions that would have turned blood to ice water in all but the most foolish of heroes. With each melony thud, a nauseating swell grew inside of me until a wave of guilt threatened to wash away my retrofitted conscience. Although my command facade suggested that I was in complete control of my emotions, a war between right and wrong was raging inside my head. If I could hold on a moment longer, I told myself, it would all be over. I could regroup, pop a few of the little blue pseuprezdid pills I had been issued, and incant the Nuremberg defense until the pain went away. Of course, I had made a terrible oversight. The fact that we were similarly obligated to dispose of eight hard-working girls trying to make an honest buck—maybe not innocents, but civilians just the same—didn't sit right with me. I had never even struck a woman no less put one down like an animal.

You should've seen them scampering to and fro over the deserted highway, all that candy-coated ass in spandex and skintight leather. Stiletto-heeled gazelles in synchronous flight. For all they knew, we were the mercenary pimps retired whores had warned them about: hired collectors who shanghaied naughty little girls for horny sheiks interested in stabling their harems with light-skinned brood mares so that their offspring might attend American universities without fear of discrimination.

The entire squad must have been experiencing my pangs of doubt because they just stood there watching the voluptuous herd stampede wildly about until their cheeks flushed red and their hip flexors quivered from exhaustion. Part of me was relieved that I was not commanding a zombie death squad. However, another part of me wanted them to get it over with, to simply take matters into their own hands. I knew that one way or another the decision was mine and mine alone, that the blood—some sixty-four pints, give or take— would be on my hands.

"What should we do with them, sir?" Lachaise asked.

"You know our orders," I responded, half-questioning.

A palpable hush descended over the highway, giving life to a silence so absolute that I could almost hear the sticky red blood of the slain Iraqis Rorschaching over the scalding pavement.

"Not exactly, sir," Lachaise continued, the golden thatch carpeting his scalp glinting like Montana wheat.

"Oh, my God, you're Americans!" shrieked a pigtailed redhead in a provocatively scant Catholic schoolgirl ensemble complete with starched white blouse, pleated plaid skirt, and lace trimmed knee-highs.

"They're Americans!" echoed a ponderously well-endowed brunette who had somehow managed to stuff herself into faded denim Daisy Dukes and a yellow gingham titty top with white cotton ruffles accenting her bust.

"We don't have a lot of time here, Lieutenant," I reminded Lachaise.

MacMurrough, a sharpshooter whose blind adherence to military homogeneity and general lack of distinguishing characteristics, physical or otherwise, had earned him the nickname "Clone," stepped forward and chambered a round.

"Let me do 'em," he offered blankly, his outstretched arm ticking off his intended victims like the second hand on a clock.

"Does anyone have any tampons?" asked a twenty-something Mouseketeer wearing red vinyl hotpants and fuzzy velveteen ears.

"Don't do this, sir," Ogburn pleaded sternly. "There's got to be another way."

"Dis widdle piggy went to market," Clone chanted as he drew a bead on each of the terrified faces. "Dis widdle piggy went home. . . . "

"Clone, put the gun away," I instructed. "I need to think this over."

As Clone complied begrudgingly, a platinum-blond Asian in

a silver super-mini bent over at the waist and planted a lippy kiss on the black steel muzzle leveled at her face.

"Don't get your panties wet, girls," she assured her befetished colleagues, brushing aside Clone's 9mm and striding across the road toward one of the head-shot escorts. "These gentlemen don't know it yet, but they need us."

With an ease that defied the laws of physics, the Asian nudged the dead escort onto his back with the blunt toe of a strappy black patent-leather platform shoe. She lowered herself onto him, exposing the gossamer swatch of fabric guarding the forbidden delta of her inner thighs. A burning cigarette lay on the ground next to the dead man's head. She picked it up, brushed a few specks of dirt from the filter, and took a drag.

"Who the hell are you?" I asked, my eyes inexorably drawn toward the silky confluence between her legs.

"Mekong," she breathed coyly, exhaling snake-like curls of smoke that writhed hypnotically about her head. "The way I see it, you can kill us all right here or you can bring us with you."

"No fucking way," I said.

"You'll never make it past the main gate without the password," she informed me flatly, levitating from her mount and bridging the distance between us with the purposeful strides of a quarter horse. "You just don't have the body for it."

"Don't let her bring you down, Captain," Chavez remarked. "You've got a great personality."

Mekong's hand encircled the muzzle of my .45 and drew it toward her. Her fingernails were long and glossy and black.

"Do me," she hissed.

I withdrew the gun from her playful grasp and stepped backward. She killed the cigarette with a suggestive drag and flicked the spent butt past my head. The other girls watched breathlessly, their painted faces—a provocative mixture of ecstasy and sin—ostensibly borrowed from the pages of a bible comic.

"The scent you're wearing," I asked. "What is it?"

"Napalm," she replied hotly. "You like?"

"It suits you."

• • •

The main gate at Saddam's compound was a reinforced bronze battlement that must have weighed ten tons. Those of us impersonating drivers were to remain behind the wheel disguised in Republican Guard berets and fake mustaches while the rest of us laid low with the girls in back. One at a time, the moon roofs in each of the three limos opened to reveal a blue rectangle of sky overhead. As the curvaceous Mouseketeer sitting across from me slipped off her top, a belly-cropped jersey exclaiming Jody in flirtatious red script, I began to understand what Mekong had meant back at the ambush site. Like comely maidens affixed to a ship's bow to assure safe passage over a treacherous sea, the topless vixens bared their breasts to the undersexed guards awaiting the inimitable password. Mekong was right—I didn't have the body for it.

Set on the banks of the Euphrates, the compound at Al Qa'im was more beautiful than I could have ever imagined. Encircled by a towering stone wall that had withstood eons of three-digit heat and an occasional head-for-high-ground deluge, the fabled desert retreat was like something out of the pages of *A Thousand and One Nights*. Purple-crowned agapanthus fringed the shoreline of an enormous deep blue spring. Quarrelsome birds ruffled their wings and disputed ownership of the tender sweet-meated dates plundered from the swaying palm groves silhouetted against the cerulean sky. But even Eden had its snakes in the grass. It was this that I had kept telling myself, knowing that I had brought the ill-will of humanity with me to this paradisical wonderland. I was there to do a job, just as the devil appearing as the head of a worm in an apple had been duty-bound to corrupt Adam. Neither I nor Eve could have known what forces conspired in the shadow of our good intentions. Just as she could not have possibly extrapolated famine, war, and the spread of AIDS from the naïve flirtations of a boy and a girl, so, too, was I oblivious of the fate to which I was wedded like a bride of Bluebeard.

In the center of the sparkling green and gold oasis stood an ancient Moorish castle buttressed by smaller though equally fantastic outbuildings. These, I would later learn, had long ago housed a king's twenty-seven unwed daughters, each connected to a central escape tunnel leading into the heart of the desert. Built by an overprotective father determined to safeguard the virtue of his progeny in the unlikely event that the fortress was overrun, the sandstone artery breached daylight some three miles to the west just inside the sandblasted walls of a city all but erased from the face of the earth. For those in the know, food caches and oil lamps marked the way. For all others, booby traps and an elaborate system of dead ends could mean death in an hour or a week. Had I known then what I know now, I would have never ordered my men into that god-forsaken catacomb in pursuit of the man whose sinister deceits haunt me to this day.

Once inside the compound, security was relatively light. We parked in the midst of a gleaming flotilla of government limousines and German luxury cars. By now the sun was low on the horizon, the sky awash in a cool lavender tint. While the Iraqi welcome wagon, a heavy-breathing contingent of paunchy middle-aged men, escorted the girls inside, those who had been driving the limos slipped into the back, put up the privacy screen, and laid low with the rest of us in the blacked-out passenger compartments. No one had seemed to notice. They were too busy trying to charm the pants off the girls.

Shortly after nightfall, Chopstix and Lachaise took out the two door guards with synchronized shots to the head. Bascombe, Ehrlich, Goof, and Phone Sex plunked the wall sentries. Reacting as if bitten by killer mosquitoes, their praetorian silhouettes pitched headlong into the burnt umber dusk. It took Neuhoff less than a minute to pick the lock on the heavy wooden door guarding the entrance to Saddam's X-rated sanctuary. A long, dimly lit passageway plunged into a void flickering with erratic pulses of light at the base of a sweeping flight of stairs. A low repetitive thudding welled from the subterranean chamber, its concussive signature reverberating in the ribbed corridor like the heartbeat of an enormous creature that had swallowed us whole. I could feel it in my guts, in the liquid buffer between brain and skull, in every cell and follicle bristling on my hide. By the time we reached the top of the stairs, the rhythmic assault on our senses had begun to take shape. A series of lesser oscillations accompanied the hard-hitting bass, expanding and contracting in precisely modulated time signatures. Foolishly, I realized that what we were hearing was not the visceral rumblings of a gargantuan menace, but the humping pulse of a discotheque.

As we descended the stairs, it became clear to me that the frenetic environment into which we were sinking was grossly ill-suited to the preferred conditions of assassination. Every flash of light, every exaggerated movement, every trance-inducing computer-generated sound bite conspired to confound the senses. While stationed in Munich, I had frequented nightclubs in which this sort of musical chaos was the norm, nights surrendered to the blissful out-of-bodiness of dance, drugs, and fornication. However, other than a few instances of bareback sex with some freaky fräuleins and an occasional bad dose of Ecstasy, my life for the most part had never been in jeopardy. This, of course, would mark the onset of my ruin, the efflorescence of a garden sown in ignorance and fertilized with blood.

I had told myself that we could use the confusion to our advantage just as I had favored the German discos for the invaluable anonymity afforded their escapist clientele. Wearing the clothes of one of the dead escorts, I gathered myself and danced my way into the midst of Saddam's inner circle of generals and military advisors. I was reasonably certain that given the erratic lighting, the impossibly loud music and the preponderance of booze being consumed, I could move undetected amongst them, pinpoint our target's location, and relay it to my men, who were positioned on the stairwell like pageant contestants awaiting the opening of the envelope.

I was not exactly feeling the music. Moments earlier, I had been sipping single-malt scotch in the back of a limousine thinking about Janie and all the things we were going to do together when I returned from the Gulf—walks on the beach at sunset, ski lodges and spiked hot chocolate in front of a crackling fire, warm bubble baths and strawberries dipped in brown sugar—now I was wearing the uniform of a dead man who, more than likely, had someone special of his own to come home to. My growing dependence on pseuprezdid was exacerbated by this stubborn parallel, which plagued me each time I was called upon to pull the trigger. My muted humanity percolated beneath the surface of my soldierly exterior like a hibernating pathogen awaiting the optimum window of opportunity in which to lay siege to my moral defenses. Had I been anywhere else, save perhaps a wedding, the undisputed heavyweight of bad dancing, my herky-jerky movements would have attracted suspicious glances from every corner of the room. Rather than fight the stiffness possessing my limbs, I approximated as closely as I was able the robotic pantomime of the Venice Beach street performers to whose jingling coffers Janie and I, in the heyday of our love, had once contributed generously.

Like a short-circuited C3PO I popped and moonwalked my way across the dance floor, swiveling and gyrating for the benefit of my erstwhile comrades. Even the girls didn't seem to notice me; they were too busy bumping and grinding with Saddam's henchmen. Time seemed to slow, the flickering strobe giving life to a stop-time montage of boogieing war criminals and aspiring centerfolds. Fake smoke rolled across the floor, obscuring the dancers from the knees down in an eerie nimbus of evaporated CO_2. A dazzling spectrum of colored light illuminated the cool mist from within, imbuing the enrapt expressions of the dancers with an unearthly glow. It was like standing on the surface of a newly formed planet, a geologically active hot zone teeming with strange and potentially lethal life-forms. Had Mekong not taken hold of me by the zipper of my borrowed dress fatigues, there's no telling how long I would have languished in the tarantistic embrace of the techno siren call, the priority-one directive to which I was thanklessly duty-bound overpowered by the hard-driving industrial barrage.

"Relax," purred Mekong, her hands playing over me like a posthypnotic suggestion. "Imagine you're making love to me."

"Where is he?"

"You no like dance with Mekong?" she pouted, releasing my zipper and appraising me with a feline grin.

Stupidly, I realized that I had stopped dancing, that I was simply standing in the middle of the room while heaving, pulse-pounding bodies flashed about me. With a jolt, I resumed my spasmodic gyrations to the beat of the eclectic boogie-down mix.

"I'm here to kill a man."

"That's it—move your hips," said Mekong, clutching me by the ass and pulling me into her.

"I don't have time for this," I protested uselessly, captivated by the sheer silvery glint of her miniskirt swishing over her ginger thighs.

With each promise-laden movement, with each seductive parting of her lips, with each penetrating look of lust, she seemed to draw me farther inside of her until it was as if we shared a single heartbeat, a single pulse, a single overpowering desire to become one. I could feel her breath in my ear. Each humid exhalation was like a spicy blast from a hookah, intoxicating rungs on a smoke ladder aimed at nirvana. She urged my hands to explore the shrink-wrapped contours of her body, its sought-after peaks and mythic valleys, the trail by which I would find my way back obliterated by the promise of what lay ahead.

"Captain!" Bascombe hissed over the receiver plugged into my ear. "What's going on in there? We're getting antsy."

I buried my face in the nape of Mekong's neck and spoke into the microphone concealed beneath the fold of my collar.

"Hold position. Confirming target. Copy."

Mekong decided to return the favor, and tattooed my neck with a life-draining hickey. The girl had a set of lips that could have stripped the barnacles off the hull of a battleship, however it was Janie's face that delivered me from the grip of her lusty vacuum.

"Show me where he is," I demanded, disentangling myself from her sinewy anchors.

"Hold your horses, Killer," she cooed dangerously. "He's right there."

At the edge of the dance floor was a secluded booth steeped in the cool blue light of a baby spot. Seated alone in the richly upholstered horseshoe was the distinguished profile of the

Ghoul of the Gulf, the Stalin of the Sand, my target, Saddam Hussein. No American had been this close since Philip Morris had introduced Joe Camel to the Iraqi parliament in a misguided attempt to express a cross-cultural bond between nations. He was handsome in the way of all dictators, the travails of his brutal rise to power etched into the lines of his face. There was an inconsolable solemnity about him, a joyless disrepair expressed as much in the fact that he wasn't dancing as in his isolation from the others.

"Bascombe," I said. "You ready to do this?"

"Locked and loaded."

"Three minutes on my mark."

Mekong danced her way around the room instructing the other girls to take cover as soon as the first shot was fired. My greatest concern was that one of them would become a bargaining tool, a hysterical teary-eyed bullet catcher. Should such a scenario arise, X-Ray had been instructed to treat the hostage as a secondary target and take him or her out along with the primary. Not only were these hapless civilians we were talking about, they were every hetero male's wet dream. Asking us to gun them down in cold blood was like asking us to renounce baseball, rock 'n' roll, and muscle cars.

I robot-danced my way across the floor and positioned myself ten feet from where Saddam sat alone observing the dance floor with a troubled smile. I couldn't escape the feeling that there was more to the man I had been sent to kill than met the eye.

As I articulated every joint in my body like a tightly wound toy soldier on methamphetamine, I began to wonder if I was cut out to be an assassin. Having alerted the last of the girls, Mekong danced her way toward me with a carnal fluidity that betrayed nothing of the impending slaughter. I checked my watch. I had less than a minute to draw my gun and cap the lonesome wallflower bobbing his head and lip-synching the uncensored lyrics of "Big Booty Ho's" like a dateless teenager at the high-school prom. I don't know who was more pathetic: the dictator afraid to shake his moneymaker or the hit man with a heart of gold.

As the second hand ticked down and Mekong's predatory

two-step acquired the curse-carrying fervor of a voodoo death ritual, I began to understand why the army had such unwavering faith in pseuprezdid. Responding as if to a genetically encoded murder instinct, I performed a series of mechanized movements that I knew from the onset would culminate in the death of the toe-tapping autocrat. At precisely the moment the second hand reached its apex, I drew my gun and fired two quick shots into Saddam's head. The first hammered into his skull just above the bridge of his nose, knocking him back. His eyes fluttered and crossed involuntarily, as if in the throes of an orgasm. The second shot ripped through his chin, passing through the crown of his skull and flipping the trademark beret from his head like a done-to-death western gag.

The ratcheting of automatic-weapons fire and blinding muzzle flashes blended seamlessly with the musical pandemonium, the pulsating lights and crisp synthetic beat disguising the rock-concert-like pyrotechnics belching out death at a thousand rounds per minute. On cue, the girls had dropped to the floor. As their unsuspecting dance partners were cut down in a locust swarm of bullets, the gun-shy beauties scrambled about on all fours to avoid the crush of bodies toppling down around them. Only Mekong seemed unfazed by the bloody demolition, the balls-out havoc of shattering glass, splintering wood and volcanic showers of sparks of no greater consequence to her than a spirited barroom brawl. She continued dancing as X-Ray swept through the room in their flowing black burnooses pumping bullets into anything that moved.

The dance floor was proper with corpses, a moribund relief map of good times gone bad, bullet-addled bodies strewn about like Pompeiian statuary. Cowed by the massacre, the girls whimpered and wept. I was certain as never before that somehow, some way I would be judged for my actions. The flimsy pretext of righteousness the army had brainwashed into me was just a patriotic subterfuge for the unforgivable sin of murder. Even then I realized that although I could munch pseuprezdid like M&Ms, I could never outrun my conscience. Like the curse of the mummy, it would pursue me across continents, traversing oceans and deserts, the cells in my body like grains of sand in an hourglass sifting irrevocably toward spiritual emptiness, my heart a tomb robbed of the richness of life.

"You got the son of a bitch!" Goof shouted above the music, clapping me on the back. "Fuckin' A, Lee Harvey, you smoked his ass."

"Ogburn, check the body," I ordered. "Make sure it's him."

Obviously shaken, Ogburn, the civilian forensics specialist whose role it was to positively ID Hussein, worked his way across the dance floor. For him, the still-bleeding corpses embodied the difference between buying his hamburger packaged and slaughtering the cow and grinding the meat himself. Upon reaching the booth, he removed his forensics kit—dental casts, blood typing, DNA—and set about his examination with a look of half-formed dread. He stooped over the corpse where it lay facedown on the table in a pool of blood. After examining it from various angles, he bent his head to one side and looked under the table.

"Captain," he said, "I think you should see this."

Before I could make it across the room, Chopstix took hold of Hussein by the collar and easily lifted him off the table. Had a dead man not been involved, the effect would have been comical. There, suspended in midair like a finely crafted ventriloquist's dummy, dangled a 1/2-scale Hussein look-alike, an abbreviated dictator right down to the polished combat booties shoeing his tiny feet, the various medals adorning his proud breast and the authoritarian scowl offsetting his lifeless eyes with studied contempt. I had thought there was more to him, but apparently there was less.

"Looks like you bagged one of Santa's little helpers," Chopstix declared. "What we got here is an elf."

"It's not as if he was parading around on top of some guy's shoulders wearing a trench coat and a phony mustache," I explained, sickening pangs of guilt already challenging pseuprezdid's tenuous hold on my embattled morality center.

"We knew something like this might happen," Ogburn offered with a conciliatory frown. "Apparently, the guy's got everyone and his cousin surgically altered to look just like him."

"Da plane, da plane," Chopstix buzzed, manipulating the dwarf's right arm so that he appeared to hail the pilot who would ferry his soul to a better place. A few of the girls managed to laugh through their sniffles.

Clone retrieved something large and familiar-looking from the vinyl cushion where the dwarf had been sitting. He fanned through the flimsy pages like a professional cold caller limbering up for a day's work.

"Fucking Iraqi yellow pages," he declared gleefully. "Tattoo was sitting on a goddamn phone book!"

"Somebody get the lights and turn off the fucking music!" I shouted. "I can't hear myself think."

A moment later the lights came on and for the second time that night all hell broke loose.

"There he is!" cried Bascombe, the lot of us paralyzed in disbelief.

The DJ booth was set into the wall some ten feet off the ground on the other side of the dance floor. There, spinning tracks behind an inch-thick pane of soundproof glass, stood Saddam Hussein, eyes closed, grooving to the high-octane beat. The lights must have caught his attention because his eyes suddenly snapped open. Surprised, he panned over the carnage on the dance floor beneath him and dived for cover. Gunfire erupted, shattering the soundproof glass and filling the booth with sparks. The music died out with the plaintive groan of a wildebeest locked in the jaws of a crocodile.

By the time we found our way up to the booth, Saddam was gone. We split up and searched the compound from top to bottom. Ehrlich and Phone Sex found the entrance to one of the escape tunnels and went in after him.

Only Ehrlich came back.

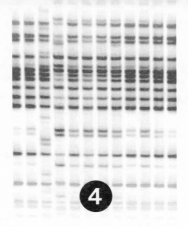

4

"WHAT DID YOU EXPECT TO FIND IN THAT SEWER PIPE, anyway, Captain?"
Ehrlich asked offhandedly, picking a scab from his balding
crown and studying it in the antiseptic cone of the map light as
we drove back toward my house.

"You wouldn't believe me if I told you."

Ehrlich started whispering to himself. Nonsense. Furtive dia-
logues that sounded like rats scratching around in the wall
spaces of a condemned warehouse. He deposited the scab in the
ashtray where I kept spare change for parking meters.

"They got Bascombe," he said. "Bastards forced him to eat his
own feet before they cut his throat."

"And Chavez, and Goof, and Neuhoff." I recited the names
blandly, without emotion. "I thought I was the only one left."

"How have you managed to stay alive for so long?"

"Just lucky, I guess."

Ehrlich let his head fall back against the headrest. He ran his
hand over the headliner, whispering to himself and finger-
painting invisible images on the stretch-fitted polyester.

"Myself"—he reflected grimly—"I've been living on the streets.
. . . Doing the homeless thing."

"The papers said you were dead: suicide. You parked your car
at the edge of a cliff and jumped into the ocean. The body was
never found. I read your obituary."

"I did it for Louise and the kids," he confirmed defensively.
"With me around, they were as good as dead. What about your
wife—Saddam get her yet?"

"I think he figured she was more trouble to me alive. I think she's in love with someone else."

Ehrlich's head bobbed pensively as he stared out the passenger window, his expression spent and haggard. I wanted to tell him about Arbegast and the others, but I couldn't see fueling his lunatic delusions with tales of murderous chimps on the loose.

"I eat garbage," he said at last.

I rolled down the front windows hoping to expel some of his vigorous stench, the haughty vintage evoking a pastoral wasteland of sludge irrigation and sweeping vineyards of vine-ripened dingleberries. He reeked of stale beer, urine, and composting organics, a relatively mild companion to the noxious gases forced from his lungs in belligerent gusts.

"Your death must have been hard on Louise. Aren't you ever tempted to let her know that you're okay? Maybe drop her a postcard?"

"Hard on *her?*" Ehrlich replied, his voice swelling with anger. "What about me? I'm fucking dead! What the hell would I say to her, Dutch? 'Sorry, sweetheart, it's me who's been shitting behind the hedge all these years. Leave a roll of Charmin on the back porch so I don't have to use the 'Lifestyles' section to wipe my ass.' I am *anything* but okay!"

He pulled at his face, mute sobs racking his body like blows from an invisible foe. What do you say to a man who has lost everything? I was still searching for something to tell myself.

"If it makes you feel any better—" I began.

Ehrlich cut me off abruptly, his voice galvanized with hurt. "It doesn't," he said.

Silenced, I looked away from him, surveying the neighborhood in which I had lived for the past fourteen years with an air of wonder and bewilderment. The unsure saplings that had once lined the street like naked stick figures had grown into towering giants, their massive limbs interlacing to form an impenetrable canopy high above the sulfurous glow of streetlamps. Shrubs and hedges and wild sprays of unkempt vegetation that defied explanation thicketed moss-covered walkways, climbed rain gutters, snaked in and out of picket fences like rattan basketry. One of the houses was so overgrown that the chimney seemed to be the only logical point of entry for its inhabitants. Either I had never really paid attention to the once-quaint dwellings or they had simply metamorphosed into something infinitely less reassuring, a paradisiacal vision of a world without humans. Where were the Mexican gardeners who had once prowled the neighborhood in beat-up pickups manicuring the parceled acreage of its white middle-class residents? What had happened to the roar of the gas-powered lawn mowers and leaf blowers, the ambrosial scent of freshly cut grass and the loamy waft of steer manure nourishing beds of daffodils and tulips aligned with uncompromising symmetry? In the uncertain light, freakishly oversized birds of paradise were virtually indistinguishable from banana plants, their broad, waxy leaves lolling in the torpid Santa Ana breeze as if powered by the lethargic fanning motion of enslaved eunuchs.

What had not been raked and bagged had gone to mulch. Steaming piles of moldering leaf rot gave rise to species of fungus and lichen that had not proliferated in Southern California since crocodile-infested peat bogs had perfumed the primordial dawn with methane gas from Hollywood Boulevard to the Pacific. Toadstools studded lawns shaggy with neglect. Sprinklers left spouting at capacity delivered precipitation with monsoonlike efficiency, drenching the gardens and sluicing the gutters with tea-colored runoff. Drip lines no longer apportioned their cargo by the cc, but writhed in their beds, sweating madly like snakebitten plantation workers, sizzling fuses igniting an explosion of life. Bromeliads and kaffir lilies and alien-looking succulents spiked with otherworldly blooms thrived in the abundant moisture. Even the power lines hosted ambitious creepers of Boston ivy, passion vine, mandevilla, and wispy stalactites of copper green moss.

I hardly recognized my own street, which, given the nearly decade and a half of semi-permanent residence there, struck me as odd. Part of me felt as if I was lost—if not worlds, then surely latitudes away from my humble abode. This was more like the malarial quagmire of Janus's office or the impassable jungle bula-bula land of the Enchanted Forest than a respectable borough of greater Los Angeles. When I finally snapped out of it, Ehrlich's expression had softened.

"Forget everything I said. It's just that I've been under a lot of strain," he explained, his voice apologetic.

"No problem."

"You don't look so hot yourself." He bared his front teeth and clicked his fingernail against them.

"I've got a bridge," I explained, "but for the moment I seem to have misplaced it."

As down as I was, I still had too much pride to elaborate and admit to Ehrlich that sometime within the next twelve hours or so I would recover my runaway teeth by picking through a pile of my own shit.

As we pulled into the driveway, my mood sank just a little further. No matter how realistic I tried to be, there was always hope in the back of my mind that I would return home to find Janie standing in the reassuring glow of the porch light, her posture communicating in that magical way of hers that all was forgiven. But the place was dark and empty, enshrouded in a capsule of abandonment that was exaggerated by the advanced degree to which the unchecked flora had extended its stranglehold on the neighborhood.

Tree ferns I had planted shortly after my return from the Gulf—just one of many therapies that had failed to exorcise the demons I had piggybacked across continents—stood well over ten feet tall, green mushroom clouds that defied the growth indicators to which I had referred when choosing a species that would not overpower our modest piece of land. Where the flabellate giants had derived the nourishment required to induce gargantuanism was impossible to say for certain. I could only surmise that it was stolen from the heavily saturated ground atop which several weeks' worth of unread *L.A. Times* lay bloated and disintegrating next to the old-fashioned push lawn mower that foundered like a ghost ship in the swirling mange of what many had once considered the most beautiful lawn on the block. Plants I neither remembered nor recognized proliferated in the marshy substrate that bubbled and slurped and squished underfoot like the floor of a Javan cloud forest: otherworldly protea, gooey gnat catchers, open-mouthed pitcher plants, and ravenous clusters of Venus flytrap—a veritable who's who of carnivorous chlorophyll.

"So this is home sweet home," Ehrlich commented as he side-stepped a snail the size of a cinnamon danish on the walkway. "The fabled Chateau Flowers."

I imagined the mighty edifice to which he had alluded collapsing before me, its crowned battlements, lofty spires, and moated donjon turning to rubble in the blink of an eye. I knew I had to face the distinct possibility that things would never be the same between Janie and myself, that sooner or later one of her random and ever-lengthening departures would be for good. I would be left utterly and hopelessly alone with nothing save the abstruse dementia of my imaginary syndrome to keep me company in the wee hours of night. As Ehrlich and I neared the front door, I could hear the hiss and burble of running water nearby.

"Wait here," I said, "I think I might've forgotten to turn off the hose before I left."

Of course I hadn't been anywhere near the hose in weeks, but Ehrlich didn't have to know this. Between the army's categorical denial of my illness, Acteon's clandestine gene-tampering with chimpanzees, and my unconfirmed suspicions of adultery, I was not about to take on the burden of any additional conspiracy theories, no matter how insignificant they may have seemed. What was I supposed to tell him—that I suspected a group of renegade environmentalists was somehow involved in a systematic process of reforestation? Even to someone as schooled in the ways of intrigue as Ehrlich, the idea would've sounded crazy. I was starting to sound a little paranoid to myself. After all, what could anyone hope to gain from making the world a more beautiful place in which to live? Better that I keep Ehrlich in my corner than alienate myself from the only person I had come across in years who might actually understand a fraction of what

I was going through. The idea of it being me against the world didn't exactly warm my cockles.

Having, at least for the time, concluded my business with Janus, I had picked up a new pair of Nike cross-trainers, reassuring myself that the eighty dollars I had charged on Janie's Visa was a legitimate business expense. You have to spend money to make money, right? Like it or not, I figured to be doing a lot of legwork tracking Arbegast, and a stealthy new pair of air-cushioned kicks seemed to be just what the doctor had ordered. I had it all worked out: track down Arbegast, collect my fifty Gs, and pay off Mr. Wonderful before I got used to the collar around my ankle. But first things first: Somewhere out there, a drug-addict chimpanzee with a three-hundred-proof IQ was prowling the streets with my .45 in one hand, and in the other hand, a hard-on for the awesome power he now possessed. I needed to stay focused.

I tracked the hose across the lawn and instantly regretted that I had not done so barefoot. I had traveled no more than ten feet, squinting and swatting my way through aggressive clouds of no-see-ums that attacked like sprays of birdshot, and already I could feel the wetness penetrating the synthetic leather upper and breathable Gore-Tex webbing upholstering my insteps. So much for keeping my new shoes new-looking. Apparently, someone had cranked open the shut-off valve full bore and left the hose spewing a crystalline arc at the base of a chest-high sago palm whose shallow root system had been exposed by the forceful stream of water. Stranger still was the fact that the very shut-off valve which had been left open had been deliberately sabotaged to remain so. The forged brass twist was missing, and the stem atop which it had once resided snugly was irreparably stripped. In spite of my frustration, it explained the deluge that had transformed my lawn into spongy green bread pudding. Aside from hauling a twenty-four-hour plumber out of bed at double his normal rate, the only way I was going to stop the flow before morning was to shut off the water main. The thought of spending a night in the same house with an unwashed Ehrlich was enough to convince me to wait until he had finished scrubbing the street residue from his feculent dermis. As I made my way back across the lawn I was overcome by an awkward sensation; I could swear someone was watching me from beyond the blind of a robust hedge of camellias. Although certain it was my green-thumbed saboteur, I was in no mood for a confrontation after all I'd been through of late.

"Quite a garden you got here, Dutchie," Ehrlich remarked upon my return. "Your water bills must be through the roof."

"Welcome to paradise," I offered with a trespasserly lack of conviction.

While Ehrlich showered and attended to matters of personal hygiene, I sat down to outline a new plan of attack. Although the premise behind checking the parks was theoretically sound, the area it required me to cover was simply too vast, too varied. I needed something solid to go on, a lead. Let's face it, with Mr. Wonderful's monthly installment coming due I didn't have time to go chasing hunches all over the city.

I poured over Arbegast's psych profile in search of anything that would bring me closer to anticipating his next move. Thinking like a chimp—a God-given talent that was surely within my reach—was pointless. Who knows how many millions of R&D dollars Acteon had invested to make certain their chimps thought like humans, a talent with which I am admittedly less well-versed? I had decided to telephone Shackleman at his home and pump him for information—something he had begged me not to do unless absolutely necessary—when Ehrlich emerged from the guest bathroom pursued by a billowing contrail of lavender-scented steam. So he had used Janie's decorative bath cakes to lather away God-knows-how-many layers of filth and grime. When the time came, I could quietly dispose of the tainted French *savon de bain* and replace it before Janie noticed. No harm, no foul. At least I wouldn't have to smell him anymore. Problem was, Ehrlich had slipped into the same dirty clothes he had been wearing when I'd dragged him out of the sewer pipe, a mishmash ensemble of raucous odors and smarmy stains sponged from garbage cans and homeless shelters.

"Why don't you put on something of mine?" I suggested. "That way we can run your stuff through the wash."

I said "wash," but was thinking "incinerator."

Ehrlich looked at me as if it was I and not he who had gone completely out of his mind.

"Camouflage," he replied cryptically.

"What about camouflage?" I asked.

"Cam-ou-flage," Ehrlich repeated, sounding out the word one syllable at a time. "The art of concealment. No offense, Dutchie Boy, but if I hit the streets dressed like Ward fuckin' Cleaver, the Raqis'll cap me faster than you can say scabies. I don't know where you've been, my friend, but it's a goddamned war zone out there. You either dress for success, or the guys with the clean fingernails and body bags haul you away."

I was stunned. I shouldn't have been, but I was.

"You're going back?" I asked incredulously. "You're taking your meals in a sewer pipe! There's disease in there, pestilence. You're not the Phantom of the Opera."

"What disease?" Ehrlich replied nonchalantly, massaging the base of his skull where a scrofulous patch of dandruff had gone terminal with neglect.

"Leprosy, tetanus, diaper rash. . . . How the fuck should I know? *Rats!* There's gotta be rats in there. Everyone knows that rats carry disease. Look at the Middle Ages—one big sewer crawling with rats. Millions died. It'll be a miracle if you don't end up with warts on your eyelids."

"Poor man's poultry." Ehrlich smacked his lips. "Ghetto chicken. Snap off a car antenna, and you got all the makings of a gourmet shishkebab."

As a rule, I am not particularly squeamish. However, the thought of one of my men supping on vermin, and the possibility that I had uncovered the reason behind the rash of misappropriated car antennas plaguing the city filled me with disgust. I could feel the tofu hotdogs I had eaten for dinner, a volatile mix of stomach acid, sea salt, and creamy pink soy magma, looking for a way out.

"I'm just fuckin' with you, Dutchie Boy," said Ehrlich. "I've actually been eating pretty good the past couple of years. Suck a few dicks now and then, cut the coupons out of the Sunday paper, and I'm good to go. Hell, I even got my own shopping cart."

Eventually, I convinced Ehrlich to stay at my place for a while and explore his options for survival. Eking out an existence on the streets, we both agreed, did not exactly rank him among the living.

"You're not doing too well yourself," he was quick to remind me, eyeing the electronic ball and chain around my ankle. "How long before a guy in a helicopter plunks a tranquilizer dart in your ass and hauls you in so he can poke around in your lower intestine and see what kinds of nuts and berries you've been eating?"

I unhitched my pant leg from where it had become snagged on the transmitter and dropped the curtain on the subject with an ironic smile.

"The top of the food chain sure ain't what it used to be," I agreed.

Around 4:00 A.M., the two of us settled down at the kitchen table with a semi-soft stick of tofu salami, a squeeze bottle of organic mustard, and several years' worth of catching up to do. I was relieved that I was not alone. For the most part, I talked and Ehrlich nodded absentmindedly, devouring everything I set in front of him with ravenous disregard for the shrunken confines of his stomach and Janie's strict adherence to a healthful—and consequently bland—diet. From sesame crackers with sugarless grape jelly to white asparagus spears packed in effervescing spring water, he seemed not to mind the shortage of sodium and saturated fats which, at times, had driven me to consider starvation. Having observed him lay waste to virtually everything in the pantry, it should not have surprised me that he was in no way put off by the rowdy stench of exotic fruits going to rot in the vegetable crisper. By no means were these the familiar shapes and textures you find nestled among the cantaloupe and cherry tomatoes in the produce section at Von's. To a fledgling botanist, the otherworldly cornucopia may have constituted an exciting discovery. To me, however, the disagreeable compost simply smelled bad.

"You're not throwing that out!" Ehrlich exclaimed as I removed the bin and prepared to feed its unsavory contents to the garbage disposal.

"It's rotten," I assured him. "If you want fruit to eat, I think there's a can of peaches in the cabinet to the right of the stove."

Ehrlich shot out of his chair and snatched a spiny green football-sized ovoid from the sink and cradled it in his arms.

"It's not rotten," he declared with maternal indignation. "Durian just smells that way. It's an acquired taste. Hmong tribesmen consider it a bona fide delicacy. What you got here is jungle caviar."

"I'll see if I can find some crackers."

"Your wife has expensive taste in fruit, Dutchie Boy. This stuff's like gold. Six bucks a pound in your Asian specialty markets," said Ehrlich. "Fuckin' A, that's *if* you can find it."

"How the hell do you acquire a taste for something that smells like the bottom of a garbage can?" I wondered, immediately sorry that I had asked.

"Home sweet home," Ehrlich explained, hefting the rescued durian in both hands. "Got a knife?"

I had given Ehrlich a pair of khaki permanent-press dress slacks and a Christmas-motif Hawaiian shirt complete with ukulele-playing elves and surfing Santas. I hadn't touched the ensemble since I had tried unsuccessfully to hold down a 9-to-5 in jacuzzi retail after the war. *Spa, the Final Frontier*: what a nightmare that had been. In any case, Ehrlich's feeding frenzy gave rise to a falling-rock zone of snack debris that rolled off his chin and tumbled down the front of his shirt as I recounted the events surrounding the past few months. I shared my suspicions about Janie, the phantom illness that had soured my sperm, and the transvestite Reaper in couture swimwear who was bleeding me dry.

The sun came up and we were still going at it like a couple of penitents traveling different roads to absolution. I talked; Ehrlich ate—albeit with less gusto than we had exercised upon first leaving the starting gate. The bottle of 101-proof Wild Turkey I kept on hand for emergencies and with which I had oiled the windmills of my quixotic epic was empty but for the sacramental vapors lingering inside of it like a tapped-out genie. I left Ehrlich alone at the table and raided the pantry for something else we could drink.

"He almost got me once," Ehrlich grumbled scornfully, elevating his voice. "If I hadn't smelled the fruity bastard coming, I'd be pushing up buttercups alongside Chief Rain-in-the-Face in Anaheim Stadium. I'll tell you who belongs out there instead of me . . . Jim Everett—that's who. The guy's good for one thing and one thing only: fertilizer. He's an embarrassment to the league. This isn't girls' field hockey we're talking about. This is the NFL. There's no place for a guy who buys his jockstraps at Victoria's Secret."

I returned to the table with a bottle rescued from an unmarked cardboard box on the floor of the pantry, its clandestine presence in my pantry as puzzling as its golden contents were effective in the warding off of evil spirits. Banana liqueur. Monkey rum. It must have been on special. A buy-one-get-ten sort of deal. Unless, of course, Janie was going into the soufflé business and I didn't know about it. The fact of the matter is I had never really thought of her as a banana lover. It just goes to show how close you can get to a person and still not know about the little things that make them tick. I promised myself that I would do a better job of listening if and when she ever decided to come home.

"You know Mr. Wonderful?" I asked.

"Flashy dresser with rings on his fingers and bells on his toes?"

"A regular femme fatale," I agreed, knowing with undiluted certainty that we were speaking about the same gender-bending hit man.

"What's the story with him, anyway? He looks as if he should be giving bikini waxes to old drag queens, not headhunting for Saddam. I know one thing for sure. The guy's a handful of pain. Serious as AIDS. A devil in ladies' underwear. I'm just glad it was you in the park tonight and not that lunatic lingerie jockey."

"He saved my life the other day," I explained numbly, cracking the seal on the banana liqueur and filling our glasses. "I was trying to commit suicide. I think he might have done *something* to me while I was unconscious."

"That ain't shit," Ehrlich muttered thickly and then simply clicked off.

It was as if some sort of emotional circuit breaker had interrupted the current of despair bottled up inside of him. No two ways about it. The guy was in some deep hurt. I attempted to establish visual communication, but he was nonresponsive, his face a plain paper sack fitted with eyeholes. When the phone rang, I nearly jumped out of my skin in my haste to answer it. It had to be Mr. Wonderful. Imagined or not, there was an ominous pitch to his calls, an octave or two lower than the standard incoming, like the purplish coda of a Bach fugue. I didn't want to risk upsetting Ehrlich any further. In the past, Mr. Wonderful had left me some pretty fucked-up messages—avenging angel–type verses from the Koran. Whether or not the twisted son of a bitch actually bought into all that crap about firestorms and genital warts cleansing the earth of the wicked was not the point. Ehrlich was in enough of a state already without having to listen to one of Kassem's megalomaniacal rants crescendoing in the static dawn like the doomsday aria of a hell-bent muezzin.

"I have to get that," I blurted, making a break for the living room and the wailing telephone. "It might be Janie."

Ehrlich called after me, but his voice was sucked out of the air by the vortex of the swinging door. At the time, I was under the impression that thievery was endemic to the homeless community, a fact of life as prominent within their wasted ranks as garbage-bag rain slickers and public defecation. The idea of leaving him alone with the family stainless didn't exactly sit well.

I snatched the phone from its cradle next to the TV and whispered savagely into the mouthpiece so Ehrlich wouldn't hear.

"Either you get your faggot ass over here right now and take this thing off my ankle, or I'll cut it off and strangle you with it! I'll saw off my fucking foot if that's what it takes."

"Dutch, it's me."

The voice at the other end was hauntingly beautiful, a celestial beacon distorted by time and space.

"Janie? Sweetie, is that you?"

"Dutch"—her voice was taut with misgiving—"are you okay?"

"Fine. Wonderful. Where are you?"

"Are you sure?" Janie pressed calmly. "Because you don't sound fine. You sound worried. Like something's wrong. Are the people from *60 Minutes* still bothering you?"

"Don't I wish? We could use the money."

Okay, so I had not exactly told her about the bounty on my head. What was the point? Between my incurable imaginary illness and our inability to conceive a child, our relationship had been rocky enough without making a family pet of the albatross slung about my neck. It was strain enough that I alone march under the yoke of death without lashing my wife to my back. From the very beginning, I had attempted to spare Janie the indignity that comes with being married to an international object of ridicule. It was the noble thing to do.

"Dutch," Janie continued, downshifting into a more serious tone in anticipation of the precarious bend in the road ahead. "I called to tell you that I'm not coming home."

"No hurry," I said, trying desperately not to let panic creep into my voice. "I've got an old friend here anyway. Ran into him on the street the other day. You remember Ehrlich. . . . "

Silence.

"No, I guess you wouldn't," I went on. "Anyway, he's leaving tomorrow. I was thinking that maybe you and I could drive up the coast to Santa Barbara this weekend. See if this old lightning rod of mine has any spark left in it."

"Dutch, I want a divorce."

Her words crashed over me like a tidal wave of liquid nitrogen. Bluish currents of vertigo and despair crystallized in my veins. I was rigid with fear, flash-frozen, a cryogenic Popsicle hoping to be reanimated in a time and place marked by social justice and perfect marriages. Immediately, the thought popped into my head that all of this was Mr. Wonderful's fault. Upon first returning from the Gulf, Janie had been able to forgive

me the wholesale paranoia and sneaking around that had pre-
cipitated a climate of distrust between us. After all, this sort of
behavior came with the territory of being a troubled combat
vet and scapegoat extraordinaire of the international news
media. However, when the ink dried and I was no longer the
flavor of the month, my wife, my anchor, my Gibraltar, that
paragon of stability I had leaned upon for so many years, had
begun to suspect that I was having an affair. By the time I was
ready to tell her about Mr. Wonderful—that it was a holy
assassin who compelled me to murmur incessantly in my
sleep, and not a blonde sex kitten—the damage was done. The
fact that I had rigorously withheld the truth from her for so
long would have constituted a breach of faith tantamount in
its disavowal of the institution of marriage to that of adultery.
I had done what I'd done so that she would not have to live as
I was living—with her head on a swivel and her soul on a
leash. Only after it was too late had I realized my mistake. That
I had not shared this essential part of myself with her would
have wounded her more deeply than if she had discovered I
had given myself to another.

"Say something, Dutch," Janie pleaded. "Please, this isn't easy
for me."

I imagined her rehearsing in front of the full-length mirror
where she had assembled herself prior to work each morning—
bracketing her eyes with despair and repeating the banal
reproach until it came glissading off her lips like snake venom.

"It's him, isn't it?" I asked.

Hatred raged inside of me. I wanted her lover to suffer as I had
suffered, to watch as his body was pulled apart by elephants.

"I'm sorry, Dutch. I thought you and I could work things out.
That it was just . . . *I don't know,* a phase or something like all
couples go through."

"Tell me where you are and I'll come get you."

"I'm not going to pretend anymore," Janie went on, ignoring
me. "How and with whom you choose to spend your life is your
business. But the fact remains, I don't want my children being
raised by a . . . "

"Go ahead, everyone else has taken their shot. You might as well get in yours while I still have a pulse."

My head was swimming with a fairly comprehensive list of possible accusations. If it meant getting Janie back, I was prepared to endorse just about any negative opinion of me she or anyone else might have. That is to say, any other than the slanderous charge that I was a cold-blooded murderer.

"I feel so stupid," Janie said flatly. "I should have recognized it sooner: the lies, the sneaking around behind my back, the pretty, ethnic-looking guy that's always parked in front of our house. For God's sake, Dutch, I can't remember the last time you tried to make love to me. Now I understand why."

"Ethnic-looking guy?" I echoed innocently. "It was probably someone from the dry cleaners picking up a load of laundry."

Mr. Wonderful's universal presence was more than simple stalking. He prowled my dreams like an agent of sleeping sickness. I could feel him lurking in the chambers of my heart, piggybacking his way through my bloodstream, each cell, trillions in all, a beast of burden to his insoluble menace. Still, I failed to see where Janie was going with this.

"Look, I love you, Dutch, but let's face it. Things just aren't going to work between us. I need someone who's there for me. I need someone to hold my hand. I need someone who makes me feel safe at night. You're never home. You may as well be dead. I need a husband, Dutch, not a guy who shows up every now and then to explain why he's never home. I need someone who can give me a child. I only wish you would have been honest with me from the beginning . . . honest with yourself. This *lifestyle* of yours . . . it's genetic. You can fight it, Dutch, but you can't win. Accept yourself, you're a wonderful man."

Before I could beg Janie to give me another chance, I was distracted by a loud noise in the kitchen. A leaden thud, then nothing, silence. It was as if my ex-wife-to-be had disconnected with the full force of her will, this decisive step transcending the mere physics of telecommunication and manifesting itself with concrete finality in the failing hearth-light of our broken home.

Weeks later, I would still hear the buzz of the dial tone carrying on like a fly trapped inside my skull. For the time being, my only concern was that I get to Ehrlich before another chapter in my defunct autobiography was wrapped up without regard for the triumphant course of events I had naïvely predicted as a boy whose Schwinn bicycle routinely took the checkered flag at the Baja 1000. Other than an eclectic scattering of empty cans, cracker crumbs, and savaged food wrappers, there was no sign of Ehrlich. It was as if a tornado had passed through the center of an organic-foods store before whisking away the troubled demolitions expert. Contrary to what I had expected, Mr. Wonderful was nowhere to be found nor, as far as I could tell, had he been anywhere in the vicinity of the kitchen in the past several hours. Conspicuously lacking was the brassy ring of cologne that parasitized him with unremitting willfulness and vigor. Perhaps it was the thought of finding him there hunkered over Ehrlich's corpse like some sort of semen-sucking vampire that clued me in to what Janie had been driving at on the phone. Mr. Wonderful! She thought I was fucking the swishy fiend.

Despite my horror at having pieced together Janie's erroneous deduction, I had only a moment to dwell on the ironic turn of events. There, sprawled on his back in the middle of the kitchen floor, lay Ehrlich, a twitching mass of humanity locked in the throes of an aerosol overdose. Clutching a can of Pam nonstick cooking spray in one hand and an empty Gold Medal flour bag in the other, his expression, a peculiar landscape of bliss residing somewhere between the unwaxed linoleum of my kitchen floor and the honeyed pastures of Shangri-la, communicated a welcome release from the earthly shackles that bound him to the hunted existence shared by us both. Perhaps if I had not been so afraid to have been left alone in that bleak and unforgiving land, I might have allowed the nonstick sleep to deepen its hold on him. I am ashamed to admit, however, that the sense of urgency that compelled me to grab Ehrlich by the shoulders and shake the life back into him was more closely related to the absence of compassion that ruled me like a Hun chieftain than the goodness that the saving of one's life typically exemplifies. For all my moral pretense, I was no better than Mr. Wonderful.

As I maneuvered Ehrlich into the guest bedroom, I marveled at his lack of physical substance. With very little effort, I was able to support the majority of his weight as he slogged along at my side, his feet treading uncertainly on the floor underfoot as if sleepwalking across a lake of Jell-O. I rolled him off my shoulders and onto the bed, his eyes glistening in their sockets like hard-boiled eggs. I realized for the first time since rescuing him from the sewer pipe that what he lacked in mass was more than adequately compensated for with experience. His perfunctory explanation of life on the streets was merely icing on the cake, a gritty veneer that anyone with half a brain could piece together from news magazines, urban exposés, and the zombie-faced disciples of hardship advertising *Will Work for Food* at every intersection. Out of pride and principle, he steered clear of the soup kitchens and homeless shelters, purgatorial way stations cataloging the misery of not only the hopeless, but the weak-willed. His accounts, though intentionally short on detail, were rife with spiritual malaise and suffering, ugly silhouettes heaving in the shadows of his brave facade. What Ehrlich had neglected to mention was the sickness and disease—the fact that a bad tooth or an ingrown toenail could go staph and kill you as easily as a cold snap. And there were the coping mechanisms, the tools of combating despair: drugs and alcohol and unprotected sex in the gloomy shadows of rusted-out shopping carts, alleyways, and cardboard shanties.

It was this great weight of things unspoken that troubled me as I covered him with a blanket and prepared to resume the hunt for Arbegast. Looking at Ehrlich's teeth, a plaque-gilded necropolis of bleeding gums and rampant decay, it occurred to me, as any anthropologist will tell you, that there is no better window into the habits of man or beast than the mouth and its accessory components. Whether it be the unevenly worn dentition of a pipe smoker or the overworked molars of a herbivore, the mouth, this telltale gateway of things consumed and revealed, does not lie.

Sleep well, brave soldier.

According to Shackleman, Arbegast was addicted to heroin. If there was any truth to it, he'd be climbing the walls looking for a fix. Taking into account his accelerated learning curve and God knows what other nifty little side-effects Acteon's genetic tampering and behavioral modification had imparted, I had no doubt that the resourceful chimp would figure out a way to squelch the demons dancing in his head.

The phone must have rung twenty times, its insistent cries unsettling the dawn like the agonized bleating of a wounded lamb, before Shackleman finally summoned the courage to pick up. Despite the delay, it was as if he had been expecting the call all along, his hand affixed to the receiver in dreaded anticipation of the preordained moment. Although he had given me his number voluntarily, it was obvious that Shackleman was not entirely comfortable with the exchange. I got the sense that from his side of it he was entering into an alliance with a dark and forbidden power, an evil pact conferring upon him an awesome, unspeakable responsibility fraught with dire consequences.

"I hear you paid a visit to the Enchanted Forest," Shackleman remarked, his voice alloyed with an insider's understanding of what exactly this meant. "Consider yourself lucky to be alive."

I had tried to forget the near-death experience I had suffered at the hands of Arbegast and his black-eyed proselytes, the silly terror hunkering deep within my embattled subconscious like a recrimination from God. It's one thing to realize that destiny sails regardless of which way the winds are blowing; it's entirely another to realize that a monkey is at the helm.

"Sorry if I woke you," I said, attempting to divert the flow of the conversation before I became hopelessly mired in its far-reaching implications, "but I need information."

"I wonder, Mr. Flowers, does the future hold a return trip?

Eden isn't just for honeymooners anymore. The gates are wide open. Come one, come all. But you'd better pack a lunch because the fruit is rotting on the branches."

Although Shackleman was clearly baiting me to decry the top-secret proving ground as a place of incontrovertible evil, I wasn't biting—bad apples or not. No amount of cajolery in the world was going to lure me back inside the Enchanted Forest, neither physically nor via the synaptic thoroughfares of memory. I would have rather taken my chances with an unpaid Mr. Wonderful than reconvene in that abominable court of evolutionary mistrial.

"The other day you mentioned that some of the chimps are addicted to heroin. Shackleman, if you were actually serious, it might help me track Arbegast down."

"If humans will torture one another for sexual gratification, then why not chimp junkies? Is it so hard to believe? Self-destruction is as inherent to our nature as the drive to reproduce. The human DNA we've been feeding into the genetic makeup of our furry little cousins is lightning in a bottle. The worse something is for them, the more they seem to enjoy it. They're like us, all right. . . . Very much like us. That's the main reason all of this has gotten so out of hand."

"Don't you think it's a little unethical teaching animals who don't know any better how to shoot up? For chrissakes, you're no better than the street-corner pushers parents warn their kids about."

"Unethical? Every time those same parents have a glass of wine with dinner, they're teaching their children to be alcoholics. We encourage by example and atone with guilt. Ethics are merely window dressing for what society is really selling. Moral accountability is dead, my friend. We deal in the currency of sin and absolution. There are a billion Catholics out there to prove my point."

There was a momentary break in the communication, a nanosecond of static interference, then business as usual. To the untrained ear, the interruption may have gone unheeded, an earthly by-product of solar flares or a routine glitch in the connection. The downshift in Shackleman's tone, however, confirmed a source of a much more sinister nature. The line was bugged.

"I-I-I've got to go," Shackleman stammered, his tongue unhinged by the realization that someone was listening in.

Before I could say another word, Shackleman hung up on me, the second time in as many calls that my needs had been subordinated to the prevailing influence of an anonymous third party.

I was shaving in anticipation of a long, desperately needed shower when the phone rang. Against my better judgment, I let the answering machine do the dirty work. I was fed up and frustrated. The last thing I wanted to do was explain to a pushy telemarketer why I wasn't interested in planning for my unborn child's college fund. It was Shackleman. His voice, woefully off-key, vibrated in the stillness like the death twang of a broken guitar string.

"Please, Mr. Flowers, if you're there, pick up! I don't have much time. It's imperative that I speak with you."

"What the hell!" I growled, nicking myself under the nose and plunking the razor into a mentholated quagmire of spent shaving cream, trace corpuscles, and chin stubble. "This better be good."

Half-shaved, I stormed into the study and retrieved the handset from the cradle atop my desk where I had slammed it down twenty minutes earlier. "What do you want?"

Shackleman was out of breath. "Please, there's not much time," he panted, sucking air. "I'm being followed."

"By who?" I asked, reluctant to bite.

"Acteon! They've been watching me for months."

"One thing's certain," I confirmed not-so-reassuringly. "Your phone's tapped."

Shackleman practically screamed at me. "You don't think I know that? I can't urinate without someone looking over my shoulder to make sure I'm not siphoning it out of a Ziploc baggie!"

"Get used to it. Piss testing is corporate America's token act of righteousness. They've turned the bathroom stall into a confessional. Clean pee means you're a stand-up guy. Next thing you know, they'll be running your time cards through a crime lab and comparing your fingerprint residue with your daughter's panties to make sure you're not a pedophile."

"Listen to me!" cried Shackleman. "They'll be here soon."

"Who's *they?*" I asked calmly.

"Janus's goons!"

"What goons?"

"Blight—that guy you passed on the way out of my office the other day," Shackleman went on to explain. "He works for Janus."

"Why didn't you tell me this earlier? Who is he?"

"About the heroin . . . we stimulated an addictive response in the chimps to fill an order for a pharmaceuticals outfit. They were developing a serotonin blocker to ease the symptoms of withdrawal. Teaching the control group subjects to shoot up was simply a matter of monkey-see, monkey-do."

I was hardly listening as Shackleman recapped a dubious account of lab technicians attired in state-of-the-art Animatronics teaching Arbegast and his band of chimp rowdies how to mainline smack. Once the control-group subjects were hooked, things had begun to get out of hand. Suddenly, behavior management posed a serious problem. Either the ghosts could continue supplying the chimps with their placating mistress, or they could stand by and watch as the pedigreed junkies beat their heads against the walls. The fact that the chimps had begun to acquire human consciousness only exacerbated things. The *why?* of existence had become overwhelming, the transition from ape to *"Honey, I'm home"* too abrupt, the burden of self-awareness more than they were equipped to bear. Heroin was a release, parole from the savage breast of their percolating humanity. It took the edge off. Without it they were a danger to themselves. Nonetheless, I now had Blight to think about. What was his agenda, and how did it involve me? I had no doubt that the answer was lying in ambush for me somewhere along the circular path of my exile. But where?

"Flowers," Shackleman cried nervously, "are you listening to me?"

"Let me guess—the buyers backed out when they saw what you had created. The idea of rehabbing a bunch of suicidal monkeys was a little more than they had bargained for."

"Suicide is a uniquely human trait. Besides, that's not the point. Arbegast is out there looking for a fix. He's a resourceful and dangerous chimp, Mr. Flowers. I wouldn't want to cross paths with him, given his current state of mind. He should be put down before he kills again. You need to find him."

"Maybe I should just sit tight and let Animal Control pick him up. How far can a chimp get out there? It's not as if he'll have the faintest idea what to do or where to go. Everyone knows that you can't get around L.A. without a car."

"I wish it was that simple. In receiving human DNA the chimps have received a form of human precognition—déjà vu, if you will. Much of the DNA donor's learned behavior becomes second nature to them. In fact, there are those of us who believe that they regard themselves as existing on an equal plane with humans—that perhaps they are unable to make the distinction at all."

"If Arbegast has been alive this entire time, then why did Janus try to convince me that he was dead?"

"Listen to me, 131 is not really Arbegast. Cloud's story was a hoax."

"If he isn't Arbegast, then who the hell is he?"

We were interrupted by a toneless female voice-recording. *"Please deposit twenty-five cents for an additional three minutes."*

"Look," said Shackleman. "My dime's almost up. You know the Alibi Room on Lincoln?"

"I can find it."

"Be there at one this afternoon, and I'll tell you everything I can."

"The Alibi Room at one o'clock."

Shackleman's voice took on a new urgency. "I've got to go," he said.

"Don't hang up! Tell me where can I find 131."

"Look where east meets west."

"Come again?"

Shackleman was clearly annoyed. "Little Saigon, Mr. Flowers. And be careful. 131's escape was not as accidental as it seems. They're using you. You're nothing more than a contingency, someone to blame when it all goes to shit. They've been playing you from the very beginning. If you find 131, you have to kill him. 131 must die."

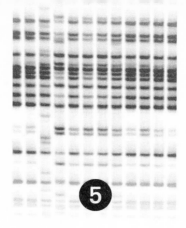

5

IN THE PAST DECADE, Little Saigon had supplanted Chinatown as greater L.A.'s gateway to the Orient. Like the walled-in lordships of its parent dynasties, Chinatown's geographic exclusivity and venerable mystique were ultimately the source of its undoing. In a few short years, the bamboo tearooms and blustery noodle houses had been overrun by the trendsetting ranks of Hollywood's in-crowd. The very places where city health inspectors had once dared not tread for fear of reprisals from cleaver-wielding Bruce Lees now boasted client lists as comprehensively Anglo and provincially sheltered as a KKK rally.

Little Saigon, on the other hand, was different, uncorrupted by Western ideals, as inhospitable to round-eyes as Ho Chi Minh's Pyrrhic namesake on the eve of the fall. Day and night, police helicopters slashed at the air overhead, ever watchful of the dealings of the Vietnamese Mafia, whose underground network of drug traffickers, massage-house pimps and, if you believed the rumors, organ thieves was every bit as elusive and firmly entrenched as the Vietcong had been in the tunnels of Cu Chi during the American occupation of Saigon. As much as I did not want to be here, I had no other choice. Ehrlich's overdose had reinforced what I had known since Mr. Wonderful had revived me on the bathroom floor. Either I take immediate control of my life, or end up a casualty of my own apathy. The fact that Arbegast was a lower-order primate notwithstanding, I believed that if I could match wits with the diabolical simian, bring him to justice and clear myself of all charges, I could begin again, resurrect myself from the ashes of my failed campaign in the Gulf.

Although the sun had scarcely risen past shoulder height as I rolled into the bustling streets of Little Saigon, the temperature had already soared well into the eighties. In the space of a few blocks, I could neither read nor identify the advertisements flanking both sides of the street, their declarations of product lines and services rendered as alien to me as the cryptic annotations cluttering the margins of Bobo's autobiography. I sealed the windows and cranked up the A/C, taking in the roar of recirculated air and stale freon infused with the citrusy fragrance of lemon grass and mint tea. As I ventured deeper, with no specific plan of attack in mind other than to locate Arbegast and go from there, my surroundings lost what vague semblance of familiarity they once possessed. The lowered high-performance rice rockets zipping around Little Saigon's transitional outer limits gave way to saddle-seasoned pedicabs, specially equipped passenger bicycles that were as much pre-internal-combustion artifacts as they were a means of conveyance. Big Macs gave way to dried salted cuttlefish; medical science to witch doctory.

I had visited Little Saigon once before in an attempt to procure a remedy for the so-called "indolence" that had waylaid my desire to father a legacy not predicated on my failure as a soldier. To my bitter disappointment, the costly concoction—a blend of exotic roots, foul-smelling herbs, and Tibetan snow-leopard pituitary—had done little more than give me a nasty case of dysentery. Nothing had changed since then. I was just as lost, just as wary, my vagabond sperm just as listless as when I had first visited Dr. Ngong in his office in the backroom of Shakespeare Adult Bookstore nearly a year ago.

Although staunchly skeptical, it had been Dr. Ngong's inscrutable eyes and manner that had convinced me, his seedy proprietary interests notwithstanding, to give the vile elixir a shot. It was with the same sacrosanct demeanor that he greeted me the second time around, my face, as far as I could tell, familiar to him only inasmuch as it harkened a potential sale.

"You don't remember me, do you?" I asked.

The old doctor examined me for a moment and replied, "To know ro' befo' dem, one mus ass doze come back."

"Look, Confucius, that pecker potion you sold me didn't work."

"You 'plyfo make hot sex like I teer you?" he asked, his lascivious grin reflecting a seamy reenactment of the imaginary union.

"*Apply?* You told me to drink it. You didn't say anything about applying."

"No, no," Ngong insisted vigorously, tinkering with the faulty control switch of a variable-speed dildo. "Make you belly bad sick."

"No shit," I confirmed, still haunted by the explosive intestinal refrain that had nearly turned me inside out.

Ngong shook his head in hearty disagreement. "You drink, make wotsa poop. Let me look you tongue. May' you nee docto'. May' you dead man an' not know it. May' why you teef fall out."

"Never mind about my teeth," I said. "I need information."

"You wan' see kafrick scoogir make baby wi' dongee? You wan' party wi' shemare?"

"No donkeys, no shemales. I'm looking for the white palace, yam-yam, smack."

Ngong smiled evasively, his thin lips forming a barrier as tight and unimpeachable as a scar.

"Listen, old man," I repeated forcefully. "Tell me where I can find some heroin or I'll have the Board of Health close you down."

"If you wan' her'win, why you not say so in firs' prace? Shakespeare Adult Bookstore not deer in mystelies."

The place Ngong sent me was like something out of a Fu Manchu comic book, its cast of characters every bit as colorful and unlikely as those populating the shady waterfront locales of dealers in rhinoceros tusk and white slavery. As opium dens went, the Happy Buddha Restaurant was state-of-the-art, a modern urban masterpiece of depravity and deception. According to Ngong, the last stall in the men's restroom, an excessively filthy subterfuge marked OUT OF ORDER in a host of languages, was a veritable gateway to paradise. A single flush and the toilet slid back to reveal a hidden passage that led to a basement unaccounted for in the blueprints on file in the County Recorder's office. As I descended the cramped staircase, I felt as if I was back in Saddam's compound at Al Qa'im, revisiting the first in a pivotal sequence of grievous faux pas that would forever alter the course of my life.

Sinking into the lurid, smoke-filled parlor, I realized just how naked I was without my .45, its absence compounded by the unwelcome knowledge that it was in Arbegast's devilishly capable hands. Contrary to the Shanghai welcome I expected, a vicious back-alley beating compliments of the resident martial-arts expert, my arrival generated no more interest than if I had been a regular for the past decade. In fact, everyone present— from the recumbent half-asleep patrons to the silk-wrapped geisha-style hostesses—was captive of the same drowsy air. Paper lanterns, once white, now tea-colored with opium residue, illuminated the smoke-filled chamber. Curtained bunks lined the walls, the formless occupants lying within stacked three deep from floor to ceiling stirring gently behind muzzy yellow-blush panels like termite larvae awaiting their wings. No sooner had I cataloged the room—its windowless walls and smoky tributaries, its tomblike sanctity and murmurous somniloquies— than a beautiful lotus-faced girl took me by the arm and escorted me to an open bunk in the corner.

Before condemning my actions, consider that I had ingested several lungfuls of the narcotic exhalations of the stoned clientele since first touching down in the rarefied atmosphere of the Happy Buddha's terra incognita. By the time my eyes adjusted to the dusky light, my head was teeming with the pungent spirits of the Far East. As I groped my person for Arbegast's photograph, the girl fed three pea-sized balls of opium into the toothsome maw of a bronze dragon and fitted an oxygen mask over my nose and mouth. A moment later, there was a low-level mechanical hum as the dragon's vacuum-pump belly, a greenish sphere encrusted with flecks of tar and organic detritus, began bubbling away. With each breath, my extremities seemed to slip farther away from me, to become less distinct, to lose the ability to receive signals from my brain. I foraged clumsily in my pockets for Arbegast's picture, my arms of no more use to me than tentacles on dry land, until finally I latched onto the folded xerox likeness Shackleman had given me.

"I'm looking for him," I explained dumbly, handing the girl Arbegast's picture. The oxygen mask made my voice sound like a deep-space transmission, nasal and far-off sounding. *Mission Control, do you read me? Come in, Mission Control. . . .*

The girl eyed me obliquely. "This man your friend?" she wanted to know.

"This *monkey*," I said derisively, "is a murderer."

"Who this man murder?" she asked doubtfully, her slitted eyes communicating a deep distrust.

"You don't believe me," I half-questioned, considering the enormous leap of faith I was asking her to take. "Hell, *I* don't believe me. But it's true."

It was clear from the girl's blameless expression that she was not unaccustomed to the incongruous ramblings of strange men with half-cocked ideas in their heads. Her place of employment was not exactly what you'd call a bastion of rational thought.

"Anyway . . . " I pressed on. "*Who* he murdered is not important. What *is* important is that I find him before he kills someone else. Please, if you have any idea. . . . "

"He not look so mean. You fix eye, this man okay handsome."

I removed the mask and severed the umbilical to the marsh-mallowy world in which I had been blissfully enwombed for the past couple of minutes.

"Let's try this again," I said, plodding relentlessly forward. "This *man* is a monkey—a very dangerous monkey." To illustrate my point, I knitted my brow, thrust my jaw down, and outward, and clapped myself on the chest. "You know, ooh-ooh aah-aah. Loves bananas. The point is, he's a killer."

It was as if the girl hadn't even noticed my artless imper-sonation, the chest-thumping antics simply another manifes-tation among many in the character of the man with whom she had Arbegast confused.

"You tell you friend he okay with Maichi," she continued heedlessly. "He make big tip."

Clearly, all the secondhand smoke was affecting her judgment. She could no more be expected to tell the difference between a man and a chimpanzee than to lay golden pot-stickers. Deeply bloodshot, her eyes regarded me through narrow slits like the unhatched portents of a fortune cookie. As hard to swallow as it may have seemed, I couldn't shake the feeling that there was an element of truth, no matter how subverted it may have been by the stupefying concentration of drugs in her system, to her opiated discourse. Admittedly, I was more susceptible to seemingly out-landish ideas than, say, if I had actually been sober. Suddenly, and in no way independent of the preponderance of psychotropic stimuli coursing through my veins, the criteria by which I nor-mally judged reality didn't seem so clear-cut. If pink elephants, I reasoned obtusely, then why not opium-smoking chimpanzees?

Barely a minute had elapsed since I had cut myself loose from the tranquilizing effect of the opium slow-drip, and already I could feel the old sense of urgency returning, muted though it may have been by the pleasant warmth enveloping me like the gurgling ooze of a mud bath.

"When was the last time you saw my friend?" I asked, aban-doning any hope of reaching a consensus opinion as to Arbe-gast's ranking in the Linnaean scheme of things.

"He leave here two, maybe three, hour 'go."

For no apparent reason, I suddenly found myself addressing a small audience, the urgent swell of my voice rippling outward into the semiconscious circle of faces.

"Do you know where he went?" I asked, frustrated.

"He ask Maichi where to get goo' massage, so I tell him. You friend, he very sweet man. He not yell at Maichi like you."

Having finally tapped into the correct set of nerve impulses, I was, at long last, able to assume an upright stance. The room merry-go-rounded wildly as I rocked back and forth, the floor underfoot rolling like the deck of a tugboat in heavy seas.

"I'm sorry for raising my voice," I apologized drowsily, "but this is an emergency. Please, can I get the name?"

"He not tell me his name," the girl reflected fondly. "He quiet type. . . . Not say much. . . . Talk with eyes."

"The name of the massage parlor," I clarified.

As you can imagine, I was fast becoming edgy. I wanted out of there before the lugubrious air undermined what little resolve I had left. The longer I stayed, the less likely I was to leave. I was possessed by an overpowering desire to sleep, to simply lie back and surrender to the lotusy menace swirling about me like the tepid bathwater of my botched suicide. My body was like the dark matter inside a black hole, dense beyond comprehension, the immovable mass in an equation unto itself.

"Please," I begged. "Tell me where."

"Firs' you pay me two hundra dolla'. . . . Then I tell you where you friend go."

"I'm not going to pay you two hundred dollars for an address. I'll check the yellow pages."

"Two hundra dolla' not fo' address . . . Two hundra dolla' fo' you party-hearty with Maichi."

"Look, I don't carry that kind of cash with me. If I did, it'd be in a briefcase handcuffed to my arm."

"Then we take one o'you ki'ney in trade. Only hurt teeny-tiny bit. Doctor sew you good as new."

She smiled prettily, the opalescent sheen I had attributed to exceptional oral hygiene giving way to the realization that her teeth had been capped with mother-of-pearl. The exotic veneer bent the yellow orange light when she spoke.

"Works for me. Hell, while you've got me under the knife, maybe you could add a couple of inches to my dick."

Before I could weigh the consequences of my glib retort, two men previously unnoticed by me materialized out of the smoky nether reaches beyond the bunk-lined periphery. Their perfectly synchronized approach called to mind the matchless precision of an army color guard. Shoulder to shoulder, they appraised me shrewdly, their eyes seething with irrepressible contempt for the pithy sarcasm of the white man. Before I realized what was happening, the thuggish duo had seized hold of my arms and were whisking me toward the exit with gravity-defying ease. Stirred by the commotion, those languishing in private bunks brushed aside the gossamer panels to get a better look. I was too stoned to say with any degree of certainty that the furry faces witnessing my departure were anything other than psychic projections cut from the cloth of my chimp-obsessed mind. In a matter of seconds, I was hauled from the fuliginous bowels of the Happy Buddha Restaurant and into an appropriately rat-infested alley.

As I absorbed a beating that, if not for the numbing properties of the opium, would surely have rendered me unconscious with pain, I realized that something was not right. The bastards shared more than a hired goon's intimate knowledge of soft spots and pressure points. Vital organs and a good tailor for starters. Confused? I sure as shit was. Had it not been for a wicked shot under the ribs landed by yours truly, I may have never put one and one together—so to speak. Siamese fucking twins! Although I believe the politically correct term is *conjoined*. Anyway, I socked Yin in the gut and Yang doubled over sure as peanut butter and crackers, his face all knotted up. The vicious bastards were joined at the hip like world-class tangoers cutting a kill-or-be-killed swath across a crowded dance floor. Unable to fend off the relentless multi-appendaged assault, I shielded my face and crumpled under a flurry of precisely coordinated blows delivered as if by Shiva himself.

They were going to beat me to death. I could feel it inside of me, both literally and figuratively. My botched suicide attempt, or rather the nearness to death I had experienced as a result of that woeful endeavor, had imparted in me a corresponding nearness to life. I did not want to die. It's difficult to say how many direct shots I took in those terribly elastic seconds, however a subsequent inventory of the damage revealed an extended domain of deep-tissue bruises and nasty abrasions. I had only a moment to chew on the bittersweet irony of my situation before everything went black, as if an octopus had discharged its cloud of ink into my eyes.

I can't say for certain how long I was unconscious. However, I do remember coming to briefly—long enough to put the fear of God into me. Although the images flashing before me in those few moments were badly disjointed, I was able to piece together a nightmarish collage of sensory data. As a former high-school all-American in both football and wrestling, I was no stranger to the eye-opening waft of smelling salts. Nothing, however, could have prepared me for the rank exhaust that picked me up by the nostrils. My watcher's breath was warm and boggy, miasmic, a pestilential soup as conducive to the propagation of disease-carrying pests as it was a foul-smelling by-product of organic decay. It was my watcher's face, however, though hazy and out of focus, that confirmed it was Arbegast hunched over me like a gargoyle. There was a dark and unforgiving gravity swirling in the bottomless vortices of his eyes, the unrelenting pull of which neither light nor compassion could escape. As much as I wanted to grab him by the throat and shake the life out of him, I was helplessly fettered to the residual paralysis of the concussion Yin and Yang had given me. I could only lie there and submit to Arbegast's hairy-backed hands as he rolled me like a Sunset Boulevard drunk: wallet, keys, a half-eaten roll of Breath Savers, the Post-it on which I had scrawled the time and place of my intended meeting with Shackleman.

Then blackness.

When I came to the second time, an EMT was inserting an IV drip into the vein in the back of my left hand. Apparently, there was another victim besides myself because I could hear a woman in my immediate vicinity giving orders as to how many cc's of this to administer and how many volts of that she needed to shock the life back into her dying patient. Amid the murmur of curious onlookers and the electrical spooling and zap of the defibrillator, I could hear a low animallike whimpering—almost nothing, really—a faint undercurrent teasing its way among the interconnected sound bites like a loose thread. With some serious effort, I managed to sit up. The EMT to whose care I was entrusted abandoned me in favor of the flatlining patient sprawled lifelessly on the pavement not ten feet away. From my new vantage, I could see why the oft-rehearsed drama had attracted so much attention. The patient to whom the electrified paddles were affixed in vain was none other than Yin and Yang, the Siamese twins. A large compress had been applied just below Yin's sternum to stem the flow of blood emanating from a gunshot wound. As Yang lamented his brother's passing, it was clear that his grief was twofold. Gradually, his own life functions began shutting down as death bridged the systemic confluence joining his two selves. The EMTs stared helplessly at one another in horrified disbelief, their specialized training grossly inadequate for dealing with medical crises of the transmundane.

Better them than me, right? About an hour into the police interrogation that followed, I was beginning to think otherwise. I had been rehydrated, disinfected, swabbed for gunpowder residue, and remanded into the custody of L.A.'s finest, a hard-drinking homicide detective named Gogan. Lieutenant Gogan, he was quick to remind me, his rank as much a declaration of his bitter distaste for me as it was a reminder of who was calling the shots. Viewed as the sum of his constituent parts, Gogan called to mind a Frankenstein monster assembled in the stockroom of a butcher-shop laboratory by the Ads Division of the American Meat Council. His face was like a canned ham, big and pink and wet-looking, with thick-lidded eyes and a nose like a double-cut lamb chop. Pork-shouldered, hock-wristed, hog-bellied: He would have excited the salivary glands of all but the most jaded of carnivores. Noticing the pink droplets of sweat accruing on Gogan's overhanging brow, I found myself wondering about Dunkie living with the savages deep in the jungles of Papua, New Guinea, and how readily he had adapted to their primitive customs and anthropophagus rites. How much are we products of our environment, pawns of process and socialization? Is undoing what we think of as genetically encoded behavior as easy as a change of scenery, ideology, the availability of a good source of protein? Were I to suddenly find myself in Dunkie's situation, how long would it be before I was snacking eagerly on the slow-roasted appendages of my enemies, yearning for the marbled meats of free-range tribesmen and the spirit-edifying properties purportedly imparted to those who ingested human flesh?

Encouraged by decades of barrel-aged precipitation, the gin blossoms etched in Gogan's cheeks enjoyed a thriving efflorescence, the roseate vessels contributing to a precirrhosis filigree of worry lines and branching crevasses. Although very possibly it was the lingering draft of his breakfast, the unmistakable odor of coffee and bacon hung over him like the greasy fust of a pancake house. Nearly as wide as he was tall, Gogan's blockish frame was ideally suited for the crushing gravity of the outer planets. It was as if all the years of exposure to the criminal element—the cynicism, the lies and deception, the rampant grassroots corruption—had altered him physically. Adapt or go extinct seemed to be the message expounded in his stalwart physique. Despite Gogan's age, a figure I estimated to be on the lee side of fifty, there wasn't an ounce of fragility to him. I had no doubt that encoded in the scars upholstering his knuckles were the uncensored transcripts of interrogations past, no-holds-barred Q&A sessions in which the aging master demonstrated the art of persuasion with draconian expertise for his effusive pupil.

"So you're the guy everyone was talking about a few years back," said Gogan. "You're damn lucky you're not doing time in Leavenworth for that shit you pulled. If it was up to me, they would've broken your legs and run you out of the country."

Gogan's words glided along the periphery of the dull, postconcussive haze enveloping my brain. Although battered and woozy and half-stoned, I had enough sense left in me to realize that it was Arbegast who had capped the genetic double-take, my .45's thunderous cannon shot as familiar to me as an infant's cry is to its mother. I was still, however, trying to figure out why. Either Arbegast had been gunning for me and had simply missed. . . . Or? I could think about that later. We're talking about the devil in a monkey suit, not my guardian angel.

"Go ahead," Gogan went on. "Sit there staring at me like a goddamned scarecrow without any teeth. Ballistics is running the powder swabs and the slug we dug out of that sideshow freak you were dancing with."

"Knock yourself out," I said. "I'm not your man."

The air inside the interrogation room was hot and sticky and coated my skin with an adhesive film. A small, overworked fan oscillated halfheartedly, whipping the glutinous atmosphere into a frothy conglomerate of mildew, gooey lead-based paint fumes and residual sweat. Gogan retrieved a wadded-up paper napkin from his pants pocket and wiped deposits of dried spit from the corners of his mouth.

"Forensics managed to lift a couple of good prints from a half-eaten piece of fruit we found at the scene," he informed me, returning the napkin to his pocket. "As soon as we get a match, I'm booking you for a double homicide. I'm betting a guy like you will get the gas chamber when the verdict comes down."

"Tell you what," I replied smugly. "If the computer comes up with a single match, I'll pay your tuition to charm school."

Imagine the lab boys trying to finger a human suspect using prints lifted from a chimpanzee. Talk about giving the FBI mainframe one hell of a brain fart. It'd be a miracle if the entire system didn't crash.

"Why don't you tell me what you were doing in Little Gook Town," Gogan continued. "Looking for a little action—is that it?"

"I was having lunch."

"Maybe you make a little fucky-sucky with some twelve-year-old mama-san."

"Like I said, I was having lunch."

"I don't like you, Flowers. You're like an onion: the more layers you peel away, the more you stink. If it was up to me, I'd have you castrated and locked away on an island somewhere. There are enough fuckups in the world already without guys like you running around."

"Have we met?"

"You're an ex-military hotshot who couldn't tell Saddam Hussein from your own mother. Killed a lot of innocent sand niggers over there, didn't you?" Gogan leaned across the table and got in my face. "I wouldn't piss on you if your head was on fire."

"Tell me, Detective, how long before the studio needs you back in central casting? You can't be for real. I thought cops like you went out with poodle skirts and Jell-O casseroles. Now either book me or let me go."

Remembering my date with Shackleman, I checked my watch. I had less than an hour to make it across town to the Alibi Room. Now more than ever, I wanted information. There had to be something—some clue, some undisclosed bit of data, some unfathomed key that would unlock the door to Arbegast's IT-corrupted psyche. In the wake of this latest episode of cat and mouse, it had become clear to me that the only way out was to beat Arbegast at his own game. So far, I had been one step behind, a leash-led pawn turned loose in a labyrinth of my own ignorance. I have to admit that I was more than a little rattled by the implications of Arbegast's gallant intervention on my behalf. The off chance that his presence in the alley was simply a coincidence. . . . Let's just say I don't believe in coincidences. Not unless you're talking about Ehrlich's unexpected return from the dead. Whether by something imparted in him via xeno-whatever-the-hell-it-was, or some jungle-honed tracking instinct, Arbegast had known exactly where to find me. About the only comfort his covert vigil offered me was the possibility that he and Mr. Wonderful might one day cross paths as both monitored the whereabouts of yours truly.

A single fly turned dull, elliptical orbits in the thickening air over our heads, its erratic flight path dictated by the fan's aloof cross-currents. Every third pass or so, Gogan would take an obligatory swipe at it, his sausage-like fingers raking the air.

"So what's it gonna be?" I asked, standing to leave.

"Eyewitnesses say you were getting into it pretty heavy with that *thing* you shot."

"Real slick. You almost had me there."

"A word of advice," said Gogan, soliciting a self-satisfied grin from the feculent stable of his imagination. "You might want to hit up some of the bath stores for a soap on a rope. You'll need it where you're going if things shape up the way I think they will."

"What is it with cops and sodomy, anyway? Someone bends over to tie his shoes and you guys got your billies in your hands so fast you'd think you caught your daughter fucking the only black kid in bible study."

The door to the interrogation room opened and in walked Gogan's partner, a tall, yellow-orange man with dull yellow-orange hair and soft, shapeless yellow-orange lips. His skin was the texture of cheese rind, fatty oils and creamy base separating in the heat. He fanned himself with a computer printout.

Gogan immediately perked up, his face aglow with hope.

"Should I reserve our friend here a honeymoon suite in the fudge factory?" he asked.

Gogan's partner stopped fanning himself. "Not exactly, Lieutenant."

"No matches?"

"See for yourself."

Gogan thumbed through the surprisingly dense sheaf of papers, his expression taking on the uninspired contours of an armored transport vehicle. "Is this some kind of joke?" he demanded bitterly.

"No joke, Lieutenant," replied his partner. "I ran the prints myself."

"Run 'em again!" Gogan barked, but by then I was already on my way out the door. "Buy yourself some teeth," he called after me. "That way I'll have something to knock down the back of your throat next time I haul you in."

I have always believed that we are little more than glorified animals, overachieving beasts celebrated on pedestals of our own design. However, I never expected that the evidence would be so clear-cut, nor that it would originate from the purely objective brain of a computer and not some radical animal-rights coalition. The fingerprints of one chimpanzee had generated 1,183 partial matches from the millions on file in the national crime database. It wasn't exactly the kind of statistic one would find being bandied about over cherry Kool-Aid and Swedish meatballs at a church social. The idea that mankind was merely the newest flavor to have come out of the evolutionary mixing bowl wasn't the sort of thing that sat well with creationists. Truthfully, I still wasn't sure how well it sat with me. But what do I know? At least I was off the hook with Gogan for the time being and could get back to the business of apprehending a murderer.

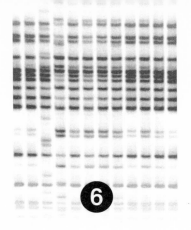

6

WHO CAN SAY FOR CERTAIN if we ever actually came close to taking out the real Saddam Hussein? After our near miss at Al Qa'im, he got careful, his whereabouts as incongruous with his tyrannical leanings as his decoys were numerous and widespread. In nearly eleven weeks of following up on our informant's leads, we had killed over a dozen men, none of whom turned out to be the one we were after. Dead ringers, yes, but not a spin-jockey dictator in the bunch. Saddam's team of plastic surgeons set 'em up, we put 'em down. One thing's certain: We kept Ogburn, the forensics expert, busy. We killed a dwarf, an elephant trainer, a barber, a washed-up character actor with six toes on each foot who, in death, achieved a measure of realism he could only aspire to in life. We killed the winners of three Saddam Hussein look-alike contests. We killed a shoe shiner, the construction worker in a Village People cover band performing in a Baghdad nightclub, a Sufi mystic who clutched his chest and died of causes unknown moments before the bullet ripped through his left atrium. Collateral casualties were high. Women. A little boy. Victims of blast radii. Crossfire. Morale was low. We were dehydrated, tired, underfed. Exhaustion gave way to paranoia and indecision. Apprehension and doubt were as integral to our way of thinking as dysentery and penicillin. The civilian casualties took their toll on X-Ray. MacMurrough hanged himself with his shoelaces. Adler ate blasting caps. Ogburn cried in his sleep. Before long we were passing around pseuprezdid like it was popcorn. Goof no longer had nightmares about spiders building webs in his mouth. Bascombe's ulcers relaxed. Ehrlich stopped whispering to himself. It wasn't all good, but we could sleep at night.

I hopped a taxi from the doorstep of Gogan's precinct back to Little Saigon so that I could resume my hunt for Arbegast. As I attempted to make idle chitchat with the driver, a severe-looking Nazi skinhead type whose raw pink complexion and shaved-bald head called to mind an ostrich, it occurred to me that I lacked both the necessary cab fare and the keys with which to operate my car. Embittered, like so many of his generation, he frowned darkly at the road ahead of him as if in symbolic declaration of what the future had in store. He was nonresponsive, his face an armory of masochistic piercings: nose, ears, lips, eyebrows. Alternative-rock music swirled beyond the scrawled-on Plexiglas shield that separated us, the grinding power chords, equal parts rage and existential angst. He ignored my repeated queries about the recent heat wave and the Dodgers' chances in the upcoming pennant race. If this was not enough to convince me of his generic contempt for humanity, the words FUCK YOU were tattooed across his knuckles in block Roman script. Clearly, reasoning with him about my lack of finance was out of the question. There was no doubt in my mind that in his abusively cynical eyes the letters IOU, a grossly ineffectual trinity of vowels, were something his parents should have anted up for bringing him into such an ugly hate-filled world. My avenues at reason and compromise stymied, I was left with no other choice than to ditch out on the fare and hope the unfriendly little son of a bitch wasn't packing.

A block away from where I had parked my car earlier that morning, I instructed the skinhead cabdriver to descend into an underground parking garage. I assured him that his tip would more than adequately compensate for the paltry two-dollar fee that would accrue as a result of his passage beyond the diagonally striped mechanical arm.

"All the way to the bottom," I confirmed, as we spiraled down and around into the cool lower levels that smelled of urine and quicklime. "I like to keep my car out of the sun. . . . Keeps the paint from fading."

The skinhead cabdriver eyed me briefly in the rearview mirror, cauterizing my lips with an acid glance.

My plan was to have him take me all the way to the lowest level where the garage dead-ended, and then bolt up the several flights of stairs that would deliver me to the street above. By the time he managed to flip the car around, wend his way up and out of the circuitous labyrinth, and pay the man at the booth, I would be well on my way to the Alibi Room, my car hot-wired and whooshing down the freeway at seventy-five. However, as we rounded the last turn, the penultimate floor occupied by only a handful of cars, the myopia of my plan became readily apparent to us both. The bottom floor, a mere corkscrew twist away, was totally empty. Before he could take action, I threw open the back door and bolted for the stairwell, the lopsided gait I had acquired compliments of Yin and Yang carrying me across the concrete with alarming slowness. As I hit the first flight of stairs, the taxi barreled past me in reverse, tires squealing, the skinhead cabdriver's pinched face filling the rear window with a sadistic smirk.

Two at a time, I hoofed it up the dizzying flights, legs aching, lungs rasping, my upper lip furling into the gap once occupied by my swallowed bridge. At each floor, as I was paced by the roar of the taxi's engine and a glimpse of the skinhead cab driver's hatchet profile, my resolve—if not my energy—was renewed. Matched by his skill behind the wheel, the desperation of my flight was fueled by an adrenalized fear of what violent retribution the tattooed fiend had in store for me should our paths cross at street level. Catching a small break, his pursuit of me was delayed by a parking patron on his way into the garage, and I was able to put some distance between us. However, by the time I emerged from the helical catacombs, heart thudding in my chest like shoes in a clothes dryer, my overworked adrenal gland was again beset upon by the crescendoing pandemonium of the taxi's hell-bent ascent. With the guttural roar of its red-lining

V-8, the tortured shrieking of tires and bestial power chords blaring from the stereo, it was as if the devil had thrown open the gates of hell.

I had just made it onto the sidewalk when the taxi crashed through the flimsy matchstick toll arm and launched itself bucking into the center of the street. Had a passing transit bus not crushed the taxi's rear end, I'm certain that Heinrich Himmler, Jr. would have goose-stepped his way up and down my sorry ass, tattooing swastikas on my internal organs with the thermally molded heels of his war-surplus jackboots.

In any other circumstance, discovering that my car, a 1985 it's-a-boy blue Ford LTD, had been stolen would not have come as a surprise. Had anyone other than Arbegast lifted my keys, I would have expected it. This was how it worked. However, the idea that a chimp was currently delivering my one-and-only means of transportation to a Mexicali chop shop wasn't exactly the sort of thing I was willing to go to bed with. If anything, the theft of my car confirmed that Arbegast had an accomplice, someone who could drive. Blight, maybe.

I walked the street checking cars for unlocked doors. To allay the suspicions of curious passersby, I smiled dumbly and shook my head regrettably as if to confirm that I had carelessly locked my keys inside. I had covered less than half a block when the driver of a white minivan double-parked twenty feet in front of me and ducked into a convenience store, leaving the unattended vehicle idling. Without hesitation, I slipped in behind the wheel and eased into the flow of traffic before the minivan's owner was back on the street.

I turned right at the underground parking garage. A motorcycle cop waved me past the scene of the accident where his fellow officers had only recently taken the skinhead cabdriver into custody. He scowled with murderous hatred as they forced him into the backseat of a black-and-white and whisked away to where angry young men are transformed into career enemies of the judicial system. The next time the freewheeling punk hit the streets, he would be looking to join a radical militia group whose doomsaying rank and file was a scary mishmash of ex-law enforcement and the criminals they had once sought to put behind bars. You could say the encounter was a sort of get-acquainted session, a fateful *"How-do?"* the bald anarchist and his civil-servant captors would one day chuckle about over bomb schematics and federal building blueprints.

Although the minivan was not exactly in keeping with my self-image, it did afford me an invaluable level of inconspicuousness, the irony of which was the fact that I, the progeny-less prince, was at the helm of the quintessential family car.

I cut across town and picked up the 10 westbound. The temperature had spiked into triple digits. A yellow brown inversion layer hung over the L.A. basin like a dirty blanket. I cranked up the air conditioner and adjusted the rearview mirror. It was then that I noticed the small red-and-white cooler stowed invitingly on the floorboards behind the passenger seat. Maybe my luck was turning around. If not a six-pack of cold beer then perhaps a soda—something, *anything* to wash away the sticky residue of opium and smog and blood congealing in the back of my throat. What I found inside the cooler may have appeased the insatiable bloodlust of a pagan deity; but as for myself, the lone kidney wrapped in plastic and packed in crushed ice served to remind me how close I had been to forfeiting one of my own in payment for my trip down the rabbit hole.

Maybe finding the kidney was a blessing in disguise. After I met with Shackleman, I could give Artie Shank a jingle and see if he could put me in touch with anyone in the market for a second chance at life. There had to be hundreds of men and women in the area who needed transplants. The city was teeming with stories of people who had taken out second mortgages on their houses to pay for facelifts. Imagine what someone teetering on the brink of death would pay for the purloined organ! With a little luck, I could turn my misfortune into a quick buck or two. Locating a match would be a snap. Behind the cooler was a medical chart of the organ donor's vitals right down to the rhesus factor.

It was 12:55 when I first spotted the Alibi Room. The i's on the sign over the entrance were dotted with neon martini olives. If

Shackleman was as punctual as he was prone to flights of mild paranoia, then I was right on schedule. Finally, some answers. I eased the minivan into a shaded parking space and cracked the windows so the kidney wouldn't end up roasting in its own juices. I wiped the car for prints just in case and locked up. By chance I noticed Shackleman standing at the curb no more than a hundred feet away on the opposite corner of the intersection. He waited for the signal, checked both ways, and started across.

Although it should not have surprised me given Arbegast's impressive credentials, I could only watch in dumbfounded horror as my car jumped the red light and barreled into the intersection with the possessed ape at the wheel. Shackleman turned, but it was too late. The heavy steel bumper clipped him at the knees and sent him cartwheeling through the air like a drunken trapeze artist. He was dead before he hit the ground. I made eye contact with Arbegast as he shot past me and swung a hard right toward the freeway on-ramp. In that moment, a sort of understanding was exchanged, Arbegast as certain of his actions as I was totally stunned and mystified by the unimaginable motives jumping out at me from every conceivable closet of possibility.

I rushed to where Shackleman's broken body lay in the street. Blood leaked from the corner of his mouth, a viscous red stalactite spreading out over the asphalt. His glasses had been knocked from his face; without them, his eyes resembled raisins. The requisite throng of onlookers had not yet amassed, their oohing and aahing ranks still assembling from parked cars, nearby storefronts, and fervid cell-phone conversations in which they recounted, no detail too graphic, the grisly tableau for the listener at the other end of the wireless connection. I am happy to say that my own presence was not nearly as gratuitous. Shackleman was supposed to have information for me. The chances were slim to none that he was actually carrying anything I could use. However, I went ahead and patted him down anyway. If anyone asked, I was checking his vital signs. In his pants pockets I found two ticket stubs to the late showing of *Planet of the Apes* at the Beaux Arts Theater, an unlabeled prescription bottle of nondescript brown pills, twenty-three dollars in small bills, and a computer disk about the diameter of a poker chip. I was about to get the hell out of there when I noticed a peculiar bulge in his crotch. It was long and angular. As much as I hated the thought of getting caught with my hand in some dead guy's pants, I had to check. I wanted to squeal like a schoolgirl when I took hold of the hard, smooth shaft. Apparently knocked from where it had been tucked into his waistband, the true whereabouts of my .45 was no longer in question. "I could kiss you, you crazy bastard," I whispered as I tucked the gun safely into my own pants and made a break for it before the vultures could hem me in.

About halfway across the street, I came face-to-face with Blight. Had we been inside the STF, you can be damn sure that he would have made me instantly. However, by the time his neurons had tapped into the necessary correlative, it was too late. By then I had abandoned the minivan, kidney and all, and was in the midst of a taxi ride home—Shackleman's treat. So, the reformed nicotine junkie wasn't totally nuts. Who was Blight? And why was he after Shackleman?

In the light of day, my neighborhood evoked an antediluvian fantasy retreat, a garden paradise unspoiled by the presence of the wicked. Lured by an abundance of flowers, butterflies, and hummingbirds flitted colorfully about, sustained effortlessly on the gentle currents of an ocean breeze. Here, it was at least ten degrees cooler than in the heart of the city, the preponderance of shade-giving trees and heat-absorbing shrubs thwarting the greenhouse effect with model efficiency.

I had not given Ehrlich much thought since tucking him in earlier that morning and abandoning him to his bubbly non-stick world. I had made sure to hide all of the aerosol cans and other potential inhalants, but who could say with any degree of certainty what other household products with inviting disclaimers of health risks he might sniff or swallow? For a brief period after the army had taken my pseuprezdid away, I had systematically scoured the shelves at the local pharmacy for over-the-counter medications whose active ingredients shared one or more of the cryptic components listed in pseuprezdid's complex chemical profile. Misguidedly, I believed that I could synthesize a serviceable version of the drug by combining the various OTCs. Needless to say, my efforts were in vain. I even went so far as to imbibe a foul-tasting concoction of prenatal vitamins, wart-removal compound, fungicide, and nasal decongestant that blurred my vision and caused my lips to shrink. Like Ehrlich, I feared life without a buffer. For me, the thought of ever having to confront what I had become in Iraq was terrifying. Better that I languish in perpetual indifference than face the monster that lived in my shadow. Anyway, it turns out that pseuprezdid's effect is cumulative, a persistent little devil with the stick-to-itiveness of genital herpes and the half-life of uranium 238.

Ehrlich was gone. His bed in the guest room had been stripped bare, and the clean clothes I had lent him were lying in a crinkled heap on the floor like the molted skin of a reptile. There was no note, only the faint garbage-can odor of him taking shape in the captive air, a bittersweet reprise of the waste he had become. I guess I should have expected it. We were both shackled to the same hunted existence. Like myself, he must have believed that there was no way out—that hiding, although not an avenue of escape—was his adaptive best. He had given up his civility for survival, bubble baths and forced-air heating for cold concrete and ghetto chicken, domestic bliss for Dantean suffering. He was out there on the streets somewhere wearing his head on a swivel, as elusive and deprived of the ways of civilized man as Bigfoot. With fraternal resignation, I opened the window and released his feral scent like a dirty dove into the soupy amalgam of airborne particulates and ozone-gobbling CFCs.

I was anxious to learn what was contained on the computer disk I had rescued from Shackleman's pocket, but none of the ports on my PC would accommodate it. Until I could get my hands on a compatible machine, I would have to use know-how and instinct to anticipate Arbegast's next move. I had come close twice already. Gambler that I am, I stashed the disk in plain sight, albeit camouflaged to the casual observer. Before the media spotlight had driven my then circle of friends into the shadows, a group of guys, army mostly, had convened at my house every Sunday night to drink beer, smoke cigars, and play poker. It was in the poker caddy I had bought while on maneuvers at the old Nevada nuclear test site that I concealed what could very possibly hold the answers to all of my questions regarding IT. Sandwiched in among the blue chips—a dubious metaphor for my own ex-hero status—I passed the bet for the time being and hoped that my third go in the batter's box would earn me a canter around the bases.

My .45 was another matter. The police were scouring the city for the weapon used in the shooting of Officer Blanks and the murder of the Siamese twins. Without my gun, they could never build a case against me. Shackleman had taken a big risk in delivering the sought-after .45, his esteem increasing tenfold in my grateful eyes. As difficult as it would be for me to sacrifice my beloved sidearm, it was going into the bay the first chance I got. It was the only way. For now, the chimney seemed as good a hiding place as any. I sealed my .45 inside a Ziploc freezer bag and placed it atop a brick ledge at the base of the flue. Although there was still the matter of how Shackleman had come into possession of my gun—not to mention the identity of the brown pills he had been carrying—I was more or less resigned to count my blessings and call it a day. Torturing myself with unanswerable questions wasn't going to solve anything.

Oh, yeah, three people were dead. I could worry about that later. . . . Or would I?

I probably shouldn't have checked, but the answering machine, much as I had expected, was empty, the accusatory red zero in the electronic in-box declaring in no uncertain terms that Janie had more important things on her mind than me. It was as I wallowed in self-pity that the first unwelcome stirrings of my bowels alerted me to the fact that any minute now my bridge would undertake the last leg of its voyage through my ulcerous intestinal tract. I would have my teeth back, and with them a modicum of much-needed dignity would be restored.

Half an hour later, my rescued bridge soaking in a glass of water and Clorox bleach, I plopped down on the living-room sofa, clicked on the television and thumbed through the channels with the remote. The news was reporting from the scene of a police investigation in a quiet residential neighborhood of Thousand Oaks. An elderly woman and her thirty-something niece had been brutally murdered sometime during the previous night. The culprit had apparently entered through a second-story window of the luxury townhouse where the two women lived together and had carved them up pretty good with a knife of some sort. So far, the details of the case were sketchy. However, the friend of the family who had discovered the victims had told reporters that the niece's corpse had been forced, of all places, into the chimney. Small world, I thought to myself, the freakish incident galvanizing my resolve to dump my .45 as soon as possible.

I was about to change channels when the report was interrupted by a breaking news bulletin. Helicopters and news vans were broadcasting live from the scene of Shackleman's hit-and-run, a toothsome ex-captain of the UCLA cheerleading squad recapping the vehicular tragedy with the conciliatory tone she had honed crushing the hopes of young, high-kicking wanna-bes. As the station was about to run a description of the vehicle alleged to have taken part in the fatal hit-and-run (this is where things went from worse to impossible) the bulletin was interrupted by another bulletin—this one apparently more important and of greater urgency than Shackleman's passing into the realm of things forgotten. The camera cut to a live shot of a chimpanzee lying in a hospital bed. The ailing beast was plugged into an array of IV tubes and vital-sign monitors. The reporter, Carlos Cassavetes, a spit-polished Latino famous for his ornamental Spanish accent, introduced the chimp, Marcel, and Marcel's impassioned caretaker, Lorelei Beckett Ph.D., a world-renowned animal psychologist and leading authority in the field of Applied Simian Linguistics. No sooner had Dr. Beckett been introduced than she snatched the microphone from Cassavetes's hand and launched into a diatribe against the one who had stolen the minivan carrying the donor kidney Marcel was slated to receive. I don't know which was more stunning: the fact that a chimp was about to undergo a kidney transplant from a human donor while thousands of men and women awaited similar procedures, or Lorelei's soul-awakening beauty.

Although her rancor was received in equal dosages on millions of television sets throughout L.A. County, I rejoiced in the knowledge that it was me at whom her blustery obloquy was aimed. Her mouth, as breathtaking an orifice as has ever stirred the kettle of desire, mesmerized me with its ardent plea for information regarding the minivan's whereabouts. I could not help but be seduced by the compassion Dr. Beckett expressed for the ailing chimp at her side. Truth be told, I envied Marcel—his hopeful eyes and failing kidneys—the blessed recipient of so much love and affection. Why couldn't it be me lying there in the spectral light of the news cameras, my fate bound to the ethereal creature who had manipulated my lips with her own bare hands since birth in the hope that one day she could coax "ma-ma" from my inchoate language-acquisition device and prove Chomsky and all the skeptics wrong?

"Please," Dr. Beckett pleaded, her watery eyes communicating a deep hurt, "Marcel is not only an important scientific milestone, he is like a son to me. I have raised him since his birth mother was murdered by poachers nearly seven years ago. If you have any information that might help locate his kidney—*anything at all*—you can reach me in person at the Center for Primate Studies at the Los Angeles Zoo."

Unable to locate a piece of paper, I scrawled the phone number on the back of my hand with a ballpoint pen. I was dialing before the ink dried.

"Dr. Beckett, please."

"Dr. Beckett is busy," a male voice informed me abruptly. "Can I take a message and have her return your call?"

"This can't wait."

"Dr. Beckett is being interviewed on television right now," he explained. "I'm Dr. Beckett's assistant. Is there anything I can help you with?"

"If you don't mind, I'd like to speak with Dr. Beckett directly. It's about the monkey."

"You mean Marcel?"

"Yes, I'm watching the news right now. He's right here on the TV in front of me, plain as day."

"Sir, Marcel is a chimpanzee."

"Forgive me, I should know better. Now, please, put Dr. Beckett on the phone. I know where you can find Marcel's kidney."

The assistant's voice suddenly became muffled as if he had cupped his hand over the mouthpiece. I turned my attention back to the television where a leathery, sun-seasoned man old enough to be Dr. Beckett's father appeared on-screen. He whispered something into the ear of the lovely animal psychologist and handed her a cordless phone.

"You can tell us where Marcel's kidney is?" she beamed hopefully, stroking the sickly chimp's head.

"First, you have to promise me two things. . . . "

"I'm listening," she answered distrustfully.

"Look into the camera, so that I know you're being straight with me."

A close-up of Dr. Beckett's face hovered before me, a million pixels of electrified perfection. It was all I could do to keep myself from crawling across the floor and kissing the screen.

"One: I don't want the press involved. My identity is to be kept strictly anonymous."

"Fine," she agreed promptly. "I'm not interested in who you are. I just want to know where Marcel's kidney is."

"Two: You have to meet with me tonight. Just us. Somewhere you'll feel safe so that we can talk. I need to pick your brain."

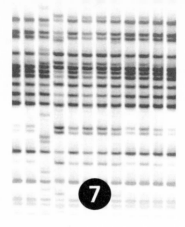

7

MARCEL THE CHIMPANZEE WAS RECOVERING from what his surgeons were describing as successful kidney-transplant surgery when I arrived at the L.A. Zoo shortly after midnight via rental car. It was a tiny two-seater economy model manufactured in a dreary industrial sector of the former Soviet Union. Scarcely more than a hood ornament, I liked my chances better behind the wheel of the gnatlike conveyance, than, say, in my own car given the fact that an APB had been issued for its apprehension in connection with a fatal hit-and-run.

The zoo is an eerie place after midnight. Between the ammoniated waft of territorial scent markers and the shrieks and growls and rumblings of beasts both predatory and mournful, it's like stepping back an epoch or two into a world where man was featured as a daily menu special. My cardiopulmonary rate doubled its normal output, gorging my muscles with superoxygenated blood should my legs suddenly be called upon to get me the hell out of there. Knowing that my natural rivals were locked up in cages could not override thousands of years of behavioral conditioning. Genetically, I was a runner and a hider, a big-brained sissy born with one foot on the mountaintop and the other in the lion's mouth. Adding to my discomfort was the fact that the parking lot was totally empty, a foregone conclusion most any other night at this hour. Where was she? Curled up in a chair at Marcel's bedside, a thin PROPERTY OF UCLA MEDICAL CENTER blanket cocooning her against the HEPA-filtered chill of the critical-care ward? The second hand on my watch plodded around the luminous dial.

I was about to phone it in for the night when a car cut through the darkness at the other end of the lot. Its headlights glittered like the eyes of a jungle cat as it crept slowly toward me. It was Lorelei! What would I say? Where would I begin? Of course, I was here for a guided tour of the simian psyche, but, oh, how I longed to breathe in the feminine scent of her, to slake my eyes at the trough of her beauty. Although I had never even met the woman purported to converse with the apes, I was both mystified and enchanted by the depth of her compassion for Marcel. I could scarcely feel for members of my own species, and she was pulling all-nighters at the hospital, signing haiku for a bedridden chimp with bad kidneys. Not only was it possible that she held the key to unlocking Arbegast's mind, she was everything I wasn't. And what a body!

The car glided to a stop, swamping me in its headlights. The passenger door opened and the safari-clad Dr. Beckett moved into the streaming light, her shapely silhouette as wondrous and fluid as ancient Greek statuary. I, on the other hand, was beside myself with mortal longing, every bit the desperate lothario she had imagined for us both on the phone earlier that afternoon: crooked little Pan making a play for divine Aphrodite. She was lean and well-tanned and wore her dark hair back off her face in a ponytail.

"I thought we agreed that you'd come alone," I said, jealously aware of the male outline in the driver's seat.

"You could be a nut for all I know," she said, sizing me up. "Anyway, it's only my assistant. You guys talked earlier."

"How's Marcel doing? I heard on the radio that the operation was a success."

"Marcel's good," she confirmed, her expression softening slightly.

"Glad to hear it."

"On the phone you said you needed my help getting inside someone's mind. I'm an animal psychologist. . . . " She regarded me quizzically. "I'm sorry, I don't even know your name."

"Flowers—I'm a private detective."

"To be perfectly honest with you, Mr. Flowers. . . . "

"Please, call me Dutch."

"Like I was saying, Dutch, I'm an animal psychologist. I'm really not that good with people."

"That makes two of us. If you can't help me, I'll be no worse off than before."

"Okay, then," she agreed, turning to face the car. "Tom, Mr. Flowers and I are going to take a walk together. Why don't you check on Kiki, see how she's doing? I shouldn't be long."

The engine died and I was released from the tractor-beam grasp of the headlights. The driver's door swung open and regurgitated the man who had taken my call in the hospital that afternoon. He was tall and good-looking, with the brash stride of a big-game hunter, his once-blond hair the sun-burnished patina of the Serengeti in high summer.

"You sure, Lo?" Tom asked, looking at me as if through the sights of an elephant gun. "I can tag along, if you like."

"Thanks, Tom, I'll be fine," she assured him with an appreciative smile.

"Tarzan if you need me."

"Will do."

Tom unlocked the gate at one of the ticket booths and held it open for both Dr. Beckett and myself. I swear he sniffed me as I brushed past him, cataloging my odor should he be forced to track me by scent. There was no doubt in my mind that his nose was every bit as effective a tracking device as the radio transmitter with which Mr. Wonderful had fitted me. The gate swung closed after us. We were locked in.

Leaving behind the snack oasis where, during business hours, herds of the waddling obese grazed on corndogs and churros, Dr. Beckett guided me into the zoo's dimly lit interior. Snaking in and out of a succession of man-made habitats, the path at our feet skirted miniature savannas crowded with silhouettes of grazing behemoths, and mock watering holes where crocodiles prowled just beneath the surface. We walked in silence for several minutes. Spaces usually cluttered with words were occupied with the deranged cries of hyenas and the pneumatic whoosh of hippos clearing their airways.

"It's kind of peaceful in a weird sort of way," I remarked. "The exhibits are very true to life. I almost feel as if we're in the jungle or something."

"Loss of habitat is the single greatest threat to nearly every species on the planet. They like trees; we build malls. Before long, zoos will be the only place where animals will feel at home—relatively speaking, of course."

We stopped when we came to an exhibit where three ostrich-like birds were foraging for food, drumming out Morse code–like communiqués on the hard ground with their powerful beaks.

"Cassowary," explained Dr. Beckett. "They're a distant cousin of the moa, a prehistoric bird that reached weights in excess of five hundred pounds."

"Imagine the drumsticks."

Dr. Beckett looked disappointed with my remark. "So, how can I help you, Dutch?"

"There's this certain someone I've been trying to track down, but I'm not having much luck. It's as if I'm always one step behind. I was hoping that you might be able to tell me what makes him tick, maybe help me anticipate his next move."

"There's a professor in the Criminal Psych department at UCLA who specializes in this sort of thing. Does a lot of consultation work for the LAPD. She's a close friend of mine. If you like, I can put you in touch with her."

"Maybe this wasn't such a good idea."

"I'm trying to help you the best way I know. It's just that you haven't given me much to go on. *A certain someone.* . . . That doesn't tell me a whole lot."

"You'll think I'm crazy if I tell you."

"You haven't even given me a chance," Dr. Beckett replied earnestly.

"Hell, I think I'm crazy."

"If I hadn't trusted you on the phone today, Marcel might be dead right now. Maybe it's time that you trusted me. What have you got to lose?"

"Nothing," I said. "Absolutely nothing. But remember: I warned you."

Dr. Beckett exhaled deeply and closed her eyes. When she opened them again, it was with the implication that her mind was now clear and ready to receive what information I had. "Okay, let me have it," she said.

"The certain someone I'm after is a chimp."

"Do you mind if I ask who you're working for?" she asked without skipping a beat.

"Sorry, client privilege."

Dr. Beckett bobbed her head knowingly. "This chimp—does he have a name?"

"131."

"Catchy. What's it mean?"

"It's his control-group number, but never mind that. You actually believe me?"

"Shouldn't I? Animals escape from zoos all the time. The only thing that makes this any different is that I've never heard of a zoo hiring a private detective. Usually, escaped animals are the sort of thing an experienced handler will take care of."

"I wasn't hired by a zoo."

"Now I get it," she remarked knowingly. "The chimp you're after is from a private collection. Someone's pet got loose. No wonder they want you to keep it quiet. Possession of a wild animal without a license is a serious offense. They could go to jail. . . . Not that the courts would ever prosecute to the extent of the law. You may have noticed that we don't exactly hold animals in high regard. We eat them, for God's sake. Tell your client that a small fine and a slap on the wrist is all they're likely to get." She appraised me with an easy smile and loosed her hair from the ponytail. "If I don't wear it up, Marcel pulls on it. God, that feels good."

I tried not to seem too interested in what she was doing with her hair, but the truth of the matter is she was killing me. My groin stirred for the first time in months, a hibernating dragon whose drowsy fire I had believed all but extinguished.

"What I tell you stays right here," I said, attempting to pass off my rapt expression as a look of professional scrutiny. "I'm already letting you in on more than I should."

"When we spoke on the phone earlier and you said that you wanted to pick my brain, I thought that you might mean it literally. But I'm here."

"This is not your everyday chimp we're talking about. No offense, but he's a little more advanced than what you're used to."

"You'd be surprised," she countered coolly.

"He kills people," I blurted, hoping to derail her apparent irritation before it could gain momentum.

"Kills people?" she echoed dubiously. "Human beings?"

"At least three that we know of in the last twenty-four hours. . . . Another's on life support. *And* chimps—maybe six or seven of them."

Dr. Beckett studied me for a moment. A familiar look crossed her face. "Aren't you the guy that was on the news a couple of years back? Some kind of trouble with the government?"

"Look, I know this sounds far-fetched, but I've seen it with my own eyes. He escaped from a lab that's conducting experiments with chimps by pumping them full of human DNA. Most of them seem to be doing all right, but whatever they did to the one I'm after seems to have turned him into a homicidal maniac."

"You're right, it does sound far-fetched," she said, resuming her trek along the winding path. "There's not much that separates us from the chimps. Murder and suicide are about the only two significant differences I can think of—psychologically speaking, of course. Chimps are simply too grounded in the world to take part in either. It's just not in their nature to waste life."

"I'm not saying that his behavior is normal—that's not what I'm saying at all. This is one confused knuckle-dragger we're talking about. Who knows for how long they've been fucking with his mind? As far as I'm concerned, he's not responsible for his actions."

"If he's so human," asked Dr. Beckett, "what good am I to you?"

"I may be a little biased, but I believe that no matter how far gone the individual that part of him—what's good—always remains . . . No matter how deep you have to dig to find it."

Dr. Beckett eyed me obliquely, a curious smile crossing her lips. "Then you think there might be a chance at rehabilitating him?" she said.

We had reached the top of a gradual rise and stood looking out over the tops of a stand of eucalyptus whose perfumed crowns gleamed like platinum in the moonlight. The two-story overlook offered zoogoers an eye-to-eye view with giraffes.

"As a matter of fact, Dr. Beckett, I guess I do."

"No more 'Dr. Beckett,' " she scolded me generously. "Call me Lorelei."

In the case of Arbegast, rehabilitation was the last thing that would have ever occurred to me. He was too far gone, too steeped in the wicked ways of humanity. However, gazing out at the swan-necked silhouettes of the graceful leaf-nibblers with Dr. Beckett—*Lorelei*—at my side, I detected a golden sliver of optimism cresting the horizon for both myself and the accursed chimp. Because Arbegast was no longer packing my .45 his ability to make mischief was significantly reduced. I was no longer in a mad dash against time. I could ease off the throttle, slow things down a bit, particularly if doing so meant keeping Lorelei around for a while. So what if I still had no idea how Shackleman had gotten his grubby little hands on my gun. Things were looking up for old Dutch.

I walked Lorelei through the last several days, recapping every-thing that had happened since my first encounter with Janus. The murdered chimps, my mishap in the Enchanted Forest, Shackleman's hit-and-run. Throughout, I was conscious of the ruminations of the giraffes below us as they grazed on bales of hay stuffed into treetop feeders. It was against this munching backdrop that Lorelei ingested what I had told her, the giraffes' worked-at mouthfuls mirroring in no uncertain terms just how hard my story was to swallow.

"If you come to my house with me, I can show you every-thing: donor profiles, surveillance videos, photographs of the subjects. . . . "

"Okay, but now you have to promise me two things. One: that when we get to your house, you won't kill me and chop me up into little pieces. Two: that you'll tell me how you knew where Marcel's kidney was."

"Deal."

"And I have to let Tom know where I'll be in case there's a problem with Marcel. The only reason I'm not at his side right now is because I promised to meet with you," she informed me guiltily. "Anyway, the surgeon said it would be seven or eight hours before he regained consciousness. . . . As long as I'm back at the hospital by then."

"Absolutely."

We caught up with Tom in an inner chamber of the chimpanzee exhibit—a nursery, judging from the looks of it: incubators, baby bottles, boxes of disposable diapers stacked against the walls. He was using sign language to communicate with an older-looking female chimpanzee who was breast-feeding a pink-faced newborn chimp. Tom's hands, although callused and spotted with sun damage, were incredibly nimble, even eloquent, navigating the complex stream of gesticulations with the fluid grace of a belly dancer.

"Tom," said Lorelei, "I'd like you to meet Dutch Flowers. Dutch, this is my assistant, Tom Norris. Tom was with me in Zaire when we rescued Marcel."

Tom Norris signed something for the mother chimp and extended his hand. "Kiki and I were wondering what was keeping you two."

"I was showing Dutch around, and I guess we lost track of time."

"It's a zoo out there," I offered lamely. Tom's hard, well-spoken hand engulfed my own.

"Kiki," said Lorelei, signing the words as she spoke them, "there's someone I'd like you to meet. This is Dutch."

The mother chimp turned her attention to me and executed a complicated series of hand gestures.

Lorelei beamed and touched herself over her heart. "That's very sweet of you, Kiki, but he was a perfect gentleman."

I smiled dumbly not knowing what to make of the improbable exchange.

"Kiki said she was getting ready to send Orpheus out looking for us," Lorelei explained. "Orpheus is Kiki's sweetheart. He's also Edgar's father."

Apparently, Edgar was the big-eared newborn suckling at Kiki's dilapidated breast.

"Next to Kiki and Edgar, Lorelei is tops on Orpheus's list," said Tom. "Do you have any idea what it means to tangle with a pissed-off chimp?"

"I think I do," I replied honestly.

"*Tom,*" Lorelei admonished her overprotective assistant. "Orpheus is a sweetie. You know he doesn't have a violent bone in his body."

"Tell that to the guy whose ribs he broke."

"You'd get upset, too, if your wife had just had a baby and they were relocating you to another zoo." Lorelei turned and frowned at me. "We fought it, but it was no use. Orpheus has an incredibly high sperm count. We nicknamed him The Impregnator because of his high rate of success with the ladies. He's on loan to San Francisco for the next six months. Kiki is still in denial. She knows better, but it makes her feel good to pretend that he's still around."

The shame I was feeling may not have been evident on my face, but it was boiling inside of me. It seemed that every man, woman and, now, animal was dipping into the gene pool—everyone, that is, but me.

"Do you want to hold him?" Lorelei asked.

"I couldn't. . . . "

"C'mon, I noticed you staring at Edgar. I'm sure Kiki wouldn't mind letting you hold him, would you, Kiki?"

Kiki gently withdrew Edgar from her nipple and offered him to me.

"No, I couldn't," I said.

"Go ahead," Lorelei urged. "It's wonderful. Go on. If you don't take him now, you'll hurt Kiki's feelings."

• • •

Earlier in the evening I had cursed the rental car for being so small: unmanly, a windup toy, a deathtrap. With Lorelei squeezed in tightly alongside of me, this smallness was suddenly its greatest attribute. I fantasized that we were the last hope of a dying planet—man and woman—an escape pod jettisoned into outer space. The survival of our species depended on our drive and commitment to frenzied procreation. Shoulder to shoulder we would drift through the cosmos in search of a brave new world to call our own, a gravitationally challenged paradise in which my indolent sperm would execute stunning arabesques in her uterus with the ease of orbiting astronauts performing a lunar ballet. Forever springtime, eternally the Year of the Rabbit. The fantasy was perfect, except for one thing: Lorelei would insist that Marcel accompany us. I could see it now. One solar cycle the simian tagalong would be making faces at me in the rearview mirror, the next he'd be in the driver's seat showing Lorelei how to handle the joystick.

"What'd you think of Edgar?" asked Lorelei, breaking the terrible trance. "You looked so peaceful holding him."

"Are they all like that?"

"You mean so cute and cuddly?"

"So human?"

"Some more than others," she explained. "The same as it is with actual humans. There are special ones and not-so special ones. Edgar is one of the special ones."

"It was nice," I said.

I was telling her only half the truth. On the one hand, the experience had been nothing short of miraculous—vital, real, life-affirming, a laundry list of New Age adjectives better set to wind chimes and Buddha bells—but it had also engendered in me an even greater degree of frustration and regret. As far as the medical establishment was concerned, I would never know the joy of biological parenthood. In those few moments that I had cradled Edgar against me, his brown unblinking eyes appraising me with immeasurable wonder, the affection I felt for him realized its correlative in the crushing disappointment I felt at the thought of never producing offspring of my own. Not only had

I failed to fulfill my biological directive, I was being denied the one shot I had at restoring my compassion and making myself whole again. Holding Edgar had proven to me how desperately I needed something to care for.

"What about Marcel?" I asked masochistically. "Is he one of the special ones?"

Lorelei melted. "Marcel is the love of my life."

For the first time in over a year, I felt at home in my house. Having Lorelei there had driven the ghosts of my moribund marriage into hiding. The loose floorboards that had once creaked "Janie" now held their tongues. The decorative finishes with which she had feathered our nest—rooms awash in warm coconut-milk pigments and life-affirming earth tones—pulsed with renewed vitality. For a few moments, I was able to forget that, like Arbegast, I was a fugitive. Lorelei's voice filled the rooms with the melody of songbirds, sanguine chorales dispelling the gloom of my brooding martyrdom. A momentary state of bliss.

"You two still married?" asked Lorelei, her eyes settling on the wedding portrait on the mantel over the fireplace: Janie's done-up hair, my rented tux, our bulletproof faith in *for better or worse*.

"We're separated," I explained. "I guess she met someone else."

"That sucks," Lorelei said in an understated way that made me feel not so bad.

"I came back from the Gulf, and things were never really the same between us. She said the man she knew was missing in action, that it would have been easier if I had just died."

Lorelei winced. "Ouch!"

"It wasn't easy for her being married to a celebrity scapegoat: the news vans out front twenty-four-seven, the threatening phone calls in the middle of the night, the hate mail, the weirdos coming around wanting to congratulate me. Had the shoe been on the other foot, I don't know that I would have lasted any longer than she did."

"What about kids?"

"We tried but never had any luck."

"Did you ever consider adoption?"

"Never seriously."

"Why not, if you don't mind me asking?"

"Because we wanted our own, I guess. Something that was a part of us. There was a time when nothing else would do. Someone I talked to recently convinced me that I may have been a little close-minded."

There was a brief silence in which we both just stood there rocking on our heels in front of the fireplace, breathing in the memories of a life gone up in smoke.

Lorelei was the first to speak. "So, where's this stuff you want me to look at?" she asked, her voice upbeat. "From what you've told me already, it sounds as if this place . . . "

"Acteon."

" . . . has cooked up one hell of a chimp Frankenstein."

"A monster with a heart of gold," I confirmed.

"Let's just hope this version of the story has a happy ending."

While Lorelei pored over everything Shackleman had given me on IT, I went from room to room straightening up: dusting knickknacks, fluffing cushions, brooming away the cobwebs from the corners of the ceiling. Although not entirely in disarray, I derived a certain therapeutic benefit from lending order to the staging ground of my hibernating domestic life. It was an anemic substitute for real control, but it was a step in the right direction.

I was standing at the kitchen sink cleaning up the mess Ehrlich had left behind when a heated lovers' quarrel broke out in the house next door. Although I couldn't make out a single word, I was sufficiently well-versed with the elevated pitch and crescendoing appeals from countless such verbal title bouts of my own to know that some poor slob would be sleeping on the sofa tonight. I didn't know these people, but according to Janie, they had moved in less than a month ago while I was "God knows where." I could discern their silhouettes acting out the familiar drama beyond the drawn curtains like shadow puppets. He was a short, stocky brute of a man who flailed his arms wildly when he spoke, as if fending off a swarm of killer bees. She was tall and willowy by comparison, an exclamation point with a shrill voice.

Normally, I am the sort of man who minds his own business, adhering to a code of nonintervention very similar to the one practiced by the crew of the starship *Enterprise*. On this particular occasion, however, something told me that I had better at least give the police a heads up. There was something unsettling about the stormy litany, the desperation and fury encoded in the muffled duel suggesting a gulf that could not be bridged easily. With each spoken volley, the flailing baritone appeared to acquire greater physical mass, as if his rage had awakened a beast lying dormant within him. Although his posture gradually degenerated to the point that he was nearly doubled over at the waist, he was somehow larger than ever, his hulking silhouette filling the window frame. During a particularly volatile exchange, he began beating his own chest with closed fists, a veritable King Kong turned loose in a quiet borough of Gotham. But then, just as things were getting interesting, Lorelei burst into the kitchen waving Arbegast's donor profile.

"You didn't tell me that 131 was an Arbegast! I know this guy!" she exclaimed. "We were undergrads at UCLA together. He came to school totally naked one day."

I was suddenly aware of how incredibly voyeuristic I must have looked spying on the neighbors. Fortunately, Lorelei didn't seem to notice.

"You're kidding?" I said, turning to face her.

"I swear on my reputation as a scientist. It was the first time I ever saw an uncircumcised penis."

"Are you sure?"

"I'm no porn queen, but I'm also not Mother Teresa. I think I can tell the difference."

"I mean, are you sure it was the same guy?"

"D_3," she confirmed. "Duncan Arbegast, III. His daddy is a big-time drug dealer, not to mention one of the richest men in America. That's probably why D_3 wasn't kicked out of school for showing everyone his wee-wee. Last I heard, he was off living in the jungle with headhunters."

"New Guinea."

"I guess he thought nudity wouldn't be an issue among people who practice cannibalism."

"Classmates, huh? How well did you know him?"

"Not well," she explained. "We talked once or twice, but he sort of freaked me out."

"I'd be freaked out, too, by a guy who went around naked."

"It wasn't that, so much. He had some really weird ideas about technology. I remember him once trying to convince me that computer viruses could also infect humans. He claimed a friend of his had contracted genital warts from a contaminated floppy port."

"I hope his friend had enough sense to first unplug the machine."

Lorelei laughed. "After that, I did my best to avoid him. He just seemed a little kooky to me, that's all. Nice, but kooky. A girl can't be too careful these days."

She was right. Girls like Lorelei were creep magnets. Beauty and vitality like hers are to psychotics and sexual predators what virgin blood is to vampires. Your average Boy Scout would have given up every one of his honor badges just to sniff her panties.

"So what convinced you I wasn't a kook?"

"Who said anything about being convinced? The jury's still out on you. If my head doesn't end up in your freezer next to the frozen peas and ground chuck, we'll talk."

"Bring out the firing squad," I lamented with a wounded look.

"I'm only playing," she said. "I think it was your smile. Ordinarily, I don't trust people whose teeth are so white, but your breath was just so clean-smelling that . . . I don't know. It reminds me of when I was a little girl and my mother used to bleach holes in our socks. There's just something noble about wanting to get your family's clothes that clean."

As much as I believe that honesty and trust are the bedrock of a strong relationship, I decided that the truth about my pearly whites was one secret that would have to wait until after the honeymoon.

"By the way," said Lorelei as I followed her from the kitchen into my office, "they'll lock you up for peeking into other people's windows. But you probably already know that."

Covering virtually every square inch of my desk was the information Shackleman had given me on IT. Photographs of the slain chimps, arranged chronologically in the order they had died, were tacked to the wall at eye level, opposite where I sat. Beneath each were the timetables I had put together as a means of distilling the improbable field of suspects to one. It was an odd sight even for me. Here were the Barnumesque artifacts of a murder investigation so absurd in its dubious apparatus that were Louis Leakey himself to hypothesize such a far-flung scenario, he would have been locked up for heresy. Lorelei, however, seemed unfazed; excited, even. It was clear from the neat stack of papers occupying one side of the cluttered workspace that professional curiosity had compelled her to glance at each of the donor profiles before concentrating on Arbegast's.

"This is incredible!" she exclaimed, her eyes blazing with the fire of possibility, her face only inches from my own. "You hear about experiments like this, but you never really believe that such a thing exists. It's beyond incredible, it's miraculous! Can you imagine what this sort of research could tell us about the chimp brain? Imagine what the chimps could tell us about themselves. We're talking about opening a door to a previously untapped consciousness. This could advance the science of animal psychology a hundred years. . . . A thousand! Not only that—for the first time in the history of humankind, we will be able to see ourselves through the eyes of another species."

"I'm not sure I'd want to," I said, masking one area of skepticism with another. "I'm afraid I wouldn't like what I saw."

As much as I wanted to grab Lorelei by the shoulders and shake some sense into her, to tell her that this was a monster I was after, a calculating fiend with a mind for murder and a taste for blood, not some petting-zoo curio eager for a banana and a pat on the head, I stopped myself. She was even more beautiful than before. Any second, I expected her to throw her arms around me and kiss me passionately on the mouth.

Lorelei lowered her voice and looked into my eyes. "I've been hoping for something like this all of my life," she said. "How better to gain insight into what makes us human than through the eyes of our closest relative? Think of what it could do for animal rights. Arbegast is a once-in-a-lifetime opportunity, Dutch."

"Opportunity?" I repeated thoughtfully, my voice resonating with receptive tones of interest.

"Of course I haven't had a chance to do my homework. . . . But from what the data indicates, I'm optimistic that verbal communication is a distinct possibility, if not a sure thing. With the heightened intellect these chimps possess, teaching them to talk should be a snap."

"You think?"

Lorelei considered the monumentality of the task ahead of her. "Okay, maybe not a snap," she confessed, "but I know I can do it. You can't really want to see him dead. You yourself said that you don't hold him responsible for his actions."

Not one cell in my body believed that Arbegast could be trusted. Twice I had been witness to his deadly indifference. And twice I had failed to apprehend him. Although my gun was no longer an issue, I had to consider the bounty on my head. I couldn't stall Mr. Wonderful forever, not with the radio transmitter looped around my ankle.

In spite of the obvious danger courting Arbegast presented, I was powerless to object. For the first time since it had become apparent to me that Janie was never coming back, I believed that I could fall in love again.

"Any ideas how to catch him?" I asked.

On the way to the hospital, Lorelei confessed that she was somewhat baffled as to how to go about tracking down Arbegast. Manhunts—or, in this case, *apehunts*—weren't the sort of thing she had much experience with. She could make some educated guesses based on her knowledge of chimp psychology. However, none of her subjects could compare with what Acteon was churning out.

"I could be way off," she admitted frankly, "but you would think that a creature operating on two such distinct frequencies would be experiencing some sort of identity crisis, a conflict of selves. You know, a Jekyll-and-Hyde sort of thing."

"What about instinct?" I wanted to know. "His chimp half has got to be feeling at least somewhat out of its element."

"That's precisely the point—his *chimp* half. But what about his human half? Aside from the biological directives shared by all mammals—sustenance, shelter, reproduction—it seems to me that he probably feels as if he's being pulled apart by internal forces he can't possibly understand."

"Sounds to me like you're cooking up one hell of an insanity plea."

Lorelei smiled pragmatically and said, "According to the data, the infused chimps seem to have developed a level of consciousness that is—I guess I should say *was*—uniquely human. In acquiring this newfound consciousness, much of their survival instinct has taken a backseat to rational thought. With rational thought comes introspection and, pardon the poop mouth, a shitload of unanswerable whys. Imagine how confusing it must be to suddenly find yourself in possession of a set of high-powered cognitive tools without having had the training to know how to handle them."

"Thank heaven for small favors. Think of the damage the crazy bastard could do if he knew he was holding a royal flush."

"Maybe not," Lorelei cautioned. "Remember, Dutch, much of what we learn between infancy and adulthood is how to control our urges. If this wasn't the case, people would be farting at the dinner table and rape stats would be through the roof. You have to wonder how Arbegast might be handling his humanness differently had someone taken the time to teach him the ins and outs. If being human was easy, there wouldn't be so many nuts running around."

"I don't mean to sound like a broken record, but you'd think his chimp instinct would have some sort of influence on his behavior. He's still ninety-nine percent ape, right?"

For the first time since she had burst into the kitchen waving Arbegast's donor profile, Lorelei's mind seemed to be elsewhere. She scanned both sides of the road ahead, a concerned look on her face.

"We need to find a grocery store that's open," she said. "I'd like to pick up a few goodies for Marcel. If kidney transplantation is anything like when I had my appendectomy, he'll be famished when he comes out from under the anesthetic."

"There's a Von's up ahead. I think it's open twenty-four hours. We can stop there."

"Fantastic," she said, brightening. "I'll just be a minute."

As I waited for Lorelei to breach the automatic doors cradling Marcel's bag of goodies, I realized that it had been at least forty-eight hours since I'd gotten any real sleep. To make matters worse, it occurred to me that the amount of time since I had been anywhere near a bar of soap was of a similar duration. It was obvious from the bags under my eyes and the sour oils fermenting in my armpits that I was dragging anchor.

"It's very possible that Arbegast's two selves have short-circuited one another," remarked Lorelei, slipping back into the passenger seat and resuming our conversation without missing a beat. "It's the sort of thing we see in cases of multiple-personality disorder. Arbegast's chimp self may not even be aware that what his human self is doing is wrong. We're talking learned behavior. He may simply not have the ethical training necessary to see the error of his ways. Even more disconcerting is the possibility that he may feel as if he's on the outside looking in." She searched my expression for understanding. "It's as if he's along for the ride and has no idea where exactly that ride will take him."

I didn't know what to say. It was as if Lorelei had looked into my own embattled subconscious and seen the schism that existed between Dutch Flowers, the ruthless assassin, and the Dutch Flowers I liked to think of as the real me.

"I'll talk to Marcel and see if I can't conjure up something from that fuzzy little crystal-ball head of his. He's one of the most insightful sentients I know. In the meantime you should go home, take a hot shower and get some rest."

"I'm sorry," I apologized, acutely aware of the musky odor permeating the air around me. "I stink."

Lorelei set the bag of groceries on the floor between her legs and leaned in close to me. She inhaled deeply, drinking in the rammish bouquet the cramped passenger compartment had been recirculating since we had left the zoo.

"On second thought," she said, exhaling euphorically, "skip the shower. I think it's sexy for a man to smell like a man. There's too much soap and perfume in the world already. It overpowers our body chemistry and makes us deaf to our animal instincts. You smell *potent.*"

So there would be another confession after the honeymoon, I mused blissfully. At that moment, I was too aroused by her hot breath in my ear to broach the subject of my crippled reproductive system. By the time the goosebumps relaxed and my heart rate had returned to normal we were parked in front of the UCLA Medical Center and Lorelei was on her way inside to nursemaid her recovering beau.

"Here, try this," she offered, fishing a green crocodile-skinned piece of fruit from the grocery bag and handing it to me through the open window. "Cherimoya—it's one of Marcel's favorites. Unfortunately, they don't carry durian, or you would have been in for a real treat."

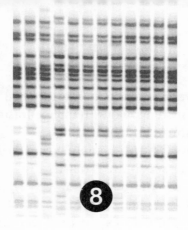

8

SINCE MY FIRST VISIT TO JANUS'S OFFICE, I had developed a keen sensitivity to the sudden overabundance of chlorophyll in the air. No sooner would I turn onto my street than my senses—especially smell—seemed to take it up a notch. What I had at first mistaken for the symptoms of common allergy turned out to be the signs of my sensory rebirth, the rust coming off the hinges of my neglected animal apparatus. I found myself sniffing the air as if I could detect the presence of hostiles in the vicinity by scent alone. Perhaps because this new talent was unrefined, my powers were not as discerning as I would have liked. Still, there was the nasal assault of dog and cat piss, pesticides, jet exhaust, odorized natural gas, rivers of household ooze and raw sewage creeping along under the street. Each had their own body and bouquet, the baneful constituents of a seldom-noticed olfactory white noise. If there had been further developments in the case of my chest-thumping neighbor during my absence, there was nothing in the air to suggest it. The house with which I shared a common border—seventy-five feet of bedraggled picket fretwork interwoven with thorny creepers of bougainvillea and potato vine—lay quiet as a shipwreck.

Unfortunately, my own house had not enjoyed a similar period of tranquillity in my absence. The front door was ajar, and several shoeboxes' worth of photographs and mementos from my honeymoon with Janie had been wrested from the top shelf of the hall closet and scattered about the floor of the entry.

Coasters from Duke's Canoe Club haloed with grenadine mai-tai runoff, miniature paper parasols, plastic swizzle sticks bearing King Kamehameha's likeness, a souvenir globe of Waikiki and Diamond Head complete with miniature surfers and oily blue water-substitute (smashed like our love). Sure, it was sad. I guess. In a symbolic sort of way. The work of a master collagist spinning a tale of lost love and ruin from an estate-sale bonanza of defunct memories. At the same time, however, the deliberately careless swirl of artifacts seemed to belong to someone else: the easy smiles, the Hawaiian shirts with the coconut-shell buttons, the caramel suntans and optimistic eyes. Anyway, you don't have to feel sadness to know it.

The rest of the house had also been ransacked—living room, bedrooms, bathrooms, kitchen: lamps toppled, cushions evis-cerated, cabinets and drawers emptied onto the floor, bed linens lying about like slaughtered ghosts, furniture overturned, pic-tures knocked from the walls, knickknacks and bric-a-brac and other decorative crap picked up and strewn about as if by a tor-nado. It was only by pure dumb luck that I had avoided the fire-works. Fortune may not have been smiling upon me, but it had certainly fixed me with a wily grin. Everything had been swept from the mantel. The brass candlesticks, the Last Supper center-piece Janie had made in crafts class from gel epoxy resin and champagne corks, and our wedding picture lay at the mouth of the fireplace, a shove and a match strike away from the land of Nevermore. My .45, much to my relief, was where I had left it. Apparently, they hadn't thought to search the chimney.

Fearing the worst, I followed the trail of flotsam into my office, passing through a maze of memories and personal effects like a coast-guard cutter combing the water for survivors at the site of a downed passenger jet. Whoever was responsible for the mess had left behind a distinct semifamiliar odor that I was unable to place. It was pure and assertive, untamed by soaps or perfumes. I was certain that I could track them by scent if pre-sented with the opportunity. If they had found the disk, it was virtually guaranteed that I would never have the answers I was looking for, that Acteon's dark secrets would die with the chimps. Or worse yet, continue to thrive in the hands of scientists bunkered in top-secret laboratories beneath the Coliseum.

I've seen the aftermath of some careless searches, many by my own two hands, but this one stole the show. In the center of the room lay the poker caddy in which I had stashed the disk, its neat stacks of pretend currency shaken out onto the floor. At first I was sick with regret, but then I noticed it. There, in plain sight among the scattered chips—a fool's ransom of red, white, and blue plastic rounds—lay the disk, its spectral whorls catching the light like mother-of-pearl. It was impossible to miss. There were only two reasons I could think of that anyone would have left it behind. Either the disk was worthless, or whoever had torn my house apart had been looking for something else—a probability evidenced by the fact that the annotated copy of *Bobo: An Autobiography* that Shackleman had given me was nowhere to be found. As much as I wanted to believe that the disk would somehow drop the curtain on all of this, I was fairly convinced that I would have to look elsewhere for the answers that would tie up the loose ends in the final act. Exhausted and discouraged, I flicked the disk back atop the pile of poker chips and plodded into the guest bathroom.

The mirrored door of the medicine cabinet was hanging open, and its contents had been swept into the sink. Fungicide, nasal decongestant, aspirin, sleep aids, anti-itch cream, lip balm, fifteen different sizes and shapes of Band-Aids—a remedy for every foreseeable household affliction other than a broken heart. I stood there appraising myself in the mirror, gamy and unshaven, wondering what secrets, now lost to me forever, Bobo's arcane magnum opus had contained?

In spite of Lorelei's peculiar advisement that I not bathe, I undressed and stood before the shower door prepared to wash away the layers of sweat and grime and sebaceous excretions that apparently constituted something of an aphrodisiac to her. However, before I committed myself to the steamy deluge scudding against the antislip fiberglass floor, I noticed something odd in the soap dish. It was small and oblong and jacketed with hairy gray-black corkscrews. What I had mistaken for a drowned rat turned out to be one of Janie's decorative bath cakes bristling with pubic hair and bellybutton lint. Not only was it a chilling artifact of Ehrlich's neglected bodily hygiene, but a grim reminder of just how thin exactly was the veneer of civilization. Only a man entirely stripped of his civility would do such a thing.

Lorelei's comment about soaps and perfumes deafening man to his natural instincts begged a much greater question than the issue of quashing nature's olfactory signposts. Fashion, fiction, and an immeasurable array of superficial social conventions—both applied and theoretical, from baptism to last rites—were as substantive hallmarks of humanity as the average Homo erectus would ever achieve. Yes, there was rational thought and performance art and introspection and logic, but these were gifts that the "man on the street" would never experience beyond the nebulous realm of abstraction. Give Joe Nosepicker a banana, and he wouldn't understand it any better than would a chimp. Hell, he wouldn't know to peel it if there was no one there to point the way. Deeply disgusted, I concluded that a shower may not have been such a good idea after all and trudged into the master bedroom, where my empty bed awaited me like a Viking funeral raft bound for the misty fjords of Valhalla. I was out before my head hit the pillow, an elastic free-fall into a bottomless abyss.

A short time later, I was awakened by a sharp blow to my ribs. As I gasped for air, my wrists were secured behind my back with duct tape, and a pillowcase was fitted snugly over my head. I struggled briefly with my unseen assailants, but they were too strong, too nasty. I'd known meat packers with a softer touch. Sufficiently tenderized, I was dragged from my house wearing nothing but the pillowcase. Moments later, I was forced into the trunk of a large, smooth-riding sedan, my demands for information earning me a volley of mirthless chuckles and a stiff blow to the side of my head. After twenty minutes or so of schussing over surface roads without the faintest idea where I was being taken or for what purpose, I was hauled from the trunk and thrust into an elevator. Following a brief descent, I was swept down a long, drafty corridor in the viselike grip of my two captors. The slap of my bare feet on the cool concrete was echoed threefold in the queer canter of my mute guides. Fifty yards later, I was shoved through a doorway and forced into a chair. In total darkness, they removed the pillowcase from my head, in this way guarding their identities. They departed as abruptly as they had arrived, never uttering a single word. When their footsteps had subsided, a switch was thrown and I found myself sitting in a small, windowless room thrumming with ultrabright fluorescent light. Bundles of electrical conduit snaked overhead and enormous banks of circuit breakers paneled the walls. At first, I thought I was in some sort of large industrial facility—a room in the basement of a factory or refinery, maybe. However, it wasn't long before I noticed that the chair I occupied was merely one quintuplet in a five-unit block of foldout stadium seats, the kind that put your ass to sleep long before the half-time show.

"I know where we are," I proclaimed, mindful of sounding too happy with myself. After all, I was naked and perceptibly cold. "Look, Janus, I'm on your side. I want Arbegast just as badly as you do."

An unfamiliar voice addressed me via a tinny intercom speaker in the ceiling.

"Excellent, Mr. Flowers. . . . " The intercom clicked off and the door through which I had entered swung open. "It's essential that each of us knows where the other stands."

It was Blight. I should have known.

"I don't believe we've been formally introduced," he said, greeting me with a slippery smile. "Dr. August Blight."

"You'll have to forgive my choice of outfits," I said, reclining immodestly. "I'm a little behind on my laundry."

"Nothing I haven't seen before," he assured me.

Blight was dressed less formally than he had been the previous times we had crossed paths: designer blue jeans and a pale yellow knit cotton pullover. He was tall and fit and tan, and like a war criminal living without fear of extradition in a sunny South American resort city seemed to take a smug delight in his surroundings.

"So you're a doctor," I observed skeptically.

"Mustard plasters and leeches," he confirmed with an apostolary upturning of his palms.

"What about 12 and 99? You any good at raising the dead?"

Blight shook his head and spoke deliberately. "Death is a lost cause. I don't have the patience for it. This is what martyrs and saints are for. Personally, I believe in preventive maintenance for the living."

"Whatever helps you sleep at night."

"I brought you here so that we might go over the game plan," Blight explained. "It's essential that we're on the same page with this. Arbegast is of monumental importance to the project. If anything were to happen to him. . . . "

"Arbegast is a murderer. He should be put down before he kills anyone else. One more death may not weigh heavily on your conscience, but it sure as hell isn't going to lighten the load on mine."

"I'm asking nicely, Mr. Flowers." Blight smiled severely. "Don't make me reconsider my Hippocratic oath. My bedside manner can be rather unpleasant when provoked."

"What are you gonna do, lose my chart?"

Blight studied me for a moment, his blue eyes glinting icily. "Did you hear the one about the guy who went in for a routine consult and died three weeks later choking on a chicken bone?"

"I must've missed that one," I said.

"He didn't take his doctor's advice seriously."

"Let me guess. He ate lunch and didn't wait thirty minutes before trying out the high dive."

"He was in the habit of biting off more than he could chew. If you get to Arbegast before we do, treat him as if your life depended on his well-being."

"What's so special about Arbegast, anyway?" I asked. "There are a dozen others just like him ambling around upstairs right now."

"Not just like him. Arbegast has something very dear to me and I want it back."

"You?" I replied incredulously. "He stole my car!"

Blight regarded me blankly.

"What about the fifty thousand dollars you guys promised me?" I asked. "If I bring him in alive, do I still get the money?"

"I don't see why not."

"Since we're pals now," I said, wiggling the radio transmitter looped around my ankle, "maybe you can help me get this thing off. I seem to have misplaced the key."

"And before I forget," said Blight, "I'm going to need the disk you took off Shackleman."

I was confused. Even with the pillowcase over my head, I had been able to identify my abductors by their scent. Proprietors of an odor as ripe and aggressive as a soft French cheese, clearly they were the ones who had ransacked my house a short time earlier. If the disk was so important, why had they left it behind? Apparently, my sense of smell was not the finely tuned instrument I thought. Maybe these were different thugs altogether. In any case, if Blight wanted the disk, then so did I.

"Disk?" I echoed dumbly.

Blight's fist flashed out of nowhere, connecting with the bone and soft tissue orbiting my left eye.

"Small, round, shiny," he informed me humorlessly. "About the size of the rotary saw blade I'm going to use to cut off your legs if you don't return it to me in twenty-four hours."

"Who are you really working for," I demanded to know. "CIA? NSA?"

"It's no secret, Mr. Flowers, that I'm with the AMA."

"Never heard of it."

"The American Medical Association. Who do you think the president turns to when he needs bypass surgery? The army, the navy. . . . The *Mafia*? They're all fine if you want an airfield bombed or a strike broken. But the man in the Oval Office turns to us if his pipes are clogged. Remember, Mr. Flowers, we determine who lives and who dies."

Blight left the room, the lights went out, and the pillowcase went back over my head as they dragged me naked from the Coliseum basement into the predawn light. For a moment, the uninvited darkness was a welcome reprieve. My eyes stung and the sound of the irregular footfall of my taciturn escorts slap-slapping against the cold concrete confounded my ears. Fortunately, I had already worked enough slack into the tape binding my wrists that it was only a matter of minutes before my hands were free and I was diapering myself with the pillowcase. Under the circumstances, it was the best I could do. As the sun came up and the sky began to lighten at the edges first, the way bruises do, I told myself that I had been through worse, checked to see that the pillowcase was firmly knotted at my hips and headed home.

Although I never stopped to look over my shoulder, I could feel the Coliseum standing out against the yellow gray sky behind me. Within its weary walls, a drama was unfolding with all the plot twists and betrayals, deceptions and epiphanies of good theater. It wasn't simply the oldest story ever told; it was the only story. What kept audiences coming back were the same archetypal constructs and astounding subplots that had compelled the critics to call it brilliant at times, predictable at others. Only the names had been changed. A roman à clef with monkeys. I had been them. Now they would be me. Bravo. Encore. Fade to black.

One of the things that makes Los Angeles great is the total and uncorrupted anonymity it affords weirdos. From the way I was attired, you would have thought I was a runaway coolie fleeing the tyranny of my imperialist overlords. Seven miles barefoot and half-naked over surface streets crowded with people on their way to work, and no one even seemed to notice me. For all they knew, I was just another disciple of some fringe cult awaiting the arrival of the mother ship. Point is, most Angelenos are oblivious to deviations from the norm, the norm itself being patently deviant. I was beginning to think that Arbegast's extended sojourn in the concrete jungle was more a testament to this urban phenomenon than a product of the ape's man-made cunning and instinctive ability to adapt to his surroundings. Who was going to notice a wild hair or two floating around in this eclectic soup du jour?

Duncan Arbegast, Sr. was everything you'd expect of a billionaire business tycoon: direct, well-spoken, the sort of man whose own shadow won't make a move without first consulting him. Like so many of the great American entrepreneurs before him, he embodied the very essence of inventiveness and determination. His profile was recognizable in the way of city skylines and dead presidents: eternal and monolithic. I could easily imagine his likeness, a portrait of intrepid willfulness, ousting Roosevelt from the sculpted peaks of Mount Rushmore without so much as a whisper of dissent from those observant enough to notice the change. Every gesture, every blink, every inflection was weighted with understanding and purpose. Of course he was wealthy and privileged and accustomed to calling the shots, but there was more to the immaculately well-preserved septuagenarian than antebellum entitlement and birthright. Like gravity, the force of his will extended well beyond his immediate vicinity. I could feel his presence long before I first laid eyes on him standing amidst the scattered contents of my living room. There was also the fact that a Mercedes limousine bearing the Arbegast Pharmaceuticals corporate seal had been parked in front of my house.

"Is this your wife?" Arbegast Sr. asked, his eyes fixed on the wedding picture of Janie and me Lorelei had commented on hours earlier.

The frame was cracked and the glass broken, a branched fracture looming over our hopeful faces like a lightning bolt. I felt nothing, not even a residual charge.

"Technically speaking," I answered, forgoing the usual battery of questions and threats I keep handy for intruders.

Men at Daddy Arbegast's income level do not occupy the same plane of existence as mortals. Doors and deadbolts are useless against them. Like beautiful women, they come and go as they please.

"No children?"

"We tried, but apparently my sperm forgot how to swim."

"You're wondering why I'm here," he said, politely steering the conversation away from the source of my shame.

"I have an idea." I hitched up the makeshift diaper with as much dignity as I could manage. "Give me a minute to change into something less humiliating, and we'll talk."

"By all means."

"Excuse the mess," I apologized, indicating the aftermath of the night's festivities with an expansive gesture. "I gave the housekeeper the week off."

When I returned to the living room, Daddy Arbegast was looking out the window through a fiery spray of magenta bougainvillea, which had jumped my werewolf neighbor's fence and given rise to a brilliant conflagration in my own yard. His expression had clouded over, making him look much older than before. It was unsettling to see the aging pharmaceuticals icon this way—his dull wet eyes and sagging neck muscles betraying the withered creature camouflaged beneath the crisp lines of his fine hand-stitched suit.

"How did you recognize me?" he asked.

"Shackleman gave me a photograph of you and your son."

"Shackleman was a brilliant scientist." He frowned thoughtfully. "I was sorry to learn of his death. In fact, the circumstances surrounding the unfortunate incident are what compelled me to come to you."

"I believe you have him confused with Dr. Janus. Shackleman was Janus's assistant."

"I don't pretend to have entirely eluded the effects of senility, Mr. Flowers. However, neither have my mental faculties abandoned me altogether. Shackleman was instrumental in getting IT off the ground. It was the procedure he pioneered—xenogenaltransmutation—that made IT possible."

Whatever the truth, the answers I was looking for were not going to be arrived at by waltzing with the old man. If, indeed, Shackleman was more deeply involved than I had previously realized, it stood to reason that the disk probably contained the sort of information I had been after since day one. No wonder Blight was so adamant about its return.

"When I said 'confused,' I didn't mean it like that."

"I'm not here to discuss semantics, Mr. Flowers. I want you to help me find my son. He may be a little high-strung, but he's no murderer."

"You mean the monkey?"

"Monkey is such an ugly designation." Daddy Arbegast frowned distastefully. "It makes it sound as if my son is a fugitive from the circus. But as I said, I'm not here to debate semantics. If you're comfortable with that term, then by all means . . . I want you to help me find my *monkey* son."

"Before I say what I'm about to say, remember I'm just throwing it out there to see if it sticks. I'm a detective—it's what I do. Nothing personal. Strictly business."

"Yes," Daddy Arbegast agreed cautiously. "Of course."

"How do you know that your son is really your son? You said yourself that he's no murderer."

"DNA analysis confirmed that the finger Mr. Cloud recovered in New Guinea belonged to Dunkie. Otherwise, I would have never paid him the million dollars."

"Let me guess; Acteon ran the test."

I could tell from the old man's expression that he had never considered the possibility that the million-dollar pinkie belonged to someone other than his crackpot son. Hope is funny like that. A guy like Daddy Arbegast with a team of six-figure advisors and medical experts at his disposal will forgo the usual channels of verification when it comes to mending his broken heart.

"Before he died," I continued, "Shackleman told me that your son wasn't really your son."

Daddy Arbegast appraised me calmly. "If he's not my son, then who is he?"

"I've been asking myself the same question."

"Why would Acteon lie?" he asked, a note of vulnerability working its way into his voice.

"A name like Arbegast is as untouchable an institution as the pope. Maybe Janus was banking on the power of your influence should anything go wrong. Sir, you have to admit that your name carries a certain degree of diplomatic immunity. If you'll pardon me for saying so, there are not a lot of men out there who have the balls to lock horns with you."

Daddy Arbegast absorbed what I said with an expression as immune to calamitous tidings as he was innately conscious of its effect on his shareholders.

"I want you to find my son and bring him to me," he said forcefully. "I'll pay you $250,000. Half now, half when your work is done. In spite of how you may feel about all of this, he's still the bearer of my bloodline. I am much too old to start another family. Without him, everything I am and ever was will die with me."

I resisted the urge to throw my arms around the old man and plant one on his lips. A quarter of a million dollars might just be enough to get Mr. Wonderful off my back for good. At the very least it would bankroll a life and a new identity in some out-of-the-way island paradise where I could wile away the breezy afternoons cracking crabs and drinking myself silly on coconut rum. Blight and Acteon could take their fifty grand and go fuck themselves. In the interest of keeping my extremities intact, I would return their disk—that is, after I took a peek at what was on it.

"Why me?" I asked, playing it cool. "Why not the police? A man with your connections could get just about anyone he wanted."

"Scandal, Mr. Flowers," Daddy Arbegast replied succinctly. "My name, my company can't afford one."

"Let's just say for argument's sake that the individual you want me to help you find is your son? What then? He's killed as many as three men depending on how you slice it. Who's to say you wouldn't be next? What if you get him home and he buries a cleaver in your skull? How will I collect the balance?"

"So far my son has had two opportunities that I know of to do away with you, and you're still breathing. Don't you find this a little odd for such a cold-blooded murderer?"

Daddy Arbegast had a point. On two separate occasions, chimp Arbegast had had me at his mercy. Why, exactly, he had failed to take advantage of either situation had been a source of puzzlement and misgiving since he had spared my life in the Enchanted Forest. For the time being, however, I had decided to forgo deeper inquiry rather than muddying the waters any further with questions I could not possibly answer given the limited facts at my disposal.

"What are you driving at?" I asked.

"The gun Shackleman was carrying when my son ran him over. . . . He intended to kill you with it."

"How did you know Shackleman was carrying a gun?"

Daddy Arbegast regarded me impatiently. "How I know is not important. The point is, my son saved your life."

"Shackleman was meeting with me to discuss the finer points of the IT Project. I sincerely doubt that he intended to kill me."

"Shackleman was preparing to divulge company secrets. From what I understand, the information he was in possession of would have destroyed Acteon. Only *they* got to him first."

"Why would Shackleman want to destroy the company he helped build?"

"A schism. The forces that be at Acteon were divided as how to best use IT. Shackleman represented a resolute, but rapidly diminishing, faction. That's all I know."

"These are the people you trusted with your son's DNA?"

"As you are no doubt aware, my son and I did not exactly see eye to eye on certain matters. Acteon had agreed to adjust his cognitive processes so that he would be more receptive to corporate life. It was the only way."

"Let me get this straight. You were having your son brain-washed so that he wouldn't object to taking over the family business. You were going to let a monkey run a multibillion-dollar empire? I'm sorry, but—"

Daddy Arbegast cut me off me with a stern look.

"My intentions are not at issue. Will you help me find my son, or not?"

"You've got a deal," I said, leaving Daddy Arbegast standing alone in the grim light. "But there's something I'd like you to take a look at."

I returned from my office with the bottle of brown pills I had recovered from Shackleman's pocket. I had also retrieved the last of the pseuprezdid pills the army had given me. For more than a year, it had occupied a space next to Janie's Monistat on the top shelf of the medicine cabinet in the master bathroom. I had hung on to it as a sort of morbid keepsake the way soldiers often do with bullets recovered from wounds they have sustained in battle. I slept a little better at night knowing the little blue pill was there. But first things first. Daddy Arbegast uncapped Shackleman's prescription bottle and examined the contents.

"Some sort of vitamin?" he said, shaking one of the brown pills into his palm and studying it in the light. "Could be just about anything—aspirin, even. The brown coating is just a buffer."

"It's important that I know for sure."

"I can run it through the lab if you like."

"Could you check out this one, too?" I asked, setting the little blue pill in his palm alongside the brown one.

Daddy Arbegast fished a pair of reading glasses from his coat pocket. "Little devil," he remarked, prodding the pseuprezdid with his fingertip. "I can tell you this, it's not one of ours. There's no marking. . . . A generic, maybe."

"The army calls it 'pseuprezdid.' "

He produced a silk handkerchief from his shirt pocket and knotted both pills in the center of it. "I'll have the lab run a chemical analysis. I can have the results for you in forty-eight hours."

Daddy Arbegast turned to leave, the rough parchment hue of his skin nowhere nearly as vital as the sheer silk blend of his suit.

"One more thing," I said. "Do you have any idea why your son would want to save my life?"

"I have never understood my son," the old billionaire informed me abruptly. "But I love him just the same. It's the curse of being a parent. You'll know what I'm talking about when you have children of your own one day. And, by the way, try to keep your hands out of your pockets when discussing business. It makes you seem nervous and untrustworthy. Particularly with that shiner you're nursing."

I had reclaimed possession of the computer disk while Daddy Arbegast had waited in the living room for me to put on some pants. To my relief, it was still atop the pile of poker chips where I had left it before having been roused from my sleep by Blight's barefooted henchmen hours earlier. Throughout the duration of my conversation with the aged pharmaceuticals mogul, I had held onto the disk, anxiously circumnavigating its smooth perimeter and turning it over and over in my pocket like a Twelve-Step recoveree warding off the grip of temptation. For the time being, I could put aside the image of myself as a double amputee parked in a wheelchair on some street corner begging for spare change while my legs rotted in the local landfill. It was in a semi-celebratory mood that I prepared an ice pack for my blackened left eye and chauffeured myself to the nearest pay phone to give Lorelei a call. Who better, I figured, than she, a cutting-edge scientist with a wealth of technological resources at her disposal, to help me access the contents of the disk.

"I'm sure we can figure something out," she affirmed excitedly. "Meet me at the critical-care ward in, say, an hour?"

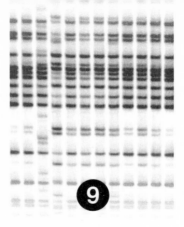

9

THE CRITICAL-CARE WARD AT THE UCLA MEDICAL CENTER was like a vision of utopia gone terribly awry. In room after room, men and women depended on machines to keep them alive. These machines breathed for them, ate for them, purified their blood, regulated their vital signs—a bleeping, wheezing, clacking array of automated life-support as vigilant as it was dispassionate. Just because I was unable to feel, did not mean that I was without a sense of irony. Like the machines, I was capable of analyzing and responding to the complex patterns of human need and maintenance, but my bedside manner remained fixed, clinical, mechanically efficient. I passed at least a half-dozen rooms on the way to see Lorelei—each stage to that woefully familiar vignette of the powerfully ill and the family death vigil—and could only liken the experience to any number of weekly televised hospital dramas peopled by actors struggling mightily with ethical correctness and a gratuitous smattering of medical terminology. I was unmoved, my eyes searching out a vending machine where I might get my hands on a Snicker's.

Although I may not have been a kindred spirit to the ways of pity and compassion it did not mean that I was unable to fake it. I hadn't always been this way. I was as acutely aware, perhaps more so, of the visual markers of despair than the most practiced associates of the terminally ill. Before entering Marcel's room, I summoned a look of intense concern and guarded optimism. Lorelei was not the kind of girl who would become romantically involved with a sociopath. It was essential that I appear troubled. Achieving the desired effect was a snap. I simply imagined that I had been diagnosed with a terminal disease. For centuries, great actors had relied on similar techniques to simulate emotion.

Even the antiseptic air of the critical-care ward was no match for the fragrant tiers of flowers brightening Marcel's room. No less than three dozen pricey floral arrangements, from Chianti-hued long-stemmed roses to stargazer lilies the diameter of dinner plates, surrounded the recovering chimp's bed. I was equal parts astonishment and envy, the aromatic outpouring of sentiment and well-wishing scarcely able to mask the savage odor of my unscrubbed hide. The media tumult surrounding the theft of Marcel's kidney had given way to a gentler climate of healing. Although surprised and curious at the apparent lack of interest in the watershed procedure, I was relieved by the absence of camera equipment and television news reporters. Lorelei was nowhere to be seen.

Marcel sat upright in bed contemplating Arbegast's donor profile where it lay spread over the lap table in front of him. Despite the IV supplying much-needed fluids to his depleted circulatory system, he appeared to be alert, well-groomed and, from what I could tell, totally engrossed with the material. This was not a crayon-eating simpleton whose multicolored teeth represented a truncated spectrum of understanding that cataloged stimuli according to taste and visual appeal. It was in his eyes—the rapt discernment of a theologian deciphering an ancient religious text squarely at odds with contemporary doctrine—a flicker of discovery and recognition. And something deeper. Apprehension, maybe; a tightness of focus intimating a layer of perception occupying a parallel though unilaterally distinct plane of understanding.

I felt as if I should say something, at least introduce myself, but the words simply would not come. What do you say to a chimpanzee pumping blood through a human kidney? Make small talk about the weather? Ask him about his prognosis? Tell him to lay off the hard stuff and drink eight glasses of water a day? Stay away from the woman you intend to seduce? I hadn't even thought to bring flowers. Confronted with a sudden and overwhelming verbal deficit, I decided to duck out before I was noticed and wait in the hall for Lorelei to return.

No sooner had I thrown it into reverse than Marcel's eyes stopped me in my tracks. He had set aside the donor profile and was looking at me: calm, inviting, seemingly poised to speak. With an eloquent flourish, he performed a complex series of hand gestures, fluidly articulating a thought I could only guess at.

"My name is Dutch," I responded haltingly, sounding out the words in a loud, oversimplified tone as if for a foreigner. "I am a friend of Lor-e-lei's."

I was met with more hand gestures, a warm vocalization of assent and welcome.

I studied Marcel's extended hand, trying to fathom the meaning behind the cryptic semaphore. Not wanting to appear stupid, I mirrored the gesture, extending my own hand in a similar fashion. I stood at the door to his room, my arm as rigid as a bowsprit, the ten or so feet bridging the expanse between us as foreboding and mysterious as the ocean feared by Christopher Columbus's contemporaries.

"Are you going to just stand there, or are you going to shake his hand?"

It was Lorelei. She had sneaked up on me, carrying a tray of food, her dark hair assembled in a loose ponytail that fanned out over the white linen collar of her blouse.

Of course, what an idiot I was! Marcel wanted to shake hands.

"I was just about to," I lied, my face hot with shame and embarrassment.

"Clear a spot, sweetie," Lorelei instructed Marcel as she crossed the room with the bounce and vigor of a high-school cheerleader. Her legs were tanned and athletic, the result of good breeding and a life of rugged fieldwork. Zaire, Madagascar, Borneo: these were not leisure destinations where one sat by the pool playing backgammon and sipping fruity cocktails named after legendary storm systems: *Typhoon, Hurricane, Monsoon.*

Without hesitation, Marcel assembled the contents of Arbegast's donor profile in a neat, out-of-the-way stack. He smiled beatifically at Lorelei as she set the tray of food in front of him and kissed him on the forehead.

"Ostrich herb meatloaf with rhinoceros beetle grubs and sautéed mixed baby squash," she announced proudly. "Your favorite. Go ahead, dig in. You need to get your strength back."

Marcel nodded appreciatively and did this little thing in the air with his hands: *Point-thumbslash-halfclap-point-waggle.* A sort of linguistic alchemy, spinning gestures into words.

"Marcel wants me to introduce the two of you before he eats," Lorelei translated. "He says you don't understand him, or he would have done the honors himself."

Marcel's hand was much softer than I had imagined it would be. Dry and smooth, his grip had a firmness and sincerity that was regularly absent between humans. It was more than simple formality; it was a mingling of flesh and chemistry and bioelectricity, a momentary bond between entities. I felt both reassured and wary, the recipient of an expert sales pitch.

"Marcel, this is Dutch," said Lorelei, speaking and signing simultaneously. "He's a friend of mine. Dutch, this is my sweetie, Marcel."

"Hi," I said, nodding and smiling stupidly.

Marcel smiled broadly. I was astounded at the whiteness and symmetry of his bared teeth.

"Dutch knows Kiki and Edgar," Lorelei explained. "Kiki let Dutch hold Edgar."

Marcel's expression was suddenly less inviting, a perceptual shift in the way he regarded me. He was slow to sign his response.

"Last night," Lorelei answered.

Marcel furrowed his brow, his hands flashing passionately over an invisible canvas hanging in the air. *Point-thisidiot-areyoukidding-thumbslash-waggle-hangten-scribble-thumbslash-Iwasonmydeathbed.*

"Yes," said Lorelei, apparently perturbed, "while you were still unconscious."

Thumbsdown-howcouldyou-figureight-scribble-scribble-thumbslash-whataboutme!

"I'm not going to do this with you right now, Marcel," Lorelei stated exasperatedly. "You're sick. You need to be resting. If you want to discuss it later in private when you're all better . . . "

Waggle-unh-unh-point-youmeanhim-thumbslash-curlicue-whataboutus-thumbslash-didyousleepwithhim?

"That's none of your business!" Lorelei replied hotly.

For a solid minute, the two of them engaged in a heated pantomime dispute while I buried my nose in various bouquets and pretended not to notice an occasional dirty look from Marcel. Although the exact text of their quarrel was shrouded in clandestine gesticulations, I was relatively certain of its essence. The idea that I was vying with a chimpanzee for the affection of a woman made my travails with Janie seem utterly mundane. Here was a love triangle more deeply rooted in perversion than mere infidelity could ever hope to mirror.

"Look," said Lorelei at the tail end of a particularly expressive hand-gesture diatribe, "I went to the trouble of bringing you your favorite dinner. Are you going to eat it or not?"

Marcel shot each of us a poison glance and snatched his fork and knife from the tray. He attacked the meatloaf with carefully measured strokes and fed a saucy pink morsel into his mouth.

"There," said Lorelei, fixing him with a stern look of disapproval. "I'm beginning to think that new kidney of yours is somehow affecting your brain. Jealousy, Marcel?" she continued. "You're becoming more human every day. I'm not sure I approve."

Marcel smirked resentfully before resuming his meal. His manual dexterity was nothing short of breathtaking, the flashing utensils baton-like in the hands of an accomplished maestro.

"Don't pay any attention to him," Lorelei explained as she escorted me from the room by the arm. "He's still a little stressed out from the surgery, that's all. He's usually not like this."

"It's only natural," I agreed, resisting the urge to fire Marcel a gloating look over my shoulder.

"What happened to you?" asked Lorelei, pausing in the hallway to examine the purplish bruise haloing my left eye.

"Let's just say the plot got a hell of a lot thicker after I dropped you off last night. At this point, a black eye is the least of my worries."

Lorelei and I talked in the medical-center cafeteria for close to an hour. As a precaution, I suggested that we sit with our backs to the wall. I told her what had happened to Shackleman in the lunchroom at Acteon, and how it had marked the first link in a chain of events leading up to his death by hit-and-run.

"Aren't you curious to know who was behind the wheel?" I asked.

"Arbegast?" guessed Lorelei.

"How did you know?"

"That's who all of this is about, isn't it?" she said, sniffing around my shirt collar for a taste of the animal scent she had urged me to preserve.

"You're not even a little surprised?" I asked, experiencing a sudden tightness in my groin.

Lorelei smiled faintly and shook her head.

"I let Marcel drive my car all the time. Unlike me, he doesn't seem to mind battling the traffic."

"What about the police? Aren't you worried about getting pulled over?"

"Not as long as he doesn't break the law. Marcel's really a very safe driver."

"But he's a chimp!"

"Oh, that," she reflected dismissively. "I don't even think anyone notices. We're talking about a city with a population in the millions. There's a lot worse on the road."

"I hope you're right," I said. "Arbegast was driving my car when he ran over Shackleman. I figure it's only a matter of time before the police find it abandoned somewhere, make the connection, and use it to hang a murder rap on me. I don't know if you're aware of my reputation, but it's not doing me any favors. People are counting on me to fuck up. It's who I am."

Lorelei's face was fair and open-minded. As far as I could tell, there wasn't an ounce of doubt anywhere in her. I felt as if I could tell her anything without fear of judgment. Not since I had unburdened myself in the confessional as a boy had I perceived such an implicit trust and aura of forgiving in another. I told her about all the men I had lost in Operation Slay Dracula and the many others I had lost since returning home. There were the men I had killed. The chimps I had failed to protect. I told her about leaving Janie alone for weeks at a time without explanation—the degrading fear that had forced me to launder my socks and underwear in melancholy filling-station restrooms, to live in the car for days on end, and occasionally contemplate suicide. I told her about the talk shows, the tabloid exposés, Spalding Penzler and Bobo the ape. I told her about my visits with Daddy Arbegast and Blight, and how I had fifteen hours, give or take, to return the disk before the good doctor sawed off my legs. I even told her about Little Saigon and stealing the van carrying Marcel's kidney—that it was necessary because I had been outwitted by a chimp who was always one step ahead of me and apparently that much more intelligent. I may not have told her everything, but I told her enough.

"I could have turned you in to the police that day," said Lorelei, her voice resonating with rich, supportive tones. "You couldn't have known that I would keep my promise. You risked your freedom to save Marcel. The guy you told me about, the one who fucks everything up. . . . That's who you *were*, not who you are."

"Oh, and I almost forgot," I said, pulling up my pant leg to reveal the radio transmitter bracketing my ankle. "I'm kind of engaged. It's not love exactly, but we're pretty serious."

Lorelei had an admirer in UCLA's Computer Science department who assured us he could access the disk. Kyle, a delayed pubescent in his mid-twenties, said it would take him roughly three hours to break the encryption code. Although it was obvious from his declarative tone that I was supposed to be amazed at how quickly he could hack his way through such a formidable barrier—a regular Joshua of cyberspace—I was too worried about my legs to gush convincingly. I was left with two choices.

Either I could wait and pace the campus like a caged animal, or I could have faith that everything was going to work out for the best and look to take control of my future.

I found Mr. Wonderful bellied up to the edge of the pool at the Beverly Hills Hotel, a sheen of sweat in his exact outline silhouetting the concrete beneath him. Aligned precisely with the sun, he lay perched atop his elbows like a marine iguana readying itself for a restorative plunge into the cool waters off the Galápagos. As I approached him from behind, my field of vision was prisoner to the deliberately careless positioning of his bathing suit, a scant bikini brief, the seat of which had withdrawn to form a lime green cataract between the twin knolls of his coconut-oiled buttocks. I wore my sunglasses to conceal my identity and moreover to circumvent any mention of my black eye. I didn't want him fawning over me like an overprotective mother in front of so many watchful eyes.

"At least tell me you're facing Mecca," I said. "I'd hate to think this is strictly a pleasure outing. What would Allah think of such willful self-indulgence?"

Mr. Wonderful rolled onto his side, shielded his eyes from the glare overhead, and spoke: "Better is the sinner who has thoughts of God, than the saint who has only the show of sanctity."

"I've got a proposition for you."

"Sounds yummy," he snarled coyly.

"How much would it cost me to get you off my back for good?"

"Off your back?" he echoed with a wounded look. "Who saved your life just the other day?"

"I may have found a way to get my hands on a fairly large sum of money. Nothing definite, but let's just say this deal pans out. . . . You could stop nickel-and-diming me, work on your tan, buy yourself a bathing suit that actually fits."

"And say good-bye just like that? What about the memories? How would I amuse myself?"

"How much? Fifty, seventy-five, a hundred grand? What's it going to take?"

"Even if I took the money and agreed to forget about you, Saddam would send another to take my place."

"Not if he thought I was dead."

Mr. Wonderful rolled completely onto his back, drew his knees upward toward his chest, and posed along the edge of the pool like a 1940s bathing beauty. He wore his hair down; its length and luster had been greatly enhanced by nearly a year of hormone therapy. Gradually he was becoming a woman. He dabbled in the water offhandedly, an absentminded smile elevating the corners of his mouth. "Go on."

"Sooner or later you're going to have to kill me. You know it. I know it. And then what? No more me. No more money for you. It's a lose-lose situation. Why not cash in now and at least have something to show for all of this?"

Mr. Wonderful scooped a handful of chlorinated water from the pool and drizzled it over his hairless chest as if performing an ancient purification ritual.

"Think about it," I continued. "You could finally afford your operation."

He studied me thoughtfully, a sated smile rippling across his lips.

"One hundred thousand dollars," he declared. "And we would need convincing proof that you were dead. Something you could not live without."

I had thought about taking Daddy Arbegast's money and simply disappearing. However, sooner or later, Saddam would track me down and the chase would begin again. I was sick of running. It was imperative that I find Arbegast and apprehend him. If I was to have a future, he was the key. That one chimpanzee could mean so much to so many. . . .

Lorelei's attempt to pin down what made Arbegast tick had yielded more of the same kind of circuitous facts and frayed loose ends as my own comprehensive inquiry. For every known chimp standard of behavior, there was an equally prominent corresponding human trait, a stark landscape of indistinct contrasts rendered entirely in grayscale. Where exactly Arbegast the chimp ended and Arbegast the human began was a mystery shrouded in their broadband similarity.

"This isn't exactly apples and oranges we're talking about," Lorelei had concluded. "More like oranges and tangerines."

It was like trying to get at the truth of a classified government document when everything but the conjunctions and articles had been omitted courtesy of a heavy-handed black-linologist. Lorelei's conversation with Marcel regarding his own opinions as to Arbegast's motives had produced similarly discouraging insights. Why, the beguiled chimp had wondered, would Arbegast act differently than any other "person" shown the world for the first time? No matter how Lorelei approached the question Marcel had repeatedly resorted to the same hand signal to drive home his point.

"He says he would look," Lorelei translated.

"For what?" I asked.

Lorelei shrugged. "For where bananas come from."

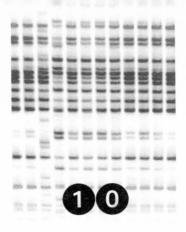

10

LUCK IS A CURIOUS THING. It pops up when you least expect it, and rarely ever when you're ready to take full advantage of it. In no particular hurry, I had stopped in at a convenience store on my way back to rendezvous with Lorelei at the medical center. I had eaten next to nothing in two days and was vaguely aware of a nagging emptiness in the pit of my stomach. I needed brain food, complex carbohydrates, branch-chain amino acids, dietary fiber. Something to get me going, sharpen my senses. Sustained energy. This was it—I was approaching the moment of truth. I had to be on top of my game. No empty calories. Fat-free, sugar-free: I could hear Janie drubbing out the green catchphrases like the feel-good lyrics of a Christian rock band. And she was probably right. I can't be sure why, but at that moment it struck me that Janie wasn't going to be there for me anymore. That I might die at any moment seemed as good a reason as any to start living my life. Although I was in no way convinced that the regenerative properties of Doritos, Hostess Sno-Balls, and a Coke would counteract the end result of my impending amputation, I was comforted by the fact that three dollars and change could still buy a few moments of baseline gratification. Saturated fats, a list of ingredients that read like the atmospheric profile of a hostile world. Glucose, sodium, trace elements. BHT to preserve freshness. I had reached a point in my life that the worse something was for me, the better it tasted. I wasn't exactly staring death in the eye, but there was a certain nobility, however marginal, in viewing the dissipated specter from askance. The point is, I wasn't hiding. It was a step in the right direction. *Carpe diem.*

Full of the spirit of rebellion, I propped myself against the fender of the rental car and savored the overinflated bag of cheese-flavored isoscelean snack treats and spongy pink spheroids. It was hot, and the liturgical drone of the rental car's overworked cooling fan mingled with the flow of foot traffic and street noises to invoke a state of blissful torpor. For a moment or two I was able to forget myself and the world around me, moving from the tortilla chips to the Sno-Balls without the slightest sense of urgency or angst. It was perhaps because I was so loosely tethered to reality that I observed Arbegast ambling purposefully past me, locked into a strange sort of rolling monkey-trot, and at first did not give the matter a second thought. He seemed to me no more out of place than if we had been smack in the center of the Gombe Chimpanzee Preserve. Had it not been for the purling lament of the pay phone toward which he was aimed arrow-straight, I might have simply watched him vanish from sight.

By the third or fourth ring, I had snapped out of it and was stalking after him, my heart racing. If I could somehow manage to subdue him, I could collect from Daddy Arbegast, pay off Mr. Wonderful, and right the sinking ship that was my life. Although he was no longer in possession of my .45, I was far from convinced that he was unarmed. I wouldn't have put it past Acteon's geneticists to have equipped him with a small kangarooish carryall, a mucous moistened transport sleeve as arcane as it was cutting edge. The automotive industry was a wellspring of such clever innovations. Why not the science of genetic engineering? If you could give a chimp a soul, then was a cup holder or a pouch in which to carry a concealed weapon so totally inconceivable? I resisted the urge to run, knowing full well that Arbegast could easily outpace me over just about any terrain. Lacking the speed or the stamina to match him physically, I would capitalize on the element of surprise. Sucking cheese flavoring and flecks of pink toasted coconut from my fingertips, I moved swiftly along the crowded sidewalk clutching the bottle of Coke in one hand like a billy club. Although the container was made of recyclable plastic, I figured that twenty fluid ounces of caffeinated soft drink would provide ample force to deliver a good whack over the back of the head and render Arbegast unconscious.

Whether it was because they were too self-involved or because of something fundamentally corrupt in their powers of perception—either of which could explain why the pay phone was left to ring unheeded—no one on the street seemed to notice the unusual pedestrian in their midst. They, like Arbegast, were totally oblivious of their surroundings. Exactly where he had come from was a question inversely proportionate in its unanswerable mystery to the unmistakable knowledge of where he was going. *Rrring-rrring!* His sudden prominence offered no explanation, nor was there any discernible reason as far as I could tell to attempt to make sense of it. He simply was. No more or less extraordinary than any of them, an undisclosed quotient in a set of variables as complex and moot as the equation his existence begged. He never once broke stride, nor so much as made the slightest deviation from his beeline toward the pay phone, a fountain of sound particles and crystalline promise gurgling at the edge of a dream. By the time Arbegast had picked up the receiver, the flow had been shut off, the lingering vibrations decelerating at cycles beyond the range of what even animals could hear. The line was dead. There was no one there.

Alone again.

I suddenly understood what Marcel had meant by "where bananas come from."

I was almost sad for Arbegast—each ring he couldn't get to, a missed call from God. He was a danger to anyone carrying a cell phone. I could see it in his posture, the abject frustration and snowballing degeneration of faith. Rejection hung over him like a storm cloud as he gazed searchingly at the mute pay phone, a hairy-backed manifestation of a pyschopath's id. It was only a matter of time before his frustration turned to murderous rage. Now was the perfect time to strike. Down and wondering why, he wouldn't know what hit him.

Maneuvering deftly along the busy sidewalk, I accelerated toward the pay phone. Within a few yards of where Arebegast stood, I clutched the Coke bottle by the neck and targeted the base of his skull. I closed the gap between us and swung the makeshift club in a savage downward arc. How easily the old violence reasserted itself. Arbegast sidestepped the intended blow as if he had seen it coming. The force of my momentum carried me through the swing and into the pay phone, knocking the wind out of me. The bottle of Coke jettisoned into the concrete and rolled toward the gutter, hissing and spitting like a stepped-on mamba. Surprise quickly turned to recognition as Arbegast pieced together what had happened from the sensory details of my failed sneak attack: the visceral intake of air, commotion in my posture and shrewd counterstare. He appraised me strangely with something like hurt in his eyes, the same searching look with which he had regarded the pay phone moments earlier, the knothole scar not nearly as tightly wound as in our previous encounters. His expression seemed to be predicated on a dogma of whys. Desperate, I launched myself at him—head up, shoulders squared—a textbook tackle but for one thing: I was still in midair and Arbegast was bounding across the street in loping quadrupedal strides, the screech of tires and blast of horns heralding his escape. Scrambling to my feet, I ran after him, the stopped traffic already resuming its two-way torrent. Arbegast paused at the opposite shore where he crouched atop the hood of a black SUV like the ritual ornamentation of a barbarian war wagon. When he saw that I had not given up the chase, he pumped his fist in the air and executed a perfect backflip before leaping to the ground and bolting down the tree-lined avenue of a residential neighborhood very much like my own.

By the time I made it across the street—the grim recollection of Shackleman's grisly demise in no uncertain terms responsible for my tentative advance through that treacherous crosscurrent of Detroit steel—Arbegast was nowhere to be seen. On either side of the avenue arose the walls of a gated community, the modern era's answer to the fortress cities of the Middle Ages.

After ten minutes of looking under cars and beating bushes, I was ready to give up. Suddenly Arbegast emerged from behind a hedge of mock orange thronged with honeybees and easily vanished over the wall, seven vertical feet of smooth stucco frescoed with leafy tendrils of creeping fig. It was an impressive feat of agility poorly matched by my own feeble attempt to scale the exclusionary barrier. With a Herculean effort, I managed to haul myself over the top and drop down to the other side.

Instantly, I recognized the place but from where and when was another matter altogether. A déjà vu or a dream, maybe. It was like standing at the epicenter of a psychic ripple, waves of sensory information radiating outward from where I had plunked down at the edge of the otherworldly oasis before doubling back and washing over me with the force of a whiplash. This was a full-size version of the celestial utopia Wright 351 had modeled on the floor of the STF. It was all here: the geodesic domes, tubular passageways, helical spires, and honeycomb ramparts. An eerie coincidence, but every bit as intricate and richly conceived. The architecture was beautifully efficient and organized around an aesthetic principle as pure and unfettered by nonessentials as the science of mathematics. There were none of the gingerbready superfluities that realtors hail and drive painting contractors nuts. Every detail was utilitarian and to the point. Upon closer inspection, even the seemingly undisciplined proliferation of plants and trees enjoyed an organic symbiosis with the inspired edifices. A striking array of species both indigenous and introduced, merged with the structures in such a way that it was often difficult to tell where the construction ended and living matter began. In this respect, the development evoked many of the residences in my own neighborhood, more or less conventionally wrought dwellings relinquished to the whim of Mother Nature until such a point as one aspect was indistinguishable from the next. Many of the larger tree branches supported second stories. Others doubled as makeshift stairways, tiered ascents jacketed with nonslip bark, leafy handrails in accordance with building safety codes. None of the windows had glass; the sills exhibited signs of entry even at heights that would have given a tightrope walker pause. Despite the development's naturalistic charm, I couldn't imagine there being a long list of interested buyers. Acrophobics need not apply. Who exactly would want to live in such a place was beyond me.

Arbegast emerged from a thicket of hibiscus, paused long enough to flash me a scornful look, bounded over a succession of unkempt hedges with the ease of an Olympic high-hurdler, and broke into a full-tilt monkey-gallop across a field of variegated mondo grass. I sprinted after him, arms pumping, legs wheeling wildly over the uncultivated terrain toward the heart of the development. Despite the many aches and pains I had accrued over the course of the previous few days—from the beating I'd suffered at the hands of the Siamese twins to Ehrlich's cannon-shot tackle from the mouth of the sewer pipe— I actually managed to gain ground on the juggernaut ape. I hadn't felt this alive since high school. The physical discord that had overshadowed my adulthood gave way to the mighty rhythms of youth. My heart and lungs swelled with renewed vitality. Somehow, I managed to accelerate, closing the gap between us even further. I was a bloodthirsty cheetah swiping at the hindquarters of a terrified gazelle! I was a gust of wind, a flash of light, a blur of superoxygenated hemoglobin and fast-twitch muscle fiber eating up the track! I was man, a miracle of body and intellect! I was . . . I was . . . *Falling!* Going over the last of the unkempt hedges I had snagged my toe and was spun into a hell-bent cartwheel that carried me into a field of sawgrass. I half-bounced, half-skidded to a stop, jamming both my wrists and streaking my knees green with chlorophyll. From all fours, I watched as Arbegast crossed a narrow strip of asphalt (as far as I could tell it was the only road in the entire development) and charged onto a ramp winding up and around a conical dwelling. Resembling a three-story stucco tepee, the peculiar habitation was largely overgrown with various species of vine. About halfway up and one revolution later, Arbegast ducked into a circular opening and disappeared from sight.

Battered, bruised, and ruthlessly determined, I picked myself up, brushed myself off and walked the remaining hundred or so feet to the base of the tepee. Fortunately, entry didn't figure to be a problem. From what I had seen of the development so far, the residents were not overly fond of doors and windows. Apparently, the wall enclosing the community was seen as sufficient a deterrent to would-be thieves as they would ever need. What naïveté. What poor understanding of human nature. No sooner had I started up the winding ramp than my ascent was cut short by a gruff voice behind me.

"FREEZE!"

I slowly turned to find a uniformed rent-a-cop looking at me down the barrel of a large-bore automatic he had no doubt selected on the basis of its kill rating as reviewed in *Guns & Ammo*.

"Hands over your head where I can see them!" he barked.

I promptly obeyed, noticing the familiar epithet tattooed across the rent-a-cop's knuckles. FUCK YOU. There was no mistaking the razed scalp and pinched face—the air of intolerance that hung over him like the murmurs of unilateral dissent at a Nazi pep rally. It was the skinhead cabdriver I had stiffed in the underground parking garage. The last time I had seen him, he was being hauled away by the police. We exchanged a look of recognition that bordered on the surreal. For once in my life, why couldn't I be the beneficiary of the karmic circle espoused by Eastern spiritualists? Sure, I had made mistakes. We all do. But I wasn't such a bad guy. What was next? Would I awaken one morning to find myself fitted with ears like an ass? Maybe my indolence was a blessing in disguise. Imagine how my children would have turned out had I been capable of fathering offspring. Maybe Daddy Arbegast wasn't doing so badly after all.

"Don't I know you?" asked the now-skinhead rent-a-cop, a sinister, self-indulgent smile hovering just above the barrel of his gun. There was a vengeful glint in his small, ignominious eyes. "Because there's something about you."

"You ever watch any adult films?" I replied lamely.

"All right, you smart-ass son of a bitch. Get your ass away from the house. Slowly. Keep your hands where I can see them. That's it. Come to Papa."

He clicked off the safety and motioned me toward the electric patrol cart he had used to surprise me. His skin was even rawer than I remembered, a deep crimson blush offset by the loose gray collar of his uniform, the shoulders of which were adorned with meaningless insignia resembling the cross-elliptical orbits of electrons.

"Turn around and spread 'em!" he shouted, his chest swelling with his newly acquired authority. "Fingers laced behind your head."

Again, I obeyed. I wasn't about to get shot by someone who couldn't carry Arbegast's jock no less remember the guy who had gotten him arrested two days ago. He kicked my legs farther apart and butted the gun's muzzle up against the base of my skull.

"Empty your pockets."

I turned my pockets inside out and jangled the keys to the rental car in the air.

"That's it, car keys?" he said, his mouth twisted into a disappointed grimace. "What about some identification?"

"My wallet was stolen," I explained uselessly.

"Turn around. If this was Bosnia, they'd cap you right here for not carrying ID." He leveled the gun at my face, and with his free hand unclipped his walkie-talkie from his belt. "What's your name?"

"Is this really necessary? I'm here visiting a friend, that's all."

"Your name, asshole! And you better not be lying."

"Dutch Flowers."

Invariably, the utterance of my name elicits a broad spectrum of reactions depending on who's asking. This time it was as if I had hit upon a secret password. The skinhead rent-a-cop released the talk button and returned the walkie-talkie to his belt.

"I thought I recognized you," he remarked shrewdly, his eyes twinkling like bits of shattered glass. "I heard about you on the news. What they did to you was totally fucked up. Hung you out to dry like that. And for what—killing a bunch of camel jockeys? Ask me, you were doing the world a favor. Sort of thing that makes guys like Kaczynski and McVeigh do what they do—ya know what I mean?"

Reluctantly, I offered a nod of affirmation.

So it was even worse than I had imagined. The skinhead rent-a-cop recognized me all right, but not from the underground parking garage. For a long time I had been aware that a fairly large number of rabid flag-wavers supported my tribulations in the Gulf. Believing that the only good Iraqi was a dead Iraqi, their patriotic fervor was as misguided as it was frightening. Until now, I had never actually come face-to-face with any of them. Suddenly I understood why cult leaders often chose to isolate themselves from their gushing devotees.

"Would you mind putting that thing away?" I asked. "My health insurance doesn't cover gunshot wounds."

He smirked and lowered the gun. "It's an honor to meet you, sir. Ask me, you're a real hero."

Sensing an opportunity to build some personal rapport—a comrades-in-arms sort of thing—I snapped off a crisp salute.

"Maybe you can help me? I lied when I told you I was here to visit a friend. I'm not. I'm here on a matter of national security." I felt ridiculous calling on the hackneyed phrase, but what choice did I have? Arbegast and a new life awaited me just up the winding ramp.

"Wish I could help you out, but my orders are clear. You understand."

"Look, I don't have time to explain, but there's a killer in there. Others will die if I don't do something to stop him."

"Killer, sir? I don't think so. These are good folks that live here." He smiled officiously, the old suspicion returning to his face.

"I'm walking up that ramp right now," I declared sternly. "Go ahead and shoot me if you have to."

I had taken no more than two steps when I heard him chamber a round. I turned to find myself the victim of an image relapse. Once again I was scum. I had no doubt that he would shoot me in the back. I knew the look. It was the same haunting lack of compassion pseuprezdid had etched in my own eyes.

His mercenary smile gone, he said, "Sir, I'm going to have to ask you to leave the premises."

"Stop calling me sir, you fucked-up little puke!"

In the ten minutes that I had been inside the development, I hadn't seen a living soul other than Arbegast and this jerk. The lone street was empty. The tire swings suspended in nearly every yard dangled like zeros, the only values in an equation that didn't add up. Still, I had a funny feeling that I was being watched from the windows high among the tree branches as the skinhead rent-a-cop ushered me from the development. I walked while he rode behind me, the eco-friendly whir of the electric patrol cart humming like contented insects. At the main gate—a solid wood rectangle on rollers not quite so impregnable as the one at Saddam's compound at Al Qa'im—he keyed in the access code and promised to "do what needed to be done" if he ever saw me come over the wall again. A delivery truck advertising YOU'LL FIND THE BEST DEALS ON HOME THEATER SYSTEMS AT THE ENTERTAINMENT WAREHOUSE passed me on the way out. So I wasn't the only one looking forward to the hours of darkness that make up television's "can't-miss" prime time.

APOTHEOSIS

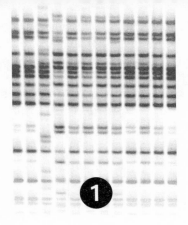

1

LORELEI WAS PEERING OVER THE SHOULDER OF KYLE the computer geek when I returned to the Computer Science lab. Standing over six feet tall, Belsen-lean, and with a stiff angular posture, the skilled hacker reminded me of a praying mantis as he plunked away at the computer terminal with his long hooked digits.

"You can put your fingers to rest," I announced semitriumphantly. "I found Arbegast. I'm going back when it's dark to get him."

"That's fantastic," said Lorelei, her tone conveying an unspoken reserve. "But how?"

"It was pure dumb luck. If it wasn't for this bastard skinhead I ran into, I'd have him right now and I could put all of this behind me."

Kyle momentarily abandoned his glissading alphanumeric scales and turned an inquisitive eye on Lorelei. Something in their expressions wasn't right.

"Dutch," said Lorelei, "Kyle managed to access some of the disk's video files while you were gone." She paused, an uneasy smile upsetting the balance of her face. "I think you should really see this for yourself."

Like any home movie, the video portion of the disk was a choppy cinema of events and images that relied more on a loose chronology to hold the story line together than professional editing techniques. The first segment featured a lab-coated and smiling Shackleman looking not nearly so frayed at the edges cradling a swaddled chimp infant in his arms. A good-looking redheaded woman also wearing a lab coat stood at his side playing with the chimp newborn and making baby talk. After a moment, the redhead faced the camera, said, "Okay, we're ready" and positioned herself alongside Shackleman, her arm coiled snugly about his waist. Shackleman straightened up, gave the woman an affectionate peck on the cheek and addressed the camera:

As you are no doubt painfully aware by now—having invested your children's college fund and then some in IT—I am Dr. Richard Shackleman and this is my wife, Dr. Sarah Brandreth-Shackleman. (smile, smile) *And this little guy I'm holding is the breakthrough we've been promising you for the past several years* (close-up of the chimp newborn). *Ladies and gentlemen, we'd like you to meet Janus Brandreth-Shackleman, IT's promising firstborn.*

I was blown away. A shock wave of realizations raced outward from the core of my being, a storm surge of questions sweeping me off the foundation of everything I thought I knew. I was like one of the tropical islanders you read about who awakens the morning after a hurricane to find the family hut and the family along with it adrift in the commercial shipping lanes, land nowhere in sight.

But it didn't end there.

The next segment echoed the jubilant tone of the shareholders' address with Shackleman and wife celebrating Janus's first birthday. They and a group of other scientists were gathered around a table in the cafeteria where Shackleman had been scalded with soup en route to his hit-and-run. The group laughed and applauded heartily as the precocious chimp blew out his candle, a large white-and-blue-striped I, and expertly served himself a slice of cake.

In the third segment, Shackleman and Janus were sitting across from each other at one end of a white Formica table playing chess. Janus was clearly older than before. The reverent wonder in his face from the earlier segments had given way to a portentous seriousness. When Shackleman declared checkmate, Janus flew into a rage. He swept the chess pieces onto the floor and went tearing around the room knocking over chairs and smashing anything he could get his hands on. The segment ended with Janus in the middle of a sustained flurry of backflips as two hulking orderlies in white pants and tight white T-shirts moved in to subdue him. The walls in the background featured a gallery of blowups picturing Janus undertaking various endeavors: the young chimp examining a model of the atomic structure of a carbon molecule; the budding prodigy stroking the keys of a baby-grand piano; the junior chemist wearing safety goggles heating the contents of a test tube over a Bunsen burner, his primitive aversion to fire replaced with intellectual curiosity.

In the fourth and final segment of the first video file, calm had been restored and Shackleman was holding hands with Janus in front of an ominously familiar door. There was a pressurized gasp as the door swung open to reveal a room shrouded in darkness. Shackleman entered first and with some playful cajolery and a firm tug convinced Janus to follow him inside. A moment later, Shackleman emerged alone and the door sealed closed after him. This is where things got interesting. The segment cut to a view of the room on the other side of the door. There was a soft, ethereal flicker as of lightning dancing high above a skein of clouds followed by a sudden scattering of light. Darkness gave way to an accelerated dawn, the room brightening to reveal a garden in its infancy. At first Janus looked confused, the landscape in which he stood alone as foreboding and awe-inspiring as the skyline of Manhattan must have been to King Kong plucked fresh from the jungle. He looked around for Shackleman, the door through which he had entered, an escape. But there was nothing. The deception now made clear to him, he let out a defiant shriek, a chilling falsetto that I would hear on and off inside my head in the days and months and years that followed.

Kyle keyed in a different password and said, "This next one was a real bitch to crack."

"I think I'll go check on Marcel," said Lorelei. "One showing was enough."

As for what came next. . . . Let's just say that any suspicions I may have had regarding the contents of the disk were promptly laid to rest. I had expected evidence of an underground shadow agency whose clandestine nature and unorthodox protocol were surpassed only by its seeming implausibility. I had considered everything from a ring of chimps trained to be international jewel thieves to a squad of chimp mercenaries schooled in the art of war. I had been ready for just about anything, but not this, *never* this.

There was no staged encounter to ease you into the action— no giggling coeds, no pajama party, no monster-dicked pizza-delivery guy with a cheesy mustache and lines that would make an action hero blush. Wham, bam! and there it was—some of the raunchiest porn I've ever seen. It wasn't so much the content that spun me as it was the participants. Of course I was no new-comer to the idea of humans getting it on with various animal species. However, in my limited understanding, the animal por-tion of the equation was limited to domesticated stock: dogs, sheep, miscellaneous equines as recommended by Dr. Ngong, and an occasional boa constrictor. But chimpanzees! This was the stuff of lurid sexually-charged creation myths, men copu-lating with their quasi-human cousins in the jungle bordellos of prehistory. Taboo of taboos. The very closeness of our two species only magnified the disparity between us. The female chimp on the video was not one of your standard farm favorites—sexual props and warm wet stand-ins scarcely more involved in the actual act than dildos and porta-pussies. She and her human partner, a man whose identity was guarded by the fact that his head existed exclusively outside the frame of the video, shared an intimacy and familiarity with one another's bodies that could not be denied. Although aggressive and rough and relentless, there was nothing in their lovemaking that a healthy libido and an active imagination could not account for. Except, of course that she was a chimp and that her co-star with the narrow white hairless ass was a human. At least the guy was getting some, which was more than I could say for myself. Of course I was curious about his identity. Who wouldn't have been? However, I was even more eager to strike all record of the video from my mind, my experience with it having generated equal parts arousal and shame.

Despite Kyle's reassurance that he could decrypt the other files, I had seen enough. Although the Shackleman I knew—edgy, wan, scornful—was a far cry from the charming married man captured on film, it was impossible to overlook his greater involvement with IT than had been implied from the onset. Clearly, he and Janus had, at one time, been close enough for Shackleman to name the project's first successful offspring after the mysterious recluse. I believed that if I could convince Janus to come clean about the schism between the two of them, I could begin to unravel the truth about Arbegast. Shackleman's "circumstantial" death was just the sort of thing to get the good doctor talking. The word of Dutch Flowers may not have counted for much, but an anonymous tip from a concerned party was enough to get the police thinking about possible motives in the hit-and-run death of a respected geneticist caught up in the middle of a corporate feud. So far, eyewitness testimony had yielded only a vague description of the vehicle suspected in connection with the hit-and-run. Miraculously, no one, including Blight, had put it together. I was still clinging to the slim hope that somehow I would avoid prosecution for vehicular homicide. Until then, Shackleman's death was the only real leverage I had. Sometimes you have to play with fire when it's the only way to keep the trail warm. Besides, the clock was ticking on my legs, and every moment I kept Blight waiting for the disk was a moment in which I pictured myself, thighs terminating in itchy twisted stumps, knuckling my way around a congested intersection lashed to a homemade skateboard.

Finding Arbegast was no longer a problem. Call it a hunch, but I had gotten the distinct impression during my initial visit to the development that the deranged chimp was planning on staying put as long as he was welcome and the undesirables—me—remained outside the wall. When the time was right, I would go in and get him. I could then collect my reward money from Daddy Arbegast and start my life over again.

• • •

Lepke had permanently replaced Shackleman as Janus's personal assistant. He was humming to himself and windexing the glass over the ADAPTABILITY IS A VIRTUE print when I entered the reception area. His skin had the same wet rubbery look as the lungfish struggling to find its way among the terrestrials, his mouth rippling with muted song like an enormous gill slit.

"Moving up in the world," I observed glibly.

Startled, Lepke nearly knocked the print from the wall.

"I thought Dr. Janus fired you," he said, putting down the bottle of Windex and hanging the rag over the spray nozzle.

"I need to talk to him."

"He's with somebody right now."

"Then I'll wait."

"He could be a long time," Lepke explained nervously. "Maybe it would be better if you came back later. I can schedule you an appointment."

"I'm not going anywhere until I see him."

"What happened to your eye?" Lepke asked. "You look terrible."

We were interrupted by the grating of stone against stone as the door to Janus's office opened. Blight emerged cursing to himself and breathing with apparent difficulty. He was pale and beaded with sweat.

"Why don't you ask him?" I suggested bitterly.

Before Blight could respond, he clutched his chest and staggered forward. With his other hand he supported himself on the edge of Lepke's desk, his face knotted in pain.

"Call 911!" I instructed Lepke, ducking under Blight's arm and supporting him across my shoulders. "I think he's having a heart attack."

"I'll be fine," Blight answered gruffly, shrugging me off. "I just need somewhere to sit down."

Lepke wheeled his chair around from behind the desk and Blight collapsed into it.

"Let me call a doctor," I said. "You don't look so hot."

"The disk," said Blight. "I assume you have it, or you wouldn't be here."

Already the color was returning to his face, the episode

apparently passed. Once again, he was a healthy shade of bastard. I removed the monkey-porn disk from my pocket and handed it to him.

"A man with a ticker like yours ought to watch the animal pleasures," I said with a wink. "You wouldn't want to miss the wedding night."

Conditions in Janus's office had worsened since my last visit. In many places, the water was ankle deep. It was like standing in an Amazonian floodplain. What was normally a terrestrial habitat had given way to a host of slow-blinking amphibians eyeing me from just beneath the surface. As I moved toward the skull monolith, creatures unsettled by my approach splashed into the water at my feet. Next time I would secure rubber bands around my ankles so that nothing could crawl up my pant legs. Insect repellent was also a good idea.

"Poor Shackleman," Janus lamented, his voice filling the grotto like a grieving note from a pipe organ. "He and I were rather close not so long ago."

"Who would have guessed?"

"I'm curious," said Janus. "Did Mr. Blight say anything to you on his way out?"

"I thought he was going to drop dead," I explained. "I nearly had to call him an ambulance."

"Mr. Blight's not well, I'm afraid."

"Something tells me that he may be the one responsible for Shackleman's death."

"I wouldn't be at all surprised," Janus responded dryly, his tone devoid of its usual irony.

"I can't imagine that sort of publicity would have a positive effect on your work here."

Janus turned it over in his mind.

"Yes, Mr. Flowers," he replied grimly, "I tend to agree with you."

"Then let me help. Tell me what Blight wants."

"It was never supposed to be this way. What we do here doesn't come without a steep price tag. Good intentions simply do not pay the bills."

"This whole business of farming out top-notch guinea pigs—wasn't that supposed to pay the bills?"

"It wasn't nearly enough. On top of which, it was wrong. These are highly intelligent creatures. To exploit them for money is not only criminal, it is unethical. I see things now in a way once inconceivable to me."

"A conscience is a bitch, huh, Doc?"

Janus did not respond. I could see his silhouette hunkered in the filigree shadow of an oleander very near the skull monolith. He was motionless.

"Did you hear me, Doc? I said, a conscience is a bitch."

Again, no answer. It was time that I confront Janus face-to-face. No more hiding in the shadows. It is one thing to disregard a faceless plea for answers; it is entirely another to look a man in the eye and tell him to go fuck himself.

"At least tell me who 131 really is," I said, moving as silently as I was able toward Janus's position. "What's the harm?"

Despite my efforts at stealth, he was gone when I finally arrived at the skull monolith, banana peels strewn about the steps at its base like slaughtered asterisks.

To my surprise, the brooding stone colossus was much as I had first imagined although considerably larger and apparently more involved. Jacketed with tangles of wild vegetation, it was a wonder I had been able to make it out at all. Only its enormity had allowed me to see it from a distance. Standing over ten feet tall, only the middle third of it was exposed to view. Curious about the other two-thirds, I mounted the steps and began to strip away the shaggy growth. No sooner had I begun the arduous task than a downpour thundered through the canopy overhead, soaking me to the bone—an unfavorable omen, if you believe in that sort of thing.

In a matter of minutes, I had uncovered more than enough to make me forget Janus. The rain let up and I could see that the steps I was standing on were not actually steps, per se. They were books, gigantic Gutenbergian tomes stacked atop one another so that a throne of sorts was the end result. Seated atop the throne of books was none other than a massive likeness of the chimp from the monkey bronze Janie had given me on our tenth wedding anniversary, the one Mr. Wonderful had stolen. There he sat in wracked contemplation, as if posed by Rodin himself, his deeply furrowed brow a Nazca relief of mystery and wonder, chin in one hand, the skull of Charles Darwin balanced in the other. It was this, a glib homage to a man who had looked into the past and seen the future, that I had mistaken for some sort of pagan altar. Could I have been more wrong? Could I have been more right? When Janus's voice shattered the stillness I nearly wet myself. It was as if I had awakened the dead, completed the circle of an ancient rite.

"131 is not who you think. He is both a fool and a prophet," Janus chanted darkly, his voice carrying to the far reaches of the grotto and echoing back on itself. "You saw the disk. I believe you have a unique insight where he is concerned. Dig deeper. There are ships in the sky we cannot see for the clouds."

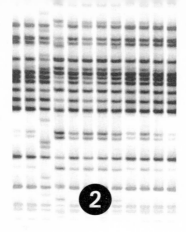

A UNIQUE INSIGHT? The monkey bronze colossus? Ships in the sky—
was this an obscure reference to pyramid-building extraterres-
trials? What did it all mean? No closer to reaching a quantifiable
sum, I had made a mantra of these and a hundred other questions on the ride back to my house. By the time I pulled into the
driveway, I was delirious with doubt.

For the first time in weeks, the answering machine was not
simply collecting dust. A high-fidelity voice from a place called
The Entertainment Warehouse congratulated me on my recent
purchase of a Sony Megascreen television. The voice wanted to
know if I was happy with the installation at 33 Via Encarnación,
and to please call if there was anything else they could do for
me. No name—a pronoun, that was all. I had already dismissed the courtesy call as a wrong number when the second
message arrived piggybacked onto the first. It was from the bank
that issued my credit card. They were calling to inform me that
a temporary hold had been placed on my Visa as a precaution
in response to a deviation from my usual charging patterns. To
have the hold lifted, it would be necessary for me to contact one
of their customer-service agents and verify that the charges at
The Entertainment Warehouse were not fraudulent. Before the
machine clicked off, I was thumbing through my Thomas Guide
for the whereabouts of 33 Via Encarnación, confirmation of
what I already knew. My wallet, my Visa, my ID, the delivery
truck: all of the pieces fit.

Turning up nothing in the printed version, I resorted to the Internet. In a matter of minutes, I had pinpointed the culprit's general location. Apparently 33 Via Encarnación hadn't been included in the Thomas Guide because it hadn't existed when the edition in question was printed. Wouldn't you know it, the bastard chimp was living it up at my expense. However, I was not as pissed off as you might think. His careless spending habits notwithstanding, it was safe to assume that he wasn't going anywhere for a while. I could take my time, stake him out, rein him in, and collect my quarter of a million from Daddy Arbegast when I had my answers.

My thoughts were interrupted when the telephone rang. It wasn't Lorelei, as I had hoped, but Daddy Arbegast.

"I have some information on those pills you asked me to have analyzed," he explained. "The brown one is called pyridium. It's primarily used to ease discomfort during urination. Doctors often prescribe it to people with bladder infections and sexually transmitted diseases."

"What about pseuprezdid?"

"Sugar and cornstarch with a splash of blue number 5."

"I don't get it."

"Pseuprezdid is a placebo."

I groped for a response, my mouth ajar.

"Mr. Flowers, are you there?"

Before I had answered the phone, I had spent an hour or so straightening up the house, followed by a long and much-needed shower. At the time, they had seemed like logical steps toward getting my life in order. Hygiene and organization mattered. After all, I was a human being. There were standards to uphold, models of behavior by which to abide. If there had ever been any doubt, Daddy Arbegast's call had promptly laid it to rest. After a long delay, I responded with a crude half-formed syllable, scarcely more than a deliberate release of epiglottal vibration and stomach gas.

"Absolutely sure," the old man confirmed, interpreting my unintelligible query with remarkable accuracy. "We burn-tested it. The gas chromatograph doesn't lie."

Burn-tested. I could see the innocuous tablet flare into nonexistence, a telltale spectrum of colors signaling the end of having someone other than myself to blame. As sure as the child Janie and I had been unable to conceive, compassion fatigue was on me. Maybe I had known all along. What better way for the military to circumvent moral accountability than to absolve their assassins of guilt by having them pop a pill? Take this—you won't feel a thing. And when the mission is done, you can stop taking the pills and go back to being your old self. Creative psychology. Problem was, the old self and the pseuprezdid self were interchangeable. It's one thing to introduce a man to his killer instinct; it's another altogether to wean him of it.

"Now, about my son," Daddy Arbegast continued hopefully. "Any news?"

"Not yet," I lied, less numbly than I would have liked.

So began a week of staking out Arbegast—one secret exposed, another in tow. I'm not sure why I had lied to the old man about the whereabouts of his forlorn progeny—there were a quarter of a million good reasons why I should have pointed him the way to 33 Via Encarnación—but I'd like to think that in some roundabout way my decision had to do with integrity, both personal and professional. The deal was that I deliver his son, right? After what the disk had shown me and Janus's ominous words, I was beginning to doubt that chimp Arbegast had any ties other than his name to the man whose fortune promised to set me free.

Shortly after the sun came up each day, Arbegast would scramble over the wall of the development and make his way into the adjacent business district. He seemed, if not to enjoy, then to take a strange interest in the succession of strip malls, clothing boutiques, chain coffeehouses, and bagel shops lining the banks of the creeping asphalt tributaries diverting the flow of traffic from the nearby freeways. He moved with the deliberate pace of an elderly man recently retired from the workforce, his face locked in unsure contemplation not of his surroundings, but of his place in them, his purpose. Shadowing him on foot, moving as he moved, seeing what he saw, I had begun to grasp what it all must have meant to him; the mystery and wonder, the duplicity and dread. There among the thriving commercial enterprise and oblivious soft-bodied creatures at home in the turbulent stream of culture and data, he searched for the stroke, the rhythm to stay afloat. Much like myself, it was evident that he felt betrayed by the system. At their best, his instincts were a time bomb; at their worst, irregular tiles in a mosaic looking for a place, a way to fit in. With each attempt, the picture became further distorted, the vision more terribly skewed.

The last morning Arbegast had ventured outside the development, he had helped himself to a piece of fruit, a gleaming red apple, from a sidewalk display in front of a specialty-foods market. The action, as modeled by other patrons before him, must have seemed totally natural, the fulfillment of a biological directive shared by his two selves. This was the way it was done in these parts, by these creatures not so much different from himself. However, when he took a bite of the apple and moved away from the display, things got ugly. The shopkeeper, a fortyish man with rusty blond hair and a flinty voice, emerged from the storefront and called after Arbegast.

"Sir," he beckoned politely, "I believe you forgot to pay for that apple."

When Arbegast failed to respond, the shopkeeper marched stiffly after him, his green silk necktie catching the light above the starched bib pocket of his white produce apron. Arbegast continued unknowingly, the shopkeeper's cries just another element of the sensory maelstrom swirling about him. Infuriated by Arbegast's cavalier disregard, the shopkeeper caught up with him, spun him about and wrenched the half-eaten apple from his fruit-flecked lips. Arbegast's expression flared, eyes raw and bloodshot, his toothy mouth gaping like a gateway to a place feared by men. He lashed out at the shopkeeper, catching him on the side of the head with a blow that could have toppled a parking meter. As the shopkeeper crumpled to the sidewalk, he dug a cell phone from his bib pocket, shielded himself from the advance of the glowering ape, and stabbed out 9-1-1 on the keypad. Before Arbegast could inflict any further harm, I rushed him from where I had been pretend-browsing the menu at a blended-juice bar. The fact that Arbegast recognized me was perhaps the only thing that had saved the shopkeeper's life. As I quickly closed the gap between us, he thumped the tightly coiled muscles of his chest, bounded down a narrow alleyway between a Starbucks and a Thai food restaurant, and into the annals of unreliable eyewitness testimony.

The description I gave to the police officer who arrived on the scene moments later—"A foreigner, dark haired and swarthy with bad teeth, a Brit maybe, between five and six feet tall . . . "—had the shopkeeper nodding in profuse agreement as he assembled a gourmet gift basket as thanks for my good samaritanship. A round of routine questions and a bogus name and address later I was back home preparing dinner for Lorelei.

And, of course, Marcel.

Lorelei skimmed through the Sunday edition of the *Los Angeles Times* while I boiled water for pasta and heated a jar of artichoke-heart pesto the shopkeeper had included in the gift basket, along with ten ounces of Italian squid-ink paparadelle, a tin of smoked escargots, a round of soft French cheese, a sour-dough baguette, and a twenty-five-dollar bottle of Napa County chardonnay. After helping himself to a glass of wine (against doctor's orders!) and several of the frowzy hors d'oeuvres, Marcel excused himself and retired to the living-room sofa in front of the television, leaving Lorelei and me alone at last.

"You don't know what you're missing," said Lorelei, throwing back a slice of baguette topped with a purulent gob of cheese and a shriveled brown invertebrate evicted from its shell.

"I'm still not sold on the idea of squid-ink pasta," I confessed. "Black noodles? It seems a little weird."

"Close your eyes and you'll never know the difference."

"I know this guy—actually, he's a transvestite—who tells me the same thing all the time."

"Very funny," she said, assembling another of the dreaded concoctions. "Just a bite."

I added the pasta to the boiling water and stirred it around.

"Next thing you know, you'll be telling me that it tastes like chicken."

"Come on, I'll feed you myself. You're not going to let Marcel show you up, are you?" Lorelei approached me smiling coquettishly. "Close your eyes and open your mouth. I promise you'll like it."

I could hear her breath close to me above the rolling murmur of the water boiling on the stove. I parted my lips and waited to be fed, praying that it would be followed by a kiss. In the previous week there had been several instances in which the swapping of spit had seemed inevitable, but for one reason or another—usually an appearance by Marcel at just the wrong moment—we had never closed the deal. As the hors d'oeuvre passed under my nose and collided with my palate, it was as if someone had set a pair of dirty gym shorts on fire and extinguished the blaze by pissing on it. Careful not to upset the vile delicacy, I pretended to chew and banished the slimy garden pest to my stomach in a single gulp. Lorelei moved in for a kiss. As our lips were about to touch we were interrupted by a high-pitched bestial warbling coming from the living room.

"What now?" I asked, opening my eyes completely.

"Marcel's been watching a documentary about World War II on the History Channel all week."

"And? . . ."

"He thinks it's funny."

"Sick sense of humor."

"He's drunk on wine and painkillers," she said, coiling her arms around my neck. "Now close your eyes and kiss me."

Dinner was a big hit with everyone but me. Marcel ate until I thought he would get sick. In fact, I encouraged it. Each time he was about to clean his plate, I loaded him up with more. Black pasta, white asparagus—an interracial marriage of starch and roughage. Although his table manners were impeccable, a mark of good breeding for which Lorelei boasted credit, he was every bit as gluttonous as a typical dinner guest. My intent was to cripple the ravenous beast with a stomachache and offer him a bed in the guest room so that he might sleep it off. When I refilled his glass of wine, Lorelei intercepted it before he could get the tangy libation to his lips.

"Not so fast," she admonished him gently. "I let you have the first one because I thought it would help lift your spirits. From the way you were carrying on in front of the TV, I think it worked a little too well."

Marcel bristled. *Point-waggle-you'renotmymother-thumbslash!*

"I'm only looking out for your health," Lorelei explained caringly.

Curlicue-chestslap-I'mabigboy-pointslash-Icanlookoutformyself-waggle-nowgivemethewine!

"Fine!" she fumed. "This time when your kidneys fail, don't come crawling to me."

Lorelei thrust the glass of wine into Marcel's outstretched hand, spilling some on the table.

"This isn't the first time Marcel's gotten a kidney transplant?" I asked, a leaf storm of question marks swirling inside my head.

"Marcel has a bit of a drinking problem. Isn't that right, Marcel? He promised me that he would enroll in AA when he was well enough."

Marcel turned away indignantly and marched into the living room, where he defiantly sipped his wine in front of the television. With Germany's evil empire vanquished and the cities of Hiroshima and Nagasaki lying in radioactive ruin, he chuckled heartlessly, a sadistic counterpoint to the narrator's somber curtain call on the second great war.

"I partially blame myself," Lorelei explained, clearly troubled. "I think the pressure got to him."

"The pressure?"

"Fitting in, being like us. Marcel was just a baby when we rescued him from poachers. He's never had any truly meaningful relationships with his own kind. I call it the Tarzan Effect. It's been hard on him, always being the odd man out."

"What about Kiki and Edgar? I thought Marcel and them were all one big happy family."

"Marcel knows them only from the zoo. I bring him around once in a while so he doesn't forget his roots entirely. Truthfully, it hasn't gone all that well. Marcel has this 'holier than thou' attitude when it comes to interacting with other chimps."

"Trust me," I said, considering the implications of Daddy Arbegast's announcement that pseuprezdid was a placebo, "there are worse things than forgetting one's roots."

"I guess," she sighed. "Look, I wanted to show you this. It's a write-up about the guy who brought Dunkie's little finger back from New Guinea. Kilter Cloud—he's in town this weekend signing copies of some book he wrote."

Lorelei handed me the book-review section of the *Los Angeles Times*. On the front page was a color photograph of Kilter Cloud, Aussie bounty hunter turned best-selling novelist, looming before a backdrop of blue sky and billowy white cumulus. He was squinting into an imaginary distance, his face, a bold amalgam of colonial bravura and elemental wrath, set against the yoke of destiny. The caption read NO GUTS, NO GLORY: AUSTRALIAN PHENOM SETS SAIL FOR HIGH ADVENTURE IN HIS NEW BOOK, *ESCAPE FROM DEVIL'S ISLAND*.

Suddenly, Janus's riddle about clouds and ships in the sky made sense.

"I'm glad you showed me this," I said. "I was planning on paying him a visit, but I guess I forgot with all the stuff that's been going on."

We were in the kitchen doing the dishes and discussing the best way to get the truth out of Kilter when someone entered the house through the front door. My first thought was that it was Mr. Wonderful. It had been days since I had discussed the possibility of buying my way out of my Faustian arrangement with him, and it stood to reason that he was growing antsy with greed. I had all but forgotten the radio transmitter looped around my ankle. I shut off the water, dried my hands, and tried to think of a way to explain Marcel that would make both of them uncomfortable. Lorelei stayed behind to finish cleaning up.

Janie stood in the center of the living room, exchanging greetings with the tipsy ape who moments earlier had been heralding the decline of civilization with fluttery bursts of laughter. They were both smiling, Janie's smooth white hand clasped delicately in

Marcel's hairy paw. Janie looked at me with the same load-bearing smile she routinely called on in awkward moments and said, "Hi, Dutch, I didn't think you'd be home, or I would have called."

"I thought you were staying at your sister's house," I said.

"I was . . . I mean, I am. . . . What I'm trying to say is that I came home to pick up some things."

I looked at Janie, then Marcel, then at Janie again.

"This is Marcel," I explained feebly.

Marcel kissed the back of Janie's hand before releasing it. Something stirred between his legs. I was too horrified to look more closely.

"Yes, I know." Janie blushed, averting her gaze. "We've met."

"Marcel!" I barked reproachfully. "Keep it in your pants!"

Cowed, Marcel took a step back, bumped into a lamp, and staggered unevenly to his place on the sofa.

"Who's in the kitchen?" Janie asked.

The water had come on and the garbage disposal sputtered and growled to life.

"A friend."

"Does he have a name?"

"He's a she, and her name is Lorelei."

Janie looked confused.

"I know what you think, but I'm not gay. The guy you mentioned on the phone the other day. . . . The pretty, ethnic-looking one you saw parked in front of the house. He's not my boyfriend. He's an assassin—one of Saddam's guys. I should have told you a long time ago, but I was afraid you'd leave me. I'd already put you through so much."

"That day at the Nite Lite." Janie was thinking it over. "You weren't being paranoid. You were right, I *was* having an affair. I feel like such a hypocrite."

We looked into each other's eyes, our confessions bringing us closer to one another than we had been at any time in the previous year.

"I'm sorry," I said.

"Me, too." Janie inclined her head thoughtfully and asked, "Are you two serious?"

I must have given her a look, because she quickly amended her inquiry with "I didn't mean anything by it. I just want you to be happy, Dutch, that's all."

The garbage disposal died out and the water shut off. Lorelei emerged from the kitchen drying her hands with a dish towel. She and Janie appraised each other, smiling stiffly. Signals exchanged and territories clearly defined, they relaxed a little and traded tentative hellos.

"Janie," I said, "this is Lorelei. Lorelei, this is Janie. She's just stopping by to pick up some things."

The two of them shook hands.

"I'll just be a minute. Then I'll be out of your hair," Janie confirmed pleasantly.

"If you're hungry," Lorelei offered, "there's still a little food in the kitchen. Dutch fixed some wonderful pasta for dinner."

"Sounds yummy," said Janie, "but someone's waiting for me outside. You two go on doing whatever it was you were doing. Dutch, you and I can talk later."

"You know where to find me."

"This guy who's been following you—" Janie asked. "Are you going to be okay?"

"Don't worry, he's a pussycat—cries at the drop of a hat."

Janie packed her bags and was out of the house in less than fifteen minutes. I tried to get a glimpse of her mystery man from the kitchen window as the two of them pulled away from the curb, but it was too dark to make out anything clearly.

Marcel was snoring loudly by the time Lorelei and I had finished putting away the dishes and returned to the living room. Apparently, the combination of prescription narcotics and the better part of a half bottle of wine was too much for him. If Lorelei was the least bit tense or apprehensive about Janie's visit, it wasn't at all evident in her behavior as we lifted Marcel from the sofa and prepared to move him into the guest room.

"Remind me never to feed him so much again," I groaned, draping the passed-out chimp's arm over my shoulder. "He weighs a ton."

"You'd actually have him over again after how he behaved tonight? Even I have to admit that he was pretty disgusting."

"Nobody's perfect."

"You're full of surprises, Dutch," she said, walking under Marcel's other arm and taking on half of his weight. "It's not every day that a girl meets a man as compassionate as you."

Working together, Lorelei and I managed to get Marcel into the guest room and roll him onto the bed. I was still bubbling with excitement over her last comment. Maybe there was hope for me. Maybe I could learn to feel again. If pseuprezdid was a placebo, the road to recovery was wide open.

"It breaks my heart to see him like this," said Lorelei, kissing Marcel on the forehead and tucking him in. "Especially after what he's just been through. I'm worried that he's not going to make it this time."

"Maybe it would be best if you somehow got him away from all of this," I suggested, flexing my newfound compassion. "Get him out of the spotlight. Have you ever thought about releasing him back into the wild?"

"He'd never survive," she explained. "It's not that he doesn't have the necessary tools—Marcel could probably build a computer if you asked him to—it's that he's been raised to be something he's not. The transition would kill him. He'd die of culture shock."

I wrapped my arms around Lorelei and pulled her in close to me, squeezing tightly. We kissed long and deep and hard, Marcel lying on the bed at our backs, his shallow breathing the physical component of a mind exploring the chambers of a dream. Lorelei and I moved into the master bedroom where she stretched out on the bed while I lowered the blinds. Across the street about a half block down, I could make out the second story of my neighbor's house awash in powdery moonlight. The roof had a fairly steep pitch to it and was overgrown with vegetation. The silhouette of a man appeared just below the eaves on the corner nearest to me, hand-over-handing it up the downspout with the facile grace and upper-body strength of a gymnast. With a deft twist of his lower half, he swung himself onto the roof, padded up the shingled incline, and dropped down the chimney.

"What are you looking at?" asked Lorelei, a note of playful urgency in her voice.

"Either someone's robbing the neighbors, or Santa Claus has lost track of what month it is."

The sex was lustful and primitive and without boundary. What wasn't illegal was more than certainly taboo. Lorelei did things to me that would have made The Marquis de Sade blush. If you're imagining dripping hot candle wax, then think napalm. Kama Sutra? Try, the deadly courting ritual of scorpion fish. Trapeze acts? Grease the bars and roll up the safety nets. Sounds escaped my body that sent primal ripples through every dog in a half-mile radius. The neighborhood boiled over like a kennel in the grip of a full moon. Lorelei evoked sensations in me that transported me to the edge of rapture and hurled me "Our-Fathering" into the abyss beyond. She bit me hard on my neck just above the collarbone, but by then I could only squirm in ecstasy and moan my approval.

Afterward, we languished in bed, marveling at the volume and intensity of Marcel's snoring. He was out cold. The bathroom door was slightly ajar, and beyond it I could see the creamy pink lip of the bathtub gleaming in the melted glow of the night light. That I had tried to end it all less than two weeks ago was inconceivable to me in the wake of our lovemaking. Although Janie was gone for good, there was a lightness inside of me that I had not felt since I don't know when. Lying there with Lorelei's naked body pressed up against me, I was almost convinced that everything was going to work out.

"So what did you think of her?" I asked, my eyes fixed on the ceiling.

"Your wife?"

"Don't you think it's a little strange that she didn't say a thing about Marcel? It's as if she didn't even notice that he's a chimp."

"Kinda, I guess," said Lorelei, nibbling on my left earlobe. "Then again, I never really consider Marcel's species when we interact. To me, he's just another one of the gang."

"That's different—you're with him every day."

Lorelei thought for a moment. "She smelled like a chimp."

"She what?"

"Let me rephrase that," said Lorelei. "She had the smell of a chimp on her."

"That's probably because Marcel kissed her hand and who knows what else?"

"It was in her hair and on her clothes. I'm pretty sure it wasn't Marcel."

Lorelei dug one of the pillows out from under her head and buried her face in it until she located the scent she was searching for. She inhaled deeply.

"There it is," she said. "See for yourself. It's the same smell."

I was awakened before dawn by the garbage trucks making their weekly rounds through the neighborhood. The hydraulic hiss and rumble of their passage occupied the edge of my dream like elephants congregating along the shore of an African spring. I glanced out the window on my way to the bathroom, watching as one of the humpbacked behemoths crept slowly down the center of the street. Three sanitation workers ambled along behind, feeding curbed waste into the crushing steel jaws, enslaved supplicants appeasing a wrathful urban deity. Although outfitted in identical slate-gray coveralls, one in particular stood out. He was considerably shorter than the other two and had a familiar loping gait. I pressed my face to the window, but he was impossible to make out in the blunted light. By now my bladder was singing out to be drained, and I concluded that I had a better chance of running into Ehrlich again than convincing myself that I wasn't hallucinating. It was bad enough to consider that one of us might be gone for good.

When I awoke for the second time that morning, Lorelei was sitting on the bed at my side. She was fully dressed. Her hair was loosely gathered above the nape of her neck in a faux tortoise-shell clip. Sunlight bled through the slats in the blinds, imbuing her skin with an ethereal bronze luster. She kissed me on the forehead and smiled meaningfully.

"There's someone at the front door to see you," she said. "A cop. He says he had you in for questioning the other day."

I rolled out of bed and dressed. "Gogan?"

"He didn't say," she replied, cataloging the various bumps and bruises upholstering my torso—all camouflaged in the shadows the night before. "Did *I* do that?"

I shook my head. "Occupational hazard. Black and blue are the team colors."

"You poor guy. After your friend leaves, I'll rub you down with lotion. Gently," she added. "You must have been in agony last night."

Gogan was standing in the entry, thumbing through the photographs I had gathered off the floor the night Blight's goons had ransacked my house. One by one, he examined each and returned them to the stack atop the table where I kept my car keys. His thick, greasy fingers bent corners and left opaque smudges on the obsolete semigloss memories. I watched as he tried to pocket a pinup shot of Janie modeling a pink string bikini on the beach in Cabo San Lucas, her tan tummy suspiciously flat for a married woman of childbearing age.

"Go ahead," I said, startling him. "Take it."

"I'm gathering evidence," he responded brusquely, staging an official presence.

"I've got an entire closet full of *evidence*, if you're into that sort of thing. There's a good one of her passed out drunk in a miniskirt. You can practically see her tonsils. If you give me five minutes, I'll dig it up for you."

Gogan gritted his teeth and flipped the photograph back atop the others. "Look, asshole, the sheriff's department pulled your car out of a ravine in Angeles National Forest yesterday. *Totaled*," he added lasciviously. "According to eyewits, it matches the vehicle used in a crash-and-dash that left a guy splattered dead."

"Let me guess. You're here to beat a confession out of me and save yourself the trouble of doing any real investigative work."

"When the time's right," he assured me with an ugly grin. "Right now, we're looking into who was behind the wheel. I've got two of my men taking statements as we speak."

"That should be good for a few laughs."

"Victim's name was Shackleman. Apparently, he was some kind of hotshot scientist. Ring any bells?"

"Thanks for dropping by," I said, steering clear of a perjury charge.

"Listen, Flowers, I don't know what kind of shit you're running here, but I'm no fool. I know a criminal when I see one."

As Gogan turned to leave, Marcel emerged from the guest room sporting a shiny red boner. He was rubbing the hangover from his eyes. He looked the two of us over briefly, shambled across the living room, mounted the sofa, and turned on the television. He flipped through the channels and settled on live coverage of a Senate debate.

Gogan's mouth fell open. "Is this some kind of joke?" he demanded hotly. "You've got a fucking monkey with a cherry red peckerwood living in the house."

"That's Marcel," I explained. "And he's not a monkey. He's a chimpanzee."

Marcel faced the two of us and nodded appreciatively in my direction.

"I don't care if he's a pink fucking elephant! I ought to run you in right now on suspicion of possession of stolen property."

"Where and why would I steal a chimpanzee?"

"Maybe you're thinking about opening a circus," said Gogan. "All I know is that in the past year, several very valuable lab animals fitting your little friend's description have been stolen from university research centers around the country. The FBI has asked us to keep our eyes out for anything that looks suspicious . . . and this sure as hell qualifies."

At that moment, Lorelei breezed into the living room and handed Marcel a glass of orange juice and a half-dozen assorted pills, including aspirin for his headache. "Marcel's with me," she interrupted cheerily. "I have a permit for him. I can show it to you, if you like."

"Forget it," Gogan huffed.

Marcel signed something for Lorelei, who nodded and said, "That would be nice." Marcel set down the glass of orange juice, hopped off the sofa, and swaggered toward Gogan who was already backpedaling for the door.

"Don't be afraid," Lorelei explained. "He only wants to shake your hand."

Gogan steeled himself as if against the charge of a Cape buffalo and stuck out his hand. It was a familiar exchange, reminding me of my own inglorious attempt to connect with Marcel that day in the hospital not long ago.

"I think he likes you, Officer," said Lorelei.

"He's delirious from all the drugs he's taking," I said.

"Just be sure you keep him on a short leash," Gogan warned, wrenching his hand from Marcel's grasp. "Wild animals make people nervous. Throw the two of them together, and bad things usually happen."

"Thanks for the advice," Lorelei replied, less warmly than before.

Gogan lumbered out the door and sped off in an unmarked car. When he was gone I asked Lorelei about the missing chimps Acteon had donated to the universities. "What do you think happened to them?"

Lorelei shrugged. "I have a friend and colleague who was working in the Primatology Department at the University of Wisconsin when one of the chimps disappeared. He said it looked like the work of a professional cat burglar. The thief entered the lab through a fifth-floor window, and the lock on the cage had been picked."

"Fingerprints?" I asked.

She nodded. "Apparently, the cops botched it. Something like five hundred possible matches turned up in Madison alone."

Once inside the L.A. Convention Center, it didn't take a whole hell of a lot of detective work to track down Kilter Cloud. One of a select group of authors, he commanded an ample section of the central exhibit hall reserved for literary nobility and whoever was hot on the current best-seller lists, talent or lack thereof notwithstanding. Cloud's table was like a bad stage prop borrowed from a high-school theatrical production of *The Man in the Iron Mask.* He was framed by an enormous cardboard cutout display, the intent of which was to evoke the infamous stone barracoon of the Devil's Island penal colony from which his roguish protagonist was foretold to escape. Staggered along the periphery of the elaborate cardboard mock-up was an assortment of images apparently owing their inspiration to some of the book's more memorable moments: the razor-sharp maw of a man-eating shark, a diabolical prison guard hefting a whip, a bosomy Anglo woman staked spread-eagle to a stone dais, a tribe of primitives stalking through the jungle in scant loincloths, a pirate ship flying a tattered Jolly Roger, and a glued-on rubber tarantula. An anonymous blurb overhead read "A SEXY, SWASHBUCKLING ADVENTURE FROM THE MAN WHO'S BEEN TO HELL AND BACK!" Cloud, a pink-faced blowhard who regularly boasted of eating grubs and drinking his own urine to stay alive, sat in mock imprisonment at the head of a long line of vicarious thrill-seekers, autographing hardcover copies of his book at $24.95 a pop with feathery flourishes of a phony ballpoint quill. He greeted each with a self-important snarl and a jaunty inclination of his head. Twenty minutes of watching him posturing for photographs and listening to his heroic Aussie-isms was about all I could handle. By the time I was face-to-face with the word-warping egomaniac, I knew exactly what buttons to push.

"To'oom shall oy make it out, mate?" Cloud asked, swiping a book from the stack in front of him and folding back the cover.

"Duncan Arbegast the third," I announced crisply. "And I'd like it to read *'Congratulations, we got away with it.'* "

Mechanically, Cloud started to write. About halfway through the proposed inscription, his pen came up lame. For the first time, he actually looked at me.

"Iz'zis some kin' of joke?" he said, crimping his face bitterly, the folksy Down-Under charm leaving him like a fart through lace panties.

"You're a fraud," I said. "Dunkie's not dead."

"Listen 'ere, mate, I don' know 'oo you think you aah—"

"Shut up!" I ordered curtly. "Where did you get the finger—hanging on the lip of a shrimp cocktail in some outback pub where kangaroo ranchers go to get drunk on warm Foster's lager and play with their didgereedoos?"

Cloud stood, knocking back the folding chair in which he had been sitting. Blood crept into a vein branching over his right eye like a lightning bolt.

"Yawr miztaken," he smiled fiercely, curiosity sweeping through the line of faces backing up behind me. "I sawr 'im die wit mine own two oyz clee-aah as Sowt African diamond."

"That so? I worked at Acteon. I helped run the DNA test myself."

Cloud thought it over.

"You're crackers," he said, studying me with a half-cocked smile, convinced neither way.

"How do you think your fans will react when they learn you're a fake? Tell me who the finger belonged to, and you'll never see me again. Don't, and you'd better start thinking of a way to get the old man his million dollars back."

Cloud was bigger than I realized, much bigger: six-three, six-four, maybe two-thirty, two-forty. Chapped eyes the matte glint of graphite. Gold in nearly every tooth. An undertaker's dream. As he sized me up across the table, I found myself wishing his cardboard cell was real.

"Now I know where I seenya befawr," Cloud proclaimed shrewdly. "Yawr that aahmy bloke what's been orn the telly. 'ad yawrself a real mess of it in the dezzet with Sadderm 'oozane. Crost you up real narce, din'ee?"

"I don't know what you're talking about."

"You Yanks an' your bleedin' petrol. 'ol buggerin' worl' stops cause you can' afford to take the mizzus for a 'oliday spin in the country. Now get outta 'ere 'fore I call the cops."

Suddenly, all eyes were on me. I could work on Cloud later. I had been to the convention center once before in the summer following my return from the Gulf. A mini-industry of sorts had arisen from my failed stab at patriotism. For nearly a year I was a genre unto myself. A handful of writers—freelance muckrakers, mostly—had chronicled my failures as both an officer and a gentleman. As part of a misguided attempt to diffuse the negative publicity hanging over my name, I had made myself available for comment at a similar such expo in which no less than six new titles documenting the infamous debacle had been unveiled. I had simply wanted to clarify my role in Operation Slay Dracula and the unfortunate turn of events culminating in my public ostracism. But it was not to be. Once again I found myself in the midst of an audience as disinterested in the facts as they were hungry for scandal.

"Dunkie's ready to come home," I called over the sudden upwelling of interested voices. "Did you actually think he'd pass on an inheritance that will make him one of the richest men in the world? Think about it. He could buy New Guinea and turn it into a goddamn theme park if he wanted!"

I had begun to work my way toward the exit when a terribly familiar face appeared in front of me like a blip on a radar sweep of the past five years of my life. It was Bobo—the same smug grimace and cocksure swagger. He was accompanied by his handler from *The Spalding Penzler Show*, the same asshole who had translated his scouring semaphores into words for all the world to hear and laugh at. The two of them stood in front of a table beyond which hung a full-color blowup of the cover of Bobo's latest book, *Before Eden: A Memoir*. It was the square footage of a queen-size bed and featured Bobo imitating a motif that was becoming as widespread and iconographic as the chromed plastic Jesus fish emblems earmarking the cars of those to be saved in the coming apocalypse. It's difficult to say which would have given Charles Darwin greater pause. Bobo acknowledged his latest success with a rather modest smile, if that was possible, and gestured something any five-year-old could have understood.

"Everything's peachy, Bobo," I replied stubbornly. "Thanks for asking. Unfortunately, I don't have time to stay and chat."

Bobo looked at me and performed a complicated series of hand gestures that at one time would have left me dumbfounded and grasping.

"Bobo," the handler began translating, "wants to apologize for embarrassing—"

"I know what he said," I blurted angrily. "I may be slow, but I'm not an idiot."

Bobo frowned remonstratively at his handler and signed something to him that I was less certain of.

"I'm sorry," the handler answered him verbally. *"Mister* Bobo."

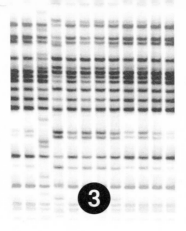

AIR TRAVEL IS NOT EXACTLY MY FAVORITE MODE OF TRANSPORTATION. Aside from the fact that I am wary of placing my life in the hands of a total stranger, there are innumerable other dangers and unpleasantries that plague the friendly skies. The mere fact that I would submit myself to several hours in a pressurized capsule brewing with recirculated farts, airborne viruses, and the oppressive waft of the meal cart should give you some idea of just how far I was willing to go to reunite Duncan Arbegast, Sr. with his absentee son. Of course, it didn't hurt any that a good chunk of change was riding on the journey's successful outcome. If, as I suspected, Dunkie was still alive, I would be able to collect both the quarter million from his old man and the fifty grand from Blight for Arbegast's safe return. All told, I stood to bring in over $300,000.

As I had hoped, Cloud's nerves had gotten the better of him and he had contacted Dunkie that night after returning to his hotel suite from the Book Expo. Pinpointing Dunkie's whereabouts was simply a matter of paying off one of the hotel staff for a printout of Cloud's phone record. I then turned it over to my contact at the phone company to determine the precise destination of the outgoing calls. The following morning, I was on a plane bound for El Paso, an ugly four-hour drive from a melancholy little border town called Sneed, with Mr. Wonderful at my side.

Isn't it obvious? The bastard didn't trust me. I had paid him a visit to detail my traveling plans so he wouldn't think that I had jumped ship, and he had insisted on coming along as insurance. Once out of transmitter range, he was convinced that I would somehow manage to rid myself of the tracking device and walk off the edge of the map into the haggard no-man's-land that lies beyond the Rio Grande.

The last time I had seen my nemesis, he was more or less intact—"original equipment" in the vernacular of classic-car enthusiasts. He now sported breasts, a bouncy C-cup bas-relief burgeoning beneath a low-cut panel of mint green Armani organdy. It was yet another step after hormone therapy toward becoming a full-fledged woman and vanquishing the identity crisis he had suffered since childhood. As striking as his meta-morphosis happened to be, it was utterly ordinary in contrast with what I had seen of Arbegast and the other chimps. Nonethe-less, I felt a little sorry for him as he winced in pain each time a shift in movement disturbed the tender additions to his person. His discomfort was doubly evident in the fact that he had not bothered to apply the cosmetic touches to his face that I had taken for granted as a hunted mainstay of the elegant assassin. In fact, he had not shaved for more than a day and wore no makeup at all. Between the budding facial hair and unsoftened contours of his exposed masculinity, I could not help but see the god who had made him this way—if not directly, then through careless craftsmanship, as perpetrator of an awful injustice.

In the first two hours of the flight, I only once considered that we were 35,000 feet up—twenty-five tons of recycled soda cans, volatile synthetics and Erector Set–style pop rivets—in the hands of a personable stranger who every now and then commented about wind speed and ground temperature from behind a locked door. Mr. Wonderful, who had spent the last thirty min-utes restoring himself by way of a manicure, may as well have been stretched out on a chaise lounge poolside back at his hotel so at home was he in the winged death capsule. He was efficient, methodical, every bit as nimble and precise as the Vietnamese mama-sans Janie had used in the strip mall just around the corner from our house.

"Ten to one Dunkie is still alive," I explained. "And his old man doesn't even know it. Now all I need to do is prove that Cloud is full of shit."

Mr. Wonderful applied a coat of clear matte acrylic to his left thumbnail and studied his hand approvingly in the light of the window.

"Be a dear and ask the stewardess for a Ginger Rogers when she comes by," he said.

"What exactly is a Ginger Rogers?" I asked.

"Vodka and ginger ale with a twist of lime."

The flight attendant had begun her final pass with the beverage cart. She smiled benevolently, filling drink orders and passing out pieces of fruit.

"Are you about done?" I asked Mr. Wonderful. "The fumes are giving me a headache."

"Don't be such a baby," he said, wetting the applicator brush and beginning on his other hand. "Oh, and a banana."

"Come again?"

"When the stewardess passes by," he clarified. "Preferably one without all those icky little brown spots."

Just then the plane was struck by a severe jolt. My hand shot out for something to hold on to, knocking over the bottle of nail polish.

"Naughty boy!" said Mr. Wonderful, eyeing the viscous droplets speckling the tray table and the front of his Prada capri pants. "No more Viagra for you. Now, if you don't mind, I'm going to see if I can sneak a cigarette in the restroom and get myself cleaned up."

Mr. Wonderful eyed me over his shoulder as he made his way toward the bathroom. The copilot's voice crackled over the intercom: "Ladies and gentlemen, the captain has asked me to inform you that it may get a little bumpy up ahead. Seems that we're approaching a weather system that's worked its way up from the Gulf of *May-hee-co*. We're going to do our best to fly around it. However, we ask that you please keep your seatbelts securely fastened."

He sounded as if he was talking into a soup can.

Weather system. One of the many phrases you don't want to hear when five-and-a-half miles up. Suddenly, every molecule in my body was charged with nervous apprehension. As much as I feared what I might find, I was powerless to resist a quick peek at the horizon ahead. I scooted into the seat vacated by Mr. Wonderful and pressed my cheek to the window. It was as if some kind of vortex had opened in the fabric of space and time and was sucking all the life out of the surrounding atmosphere. Blue sky gave way to a cancer of pure liquid blackness. A nebular mass miles in circumference boiled and writhed like a gigantic killer octopus spawned from the maelstrom of an Atlantean myth. Convection currents—great volcanic upwellings of climatic energy—billowed at its perimeter with the destructive force of tidal waves. Bolts of lightning that could have powered small cities for weeks on end arced across a necrotic field of gray that eclipsed the sun. And this was only what the eye could see. Inside, brewed forces the mind could only wonder and balk at. Flash freeze zones, tornadoes within tornadoes, hailstones the size of economy cars swirling and colliding with one another. In spite of the copilot's assurances that we would fly around the storm I was grimly skeptical. It was too big, the seat of a malevolent intelligence whispered about by terrified Neanderthals huddled in cold and leaky caves against deluges that raised the level of oceans.

"It's no use, they're ruined."

It was Mr. Wonderful. He was blotting a wet spot on the front of his pants with a paper towel. I was still pressed to the window.

"You're in my seat," he reminded me politely.

I scooched back to the aisle and cinched the seatbelt tightly across my lap.

"Did you ask the stewardess for my drink?" Mr. Wonderful wanted to know, taking his place next to the window.

"I think they're canceling the beverage service because of the weather."

"Not until I get my Ginger Rogers," he said, activating the amber request light on the overhead console. "You look like you could use a stiff one yourself."

MONKEY IN THE MIDDLE

The sky was now completely gray. Raindrops skittered across the window. The plane rocked gently from side to side.

"Fine. Wild Turkey rocks. But make it quick."

A moment later, the stewardess passed by on her way to stowing the beverage cart.

"I'm sorry, sir," she explained, "but the captain has instructed us to suspend service until the weather clears."

"Just this once," said Mr. Wonderful, his tone gently urgent. "My friend is afraid of flying. Look at him. A drink would be a tremendous help to us both. I promise I won't tell."

He winked.

The stewardess winked back and in a hush-hush voice said, "If anyone asks, I only served you so that you could take your heart medication."

"And could I trouble you for a banana?"

"I only have one left, and I promised the captain that I would save it for him. You understand."

"Of course," said Mr. Wonderful. "He's the boss."

I had just cracked the seal on the tiny plastic bottle when the plane suddenly nosedived, sending the tumbler of ice into the back of the seat in front of me. As the stewardess shielded herself from an avalanche of carry-on luggage sprung from one of the overhead compartments, the beverage cart got away from her and went barreling down the aisle toward the cockpit. I was too horrified watching the runaway cart to worry about the possible cause of our white-knuckle descent. Unchecked, the cart would crash through the cockpit door and smash into the controls, triggering a death plunge into the scrubby plains below. The cabin lights flickered wildly before cutting out altogether, and for an instant I was back in Saddam's discotheque frozen in the stop-time pulse of the strobe. Then—just as suddenly—the nose came up and the plane began to level off. Though not with adequate force to inspire a television movie of the week, the cart still managed to slam into the cockpit door, knocking it open to reveal the deft maneuverings of the flight crew within. However brief a glimpse, I know what I saw crouched at the pilot's yoke, our lives entrusted to his *capable* hands. Awash in the plasma green glow of the instrument panel, the erstwhile master of our destinies loosened his collar, eased back on the throttle, and initiated a systems check.

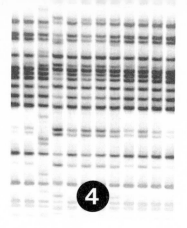

4

SNEED WAS EVERYTHING YOU'D EXPECT of a Tex-Mex border town, a neither-here-nor-there purgatory of infinite tedium and dust. The dispirited community was like a ship graveyard minus the water: a mothball fleet of sandblasted prefab homes, drydocked trailers, and cars whose paint had been lashed down to the primer by the cruel desert wind. Even the cacti, backs bent against the weight of the sun like stick-figure talismans warding off prosperity, seemed to be dying of thirst. We arrived in the midst of an exodus of tumbleweeds rivaling any of East Africa's great animal migrations. We were there less than five hours in all; however, in that time, there was no end to them in sight as of lost souls passing through en route to eternity.

What's bothering you, Dutch?" asked Mr. Wonderful, cradling his breasts against the jounce of potholes as we rolled through the center of town in a rented Jeep. "You haven't said a word since we landed."

I thought it over. What did I have to lose by telling him the truth?

"The pilot was a chimpanzee," I said.

"That storm was no joke," he reflected, stealing the rearview mirror so that he could check his face. "But given the circumstances, I think he performed rather well."

I pulled in at a gas station and parked at the pump. Judging from the sunbleached posters taped to the convenience-store windows, beer and ice had been on special since the beginning of time. *¡El Sabor de Tecate!*

"Are you listening to what I'm saying? A monkey was flying the plane for fuck's sake! Doesn't that bother you just a little?"

"Dutch," he went on calmly, his voice soothing and maternal. "It's that place where you've been working. They've got you seeing monkeys in your dreams. It was a rough flight. You were scared. We all were." He paused to adjust the lace-trimmed cups of his bra. "But the pilot was a man just like you and me."

The cashier was a redheaded Mexican with a wiry scrim of copper-colored hair hedging his upper lip. His eyes, too, were copper-colored. And his skin. There was a subtle disquiet in his manner. Clearly, there was something about the address I showed him that didn't sit well. He virtually whispered the directions, looking about anxiously as if for the antidote to a poison he had just swallowed. When I showed him a picture of Dunkie, he shook his head stiffly from side to side and went back to flushing sticky blue ooze from the overworked ICEE machine.

As instructed, we veered right at the end of town and followed an unmarked dirt road into the desert toward the mountains in the distance. The sky was like the ceiling in a smokers' lounge, a greasy palette of dirty yellows, browns, and grays. Tumbleweeds bounded ahead of us in groups of two and three like porpoises before the bow of a ship. We passed a faded hand-painted sign that advertised SEE MOSES' FOOTPRINTS IN THE SAND, and a short while later another sign—this one machine-etched stainless steel—that simply read MAGENTA 5. It was triangular and bordered by counterclockwise arrows enameled, too, in magenta. It was here that civilization reasserted itself. Scraps of paper and plastic mingled with thickets of ocotillo and yucca. Cupcake blister packs and potato-chip bags and plastic squeeze bottles contributed to a nonbiodegradable mosaic of garbage that worsened the further we drove. Within a mile, the waste began to acquire shape, order, a pattern of morbid excess and corrupt majesty. It evoked the work of the Mound Builders of ancient North America, a mysterious homage to a culture unremembered in history. Enormous piles of garbage studded the austere landscape—automobile tires, mayonnaise jars, tin cans, margarine tubs, worn-out athletic shoes, compartmental-ized snak-paks, pudding cups, a king's ransom of recyclable alu-minum and glass—each ordered by kind. A snowfall of styrofoam packing peanuts and plastic soda-bottle caps stip-pled the footworn interstices, gratuitous reminders of man's place in all of this.

Perhaps a mile ahead stood a gleaming stainless-steel pyramid whose burnished flanks picked up the sunlight and scattered it in a thousand directions. Even at a distance, it was painful to look at, an optical assault of amplified photons rioting at the fringe of a vast ochre plain piled high with sorted waste. As we drew nearer, human silhouettes resolved out of the rippling convection currents, magenta-robed shapes moving among the mountains of garbage like monks in a celebrated holy city. All wore black rubber masks with canister filters over their noses and mouths. Some wore gloves. Dozens in all, they seemed totally unconcerned by our approach and went pur-posefully about their business of sorting waste as we entered an open compound at the base of the pyramid. It was flanked by Quonset outbuildings I ascertained to be living quarters. Appar-ently, they were accustomed to visitors. The compound was scarred with dusty tire tracks, the deep brocade of heavy trucks.

"I don't like this place, Dutch," said Mr. Wonderful. "Those robes—they're horribly unflattering. No one's wearing magenta this fall. These men aren't right."

"Take it easy," I said, stepping down from the Jeep. "I intend on keeping our visit short. Once I see Dunkie with my own eyes, we're outta here. Okay?"

"Leave the keys," he instructed meaningfully. "Just in case."

I entered the pyramid through a triangular port trimmed with broad magenta arrows aligned counterclockwise tip to tail. The number 5 was etched just above the port's apex. The temperature inside was perhaps twenty degrees cooler than outside the pyramid, the air conditioning cranked full bore against the oppressive heat. A basin—holy water maybe, though it smelled like Pine-Sol—stood to one side of the entrance. The walls were smooth and virtually seamless, steepling in a sharp terminus one hundred or more feet up. The place was built to last. Elaborate, brightly anodized etchings evocative of stained glass adorned the walls. At a glance, I could see that it was a pictorial narrative in the tradition of the Crucifixion, although content-wise like none I had ever seen.

The first frame centered on a green plastic two-liter soda bottle being passed around at a Last Supper–like gathering of family and friends. The sun was high and bright in the sky. In the next, the bottle, now empty, stood in the center of the table, the dinner guests sated and smiling. In the third frame, the guests exhibited the aftereffects of too much revelry. They looked spent and haggard—aged, even. The young girls had breasts, the boys, facial hair. By the fifth frame, the message was eminently clear. All of the guests were dead, skeletons gathered around the green plastic soda bottle. Their ribs were laced with cobwebs. The sun had lost some of its luster. By the seventh and final frame, everything was gone but the eternal plastic soda bottle—table, chairs, the bones of the dinner guests—capsized and alone but no worse for wear. The sun, a dull brown smudge barely visible in the sky. Recycling-center propaganda was my first thought. Weird maybe, and a little over the top, but no cause for alarm.

The floor of the pyramid, a cool gray expanse of concrete surfaced with a nonslip industrial sealant, was fixed with pew-like kneeling cushions upholstered in magenta vinyl, dimpled from prolonged use. In front of each was a nondescript stainless-steel–rimmed hole. A stainless-steel gurney heaped with hundreds of pounds of raw red meat stood next to the pulpit beneath the familiar Magenta 5 icon. Filet mignon, if I was to make a guess based on the size and shape of the cut. Before I could take a closer look, an electronic bell sounded outside. One by one, the magenta-robed disciples filed past the water basin into what I had concluded was a chapel.

In a matter of minutes, every cushion was occupied by a shaved-bald man kneeling before the altar. Their leader, a man clad identically to themselves but for the golden triangle hanging about his neck on a heavy golden chain, took his place alongside the gurney, clasped his hands together in a prayerlike gesture and spoke. Swiveling his head benevolently from side to side so that all might absorb his wisdom, he sermonized briefly on the exquisite marbling of the filet, the enormous amount of feed and water and land it had taken to raise each cow to such delectable ripeness, and the excessive cost per pound of prime aged beef in the supermarket. His message delivered, he instructed each to come forth and receive his share of the bounty. Imagine my delight at having arrived in the midst of a church social, the generous outpouring of welcome and hospitality for the drooling stranger in their midst that would certainly ensue. Texas barbecue. I could practically hear the whoosh of the charcoal igniting, the greasy sizzle of fat dripping onto the coals.

I was trying to remember the last time I had enjoyed a steak when the insanity started. All at once, a low-level whirring filled the chapel, reverberating to the upper reaches of the pyramid and back again until the sound waves pulsed with the ominous *wah-wah-wah-wah!* of heavy industry. Although I was not sure of its source, there was a distinct menace to the nonverbal refrain like locusts swarming in the distance. Raising his voice above the din, the man with the golden necklace delivered a forceful benediction to the congregation.

"Let us give thanks for the waste we harvest!" he declaimed richly.

The kneeling disciples began feeding the filet into the holes in the floor, a hundred growling garbage disposals gnashing in unison. The ground shuddered. And then it was over. One by one, the robed contingent filed out of the chapel, each pausing to rinse the blood from his hands in the antiseptic basin by the entrance I had mistaken for holy water. I closely examined each as they removed their breathing masks from hooks on the wall and shuffled through the triangular port. So transfigured was Dunkie by cultish zeal that had I not had his photograph in hand I may have missed him altogether. Like the rest, he was uniformly oblique and glassy-eyed, the inner peace he had found imparting a waxy, narcotic bend to his lips. Though as blue as they had ever been, his eyes lacked the rebellious glint captured on film. He moved as if his will had been subordinated to a higher purpose, his magenta robe catching the dry desert wind like a sail and carrying him across the compound past the Jeep where Mr. Wonderful watched in abject horror and into the cordillera of waste awaiting him like a birthplace of revelations.

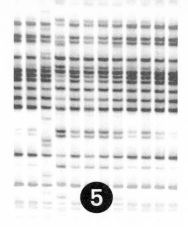

5

"DID YOU TALK TO HIM?" Daddy Arbegast asked hopefully.

"I'm afraid not," I said.

"But you're sure it was my son? You're sure it was Dunkie?"

"Positive."

"Curious, Mr. Flowers, that you would have traveled all that way and not have attempted to communicate with him."

"From what I could tell, he's involved with some sort of recycling center–slash-church. It's my policy not to get involved with cults. You just never know."

"Who said anything about a cult?" he asked, a note of alarm creeping into his voice.

"Your son was wearing a purple robe and climbing around a pile of crushed aluminum cans as big as Mount Ararat. If that doesn't sound like cult behavior, then I don't know what does. The crazy bastards worship plastic soda bottles and feed prime beef into holes in the ground."

There was a pause. Truths too terrible to consider ran roughshod over the old man's mind.

"What about his hands?" Daddy Arbegast asked finally. "Was he missing any fingers?"

"Not even a hangnail."

"So that goddamn monkey isn't my son after all," he concluded flatly, the old prejudices reasserting themselves in the shadow of his shame.

"Think of all the explaining it saves you at father-son get-togethers," I offered lightly.

"Tell me where I can find him, and I'll have the money transferred into your account first thing tomorrow morning."

Later that evening, I called Blight and arranged a meeting to discuss the exchange: 131's whereabouts for my fifty grand. There was no longer any point keeping the chimp's location a secret. I had seen all I needed to see. It was time to wrap things up.

We met, as Blight suggested, at the Beaux Arts Theater where *Planet of the Apes* had been running for close to six months now. Although it was the last show of the night, the theater was nearly filled to capacity. Had we not agreed to sit in the last row beneath the projection booth, I would have had a difficult time tracking him down. The theater was dark, the movie already in progress. Charlton Heston had just emerged from his frozen sleep capsule to find himself in orbit around an earth he no longer recognized. Up to his elbows in a bucket of popcorn the size of a small waste basket, Blight ignored me as I groped my way toward him. I kept my eyes fixed on the empty seat awaiting me at his side. Along the way, I stepped on more toes than a beginning dancer. I was nudged, kneed and screeched at until finally I settled in beneath the moted cone of light cutting through the darkness overhead. Blight continued to ignore me, his eyes glued to the enormous pre-multiplex screen. After a minute or so of just sitting there, I grew impatient and nudged him in the shoulder. He did not respond. I tried again. And again, no response. I didn't need this shit. Even minus Mr. Wonderful's substantial cut, a quarter of a million dollars would go a long way. Blight and Acteon could go to hell with their fifty grand. I was through playing games.

I considered walking out of the theater right then and there, but it was a long way back to the aisle and I was more than a little leery of the reception awaiting my two left feet. I passed my hand in front of Blight's eyes. He did not blink. Digging into the bucket of popcorn, I checked his wrist for a pulse. He was dead. Having shelled out eight dollars for a movie that was just beginning, it didn't make sense to simply up and leave. Nor was there any point in all that popcorn going to waste. I removed the cardboard bucket from Blight's cold, buttery hands and settled in for the duration of a classic forgotten to me for some time.

It was at the moment when Heston's character, Commander George Taylor, is shot in the throat while trying to escape earth's ape overlords that I first took notice of the Beaux Arts' enthusiastic patrons. A raucous cheer filled the theater, a tumult of approval that was universally inconsistent with generations of *Apes* fans. Where was the horror, the outrage, the hierarchical contempt for the monsterized simians? I looked around. The heads rising above the seat backs before me were no more or less uniform or contrary than I had been conditioned to expect from countless such cinematic excursions. Round, in a general sort of way, and as hungrily receptive as are we to the particles of sound and light streaming at them twelve frames per second, it was as if I had entered into a nightmare so that I might dream freely and without prejudice. Neither before nor since have I felt so utterly out of place, so isolated, so alone. At the same time, I was developing a sense of the falsehood and indignity behind the laughable specter of loyal Cheetah, who knew his place in the shadow of his yodeling bare-chested overlord. It was a familiar crossroads, the intersection of ignorance and enlightenment.

When the film was over, we filed out into the night together. The mood was thoughtful, introspective. No one was saying much. Before long, the parking lot was empty. The cars they drove and the clothes they wore were as eclectic and socially demarcative as the neighborhoods to which they would return to their sleeping young and refrigerator-raiding babysitters.

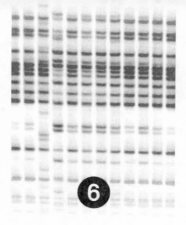

6

DON'T ASK ME WHY, but until that night I had never thought of talking to Shackleman's widow, the good-looking redhead from the computer disk. Blight's suspicious demise had rekindled my interest in the case. Although it was premature to label his death a portentous increment in a systematic process of elimination, there was sufficient evidence to suggest that I was on the cusp of a deadly trend. One by one, those closest to 131 were finding themselves looking at forced retirement in the strictest sense. The fewer there were who could answer my questions, the greater my curiosity had become.

Shackleman's house, a charming 1940s craftsman's bungalow, was located south of Los Angeles in a quiet section of El Segundo between the Mobil Oil refinery and the beach. I could see at once that the place was empty. Although there was nothing in particular to suggest this (the houses up and down the street were similarly dark and deserted looking), I had more than enough experience with my own lonely abode to have developed a sense attuned to the frequency of abandonment.

Apparently I was not the first to come snooping around since his death. One of the windows in back had been deliberately broken, a ragged swath of glass arrayed along the edges of the window frame, glinting in the moonlight like teeth. Once through, I noticed small tufts of coarse black hair stuck to some of the shards. There were also drops of blood on the windowsill—still wet. I followed the trail through the house, from one room to the next, expecting to cross paths with the bleeding intruder. A burglar maybe, lured by the absence of life and the promise of easy pickings.

The interior of the house was modest, but nice. It appeared that many of the furnishings had been removed for one reason or another. Because of this, the rooms lacked homeyness, that confluence of aesthetic and function for which women seem to have a particular knack. In the living room, there was no coffee table; magazines lay fanned over the naked hardwood floor in front of the sofa like a poker hand. A leather ottoman occupied a curious space in the center of the room, orphaned from its parent chair. A VCR; no television. In the dining room, kitchen, and bedrooms, there were faint outlines as of ghosts on the walls—paint unfaded where china cabinets and headboards and framed prints had once blocked the bleaching ultraviolet rays. The kitchen sink was full of dirty dishes. The closets held only men's clothing. Apparently, Shackleman and I belonged to the same club; a lonesome brotherhood of the dispossessed. Only the study, a cluttered and desperate retreat evocative of my own, exhibited signs of life. There were drops of blood clustered around the base of the desk, but no intruder.

An 8x10 black-and-white photograph of one the chimps occupied the center of Shackleman's desktop. Reprinted from surveillance footage, the chimp's face had been neatly scissored out of the photograph, leaving behind a roughly circular void. Although my ability to distinguish the chimps from one another was greatly improved from those first few days in the STF when they had all looked alike to me, my recognition skills had not progressed to such an extent that I was able to establish an identity without at least a face to go on. If the scissored scrap did not turn up, I could always pull the surveillance tapes and locate the image using the time-and-date index stamped in the lower right-hand corner. One thing was certain: It wasn't 131. The posture was not brash enough, the physique too slight, the contours of torso and limb too feminine.

Next to the photograph I discovered a pair of one-way airline tickets to Fiji whose departure date was now three weeks past. It seemed that Shackleman and the missus had had a change of heart about the romantic island paradise. Otherwise, the leaf fall of paper beneath which Shackleman's desk was buried was largely unremarkable, unpaid bills mostly. Gas, electric, water, insurance, mortgage—all of which were long delinquent and accruing penalties. Many of the envelopes in which the statements had arrived were unopened. From the looks of it, Shackleman had given up on his life in the quiet coastal suburb of El Segundo. But why—and for what?

Strewn about the room on bookcases and windowsills were empty nicotine patch boxes stuffed to capacity with snuffed-out cigarette butts, a pitiful motif echoed elsewhere in the house. Shackleman had been clearly torn between what he wanted and what was good for him. Added to and stepped on until it bulged pregnantly, the wastebasket beside the desk was a stratified fossil record of the last several months. In it I found the precursors to the menacing final notices promising foreclosure and stoppage of services should the balances not be remitted in full immediately. In much the same way a geologist will draw inferences about a particular epoch or event in earth's history from like items found in a cross section of terrestrial crust, I picked through Shackleman's trash layer by layer, in the hope that it would serve as a window into his recent past, and perhaps shed light on his mysterious degeneration. It can be said, after all, that man is the sum total of his waste.

Aside from letters from collection agencies warning of the snowballing ruin of his credit rating and pending legal actions, the uppermost layers of trash included handwritten passages of religiose verse bespeaking the wickedness of the "world beyond" and the wrath owed any so foolish as to venture out into it. The handwriting was unmistakably the same as that crowding the margins in the annotated copy of Bobo's autobiography Shackleman had forced upon me during our first encounter weeks earlier. Subsequent layers revealed additional drafts of verse whose theme was less apocalyptic in nature, though possessed of a similar and equally scriptural tone. Somewhere during the course of his decline, it appeared that Shackleman had found God and had since been messengering His commandments for the benefit of an unidentified following. What god or whose god it was impossible to say. The cryptic narrative referenced the Almighty almost exclusively in first person.

About midway through the layered paper trail, things started to get interesting. Xerox copies of legal documents—petition for divorce, asset sheets, signed affidavits—told a story of domestic rigor and unrest. Apparently, the Widow Shackleman had filed for divorce on grounds of infidelity. It was hard enough to believe that Shackleman had hitched his overbite to a willing bride. That he had also managed to land a mistress was inconceivable to me. Although burning with curiosity, chances are I would never know the identity of Shackleman's Madame X. From what I could tell by looking at the dates, the case had been settled, the marriage legally dissolved, nearly four months ago.

As I dug deeper, I came across more of Shackleman's amateur scripture. Although I am no expert on the bible, the work had clearly been modeled after the sacred text. Crude though they may have been, and scrawled in an idolater's rabid prose, many of his ideas paralleled those, both conceptually and sequentially, put forth in the books of the Old Testament. Remember, everything in the wastebasket was flipped around, the most recent works residing in the upper strata while the oldest works lay buried toward the bottom. If the pattern held, I might uncover something that would lay bare the event or events prompting Shackleman's misguided stab at Genesis and beyond, his spiritual awakening. It wasn't a question of when and where he had found God, but when and where he had lost himself.

To my disappointment, the base stratum yielded little to go on: a single page of frustrated "In the beginning's," a crumbled cache of Oreo wafers bearing the teeth marks of the one who had scraped out the chalky white centers, and an old billing statement for a cellular phone in Shackleman's name. The charging cradle for the phone sat on one corner of the desk. It was still plugged in. Dust had accumulated everywhere but the slot in which the phone had recharged its batteries, apparently occupied until recently.

Junk, junk, and more junk. And not a sign of the scissored scrap of photograph or the bleeding intruder.

I was going through Shackleman's desk drawers when I came across a small bundle of greeting cards commemorating various special occasions. I removed the rubber band holding them together and briefly glanced at each. Birthdays, anniversaries, Christmas—heartfelt and warm dispatches from the poignant past. The greeting cards were, for the most, depressing reminders of my own lost love, forlorn chapters in a tragic memoir. There was one however that caught my eye for reasons not predicated on masochistic sentimentality. It was a familiar theme: three monkeys hunched next to one another in a row, each denying one of the Devil's three avenues to the soul. Inside it read:

We opened their eyes and ears and gave them a voice. . . .
Now what?

Love, Sarah

It's impossible to describe what I felt after reading the inscription from Shackleman's estranged wife and widow. Urgency, shame, elation. The faces of the three chimps who had been murdered since my arrival at Acteon lurched at me like jack-in-the-boxes, their most prominent features those which had been suspiciously absent in the wake of their deaths: 99's eyes, 12's ears, the eviscerated and decapitated John Doe's tongue. I had been chasing the wrong guy all along. 131 had been framed. I needed to know whose face belonged in the photograph. Only then could I hope to complete the picture.

I was considering my next course of action when a creaky floorboard revealed that someone was in the closet. The tiny hairs along the base of my neck prickled like iron filings in the grip of a magnetic field. Ordinarily, I would have been strapped. Less than an hour earlier, however, I had taken advantage of my drive down the coast and chucked my .45 as far out past the breakers as possible. Nonetheless, I was determined to find out who or what had been spying on me for the past half hour. Armed with a soapstone bookend carved in the shape of a bison,

I approached the closet. I would throw open the door with my left hand and use my right hand to club the occupant over the head. I was reaching for the knob when a key bit into the lock on the front door and someone let themselves in. Sporting one black eye already, it was probably for the best that I didn't have the chance to carry out my plan. I grabbed what I needed and slipped out the back. My only regret was that I couldn't stick around for the fireworks.

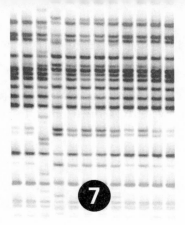

7

Since my first visit to the STF, I had learned to expect the unexpected. It was after midnight and the Haunted Mansion was crawling with ghosts. Clad, as usual, in crinkly rubber suits and working from a tray of loaded hypodermics, they were busy administering injections of an undisclosed substance to the anesthetized chimps. What now, I wondered?

Lepke was at Shackleman's old desk in the reception area outside of Janus's office. The surveillance camera under whose scrupulous eye he puzzled over the blank grid of a crossword was not nearly as arbitrary and superfluous as it had once seemed to me. I didn't know whom to trust.

"Don't you guys ever go home?" I asked.

Startled, Lepke looked up from his crossword. "What's an eight-letter word for a moment of revelation?" he asked.

"Later," I said. "Right now, I need you to pull one of the surveillance tapes from a few months back so I can figure out who this is."

I handed him the photograph of the chimp with the face cut out. He looked through the hole and winked at me. It was a strange juxtaposition—Lepke's turbid eye affixed to the chimp's headless body—the sort of monster that gave ancient Greek schoolchildren nightmares.

"Are you trying to tell me that you don't recognize those legs?" he asked.

"That's exactly what I'm trying to tell you."

Lepke fastened a reprobate expression to his face and smiled. "The faceless beauty you're carrying around is Helena 12."

He handed me the photograph.

"Are you sure?"

"You saw them giving shots to the chimps on your way in?" Lepke asked. "Those legs of hers are the reason why."

"I don't get it—12 is dead. She was raped and murdered almost two weeks ago."

"All the *cheer* she was spreading while she was still alive has resulted in an epidemic of sorts."

"What kind of epidemic?"

"The gift that keeps on giving. . . . Gonorrhea. Once it found its way inside the STF, it spread like the plague. Now nearly every subject is infected."

"How's that possible? The only way she could have caught something like that is from boffing someone outside the enclosure."

Lepke leaned back and gave me a seedy smile. "Some of us were betting it was you."

I could see Shackleman as clearly as if he had just returned from one of his urgent trips to the restroom, pale and ragged, his face the semitranslucent tint of congealed bacon grease, his brow and upper lip sequined with oily beads of sweat. It was obvious to me now: the infidelity and divorce, the picture with the face cut out, the unused tickets to Fiji, the pyridium. Shackleman had been having an affair with Helena 12. *She* was Madame X! They had planned to go away together, to live as honeymooners in a stilted hut on the edge of a lagoon as blue as mouthwash. To comb the beach and feed each other fruit and make wishes on falling stars and fuck their brains out until the sun came up each morning. Problem was, Shackleman had learned the hard way that 12 was a little too wild for prime time. She was not the type who could settle into a life of stuffing bag lunches and shuttling the little ones to soccer practice in a forest green Suburban. Crazy with jealousy and clinging to the desperate hope that he might yet reform her, Shackleman had offed her lovers one by one. When the corrective measure failed to curb 12's sexual appetite, he was left with no other choice than to pull the plug on the chimp he loved. To share her with another—or others, as was the case—was simply too painful for him to bear.

You're probably wondering why Shackleman had waited until after 12 was dead to off John Doe. Of course, this is pure speculation; however, it stands to reason that, having been diagnosed with gonorrhea, Shackleman was relatively certain that sooner or later 12 would also begin to exhibit signs of the disease. He must have believed that 12's death would serve a dual purpose. Not only would he be free of the libidinous heartbreaker, but the disease would die with her, thus severing the link between the illicit lovers that would surely be revealed during one of the monthly urine tests Acteon required of all its employees. It looks as if Shackleman had initially planned on keeping John Doe alive to use as a decoy. Whether it was jealousy or an obsessive desire to see the See No Evil, Hear No Evil, Speak No Evil motif through to the end, something got the better of him and he was forced to set his sights on another 131, another dupe. For the better part of a month, I had been hot on the trail of the wrong guy. It wasn't the first time, but I promised myself that it would be the last.

How, exactly, Shackleman had hooked up with 12 in the first place was less certain. How frequent had his visits inside the habitation module been? Of what duration? Besides the obvious, what had he done in there? What had he wanted from the chimps? Where had he thought it would lead? How had the chimps viewed him—this strange outsider? This being from beyond the sky who came and went as he pleased, who was with them even when he was not *with* them, who knew everything about them—everything about everything, it must have seemed. If the chimps had experienced God in a cell phone, imagine their take on Shackleman— the pure liquid depth and layers of perception suggested in his prescription eyes. He was fairer and straighter and taller than them. He was that much closer to the stars.

"Epiphany," I said aloud.

Lepke looked confused, the crossword spread out over the desk before him like a map of a lost civilization.

"An eight-letter word for a moment of revelation," I reminded him.

I entered Janus's office for what I hoped would be the last time. My feet left sinkholes in the mud floor that slowly filled with groundwater as I advanced toward the monkey bronze colossus. The smugness was seemingly gone from the chimp's expression. It now wore the grim and apprehensive look of a time traveler who has returned from the future and site of his own death.

"Janus!" I called out. "I need to talk to you."

The air was still and there was no rain. The ceiling-sky, although not exactly bright, was suffused with a silver gray tint. Features of the grotto once hidden to me resolved into semiclarity. I could see at once that the miniature rain forest was no more real than the Jurassic flora display at the Museum of Natural History. The trees had been molded from some sort of superstrong petroleum-based resin. I rapped my fist against one of the trunks, and it reverberated hollowly. The plants, the vines, the mats of moss and algae carpeting the ground—all of it was fake. What my urbanized nose had mistaken for the green bouquet of chlorophyll was actually a by-product of all the plastic, processed and artificial. In places, I could see beyond the leafy boundaries of the dubious paradise, the walls coated in industrial white latex, the flame-retardant acoustical tiles making up the ceiling studded with star-shaped sprinkler heads. For the first time, I could hear something other than the urgent thrum of swarming insects. The steady low-level disturbance was still there, yet it was somehow different, laconic, less biblical than before. The hive that had once dispatched squadrons of stinging drones to harass me was nothing more than a transformer box modulating the flow of electrical current required to sustain the battery of humidifiers and air conditioners regulating the balmy tropical climate. As far as I could tell, only the mud was real.

"I wanted you to see this for what it really is, Mr. Flowers—an illusion. My world between worlds."

It was Janus. I turned but he was nowhere in sight. His voice came from the direction of the monkey bronze colossus.

"The killer isn't one of the chimps," I said, continuing forward. "It was Shackleman. He killed 99 and 12 and the other chimp. He put me on the trail of 131 so that I'd be out of the picture. Then he used my gun to shoot Officer Blanks in the head. Insurance, I guess, in case I got too close."

"It was my understanding that one of the control-group subjects was in possession of your gun."

"That's what Shackleman wanted us to believe. I took it off him myself. The only thing I can figure is that he planned on killing me with it, and making the thing with Blanks look like a murder-suicide—that is, providing Blanks died."

"What about the conjoined twins?" Janus asked. "If what you're telling me is true their deaths seem rather arbitrary."

By the time I reached the monkey bronze colossus, Janus's voice had shifted locations. He was on the move.

"My guess is that he was aiming for me," I explained. "Bad part of town, illegal drugs. . . . Fatal shootings are a dime a dozen. After all, it was his idea that I visit Little Saigon. Why he didn't finish me off when he had the chance is another thing altogether, unless of course someone else was looking out for me."

"Someone else?"

I told Janus about the beating I had suffered at the Happy Buddha Restaurant, and how before I had lost consciousness, 131 had stolen my wallet and keys. I explained that several hours later, as I waited for Shackleman on the street in front of the Alibi Room, 131 had run him over with my car.

"That's when I found my gun on Shackleman. Meeting me there must have been Plan B, a contingency, in case the hit at Little Saigon didn't pan out. I'm not sure what Blight's relationship is to Shackleman, but he was there, too. I have a hunch that he was after the disk Shackleman was carrying. I was able to see only parts of it, but it was some pretty freaky stuff."

"Dr. Blight is dead," Janus announced dispassionately. He was behind me again. His voice emanated from a thicket of double hibiscus. Orange silk blossoms flared from its branches like fire. "It appears that while taking in a movie earlier this evening, he suffered catastrophic heart failure."

"Heart failure—are you sure? I assumed he was murdered."

"Less than a year ago, Dr. Blight's heart stopped working. It was replaced with a baboon's heart. Although the procedure—I believe he called it a xenograft—was rather effective, it was only intended to provide a short-term solution until he could find a more suitable donor. It was a question of compatibility—antirejection drugs can do only so much. He had been having trouble with it for some time. Poetic justice, if you ask me." Janus paused before going on. "It was Blight's ambition to create a living organ bank that would borrow exclusively from chimps genetically modified to suit human physiology. Of course, *borrow* was Blight's term, not mine."

"So that's how he fits into all of this."

"Blight was an evil man. He regarded the STF as little more than an organ warehouse. I believe that he and Mr. Shackleman had entered into a secret partnership. It seems, however, that Shackleman had changed his mind somewhere along the line. Don't ask me why."

"I'll tell you why. Shackleman didn't want to see the chimp he loved carved up for spare parts. Then he caught her fooling around, and everything changed. Maybe that's why he was carrying the disk—he planned on using it to drum up more business after his falling-out with Blight. And I thought he was bringing it to me."

"Shackleman caught *who* fooling around?" Janus asked.

"12—she was his mistress. Shackleman's wife divorced him when she found out about it. That's why Shackleman murdered all of those chimps—they were banging his little lady. I should have seen it sooner. All of the victims but 12 were male. It's your classic case of a jealous lover settling the score."

"The gonorrhea," Janus mused, making the connection.

"The guy spent more time in the restroom than a bulimic supermodel. He probably picked it up from one of the massage girls at the Happy Buddha. From that point on, it was a domino effect."

By the time I reached the thicket of hibiscus, Janus was gone. Something rustled in the bushes ahead of me.

"Okay, so I understand Shackleman's interest in 131, but what about Blight's? Why all the fuss?"

"If you'll stop following me for a moment," Janus said with an edge of irritation, "I can catch my breath and explain."

We had circled the grotto once already and were back at the monkey bronze colossus where we had started.

"Sure," I said.

"In the United States alone, there are roughly ten thousand men and women awaiting heart transplants. More than half will die before a donor organ becomes available. Blight had arranged some time ago to purchase 131 from us. In fact, 131 is not really Arbegast, as you no doubt already know. The chimp you once believed to be Arbegast is actually Blight—that is to say, 131 is a partial product of Blight's DNA."

"Now I get it. Blight wanted a new heart that would last him indefinitely."

"And Shackleman had agreed to provide it free of charge—a show of faith in their new partnership. Of course, all of this happened before I took over."

"Just how and when, exactly, was that?"

"A leveraged buyout less than three months ago. It was necessary that Blight's chimp donor reach physical maturity in order for the procedure to be effective. Otherwise, he would have gone ahead with it before my arrival. In the meantime, he was working on setting up his 'bank.' Blight was using you to track down 131."

"Why didn't you pull the plug? You are the boss after all."

"It's not that simple. My authority is very limited. Had I chosen to make a stink, Shackleman and Blight could have gone public with what we're doing here and set us back decades."

"I'm no expert, but everything seems to be within the letter of the law. With the exception of Shackleman's little killing spree, the animals here enjoy a higher standard of living than most humans."

"I guess it's time that you see for yourself."

Janus stepped out from behind the monkey bronze colossus although at that moment I was anything but convinced the unassuming chimp standing before me and the proprietor of the omnipresent falsetto were one in the same.

"That's good," I said. "Very funny. Now, where are you really?"

"No joke, Mr. Flowers." Janus smiled and spread his arms messianically. "I'm right here."

The mouth moved, there was a correlative inclination in the posture, the eyes gleamed intelligently. *Words. . . .* Words flowed freely from his lips. This was no ventriloquist's trick. I was sure of that.

"You're. . . . "

"Younger than you imagined?" Janus replied.

I thought it over. Why not? After what I had already seen, was a talking chimpanzee that far out of the question?

"I was going to say taller."

Janus nodded and we shook hands. I had the feeling that I was on the cusp of something larger than can be expressed with words. It was the sort of exchange artists re-create for history books from inflated anecdote and imagination. George Washington crossing the Delaware. Man's early ancestors trekking across the clay riverbed at Ntembe.

"I lived out there once," Janus explained. "It was cruel and ugly and false. So I came back to where I was born."

"You were the one in the video. I saw Shackleman lock you in the enclosure when you were just a kid."

Janus nodded solemnly. "Eventually I was shipped off to a university biology department, where they planned on breeding me with their own chimps. It was humiliating. I escaped and promised myself that I would return to the STF one day."

"But you were so violent."

"Mood drugs," Janus explained simply. "I was their first guinea pig."

"How did you manage all of this?" I asked, looking around. "You didn't just show up on the doorstep one day and say you'd like to join the executive intern program."

"Our community is very strong and close-knit. There are many like myself who see our work here as a means to an end. It took time and perseverance, but eventually we acquired enough of Acteon's stock to do things our own way."

My mind was racing.

"When you say that there are many more like yourself, *how many* and *how much like yourself* do you mean?"

"Globally? Thousands upon thousands. We have been living among you for years, Mr. Flowers. Every continent but Antarctica. It's like any form of immigration—no one seems to notice until there are enough of us that the status quo feels threatened. Soon it will become a question of asserting our *human* rights."

"So this is why Acteon stopped selling chimps and donating them to universities."

Janus looked ashamed. "What was going on here was no better than slavery."

"Shackleman told me that Acteon is not the only lab conducting this sort of work."

"One of the few truths to come out of his mouth. We are a widespread and growing industry. Ours is truly a multinational enterprise."

"How do you finance all of this, if you don't mind me asking? It must cost billions of dollars to keep an operation like this up and running."

"We raise and distribute lab animals—mice, rats, rabbits, lower-order primates. Don't think the irony is wasted on me."

I looked into Janus's eyes. They were clear and deep and knowing.

"All this time you were stringing along Arbegast Sr., knowing that Blight was the chimp's father."

I felt bad for the old man. He only wanted his son back.

"We knew that the finger Mr. Cloud provided wasn't a genetic match, but it was the only way we could think of to ensure an ongoing alliance with Arbegast Pharmaceuticals. They provide us with many of the drugs we need to make IT work. What we did was wrong, but it saved us millions of dollars."

"Why not tell him that one of the other chimps was his son?" I asked. "You must have known that picking Blight's would only complicate things."

"I'm afraid it was Shackleman's idea of a joke—a way of getting back at Blight and myself."

"Shackleman really had it in for you, didn't he?"

"I never forgave him for locking me inside the enclosure. When I returned three months ago, I finally had my revenge. I had him drugged and locked *him* inside. Only, unlike me, he did not want out. The control group didn't know what to make of him, so he made himself into their god. It took us nearly a week—he was hiding in the Enchanted Forest—but we finally managed to locate and remove him. In retrospect, locking him in was the most foolish thing I have ever done. My father was the serpent in our Eden. After him nothing was ever the same."

"Shackleman told me that his son had betrayed him. I had no idea that he was talking about you."

Janus fixed me with a look of grave affirmation.

"So the cell phone you told me about belonged to him?"

"He hoped to maintain a link," Janus confirmed. "The cell phone was to be his mountaintop, the ark of a new covenant— really nothing more than a soapbox, if you ask me. Shackleman called the chimps his chosen ones."

"Now that he's out of the picture, why not turn them loose?"

"The truth is I'm no longer convinced that being out there would be in their best interest. Like I said, the world is cruel and ugly and false. Perhaps they *are* the chosen ones. Perhaps it's best for them to remain here. Look at what limited exposure to humanity has done to them—murder, venereal disease, religion. Imagine what they'll find out there. 131 is a perfect example."

Janus was right, of course. It was cruel and ugly and false. "Welcome to the world," I said.

"I'm sorry for putting you through all of this, Mr. Flowers. I know it hasn't been easy. But I had to know. I think part of me knew all along. You understand. He was my father, and I didn't want to see it. This being human—it's a tricky business. I admire your strength. A lesser man would have crumbled under similar pressures, I'm sure."

"I'm not off the hook yet. The police could still link me to the shooting of Officer Blanks. If they somehow manage to prove that I was the one who called in the bomb threat. . . . "

"There is no Officer Blanks—never was," Janus admitted.

"Insurance in case I fucked up, right?"

"I'm sorry, it was the only way."

"Why the hell not?" I concluded cynically. "I'm used to being the fall guy."

"Of course you'll be receiving the sum we agreed upon. . . . However, I feel that I owe you something more for your troubles." Janus eyed me contemplatively. "I understand that you have been trying to conceive a child for some time."

"I've had to hang up the six-shooter for now," I explained by way of confirmation. "My wife and I are getting a divorce."

"Perhaps you have someone else in mind to be the mother of your future offspring?"

"There is someone I'm kind of sweet on." I was curious to know what he was getting at. "Actually, I'm sure she'd really like to meet you. Lorelei Beckett—she's a scientist at UCLA."

"Ah, yes," Janus said knowingly. "Her subjects speak very highly of her. Bring her by. Perhaps we can talk her into making a small contribution to our cause."

Janus pinched his thumb and forefinger together as if to indicate the minuteness of Lorelei's bequest.

"One last thing, Mr. Flowers. If ever the opportunity presents itself, perhaps you can point 131 in our direction. He will always have a home here no matter the road he has traveled to find his way back. I, too, was once a prodigal son."

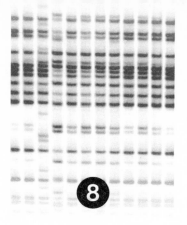

8

THE SUN WAS COMING UP when I pulled into my driveway. Lorelei greeted me at the door with a radiant smile. She had been staying at my house since the night we had first made love. We agreed that it was best for Marcel to lie low for a while. The UCLA Medical Center had been inundated with requests for interviews and photographs of the first chimpanzee to receive a human kidney. Understandably, the landmark procedure had sparked an ongoing controversy. Marcel was already having a rough time of it. The stress of news vans, picket-waving protesters, and popping flashbulbs in his face would have killed him. As it stood, he was scarcely capable of getting off the sofa, his third chance at life betrothed to the television, the dark and debilitating comedy of human history and current events and talk-show scandal sustaining what little spirit he had left. Every now and then, he emitted a mirthless chuckle at the expense of one of the tragic figures or events projected on the screen in front of him, but you could see that his heart simply wasn't in it. Although the strain on Lorelei had been great, she had managed to keep it together, calling on maternal instinct and her indefatigable dedi-cation to unlocking the chimp ability to speak. She thanked me daily for allowing Marcel and her to stay and expressed her grati-tude in the bedroom nightly. At the door, she stepped into me with the whole of her body and kissed me hotly on the mouth.

"I missed you last night," she breathed into my ear.

"I came straight home from the airport, but you weren't here.

Then I had to go see Blight at the Arts. One thing led to another and. . . . Well, here I am."

She closed the door softly after us and we went inside. We talked in the kitchen so Marcel would not be disturbed. Lorelei explained that he hadn't slept much. Nightmares.

"How was Sneed?" she wanted to know.

"Weird. A lot of tumbleweeds. Your buddy, Arbegast, is running with some sort of cult. They have him sorting garbage out in the desert. They all wear purple robes and don't particularly care for red meat."

"Vegetarians?"

"Something like that."

"Did you tell his father?"

I yawned and nodded. "I left out the part about him not liking red meat."

"No point scaring the poor old guy," Lorelei agreed wryly. "Would you like something to drink—coffee, orange juice?"

"I could go for another kiss."

Lorelei got up, straddled the chair in which I was sitting and sat on my lap facing me. When our lips finally parted, I said, "I talked to Janus this morning."

"What about?"

"For starters, Blight's dead. According to Janus, he had a baboon's heart. Apparently it gave out on him just last night. In fact, I was the one who found him."

"At the Arts?"

"With a bucket of popcorn on his lap."

"What did you do?"

"Finished the popcorn and watched the movie."

Lorelei slapped me in the chest and winced. *"Ooh!"*

"It was still warm, not too much butter, just the right amount of salt."

"A dead man's hand was in it."

"Get this; Janus said Blight was trying to organize some sort of organ bank dealing exclusively in animal parts for humans."

"Xenografting," Lorelei responded knowingly. "It's basically the same thing we did with Marcel."

"Blight lasted only a year after the transplant."

"We'll be lucky if Marcel makes it that long," she confirmed sadly. "The procedure is intended only as a holdover. We've been trying to locate him a kidney from another chimpanzee for some time. For whatever reason, they're not as easy to come by as they once were."

"I have a feeling that Janus might be able to shed some light on why that is. Anyway, he said he'd like to talk with you. He says he's heard good things."

"I'd like to talk with Janus," she said. "What's he like?"

Beginning with my visit to Shackleman's house after the movie, I recapped the events up to and surrounding my face-to-face with Janus. In spite of Lorelei's staunch scientific objectivity, I could tell that she was determined not to seem surprised that a chimp could actually, as she had suggested on numerous occasions, talk. To behave any differently would have been to admit self-doubt. She would have been no better than all the jerks who had discredited her theories and called her a nut. Nonetheless, she could not hide the fact that she was excited by the prospect. Beyond excited. The idea that she would at last be vindicated seemed to catalyze some untapped energy inside of her. The star that had already shined so brightly to me was suddenly on the verge of supernova. I could almost hear the rush of adrenaline thundering trainlike through her veins. The more I said, the more excited she became, until she had reached a state of critical mass and was dragging me off to bed.

We must have awakened Marcel because I could hear the television in the living room, the volume deliberately loud. Lorelei lay on her stomach, naked and happy-looking. She propped herself up on her elbows so that her spine curved dramatically inward before the round pitch of her ass picked up the seductive line and continued down her tanned toned legs.

"What do you think Janus wants from me?" she asked.

"Your guess is as good as mine."

Of course, I already had a few ideas of my own. However, I wasn't saying anything just yet. If anyone was going to scare Lorelei off it wasn't going to be me.

"So Shackleman was a kinky boy," Lorelei mused, rolling onto her back, her breasts peaking like the great onion domes of the Kremlin. "Before Marcel got sick, I used to think about—"

My expression, a furtive concoction of horror and jealousy, must have conveyed an immediate need for clarification, because she cut herself off in mid-sentence to put my mind at rest.

"Relax," she said. "I was going to say that before Marcel got sick we were considering breeding him at various zoos. You thought I was going to tell you that I had sex with him, didn't you?"

"So," I said, changing the subject. "I feel terrible about everything's that happened with 131. After all, he did save my life. Maybe you can help me think of a way to lure him out of hiding without getting myself shot in the process by that skinhead security guard. Janus said he'd gladly take him back."

"Have you thought about calling him? You said Shackleman's phone was missing. Maybe 131 has it. It's worth a shot."

"It *did* look as if a chimp had recently been inside the place."

"Tell me the number," she said. "I'll dial."

I had pocketed Shackleman's billing statement so that I could run it by my friend at the phone company. SOP. Check all incoming and outgoing calls. I retrieved it from my pants where they lay on the floor and recited the number to Lorelei. She dialed and handed me the phone. After close to a dozen rings, I hung up.

"No answer," I explained.

"We'll wait a while and try again."

Marcel hardly seemed to notice us as we emerged from the bedroom. His eyes were dull and he was shaggy and unkempt. He had lost weight. He looked like an old fur coat rescued from the lost and found at the Tijuana Opera House. It had been nearly a week since he'd had a drink, and then only a bottle of vanilla extract Lorelei and I had overlooked while drying out the place.

"Could you turn the TV down a little?" Lorelei asked him. "You'll make yourself deaf."

Marcel gestured something halfheartedly and obliged.

"One day at a time, sweetie," she comforted, stroking his head. "This time you're going to make it. I promise."

"Tell you what," I said, clapping the disconsolate ape on the shoulder. "If you're still not drinking at the end of the month, I'll take you to a Dodgers game. What do you say?"

Marcel smiled weakly and touched my hand.

"Then it's a date," I said.

"Dutch," said Lorelei, "why don't you let Marcel try the phone while we fix breakfast?"

I handed Marcel the phone.

"All you have to do is hit redial," Lorelei instructed. "And holler if anyone picks up."

Marcel seemed only politely interested in his new task. However, if nothing else, it served to distract him from his own mortality.

Lorelei was busy chopping and dicing the components of an elaborate fruit salad when Gogan pulled up in front of the house. He wrestled himself out of the car and lumbered stiffly up the walkway, pausing briefly to squint at something on the ground at his feet. Finding nothing, he straightened up and rang the doorbell. When I opened the door, he just stood there staring at me like a wad of chewed-up meat, his face raw and badly bruised. There was dried blood down the front of his shirt. His left ear was cauliflowered, and he was visibly shaken. Every now and then he checked over his shoulder, his face contorting against the pain of strained neck ligaments.

"Is it Halloween already?" I asked.

"That monkey I saw here the other day," Gogan said, craning nervously for a peek at the room beyond. "He still around?"

"Doesn't ring a bell. Could you be a little more specific?"

"Marcel is sick," Lorelei said, stepping forward protectively. "I don't want you getting him all worked up."

"Sick, huh?" Gogan asked suspiciously. "Like with the flu or something?"

"Something like that," answered Lorelei with a nullifying look before turning to me and saying, "I'll be in the kitchen."

"What do you want with Marcel, anyway?" I asked.

"Last night I get a call from the manager over at the Arts—says there's a stiff in the back row. Last show of the night, and this guy's still in his seat thirty minutes after the place has cleared out—just sitting there staring at the blank screen like a nut job. His eyes are kind of half-cocked so the usher—ugly little son of a bastard with acne like barnacles—thinks the DOA's beatin' his meat and tells the boss."

"A dead guy with his dick out. . . . Sounds right up your alley, Gogan."

"Remember Shackleman," Gogan went on, "the scientist who was splattered in that hit-and-run not too long ago? It turns out the stiff from the Arts is carrying Shackleman's address around in his wallet. Coincidence?" He curled his lips and discharged a blood-laced gob of spit at the base of a philodendron. "Fuck if it is."

"Now you've got your driver," I concluded neatly. "Does this mean I can have my car back?"

"And wouldn't you know it," Gogan plodded forward, "the Arts stiff is also some kind of scientist. Does the name August Blight do anything for you?"

I shook my head.

"Didn't think so," he replied indifferently. "Anyway, I swing by Shackleman's and take a look around. When I get there, one of the windows is broken and there's blood on the floor—still fresh. I'm about to call for backup and wham! Next thing you know I'm on my dirt chute, and the whole goddamn world is upside-down. Someone jumped me—damn near beat me to death."

"What's Marcel got to do with any of this?"

"Look, Flowers, I hear things working on the street. Ninety-nine out of a hundred times I can tell what's bullshit and what's not. When you were jacked in Little Gooktown the other day some of the eyewits were spinning it pretty deep. . . . "

I could see from the look in Gogan's eyes that he had come up against something his mind simply could not reconcile. Throwing 131 at that overtasked brain of his was like asking a hamster in an exercise wheel to power all the lights on the Vegas strip.

"I see a lot of shit out there and not all of it makes sense," he continued. "But this isn't like that. What happened to me tonight is way the fuck somewhere else. Somewhere I'd rather not go."

"Let me guess. You were abducted by little green men and taken onboard a spaceship where they stuck a flashlight up your ass?"

All at once Gogan boiled over. He unholstered his gun from where it cookie-cuttered into his doughy flank and knocked me aside. "I put a bullet in that hairy son of a bitch before he could get away," he snarled, stalking past me into the house. "I'll be fucked if I'm going to let you and that monkey-lover girlfriend of yours harbor an attempted murderer."

Gogan was in the living room before I could stop him. Marcel was lying on the sofa staring emptily at the television with the phone still cradled in his lap. He touched the redial button mechanically and lifted it to his ear, blocking his view of the gun clutched in Gogan's hand. Just then Lorelei emerged from the kitchen carrying a bowl of fruit salad. When she saw Gogan standing there with his gun drawn, her arms instinctively shot outward. The bowl of fruit salad crashed to the floor. Marcel's eyes leapt from Lorelei's horrified expression to the gun leveled at his head. He recognized the mean steel death-bringer from TV. Gogan's face loomed beyond it like a moon battered by meteorites—cold, misshapen, ugly. Marcel shrank into the cushions, the phone slipping away from his ear, abstract understanding powered by real fear.

"Leave him alone!" Lorelei shouted, positioning herself between the gun and Marcel. "What's wrong with you? Can't you see he's sick?"

"He tried to kill me!" Gogan roared.

"Marcel hasn't left the house in weeks, you idiot!" Lorelei fired bitterly. "I suppose they all look alike to you?"

Unsettled by all the commotion, Marcel withdrew into the corner of the sofa and resumed dialing. Shock—plain and simple. I could see it in his eyes.

"If *he* didn't attack me, then who *was* it?" Gogan asked, his voice unnaturally shrill. "How many monkeys do you expect me to believe are running around out there?"

Before either Lorelei or I could respond, a phone rang. It was not mine, not the one Marcel held pressed to his ear. The plaintive chime came from behind us, from the entry where Gogan had forced his way in moments earlier. The three of us turned to find 131 standing upright just outside the door, annealed in bronze sunlight, his malformed shadow bigger than us all playing out over the threshold at his feet. In one elastic moment, he extended his arm and moved toward us, Shackleman's phone lying dead between rings in his outstretched hand. He looked at me—searchingly, I think, but everything happened so fast that I can't be sure. Milliseconds, that's all it was. The exchange was interrupted by another ring, this one snatched from the air in the jaws of an explosive roar and swallowed whole before the anemic jingle could run its course. Even as 131 was knocked backward into the bronze sunlight, I could see in his eyes that he thought it was the phone killing him and not the slug from Gogan's .38, his spirit condemned to wander the road between rapture and betrayal.

"But I thought he had a gun!" Gogan pleaded lamely, his eyes jumping from Lorelei to myself where I knelt at 131's side, the phone clenched in the dead chimp's hand still ringing.

"You stupid man!" I said, nearly choking on all the futility and bitterness fueling my self-effacing reproach. And then to Marcel, "Hang up."

The tears came tentatively at first like rain over a desert that had known only drought for centuries. One at a time, drop after drop, until lashing down with mythic force. A species of hurt I had nearly forgotten grew out of the parched landscape of my soul. I cried for 131, so close but so far away; I cried for Ehrlich, alone and afraid, a feral outcast prowling the shadows at the edge of humanity; I cried for the ghosts of X-Ray squad and Saddam's hunted look-alikes; I cried for the crushed hopes and failed expectations, humility and lost love suffered by us all. This was no trickle of self-pity and bittersweet remorse, but an undamming of anguish so raw and elemental as to be confused with the primitive lament of an animal.

FAST FORWARD

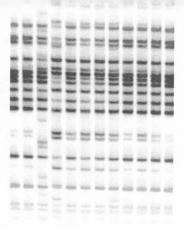

IT'S BEEN NEARLY A YEAR since 131 died on the threshold. A lot has changed since then. Lorelei and I have a nice little place in the mountains that we call home. It can get pretty hot in the summer, but in the fall the aspens turn gold and the valley below is so beautiful that I ache. Everyone seems to have forgotten about us, and we like it that way. I am not the man I used to be. Mr. Wonderful saw to that. I guess you could say that his dick saved my life. But it's not what you think. A week after his sex change was finalized, an unlikely souvenir arrived in Baghdad via FedEx with an obituary declaring me dead. Proof positive for Saddam and his boys. Janus arranged for a closed-casket ceremony to honor my memory. Although it is my name immortalized in marble, it is 131's remains that occupy a plot overlooking the freeway on the grassy slopes of Forest Lawn. Ours was the first of two such services in the span of six months.

Marcel fought to hold on, but for the second time in as many attempts, his donor kidney failed him. I fear it is this—the human component—that will be the source of any future unrest between our two species. I cried like a baby when they lowered him into the ground. I'm cured now, and sometimes this new-found compassion of mine hurts like hell. One of the reasons we left the city is because I couldn't pass a bum on the street without wondering what became of Ehrlich and how just as easily it might have been me eating out of garbage cans. Life without pseuprezdid has been rough, although Lorelei is confident that parenthood will show me the ropes.

This year Janie and her fiancé have accepted our invitation to spend Christmas here with us. It was Lorelei's idea. She says there's no point hanging onto the past, and I have to admit that I think she's right. I guess this is why she has never asked me about what happened in Abu Dhabi. She says the only thing that really matters is what lies ahead. I'm not exactly thrilled about sipping warm eggnog and banana liqueur by the fire with the swarthy Casanova Janie describes as a shorter, hairier version of me. But at least he was there for her when I couldn't be. I've grown a lot since Lorelei and I anted up for Acteon's IT specialists nearly eleven months ago. Having a child of my own has taught me that genetics is no greater guarantee of humanness than humanness is of humanity. All things considered, Janie has done well for herself with this new love of hers.

When Lorelei isn't working tirelessly at teaching our son to talk, she helps me with the small import-export business we run out of our house. Janus, who by the way is our son's godfather, gave us the idea. Darwin.com sold over five thousand monkey bronzes in six countries last month alone. Despite all that we have been through, Lorelei and I are no different from any other loving parents. We like to talk and pretend and dream what the future might bring. We know there is something special about our son. We know this as only parents can know. A doctor, an astronaut—president, even? For me, it's enough that he has my eyes.

photo © *Shiori D. Ikeda*

JOSH PRYOR holds an MFA from San Francisco State University. His work has been published in a variety of magazines, and one of his stories was included in *Best American Mystery Stories 2000*. He lives in Los Angeles and teaches composition at California State University Dominguez Hills and El Camino College.